Praise for the Leviathan series

Leviathan

★ "Enhanced by Thompson's intricate black-and-white illustrations, Westerfeld's brilliantly constructed imaginary world will capture readers from the first page. Full of nonstop action, this steampunk adventure is sure to become a classic."
—*School Library Journal*, starred review

2010 Locus Award for Best Young Adult Fiction
2010 ALA/YALSA Best Books for Young Adults
2010 ALA Notable Children's Book
School Library Journal Best Books of 2009

Behemoth

★ "The action is nonstop in Westerfeld's thrilling sequel to last year's *Leviathan*—fans of that book won't be disappointed."
—*Publishers Weekly*, starred review

Goliath

★ "[A] thrilling and fitting conclusion."
—*The Bulletin*, starred review

A Goliath's Polyp

System for Peace

Also by Scott Westerfeld

The first books in the Leviathan trilogy:

Leviathan

Behemoth

And don't miss:

The Manual of Aeronautics:
An Illustrated Guide to the Leviathan Series

The Uglies series:

Uglies

Pretties

Specials

Extras

Written by

MR. SCOTT WESTERFELD

Illustrated by Mr. Keith Thompson

SIMON PULSE

New York · London · Toronto · Sydney · New Delhi

SIMON PULSE
An imprint of Simon & Schuster Children's Publishing Division
1230 Avenue of the Americas, New York, NY 10020
First Simon Pulse paperback edition August 2012
Copyright © 2011 by Scott Westerfeld
SIMON PULSE and colophon are registered trademarks of Simon & Schuster, Inc.
Also available in a Simon Pulse hardcover edition.
For information about special discounts for bulk purchases, please contact
Simon & Schuster Special Sales at 1-866-506-1949
or business@simonandschuster.com.
The Simon & Schuster Speakers Bureau can bring authors to your live event.
For more information or to book an event contact the Simon & Schuster Speakers
Bureau at 1-866-248-3049 or visit our website at www.simonspeakers.com.
Designed by Mike Rosamilia
The text of this book was set in Hoefler Text.
Manufactured in the United States of America
2 4 6 8 10 9 7 5 3 1
The Library of Congress has cataloged the hardcover edition as follows:
Westerfeld, Scott.
Goliath / written by Scott Westerfeld ; illustrated by Keith Thompson.
p. cm.
Sequel to: Behemoth.
ISBN 978-1-4169-7177-1 (hardcover)
Summary: Alek and Deryn encounter obstacles on the last leg
of their round-the-world quest to end World War I, reclaim Alek's
throne as prince of Austria, and finally fall in love.
[1. Imaginary creatures—Fiction. 2. Princes—Fiction. 3. War—Fiction.
4. Genetic engineering—Fiction. 5. Science fiction.]
I. Thompson, Keith, 1982– ill. II. Title.
PZ7.W5197Go 2011
[Fic]—dc22
2011015892
ISBN 978-1-4169-7178-8 (pbk)
ISBN 978-1-4424-3436-3 (eBook)

To everyone who loves
a long-secret romance,
revealed at last

GOLIATH

◦ ONE ◦

"Siberia," Alek said. The word slipped cold and hard from his tongue, as forbidding as the landscape passing below.

"We won't be over Siberia till tomorrow." Dylan sat at the table, still attacking his breakfast. "And it'll take almost a week to cross it. Russia is barking *big.*"

"And cold," Newkirk added. He stood next to Alek at the window of the middies' mess, both hands wrapped around a cup of tea.

"Cold," repeated Bovril. The creature clutched Alek's shoulder a little tighter, and a shiver went through its body.

In early October no snow lay on the ground below. But the sky was an icy, cloudless blue. The window had a lace of frost around its edges, left over from a frigid night.

Another week of flying across this wasteland, Alek thought. Farther from Europe and the war, and from his destiny. The *Leviathan* was still headed east, probably toward the empire of Japan, though no one would confirm their destination. Even though he'd helped the British cause back in Istanbul, the airship's officers still saw Alek and his men as little better than prisoners. He was a Clanker prince and they were Darwinists, and the Great War between the two technologies was spreading faster every day.

"It'll get much colder as we angle north," Dylan said around a mouthful of his breakfast. "You should both finish your potatoes. They'll keep you warm."

Alek turned. "But we're already north of Tokyo. Why go out of our way?"

"We're dead on course," Dylan said. "Mr. Rigby made us plot a great circle route last week, and it took us all the way up to Omsk."

"A great circle route?"

"It's a navigator's trick," Newkirk explained. He breathed on the window glass before him, then drew an upside-down smile with one fingertip. "The earth is round, but paper is flat, right? So a straight course looks curved when you draw it on a map. You always wind up going farther north than you'd think."

"Except below the equator," Dylan added. "Then it's the other way round."

Bovril chuckled, as if great circle routes were quite amusing. But Alek hadn't followed a word of it—not that he'd expected to.

It was maddening. Two weeks ago he'd helped lead a revolution against the Ottoman sultan, ruler of an ancient empire. The rebels had welcomed Alek's counsel, his piloting skills, and his gold. And together they'd won.

But here aboard the *Leviathan* he was deadweight— a waste of hydrogen, as the crew called anything useless. He might spend his days beside Dylan and Newkirk, but he was no midshipman. He couldn't take a sextant reading, tie a decent knot, or estimate the ship's altitude.

Worst of all, Alek was no longer needed in the engine pods. In the month he'd been plotting revolution in Istanbul, the Darwinist engineers had learned a lot about Clanker mechaniks. Hoffman and Klopp were no longer called up to help with the engines, so there was hardly any need for a translator.

Since the first time he'd come aboard, Alek had dreamed of somehow serving on the *Leviathan*. But everything he could offer—walker piloting, fencing, speaking six languages, and being a grandnephew of an emperor—seemed to be worthless on an airship. He was no doubt more valuable as a young prince who had famously switched sides than as an airman.

It was as if everyone were *trying* to make him a waste of hydrogen.

Then Alek remembered a saying of his father's: The only way to remedy ignorance is to admit it.

He took a slow breath. "I'm aware that the earth is round, Mr. Newkirk. But I still don't understand this 'great circle route' business."

"It's dead easy to see if you've got a globe in front of you," Dylan said, pushing away his plate. "There's one in the navigation room. We'll sneak in sometime when the officers aren't there."

"That would be most agreeable." Alek turned back to the window and clasped his hands behind his back.

"It's nothing to be ashamed of, Prince Aleksandar," Newkirk said. "Still takes me *ages* to plot a proper course. Not like Mr. Sharp here, knowing all about sextants before he even joined the Service."

"Not all of us are lucky enough to have an airman for a father," Alek said.

"Father?" Newkirk turned from the window, frowning. "Wasn't that your uncle, Mr. Sharp?"

Bovril made a soft noise, sinking its tiny claws into Alek's shoulder. Dylan said nothing, though. He seldom spoke of his father, who had burned to death in front of the boy's eyes. The accident still haunted Dylan, and fire was the only thing that frightened him.

Alek cursed himself as a *Dummkopf*, wondering why he'd mentioned the man. Was he angry at Dylan for always being so good at everything?

He was about to apologize when Bovril shifted again, leaning forward to stare out the window.

"Beastie," the perspicacious loris said.

A black fleck had glided into view, wheeling across the empty blue sky. It was a huge bird, much bigger than the falcons that had circled the airship in the mountains a few days before. It had the size and claws of a predator, but its shape was unlike any Alek had seen before.

It was headed straight for the ship.

"Does that bird look odd to you, Mr. Newkirk?"

Newkirk turned back to the window and raised his field glasses, which were still around his neck from the morning watch.

"Aye," he said a moment later. "I think it's an imperial eagle!"

There was a hasty scrape of chair legs from behind them. Dylan appeared at the window, shielding his eyes with both hands.

"Blisters, you're right—two heads! But imperials only carry messages from the czar himself. . . ."

Alek glanced at Dylan, wondering if he'd heard right. *Two heads?*

The eagle soared closer, flashing past the window in

a blur of black feathers, a glint of gold from its harness catching the morning sun. Bovril broke into maniacal laughter at its passage.

"It's headed for the bridge, right?" Alek asked.

"Aye." Newkirk lowered his field glasses. "Important messages go straight to the captain."

A bit of hope pried its way into Alek's dark mood. The Russians were allies of the British, fellow Darwinists who fabricated mammothines and giant fighting bears. What if the czar needed help against the Clanker armies and this was a summons to turn the ship around? Even fighting on the icy Russian front would be better than wasting time in this wilderness.

"I need to know what that message says."

Newkirk snorted. "Why don't you go and ask the captain, then?"

"Aye," Dylan said. "And while you're at it, ask him to give me a warmer cabin."

"What can it hurt?" Alek said. "He hasn't thrown me into the brig yet."

When Alek had returned to the *Leviathan* two weeks ago, he'd half expected to be put in chains for escaping from the ship. But the ship's officers had treated him with respect.

Perhaps it wasn't so bad, everyone finally knowing he was the son of the late Archduke Ferdinand, and not just some Austrian noble trying to escape the war.

"What's a good excuse to pay the bridge a visit?" he asked.

"No need for excuses," Newkirk said. "That bird's flown all the way from Saint Petersburg. They'll call us to come and fetch it for a rest and a feeding."

"And you've never seen the rookery, your princeliness," Dylan added. "Might as well tag along."

"Thank you, Mr. Sharp," Alek said, smiling. "I would like that."

Dylan returned to the table and his precious potatoes, perhaps grateful that the talk of his father had been interrupted. Alek decided he would apologize before the day was out.

Ten minutes later a message lizard popped its head from a tube on the ceiling in the middies' mess. It said in the master coxswain's voice, "Mr. Sharp, please come to the bridge. Mr. Newkirk, report to the cargo deck."

The three of them scrambled for the door.

"Cargo deck?" Newkirk said. "What in blazes is that about?"

"Maybe they want you to inventory the stocks again," Dylan said. "This trip might have just got longer."

Alek frowned. Would "longer" mean turning back toward Europe, or heading still farther away?

As the three made their way toward the bridge, he sensed the ship stirring around them. No alert had sounded, but the crew was bustling. When Newkirk peeled off to descend the central stairway, a squad of riggers in flight suits went storming past, also headed down.

"Where in blazes are they going?" Alek asked. Riggers always worked topside, in the ropes that held the ship's huge hydrogen membrane.

"A dead good question," Dylan said. "The czar's message seems to have turned us upside down."

The bridge had a guard posted at the door, and a dozen message lizards clung to the ceiling, waiting for orders to be dispatched. There was a sharp edge to the usual thrum of men and creatures and machines. Bovril shifted on Alek's shoulder, and he felt the engines change pitch through the soles of his boots—the ship was coming to full-ahead.

Up at the ship's master wheel, the officers were huddled around the captain, who held an ornate scroll. Dr. Barlow was among the group, her own loris on her shoulder, her pet thylacine, Tazza, sitting at her side.

A squawk came from Alek's right, and he turned to find himself face-to-face with the most astonishing creature. . . .

The imperial eagle was too large to fit into the bridge's messenger cage, and it perched instead on the signals table. It shifted from one taloned claw to the other, glossy black wings fluttering.

And what Dylan had said was true. The creature had two heads, and two necks, of course, coiled around each other like a pair of black feathered snakes. As Alek watched in horror, one head snapped at the other, a bright red tongue slithering from its mouth.

"God's wounds," he breathed.

"Like we told you," Dylan said. "It's an imperial eagle."

"It's an *abomination*, you mean." Sometimes the Darwinists' creatures seemed to have been fabricated not for their usefulness, but simply to be horrific.

Dylan shrugged. "It's just a two-headed bird, like on the czar's crest."

"Yes, of course," Alek sputtered. "But that's meant to be *symbolic*."

"Aye, this beastie's symbolic. It's just breathing as well."

"Prince Aleksandar, good morning." Dr. Barlow had left the group of officers and crossed the bridge, the czar's scroll in her hand. "I see you've met our visitor. Quite a fine example of Russian fabrication, is it not?"

"Good morning, madam." Alek bowed. "I'm not sure what this creature is a fine example of, only that I find it a bit . . ." He swallowed, watching Dylan slip on a pair of thick falconer's gloves.

"TWO-HEADED MESSENGER."

"Literal-minded?" Dr. Barlow chuckled softly. "I suppose, but Czar Nicholas *does* enjoy his pets."

"Pets, fah!" her loris repeated from its new perch on the messenger tern cages, and Bovril giggled. The two creatures began to whisper nonsense to each other, as they always did when they met.

Alek pulled his gaze from the eagle. "In fact, I'm more interested in the message it was carrying."

"Ah . . ." Her hands began to roll up the scroll. "I'm afraid that is a military secret, for the moment."

Alek scowled. His allies in Istanbul had never kept secrets from him.

If only he could have stayed there somehow. According to the newspapers, the rebels had control of the capital now, and the rest of the Ottoman Empire was falling under their sway. He would have been respected there—useful, instead of a waste of hydrogen. Indeed, helping the rebels overthrow the sultan had been the most *useful* thing he'd ever done. It had robbed the Germans of a Clanker ally and had proven that he, Prince Aleksandar of Hohenburg, could make a difference in this war.

Why had he listened to Dylan and come back to this abomination of an airship?

"Are you quite all right, Prince?" Dr. Barlow asked.

"I just wish I knew what you Darwinists were up to," Alek said, a sudden quiver of anger in his voice. "At least if you were taking me and my men to London in chains, it would make sense. What's the point of lugging us halfway around the world?"

Dr. Barlow spoke soothingly. "We all go where the war takes us, Prince Aleksandar. You haven't had such bad luck on this ship, have you?"

Alek scowled but couldn't argue. The *Leviathan* had saved him from spending the war hiding out in a freezing castle in the Alps, after all. And it had taken him to Istanbul, where he'd struck his first blow against the Germans.

He gathered himself. "Perhaps not, Dr. Barlow. But I prefer to choose my own course."

"That time may come sooner than you think."

Alek raised an eyebrow, wondering what she meant.

"Come on, your princeliness," Dylan said. The eagle was now hooded and perching quietly on his arm. "It's useless arguing with boffins. And we've got a bird to feed."

· TWO ·

The eagle turned out to be quite peaceable, once Deryn had stuffed a pair of hoods over its cantankerous heads.

It sat heavy on her gloved arm, a good ten pounds of muscle and guts. As she and Alek walked aft, Deryn soon found herself thankful that birds had hollow bones.

The rookery was separate from the main gondola, halfway back to the ventral fin. The walkway leading there was warmed by the gastric channel's heat, but the freezing wind of the airship's passage sent ripples through the membrane walls on either side. Considering the fact that they were inside a thousand-foot-long airship made from the life threads of a whale and a hundred other species, it hardly smelled at all. The scent was like a mix of animal sweat and clart, like a stable in summer.

Beside her, Alek kept a wary eye on the imperial eagle.

"Do you suppose it has two brains?"

"Of course it does," Deryn said. "What use is a head without a brain?"

Bovril chuckled at this, as if it knew that Deryn had almost made a joke about Clankers in this regard. Alek had been in a touchy mood all morning, so she hadn't.

"What if they have a disagreement about which way to fly?"

Deryn laughed. "They settle it with a fight, I suppose, same as anyone. But I doubt they argue that much. A bird's attic is mostly optic nerve—more eyesight than brainpower."

"So at least it doesn't *know* how horrid it looks."

A squawk came from beneath one of the hoods, and Bovril imitated the sound.

Deryn frowned. "If two-headed beasties are so horrible, how come you had one painted on your Storm-walker?"

"That was the Hapsburg crest. The symbol of my family."

"What's it symbolic of? Squeamishness?"

Alek rolled his eyes, then launched into a lecture.

"The two-headed eagle was first used by the Byzantines, to show that their empire ruled both east and west. But when a modern royal house uses the symbol, one of the heads symbolizes earthly power, the other divine right."

"Divine right?"

"The principle that a king's power is bestowed by God."

Deryn let out a snort. "Let me guess who came up with that one. Was it a *king*, maybe?"

"It's a bit old-fashioned, I suppose," Alek said, but Deryn wondered if he believed it anyway. His attic was full of all kinds of old yackum, and he was always talking about how providence had guided him since he'd left home. How it was his destiny to stop this war.

As far as she could tell, the war was too big for any one person to stop, prince or commoner, and fate didn't care a squick about what anybody was *meant* to do. It was Deryn's destiny to be a girl, after all, stuffed into skirts and stuck with squalling brats somewhere. But she'd avoided that fate well enough, with a little help from her tailoring.

Of course, there were other fates she hadn't escaped, like falling for a daft prince in a way that filled her head with unsoldierly nonsense. Like being his best friend, his ally, while a steady, hopeless longing pulled at her heart.

It was just lucky that Alek was too wrapped up in his own troubles, and the troubles of the whole barking world, to notice. Of course, hiding her feelings was made a bit easier by the fact that he didn't know she was a girl. No one aboard did except Count Volger, who, despite being a bum-rag, at least had a knack for keeping secrets.

They arrived at the hatch to the rookery, and Deryn reached for the pressure lock. But with only one free hand, the mechanism was a fiddle in the darkness.

"Give us some light, your divine princeliness?"

"Certainly, Mr. Sharp," Alek said, pulling out his command whistle. He gave it a studious look, then played the tune.

The glowworms behind the airship's skin began to flicker, and a soft green light suffused the corridor. Then Bovril joined in with the whistle, its voice as shimmery as a box of silver bells. The light grew sharp and bright.

"Good job, beastie," Deryn said. "We'll make a middy of you yet."

Alek sighed. "Which is more than you can say for me."

Deryn ignored his moping and opened the rookery door. As the ruckus of squawks and shrieks spilled out, the imperial clutched her arm tighter, its talons sharp even through the leather of the falconer's glove.

She led Alek along the raised walkway, looking for an empty space below. There were nine cages altogether, three underneath her and three on either side, each twice as tall as a man. The smaller raptors and messengers were a blur of fluttering wings, while the strafing hawks sat regally on their perches, ignoring the lesser birds around them.

"God's wounds!" Alek said from behind her. "It's a madhouse in here."

"Madhouse," Bovril said, and leapt from Alek's shoulder to the handrail.

Deryn shook her head. Alek and his men often found

"SECRETS IN THE ROOKERY."

the airship too messy for their liking. Life was a tumultuous and muddled thing, compared with the tidy clockwork of Clanker contraptions. The ecosystem of the *Leviathan*, with its hundred interlocking species, was far more complex than any lifeless machine, and thus a bit less orderly. But that was what kept the world interesting, Deryn reckoned; reality had no gears, and you never knew what surprises would come spinning out of its chaos.

She'd certainly never expected to help lead a Clanker revolution one day, or be kissed by a girl, or fall for a prince. But that had all happened in the last month, and the war was just getting started.

Deryn spotted the cage that the rook tenders had emptied, and pulled the loading chute into place above it. It wouldn't do to put the imperial in with other birds—not while it was hungry.

In one swift motion she snatched the hoods off and pushed the beastie into the chute. It fluttered down into the cage, spinning in the air like a windblown leaf for a moment. Then it came to rest on the largest perch.

From there the imperial eyed its fellow creatures through the bars, shifting from foot to foot unhappily. Deryn wondered what sort of cage it lived in back at the czar's palace. Probably one with gleaming bars, with fat mice served up on silver platters, and no smell of other birds' clart thickening the air.

"Dylan," Alek said. "While we have a moment alone . . ."

She turned to face him. He was standing close, his green eyes glinting in the darkness. It was always hardest meeting Alek's gaze when he was dead serious like this, but she managed.

"I'm sorry about bringing up your father earlier," he said. "I know how that still haunts you."

Deryn sighed, wondering if she should simply tell him not to worry. But it had been a bit tricky, what with Newkirk mentioning her uncle. It might be safer to tell Alek the truth—at least, as much of it as she possibly could.

"No need to apologize," she said. "But there's something you should know. That night I told you about my da's accident, I didn't quite explain everything."

"How do you mean?"

"Well, Artemis Sharp really was my da, just like I said." Deryn took a slow breath. "But everyone in the Air Service thinks he was my uncle."

She could see from Alek's expression that it made no sense at all, and without her even trying, lies began to spin from her tongue.

"When I signed up, my older brother Jaspert was already in the Service. So we couldn't say we were brothers."

That was blether, of course. The real reason was that Jaspert had already told his crewmates about his only sibling, a younger sister. A brother popping out of thin air might have been a squick confusing.

"We pretended to be cousins. You see?"

Alek frowned. "Brothers don't serve together in your military?"

"Not when their father's dead. You see, we're his only children. And so if we both . . ." She shrugged, hoping he'd believe it.

"Ah, to keep the family name alive. Very sensible. And that's why your mother didn't want you signing up?"

Deryn nodded glumly, wondering how her lies always got so barking complicated. "I didn't mean to mix you up in a deception. But that night I thought you were leaving the ship for good. So I told you the truth, instead of what I tell everyone else."

"The truth," Bovril repeated. "*Mr.* Sharp."

Alek reached up and touched his jacket pocket. Deryn knew that was where he kept his letter from the pope, the one that could make him emperor one day. "Don't worry, Dylan. I'll keep all your secrets, as you've kept mine."

Deryn groaned. She hated it when Alek said that. Because he *couldn't* keep all her secrets, could he? He didn't know the biggest of them.

All of sudden she didn't want to lie anymore. Not *this* much, anyway.

"Wait," she said. "I just told you a load of yackum. Brothers can serve together. It's something else."

"Yackum," Bovril repeated. Alek just stood there, concern on his face.

"But I can't tell you the real reason," Deryn said.

"Why not?"

"Because . . ." she was a commoner, and he was a prince. Because he'd run a mile if he knew. "You'd think less of me."

He stared at Deryn a moment, then reached out and took her shoulder. "You're the best soldier I've ever met, Dylan. The boy I'd have wanted to be, if I hadn't wound up such a useless prince. I could never think badly of you."

She groaned, turning away and wishing an alert would sound, an attack of zeppelins or a lightning storm. Anything to extract her from this conversation.

"Listen," Alek said, dropping his hand. "Even if your family has some deep, dark secret, who am I to judge? My granduncle conspired with the men who killed my parents, for heaven's sake!"

Deryn had no idea what to say to that. Alek had got it all wrong, of course. It wasn't some musty family secret; it was hers alone. He would always get it all wrong, until she told him the truth.

And that, she could never do.

"Please, Alek. I can't. And . . . I've got a fencing lesson."

Alek smiled, the perfect picture of a patient friend. "Anytime you want to tell me, Dylan. Until then, I won't ask again."

She nodded silently, and walked ahead of him the whole way back.

"Rather late with my breakfast, aren't you?"

"Sorry about that, your countship," Deryn said, plunking the tray down on Count Volger's desk. A splash of coffee sloshed out of the pot and onto the toast. "But here it is."

The wildcount raised an eyebrow.

"And your newspapers as well," she said, pulling them from beneath her arm. "Dr. Barlow saved them especially for you. Though I don't know why she bothers."

Volger took the papers, then picked up the soggy piece of toast and shook it. "You seem to be in rather a lively mood this morning, Mr. Sharp."

"Aye, well, I've been busy." Deryn frowned at the man. It was lying to Alek that had put her in a huff, of course, but she felt like blaming Count Volger. "I won't have time for a fencing lesson."

"Pity. You're coming along so well," he said. "For a girl."

Deryn scowled at the man. Guards were no longer posted outside the Clankers' staterooms, but someone passing in the corridor might have heard. She crossed to shut the cabin door, then turned back to the wildcount.

He was the only person on the airship who knew what she really was, and he generally took care not to mention it aloud.

"What do you want?" she said quietly.

He didn't look up at her, but instead fussed with his breakfast as if this were a friendly chat. "I've noticed the crew seems to be preparing for something."

"Aye, we got a message this morning. From the czar."

Volger looked up. "The czar? Are we changing course?"

"That's a military secret, I'm afraid. No one knows except the officers." Deryn frowned. "And the lady boffin, I suppose. Alek asked her, but she wouldn't say."

The wildcount scraped butter onto his half soggy toast, giving this a think.

During the month Deryn had been hiding in Istanbul, the wildcount and Dr. Barlow had entered into some sort of alliance. Dr. Barlow made sure he was kept up with news about the war, and Volger gave her his opinions on Clanker politics and strategy. But Deryn doubted the lady boffin would answer this question for him. Newspapers and rumors were one thing, sealed orders quite another.

"Perhaps *you* could find out for me."

"No, I couldn't," Deryn said. "It's a military secret."

Volger poured coffee. "And yet secrets can be *so* difficult to keep sometimes. Don't you think?"

Deryn felt a cold dizziness rising up inside, as it always did when Count Volger threatened her. There was something *unthinkable* about everyone finding out what she was. She wouldn't be an airman anymore, and Alek would never speak to her again.

But this morning she was not in the mood for blackmail.

"I can't help you, Count. Only the senior officers know."

"But I'm sure a girl as resourceful as you, so obviously adept at subterfuge, could find out. One secret unraveled to keep another safe?"

The fear burned cold now in Deryn's belly, and she almost gave in. But then something Alek had said popped into her head.

"You can't let Alek find out about me."

"And why not?" Volger asked, pouring himself tea.

"He and I were just in the rookery together, and I almost told him. That happens sometimes."

"I'm sure it does. But you *didn't* tell him, did you?" Volger tutted. "Because you know how he would react. However fond you two are of each other, you are a commoner."

"Aye, I know that. But I'm also a soldier, a barking good one." She took a step closer, trying to keep any quaver out of her voice. "I'm the very soldier Alek might have been, if he hadn't been raised by a pack of fancy-boots like you. I've got the life he missed by being an archduke's son."

Volger frowned, not understanding yet, but it was all coming clear in Deryn's mind.

"I'm the boy Alek wants to be, more than anything. And you want to tell him that I'm really a *girl*? On top of losing his parents and his home, how do you think he'll take that news, your countship?"

The man stared at her for another moment, then went back to stirring his tea. "It might be rather . . . unsettling for him."

"Aye, it might. Enjoy your breakfast, Count."

Deryn found herself smiling as she turned and left the room.

⊙ THREE ⊙

As the great jaw of the cargo door opened, a freezing whirlwind spilled inside and leapt about the cargo bay, setting the leather straps of Deryn's flight suit snapping and fluttering. She pulled on her goggles and leaned out, peering at the terrain rushing past below.

The ground was patched with snow and dotted with pine trees. The *Leviathan* had passed over the Siberian city of Omsk that morning, not pausing to resupply, still veering northward toward some secret destination. But Deryn hadn't found time to wonder where they were heading; in the thirty hours since the imperial eagle had arrived, she'd been busy training for this cargo snatch-up.

"Where's the bear?" Newkirk asked. He leaned out past her, dangling from his safety line over thin air.

"Ahead of us, saving its strength." Deryn pulled her gloves tighter, then tested her weight against the heavy cable on the cargo winch. It was as thick as her wrist—rated to lift a two-ton pallet of supplies. The riggers had been fiddling with the apparatus all day, but this was its first real test. This particular maneuver wasn't even in the *Manual of Aeronautics*.

"Don't like bears," Newkirk muttered. "Some beasties are too barking *huge*."

Deryn gestured at the grappling hook at the end of the cable, as big as a ballroom chandelier. "Then you'd best make sure not to stick that up the beastie's nose by accident. It might take exception."

Through the lenses of his goggles, Newkirk's eyes went wide.

Deryn gave him a punch on the shoulder, envying him for his station at the business end of the cable. It wasn't fair that Newkirk had been gaining airmanship skills while she and Alek had been plotting rebellion in Istanbul.

"Thanks for making me even *more* nervous, Mr. Sharp!"

"I thought you'd done this before."

"We did a few snatch-ups in Greece. But those were just mailbags, not heavy cargo. And from horse-drawn carriages instead of off the back of a barking great bear!"

"That does sound a bit different," Deryn said.

"Same principle, lads, and it'll work the same way," came Mr. Rigby from behind them. His eyes were on his pocket watch, but his ears never missed a thing, even in the howling Siberian wind. "Your wings, Mr. Sharp."

"Aye, sir. Like a good guardian angel." Deryn hoisted the gliding wings onto her shoulders. She would be carrying Newkirk, using the wings to guide him over the fighting bear.

Mr. Rigby signaled to the winch men. "Good luck, lads."

"Thank you, sir!" the two middies said together.

The winch began to turn, and the grappling hook slid down toward the open cargo bay door. Newkirk took hold of it and clipped himself onto a smaller cable, which would hold their combined weight as they flew.

Deryn let her gliding wings spread out. As she stepped toward the cargo door, the wind grew stronger and colder. Even through amber goggles the sunlight made her squint. She grasped the harness straps that connected her to Newkirk.

"Ready?" she shouted.

He nodded, and together they stepped off into roaring emptiness. . . .

The freezing airstream yanked Deryn sternward, and the world spun around once, sky and earth gyrating wildly. But then her gliding wings caught the air, stabilized by the dangling Newkirk, like a kite held steady by its string.

The *Leviathan* was beginning its descent. Its shadow grew below them, rippling in a furious black surge across the ground. Newkirk still grasped the grappling hook, his arms wrapped around the cable against the onrush of air.

Deryn flexed her gliding wings. They were the same kind she'd worn a dozen times on Huxley descents, but free-ballooning was nothing compared to being dragged behind an airship at top speed. The wings strained to pull her to starboard, and Newkirk followed, swinging slowly across the blur of terrain below. When Deryn centered her course again, she and Newkirk swung back and forth beneath the airship, like a giant pendulum coming to rest.

The fragile wings were barely strong enough to steer the weight of two middies. The *Leviathan*'s pilots would have to put them dead on target, leaving only the fine adjustments for Deryn.

The airship continued its descent, until she and Newkirk were no more than twenty yards above the ground. He yelped as his boots skimmed the top of a tall pine tree, sending off a burst of needles shiny with ice.

Deryn looked ahead . . . and saw the fighting bear.

She and Alek had spotted a few that morning, their dark shapes winding along the Trans-Siberian Trailway. They'd looked impressive enough from a thousand feet, but from this altitude the beast was truly monstrous.

Its shoulders stood as tall as a house, and its hot breath coiled up into the freezing air like chimney smoke.

A large cargo platform was strapped to its back. A pallet waited there, a flattened loop of metal ready for Newkirk's grappling hook. Four crewmen in Russian uniforms scampered about the bear, checking the straps and netting that held the secret cargo.

The driver's long whip flicked into the air and fell, and the bear began to lumber away. It was headed down a long, straight section of the trailway aligned with the *Leviathan*'s course.

The beastie's gait gradually lengthened into a run. According to Dr. Busk, the bear could match the airship's speed only for a short time. If Newkirk didn't get the hook right on the first pass, they'd have to swing around in a slow circle, letting the creature rest. The hours saved by not landing and loading in the normal way would be half lost.

And the czar, it seemed, wanted this cargo at its destination barking fast.

As the airship drew closer to the bear, Deryn felt its thundering tread bruising the air. Puffs of dirt drifted up from the cold, hard-packed ground in its wake. She tried to imagine a squadron of such monsters charging into battle, glittering with fighting spurs and carrying a score of riflemen each. The Germans must have been *mad* to provoke this war, pitting their machines not only against the airships and kraken of Britain, but also the huge land beasts of Russia and France.

She and Newkirk were over the straightaway now, safe from treetops. The Trans-Siberian Trailway was one of the wonders of the world, even Alek had admitted. Stamped flat by mammothines, it stretched from Moscow to the Sea of Japan and was as wide as a cricket oval—room enough for two bears to pass in opposite directions without annoying each other.

Tricky beasties, ursines. All last night Mr. Rigby had regaled Newkirk with tales of them eating their handlers.

The *Leviathan* soon caught up to the bear, and Newkirk signaled for Deryn to pull him to port. She angled her wings, feeling the tug of airflow surround her body, and she briefly thought of Lilit in her body kite. Deryn wondered how the girl was doing in the new Ottoman Republic. Then shook the thought from her head.

The pallet was drawing near, but the loop Newkirk was preparing to grab rose and fell with the bounding gait of the giant bear. Newkirk began to lower the grappling hook, trying to swing it a little nearer to its target. One of the Russians climbed higher on the cargo pallet, reaching up to help.

Deryn angled her wings a squick, drawing Newkirk still farther to port.

"HOOKING THE PACKAGE."

He thrust out the grappling hook, and metal struck metal, the rasp and clink of contact sharp in the cold wind—the hook snapped into the loop!

The Russians shouted and began to loosen the straps that held the pallet to the platform. The bear's driver waved his whip back and forth, the signal for the *Leviathan*'s pilots to ascend.

The airship angled its nose up, and the grappling hook tightened its grip on the loop, the thick cable going taut beside Deryn. Of course, the pallet didn't lift from the fighting bear's back—not yet. You couldn't add two tons to an airship's weight and expect it to climb right away.

Ballast began to spill from the *Leviathan*'s ports. Pumped straight from the gastric channel, the brackish water hit the air as warm as piss. But in the Siberian wind it froze instantly, a spray of glittering ice halos in the air.

A moment later the ice stung Deryn's face in a driving hail, pinging against her goggles. She gritted her teeth, but a laugh spilled out of her. They'd hit on the first pass, and soon the cargo would be airborne. And she was flying!

But as her laughter faded, a low growl came rumbling through the air, a sovereign and angry sound that chilled Deryn's bones worse than any Siberian wind.

The fighting bear was getting twitchy.

And it stood to reason. The frozen clart of a thousand beasties was raining down onto its head, carrying the scents of message lizards and glowworms, Huxleys and hydrogen sniffers, bats and bees and birds and the great whale itself—a hundred species that the fighting bear had never smelled before.

Its head reared up and let out another roar, and the great brown shoulders rippled with annoyance, tossing the Russian crewmen into the air. They landed safely, as sure-footed as airmen in a storm.

The grappling hook clanked in its loop as the bear jerked about, and the cargo line snapped and quivered beside Deryn. She threw her weight to the left, trying to pull herself and Newkirk to safety.

The driver's whip rose and fell a few times, and the bear settled a little. As more ballast glittered in the air above, the cargo finally began to lift.

The last one of the fighting bear's crewmen leapt from the pallet, then turned to wave. Deryn saluted him back as the bear slowed to a halt. The cargo spun in the air now, skimming just above the ground.

Deryn frowned. Why wasn't the *Leviathan* climbing faster? They didn't have much time before the next bend in the trailway, and she, Newkirk, and the cargo were still below treetop level.

She looked up. The spray of water had stopped. The ballast tanks were empty. The Clanker engines were roaring and belching smoke, trying to create aerodynamic lift. But the airship was climbing too slowly.

Deryn frowned. Dr. Busk, the head boffin himself, had done the calculations for this snatch-up. He'd cut it close, to be sure, with a long trip still ahead of them. But Deryn and Mr. Rigby had supervised the ejecting of supplies over the tundra, bringing the ship to *exactly* the right weight. . . .

Unless the cargo pallet was heavier than the czar's letter had promised.

"Barking *kings*!" Deryn shouted. Divine right didn't change the laws of gravity and hydrogen, that was for certain.

She heard the shriek of a ballast alert above, and swore. If anything tumbled from the bay doors now, she and Newkirk would be plumb in its path.

"We're too heavy!" she shouted down.

"Aye, I noticed!" the boy cried back, just as the trailway veered to the right beneath him.

Instantly the pallet clipped the top of an evergreen, and Newkirk was swallowed by an explosion of pine needles and snow.

"We need to toss some of that cargo!" Deryn cried, and angled her wings to the right. When she and Newkirk were over the pallet, she snapped a safety clip onto the cargo line, then shrugged out of the gliding harness.

She and Newkirk slid down, screaming, their boots thudding against the cargo as they landed.

"Blisters, Mr. Sharp! Are you trying to kill us?"

"I'm saving us, Mr. Newkirk, as usual." She unclipped herself and rolled onto the pallet. "We have to throw something off!"

"Full marks for stating the obvious!" Newkirk shouted, just as the pallet smashed into another treetop. The collision sent the world spinning, and Deryn fell flat, grasping for handholds.

Pressed against the cargo, her nose caught a whiff of something meaty. Deryn frowned. Was this pallet full of *dried beef*?

She raised her head and looked about. There was nothing obvious to toss overboard, no boxes to cut free. Just heavy netting covering the shapeless brown mass. It would take long minutes to cut into it with a couple of rigging knives.

"Blisters," Newkirk cried.

Deryn followed his gaze upward, and swore again. The ballast alert was in full swing. Fléchette bats were taking to the air, and dishwater was being flung from the galley windows. A barrel emerged from the cargo bay door and came tumbling down at them.

Deryn tightened her grip in case the barrel hit and sent them spinning—or would the whole pallet simply break apart?

But the barrel flashed past a few yards away, exploding into a white cloud of flour against the hard-packed tundra.

"Over here, Mr. Sharp!" Newkirk called. He had scrambled to the far side of the pallet, one foot dangling off the edge.

"What've you found?"

"Nothing!" he shouted. When Deryn hesitated, he added, "Just *come here*, you blithering idiot!"

As she headed toward Newkirk, the pallet began to tip beneath her weight. Her grasp on the netting slipped for a moment, and she skidded toward the edge.

Newkirk's hand shot out and stopped her.

"Grab hold!" he shouted as the pallet tipped farther.

Finally Deryn understood his plan—their weight was pulling the carefully balanced pallet sideways, turning it into a knife blade skimming through the trees. It was a much smaller target for the debris raining down, and the bulk of the cargo was above the two middies, protecting them from any direct hits.

Another barrel went by, barely missing, shattering in the airship's wake. A few ice-laden treetops shot past, but the *Leviathan* was finally climbing, lightened enough to pull them a few crucial yards higher.

Newkirk grinned. "Don't mind being saved, do you, Mr. Sharp?"

"No, that's quite all right, Mr. Newkirk," she said,

"RETURNING WITH THE GOODS."

shifting her hands for a better grip. "You owed me one, after all."

As the treetops slowly dropped away, Deryn climbed back up, leveling the pallet again. As they were winched higher, she took a closer look at what was beneath the cargo netting. It appeared to be nothing but dried beef, slabs and slabs of it all crushed together.

"What does this smell like to you?" she asked Newkirk.

He took a sniff. "Breakfast."

She nodded. It did smell just like bacon waiting to be tossed into a pan.

"Aye," she said softly. "But breakfast for *what?*"

○ FOUR ○

"We're still traveling west-northwest." Alek looked at his notes. "On a heading of fifty-five degrees, if my readings can be trusted."

Volger scowled at the map on his desk. "You must be mistaken, Alek. There's nothing along that course. No cities or ports, just wilderness."

"Well . . ." Alek tried to remember how Newkirk had put it. "It might have to do with the earth being round, and this map being flat."

"Yes, yes. I've already plotted a great circle route." Volger's index finger swept along a line that curved from the Black Sea to Tokyo. "But we left that behind when we veered north over Omsk."

Alek sighed. Did *everyone* but him understand this "great circle" business? Before the Great War had changed everything, Wildcount Volger had been a cavalry officer in the service of Alek's father. How did he know so much about navigation?

Through the window of Volger's stateroom, the shadows were stretching out ahead of the *Leviathan*. The setting sun, at least, agreed that the airship was still angling northward.

"If anything," Volger said, "we should be headed southwest by now, toward Tsingtao."

Alek frowned. "The German port in China?"

"Indeed. There are half a dozen Clanker ironclads based there. They threaten Darwinist shipping all across the Pacific, from Australia to the Kingdom of Hawaii. According to the newspapers that Dr. Barlow has so kindly provided me, the Japanese are preparing to lay siege to the city."

"And they need the *Leviathan*'s help?"

"Hardly. But Lord Churchill won't let the Japanese be victorious without British assistance. It wouldn't be seemly for Asians to defeat a European power all alone."

Alek groaned. "What a colossal exercise in idiocy. You mean we've come all this way just to wave the Union Jack?"

"That was the intent, I'm certain of it. But since the czar's message arrived, our course has changed." Volger drummed his fingers on the map. "There must be a clue in that cargo we picked up from the Russians. Has Dylan told you anything about it?"

"I haven't been able to ask him. He's still taking the pallet apart, because of the ballast alert."

"Because of the what?" the wildcount asked, and Alek found himself smiling. At least he understood *something* that Volger didn't.

"Just after we picked up the cargo, an alert sounded—two short rings of the Klaxon. You may remember that happening in the Alps, when we had to throw my father's gold away."

"Don't remind me."

"I shouldn't have to," Alek said. Volger had almost doomed them all by smuggling a quarter ton of gold aboard. "A ballast alert means the ship is overweight, and Dylan has been in the cargo bay with Dr. Barlow all afternoon. They must be taking apart the cargo, to find out why it's heavier than expected."

"All very logical," Volger said, then shook his head. "But I still don't see how one cargo pallet can matter to a ship three hundred meters long. It seems absurd."

"It isn't absurd at all. The *Leviathan* is aerostatic, which means it's perfectly balanced with the density of the—"

"Thank you, Your Serene Highness." Volger held up one hand. "But perhaps you could recount your aeronautics lessons another time."

"You might take an interest, Count," Alek said stiffly.

"Seeing as how aeronautics is keeping you from crashing into the ground at this very moment."

"Indeed it is. So perhaps we'd best leave it to the experts, eh, Prince?"

Several sharp retorts came to mind, but Alek held his tongue. Why was Volger in such a foul mood? When the *Leviathan* had first turned east two weeks ago, he'd seemed pleased not to be headed toward Britain and certain imprisonment. The man had gradually adapted to life aboard the *Leviathan*, exchanging information with Dr. Barlow, even taking a liking to Dylan. But for the last day Volger had seemed cross with everyone.

For that matter, Dylan had stopped delivering breakfast to the wildcount. Had the two of them had a falling-out?

Volger rolled up his map and shoved it into a desk drawer. "Find out what was in the Russian cargo, even if you have to beat it out of that boy."

"By 'that boy' I assume you mean my good friend, Dylan?"

"He's hardly your friend. You'd be free now if it weren't for him."

"That was my choice," Alek said firmly. Dylan might have argued for Alek to return to the ship, but it was no use blaming anyone. Alek had made the decision himself. "But I'll ask him what they found. Perhaps you could inquire with Dr. Barlow, since you two are on such good terms."

Volger shook his head. "That woman tells me only what she finds it convenient for us to know."

"Then, I don't suppose there are any clues in your newspapers. Anything about the Russians needing help in northern Siberia?"

"Hardly." Volger pulled a penny paper from the open desk drawer and shoved it at Alek. "But at least that American reporter has stopped writing about you."

Alek picked up the paper—the *New York World*. On its front page was a story by Eddie Malone, an American reporter that he and Dylan had met in Istanbul. Malone had learned certain secrets of the revolution, so Alek had traded his life story for the man's silence. The result was a stream of articles about Alek's parents' assassination and his escape from home.

It had all been most distasteful.

But this story wasn't about Alek. The headline read A DIPLOMATIC DISASTER ABOARD THE *DAUNTLESS*!

Below those words was a photograph of the *Dauntless*, the elephant-shaped walker used by the British ambassador in Istanbul. German undercover agents had taken it on a rampage during the *Leviathan*'s stay there, causing a near-riot for which the British had been blamed. Only Dylan's quick thinking had saved the situation from total calamity.

"PONDERING."

"But that was, what, seven weeks ago? Is this what they call news in America?"

"This paper took its time getting to me, but yes, it was old news from the start. Apparently this man Malone has run out of your secrets to spill."

"Thank heavens," Alek murmured, following the story to a page inside. Another photograph was printed there: Dylan swinging from the metal trunk of the elephant, flailing at one of the Germans.

"'A Daring Midshipman Handles the Situation,'" he read aloud, smirking. For once it was Dylan in the limelight instead of him. "May I keep this?"

The wildcount didn't answer—he was glaring at the ceiling, where a message lizard had appeared.

"Prince Aleksandar," the creature said in Dr. Barlow's voice. "Mr. Sharp and I would like the pleasure of your company in the cargo bay, if possible."

"The cargo bay?" Alek said. "Of course, Dr. Barlow. I'll join you shortly. End message."

Volger waved his hand to shoo the lizard away, but it had already scuttled off into a message tube. "Excellent. Maybe now we'll get some answers."

Alek folded up the newspaper and slipped it into a pocket. "But why would they need me?"

"For the pleasure of your company, of course." The wildcount shrugged. "Surely a lizard wouldn't lie."

◉　　◉　　◉

The cargo bay smelled like a tannery, a mix of old meat and leather. Long strips of dark brown were piled everywhere, along with a few wooden crates.

"Is *this* your precious cargo?" Alek asked.

"It's two tons of dried beef, a hundredweight of tranquilizers, and a thousand rounds of machine-gun ammunition," said Dylan, reading from a list. "And a few boxes of something else."

"Something unexpected," Dr. Barlow said. She and Tazza were in the far corner of the bay, staring down into an open crate. "And quite heavy."

"Quite," the loris on her shoulder said, eyeing the crate with displeasure.

Alek looked around for Bovril. It was hanging from the ceiling above Dylan's head. He held his hand up, and the creature crawled down onto his shoulder. Count Volger, of course, did not permit abominations in his presence.

"*Guten Tag,*" the creature said.

"*Guten Abend,*" Alek corrected, then turned to Dr. Barlow. "May I ask why the czar wanted us to pick up a load of dried beef?"

"You may not," she said. "But please take a look at this unexpected cargo. We need your Clanker expertise."

"My *Clanker* expertise?" Alek joined the boffin beside the crate. Nestled in the packing straw was a jumble of metal parts, shiny and glinting in the darkness. He knelt, reached inside, and pulled one of the parts out. Tazza gave it a sniff and made a whining noise.

It was some kind of electrikal part, about as long as a forearm and topped with two bare wires.

"The czar didn't tell you how to put this all together?"

"There wasn't meant to be any machinery at all," Dylan said. "But there's almost half a ton of parts and tools in here. Enough to drag poor Mr. Newkirk into a pine tree!"

"And all of it Clanker-made," Alek murmured. He stared at another part, a sphere of handblown glass. It fit atop the first part with a satisfying click.

"This looks like an ignition capacitor, like the one aboard my Stormwalker."

"Ignition," Bovril repeated softly.

"So you can tell us the purpose of this device?" Dr. Barlow asked.

"Perhaps." Alek peered down into the crate. There were dozens more parts there, and two more boxes to come. "But I'll need Klopp's help."

"Well, that is a bother." Dr. Barlow sighed. "But I suppose the captain can be convinced. Just see that you're quick about it. We reach our destination tomorrow."

"That soon? Interesting." Alek smiled as he spoke— he'd just seen another part that would fit onto the other two. It was tightly wound with copper wire, at least a thousand turns, like a voltage multiplier. He whistled for a message lizard, then sent it to fetch his men, but didn't wait for them.

In a way it was easy, guessing how the pieces fit together. He'd spent a month helping to keep his Storm-walker running in the wilderness with repaired, stolen, and improvised parts. And the metal and glass pieces before him were hardly improvised—they were elegant, with lines as sinuous as the *Leviathan*'s fabricated wood furniture. As Alek worked, his fingers seemed to grasp the pieces' connections, even though he didn't know the purpose of the whole yet. By the time Klopp and Hoffman had arrived, he'd made a fair start of it.

Perhaps His Serene Highness Aleksandar Prince of Hohenberg wasn't such a waste of hydrogen after all.

◎ FIVE ◎

By early the next morning the device was nearly done. The few remaining parts—the knobs and levers of the control panel—were spread across the floor. The dried beef had been removed from the cargo bay to make room, but the scent of new leather remained.

Alek, Dylan, Bauer, and Hoffman had worked without sleep, but Master Klopp had spent most of the night snoozing in a chair, awakening only to shout orders and curse whoever had designed the device. He had declared its graceful lines too fancy, an affront to Clanker principles. Bovril sat on his shoulder, memorizing new German obscenities with glee.

Since the night of the Ottoman Revolution, Klopp had used a cane, grimacing whenever he had to stand up. His battle-walker had fallen during the attack on the sultan's Tesla cannon, struck by the Orient-Express itself.

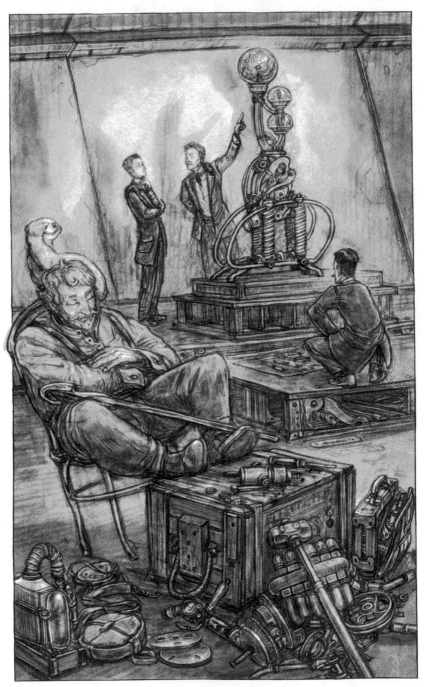

"ASSEMBLAGE OF THE DEVICE."

Dr. Busk, the *Leviathan*'s surgeon, had said it was lucky the man could walk at all.

The revolution had lasted only one night, but the cost had been high. Lilit's father had been killed, along with a thousand rebel soldiers and countless Ottomans. Whole neighborhoods of the ancient city of Istanbul lay in ashes.

Of course, the battles going on in Europe were ten times worse, especially those between Alek's countrymen and the Russians. In Galicia a horde of fighting bears had met hundreds of machines, a vast collision of flesh and metal that had left Austria reeling. And, as Dylan kept saying, the war was only just beginning.

Newkirk brought them breakfast just as sunlight began to trickle in around the edges of the cargo door.

"What in blazes is that contraption?" he asked.

Alek took the coffeepot from Newkirk's tray and poured a cup.

"A good question." He handed the coffee to Klopp, switching to German. "Any fresh ideas?"

"Well, it's meant to be carried about," Klopp said, poking at its long side handles with his cane. "Probably by two men, perhaps a third to operate it."

Alek nodded. Most of the crates had been full of spare parts and special tools; the device itself wasn't so heavy.

"But why not mount it on a vehicle?" Hoffman asked. "You could use the engine's power and save fiddling about with batteries."

"So it's designed for rough terrain," Klopp said.

"Lots of that in Siberia," Dylan spoke up. After a month among Clankers in Istanbul, the boy's German was good enough to follow most conversations now. "And Russia is Darwinist, so vehicles have no engines."

Alek frowned. "A Clanker machine designed for use by Darwinists?"

"Custom made for wherever we're headed, then." Klopp gently tapped the three glass spheres at its top. "These will react to magnetic fields."

"Magnetic," Bovril said from Klopp's shoulder, rolling the word around in its mouth.

Ignoring the engine grease under his fingernails, Alek took a piece of bacon from Newkirk's tray. The night's work had left him ravenous. "Meaning what, Master Klopp?"

"I still don't know, young master. Perhaps it's some kind of navigating machine."

"Awfully big for a compass," Alek said. And far too beautiful for anything so mundane. Most of the pieces had been milled by hand, as if its inventor hadn't wanted mass-produced parts to sully his vision.

"If I may ask something, sir?" Bauer asked.

Alek nodded. "Of course, Hans."

Bauer turned to Dylan. "We might understand this machine better if we knew why the czar tried to sneak it past you."

"Dr. Barlow reckons the czar doesn't know about this machine," Dylan said. "You see, the man we're headed toward has a reputation. He's a bit mad. The sort of fellow who might bribe a Russian officer to smuggle something for him, without thinking of the consequences. The lady boffin never liked the fellow, she says, and this just confirms that he's a . . ." He shrugged and switched to English, "A bum-rag."

"Bum-rag," Bovril said, and giggled.

"But who *is* he?" Alek asked in English.

Dylan shrugged again. "A Clanker boffin of some kind. That's all Dr. Barlow will say."

Alek finished his bacon, then looked at the parts scattered all around them and sighed. "Well, let's finish and see what happens when we turn it on."

"Is that a good idea?" Dylan looked down at the batteries, which Hoffman was charging with the power lines for the airship's searchlights. "It's stored enough electricity to throw sparks, or even explode. And we're hanging from a million cubic feet of hydrogen!"

Alek turned to Klopp and said in German, "Dylan thinks this could be dangerous."

"Nonsense." Klopp prodded the battery case with his cane. "It's designed to run for a long time at low voltage."

"Or designed to *look* that way," Dylan said, then switched to English. "Newkirk, fetch Dr. Barlow, would you?"

The other middy nodded and scampered off, looking happy to leave the Clanker device behind.

As they waited, Alek put together the control panel, polishing every piece with his sleeve. It was good to feel useful again, to have built something, even if he had no idea what it was.

When Dr. Barlow arrived, she walked once around the machine, both she and the creature on her shoulder inspecting it closely. The two lorises jabbered to each other, Bovril repeating the names of electrikal parts that it had learned during the night.

"Well done, all of you," Dr. Barlow said in her flawless German. "I take it this is a magnetic device of some kind?"

"Yes, ma'am." Klopp glanced at Dylan. "And I'm certain it won't explode."

"I should hope not." Dr. Barlow took a step back. "Well, we haven't much time. If you please, Alek, let's find out what it does."

"If you please," her loris added imperiously, which made Bovril giggle.

Alek took a slow breath, his hand pausing over the power switch. For a moment he wondered if Dylan might be right. They had no idea what this machine was.

But they'd spent all night putting the device together. There was no point in letting it sit here. He turned the power switch. . . .

For a moment nothing happened, but then a flickering glow appeared in each of the three glass spheres on the machine's top. In the drafty cargo bay Alek felt heat emanating from the machine, and a soft whine built in his ears.

The two lorises began to imitate the sound, and then Tazza joined in, until the cargo bay was humming. A sliver of light came into being inside each of the glass spheres, an electrikal disturbance, like a tiny, trapped bolt of lightning.

"Most intriguing," Dr. Barlow said.

"Aye, but what *is* it?" Dylan asked.

"As a biologist, I'm sure I don't know." The lady boffin lifted Bovril from Klopp's shoulder. "But our perspicacious friend has been watching and listening all night."

She placed the loris on the floor. It immediately clambered onto the machine, sniffing the batteries, the control panel, and finally the three glass spheres. While it moved, it kept up a steady nonsense conversation with

Dr. Barlow's loris, the two beasts repeating the names of electrikal parts and concepts to each other.

Alek watched with bemusement. He'd always wondered how Dr. Barlow had expected these creatures to keep the Ottomans out of the war. They were charming enough but hardly likely to sway an entire empire toward Darwinism. He half suspected they had been only a ruse, an excuse to take the *Leviathan* to Istanbul, and that the real plan had always been to force the strait with the behemoth.

But was there more to these lorises than met the eye?

Finally Bovril reached out a hand toward Dr. Barlow, who only frowned. But the beast on her shoulder seemed to understand. It slipped its tiny hands behind the woman's head and unclasped her necklace.

Dr. Barlow raised an eyebrow as the creature handed her jewelry over to Bovril.

"What in blazes—," Dylan began, but the lady boffin waved him silent.

Bovril held the necklace close to one of the glass spheres, and a trickle of lightning leapt out, creating a shivering connection between the pendant and the glass sphere.

"Magnetic," Bovril said.

The creature swung the pendant, and the tiny finger of light followed it back and forth. When Bovril pulled the necklace away, the lightning seemed to lose interest, retreating back into its glass sphere.

"God's wounds," Alek said softly. "That's quite odd."

"What's that necklace made of, madam?" asked Klopp.

"The pendant is steel." Dr. Barlow nodded. "Quite ferrous, I should think."

"So it's for detecting metal." Klopp pushed himself to his feet, then brought his cane up. As its steel tip drew close to one of the spheres, another trickle of lightning leapt out to meet it.

"Why would you need such a thing?" Dylan asked.

Klopp fell back into his chair. "You might use it to discover land mines. Though it's quite sensitive, so perhaps you could find a buried telegraph line. Or a buried treasure! Who knows?"

"Treasure!" Bovril declared.

"Telegraph lines? Pirate treasure?" Dylan shook his head. "Those hardly sound like things you'd find in Siberia."

Alek took a cautious step closer, squinting at the machine. The three glass spheres had settled into a jittering pattern, each tiny finger of lightning pointing in a different direction. "What's it detecting now?"

"One's aimed straight back at the stern," Dylan said. "And the other two are pointed up and toward the bow."

The two lorises made a rumbling sound.

"Of course," Hoffman said. "Most of the *Leviathan* is wood and flesh. But the engines are full of metal."

Dylan whistled. "They must be two hundred yards away."

"Yes, it's a clever machine," Klopp said. "Even if it was designed by a madman."

"I just wonder what he's looking for." The lady boffin stroked Tazza's fur as she contemplated the device, then turned and walked toward the door. "Well, I'm sure we'll find out soon enough. Mr. Sharp, see that all this is hidden away in a locked storeroom. And please don't mention it to the crew, any of you."

Alek frowned. "But won't this . . . boffin fellow be wondering where it is?"

"Indeed." Dr. Barlow gave him a smile as she slipped through the door. "And watching him squirm with curiosity should prove most interesting."

Alek headed back toward his stateroom soon after, wanting to get an hour's sleep before they arrived at their destination. He should have gone straight to Count Volger, he supposed, but he was too exhausted to endure a barrage of questions from the man. So instead Alek whistled for a message lizard when he reached his room.

When the creature appeared, Alek said, "Count Volger,

we shall arrive at our destination within the hour. But I still have no idea where that is. The cargo contained a Clanker machine of some kind. More later, when I've had some sleep. End message."

Alek smiled as the creature scuttled away into its tube. He'd never sent Volger a message lizard before, but it was high time the man accepted that the beasts were part of life here aboard the *Leviathan*.

Not bothering to remove his boots, Alek stretched out on his bunk. His eyes closed, but he could still see the glass tubes and shining metal parts of the mysterious device. His exhausted mind began to play a game of putting together its pieces, counting screws and measuring with calipers.

He groaned, wishing the thoughts would let him sleep. But mechanikal puzzles had taken over his brain. Perhaps this proved he was a Clanker at heart and there would never be a place for him aboard a Darwinist ship.

Alek sat up to pull off his jacket. There was something large in the pocket. Of course. The newspaper he'd borrowed from Volger.

He pulled it out; it was folded open to the photograph of Dylan. In all the excitement about the strange device, he'd forgotten to show it to the boy. Alek lay back down, his bleary eyes skimming across the text.

It really was the most atrocious writing, as breathless and overblown as the articles Malone had written about Alek. But it was a relief to see someone else's virtues extolled in the reporter's purple prose.

Who knows what rampant destruction might have been visited upon the crowd had the valiant midshipman not acted so quickly? He surely has bravery running in his veins, being the nephew of an intrepid airman, one Artemis Sharp, who perished in a calamitous ballooning fire only a few years ago.

A little shudder went through Alek at the words— Dylan's father again. It was strange how the man kept coming up. Was there some clue about the family secret here?

Alek shook his head, dropping the newspaper to the floor. Dylan would tell him the family secret when he was ready.

More important, Alek hadn't slept a wink all night. He lay back down, forcing his eyes closed again. The airship would reach its destination soon.

But as Alek lay there, his mind would not stop spinning.

So many times Dylan would come close to telling him something momentous. But each time he pulled away. No matter what promises Alek made, however many secrets of his own he told Dylan, the boy didn't trust him completely.

Perhaps he never would, because he simply couldn't bring himself to confide in a prince, an imperial heir, a waste of hydrogen like Alek. No doubt that was it.

It was a long, restless time before he finally fell asleep.

◦ SIX ◦

It was Newkirk who spotted them first.

He was up in a Huxley ascender, a thousand feet above the *Leviathan* in the cold white sky. His flight suit was stuffed with old rags to keep him from freezing, making his arms and legs bulge, like a tattie bogle waving semaphore flags. . . .

T-R-E-E-S—A-L-L—D-O-W-N—A-H-E-A-D.

Deryn lowered her field glasses. "Did you get that, Mr. Rigby?"

"Aye," the bosun said. "But I've no idea what it means."

"*T-R-E-E-S,*" Bovril added helpfully from Deryn's shoulder. The beastie could read semaphore as fast as any of the crew, but couldn't turn letters into words. Not yet, anyway.

"Perhaps he's seen a clearing. Shall I go up to the bow for a look, sir?"

Mr. Rigby nodded, then signaled to the winch man to give Newkirk more altitude. Deryn headed forward, making her way through the colony of fléchette bats scattered across the great airbeast's head.

"*D-O-W-N*," Bovril said.

"Aye, beastie, that spells 'down.'"

Bovril repeated the word, then shivered in the cold.

Deryn was feeling the cold too, on top of her night of missing sleep. Barking Alek and his love of contraptions. Sixteen long hours putting the mysterious machine together, and they still had no idea what its purpose was! An utter waste of time, and yet it was the happiest she'd seen Alek since the two of them had returned to the *Leviathan*.

Gears and electricals were all the boy really cared about, however much he claimed to love the airship. Just like Deryn, who'd spent a whole month in Istanbul without ever feeling at home among walkers and steam pipes. Perhaps Clankers and Darwinists would always be at war, if only in their hearts.

When she reached the prow of the ship, Deryn raised her field glasses to scan the horizon. A moment later she saw the trees.

"Barking spiders." The words coiled like smoke in the freezing air.

"Down," Bovril said.

Ahead of the airship was an endless fallen forest. Countless trees lay on their sides, plucked clean, as if a huge wind had blown them over and stripped their branches and leaves. Strangest of all, every stripped-bare trunk was pointed in the same direction: southwest. At the moment, straight at Deryn.

She'd heard of hurricanes strong enough to yank trees up from the ground, but no hurricane could make landfall here, thousands of miles from any ocean. Was there some manner of Siberian storm she'd never heard of, with icicles flying like scythes through the forest?

She whistled for a message lizard, staring uneasily at the fallen trees while she waited. When the lizard appeared, Deryn made her report, trying to keep the fear from her voice. Whatever had cut down these full-grown evergreens, which had been as hard as nails and sunk deep into the frozen tundra, would tear an airship to bits in seconds.

She made her way back to the winch, where Mr. Rigby was still taking signals from Newkirk. The Huxley was almost a mile above the ship now, its swollen hydrogen sack a dark squick upon the sky.

The bosun dropped his glasses. "At least thirty miles across, he says."

"Blisters," Deryn swore. "Might an earthquake have done this, sir?"

Mr. Rigby gave this a think, then shook his head. "Mr. Newkirk says all the fallen trees point outward, toward the edges of the destruction. No earthquake would've been that neat. Nor would a storm."

Deryn imagined a great force spreading out in all directions from a central point, knocking down trees and stripping them as clean as matchsticks as it passed.

An explosion . . .

"But we can't stand here theorizing." Mr. Rigby raised his field glasses again. "The captain has ordered us to prepare for a rescue. There are people down there, it seems."

A quarter hour later Newkirk's flags began to wave again.

"*B . . . O . . . N . . . E . . . S*," Bovril announced, its sharp eyes needing no field glasses to read the distant signals.

"God in heaven," Mr. Rigby breathed.

"But he can't mean '*bones*,' sir," Deryn said. "He's too high up to see anything as small as that!"

She stared ahead, trying to think what letters poor shivering Newkirk might have sent wrong. *Domes? Homes?* Was he was begging for some hot *scones* to be sent up?

Deryn wished she could be aloft herself, and not stuck down here wondering. But the captain wanted her standing by for a gliding descent, to prepare for a landing in rough terrain.

"Did you feel that shudder, lad?" Mr. Rigby pulled off a glove, kneeling to place his bare hand on the ship's skin. "The airbeast is unhappy."

"Aye, sir." Another shiver passed along the cilia on the membrane, like a gust of wind through grass. Deryn smelled something in the air, the scent of corrupted meat.

"Bones," Bovril said, staring straight ahead.

As Deryn raised her field glasses, she felt a trickle of cold sweat inside her flight suit. There they were on the horizon, a dozen huge columns arcing into the air. . . .

It was the rib cage of a dead airbeast, half the size of the *Leviathan* and gleaming white in the sun. The ribs looked like the skeletal fingers of two giant hands, clutching the wreck of a gondola between them.

No wonder the giant creature beneath her feet was twitchy.

"Mr. Rigby, sir, there's an airship wreck ahead."

The bosun dropped his gaze to the horizon, then let out a whistle.

"Do you think it got caught in the explosion, sir?" she asked. "Or whatever it was?"

"No, lad. Airbeast bones are hollow. The force that snapped all these trees would've shattered them. The poor beastie must have come along afterward."

"Aye, sir. Shall I whistle for another lizard and inform the bridge?"

In answer the engines slowed to quarter speed. After two days at full-ahead, the great forest around them seemed to echo with the sudden quiet.

Mr. Rigby spoke softly. "They know, lad."

As the *Leviathan* drew closer to the dead airbeast, Deryn spotted more bones among the fallen trees below. The skeletons of mammothines, horses, and smaller creatures were scattered like tenpins across the forest floor.

A growling chorus rolled up through the freezing air. Deryn recognized the sound at once, from during the cargo snatch-up, when the ballast had put too many smells into the wind.

"Fighting bears ahead, sir. Angry ones."

"Angry's not the word, Mr. Sharp. Have you noticed that we haven't spotted any caribou or reindeer herds since we reached this place? With the forest fallen, there isn't much hunting hereabouts."

"Oh, aye." Deryn looked closer at the bones of the smaller beasties. They'd all been gnawed clean, and when the distant roars came again, she heard the hunger in them.

The bears came into sight soon, a dozen at least. They were skinny and hollow-eyed, their fur matted and their

faces scarred, as if they'd been fighting among themselves. A few of them stared up at the *Leviathan*, scenting the air.

The Klaxon began to sound, the long-short ring of an upcoming ground attack.

"That's a bit odd," Mr. Rigby said. "Do the officers think aerial bombs can hit those beasties?"

"We're not dropping bombs, sir. That secret Russian cargo was mostly dried beef."

"Ah, for a distraction. Nice of the czar to provide a bit of help."

"Aye, sir," Deryn said, though she wondered how long two tons of beef would distract a dozen starving bears the size of houses.

"There we are, lad," Mr. Rigby said with satisfaction. "An encampment."

She raised her field glasses again.

Here, deep in the devastated area, a large circle of trees remained standing. They were stripped bare like the others, as if the blast had come from directly above. In a clearing among them was a handful of simple timber buildings, surrounded by barbed wire. Wispy columns of smoke rose from their chimneys, and small forms were spilling out, waving at the airship overhead.

"But how are these people still alive, sir?"

"I've no idea, Mr. Sharp. That wire wouldn't hold back a single bear, much less a dozen." The bosun lifted Bovril from her shoulder. "I'll have this beastie taken down to the lady boffin. Go prepare your Huxley for descent."

"Aye, sir," Deryn said.

"Get those men set for a rope-and-winch landing, and be quick about it. If we come about and you're not ready, we'll have to leave you all behind."

As she glided toward the ground, Deryn took a closer look at the fallen forest.

Lichen was growing over the snapped-off tree stumps, so the destruction had happened months ago, perhaps years. That was comforting, she supposed.

But this was no time for pondering. The *Leviathan* was already headed back, preparing to scatter the dried beef a few miles away. Hopefully searching through the broken trees for food would keep the beasties busy for a while.

Deryn landed the Huxley softly, just inside the ring of barbed wire. About thirty men had come out to greet her, hungry- and astonished-looking, as if they couldn't quite believe that rescue had arrived. But a half dozen of them took hold of the Huxley's tentacles with the efficiency of experienced airmen.

Among those watching was a tall, slender man with dark hair, a mustache, and piercing blue eyes. The others' furs were threadbare, but he wore a fine traveling coat and carried a peculiar walking stick. He watched as the

Huxley was secured, then he addressed Deryn in an unfamiliar accent.

"You are British?"

She struggled out of the piloting harness and made a bow. "Aye, sir. Midshipman Dylan Sharp, at your service."

"How annoying."

"Excuse me?"

"I specifically requested that no powers other than Russia be involved in this expedition."

Deryn blinked. "I don't know about that, sir. But you *do* seem to be in a spot of bother."

"I will grant you that." The man pointed his walking stick at the airship overhead. "But what on earth is a *British* airship doing in deepest Siberia?"

"We're barking rescuing you!" Deryn cried. "And we haven't any time to debate the matter. The ship will

be dropping food for those beasties a few miles from here, like a trail of breadcrumbs leading away from us. But it won't keep them busy for long."

"There is no need for haste, young man. This compound is quite secure."

Deryn looked at the coils of barbed wire a few yards away. "I doubt that, sir. Those bears have already eaten one airbeast. If they get wind of another on the ground, that wire won't stop them!"

"It will stop any living creature. Observe." The man strode toward the fence, extending his walking stick before him. When he prodded the wire with the stick's metal tip, a flurry of sparks shot into the air.

"What in blazes?" Deryn cried.

"An invention of mine, a crude improvisation with many defects in its current form. But necessary under the circumstances."

Deryn looked up at her Huxley in horror, but the other men had already pulled it a fair distance from the wire. At least they weren't *all* barking mad down here.

"I shall call it the 'electrical fence,' I think." The man smiled. "The bears are quite wary of it."

"Aye, I'm sure they are!" Deryn said. "But my airship's a hydrogen breather. You'll have to turn that electricity off, or you'll blow us all to bits!"

"Well, obviously. But the bears won't know that the

fence has been disarmed. The work of Dr. Pavlov is quite instructive in this case."

Deryn ignored his blether. "This clearing's too small for my airship, anyway. We'll have to get out of these trees and into the fallen area." She turned in a slow circle, counting the men around her. There were twenty-eight in all, perhaps a thousand pounds heavier than the cargo the airship had just dropped. "Is this everyone? It'll be tricky, making a quick ascent with this much weight."

"I'm aware of the difficulties. I arrived here by airship."

"You mean that dead airbeast we saw? What on earth happened to it?"

"We fed it to the bears, Mr. Sharp."

Deryn took a step back. "You *what?*"

"In outfitting my expedition, the czar's advisers didn't take into account the desolation of this region. We were undersupplied, and the bears of my cargo train began to lack for hunting. I was too close to a breakthrough to abandon the project." He twirled his walking stick. "Though, if I'd known a *British* ship would come meddling as a result, I might have chosen otherwise."

Deryn shook her head, still not believing. How could he have done such a thing to a poor innocent beastie? And how had the czar dared to send a British airship to rescue this madman, after he'd fed his own ship to the bears?

"Pardon me for asking, sir, but who in blazes are you?"

The man stood straighter, extending his hand with a courtly bow.

"I am Nikola Tesla. Pleased to meet you, I suppose."

⬡ SEVEN ⬡

The *Leviathan* was a few miles distant when its bomb bay doors opened. Bales of dried beef fell in ten-second intervals. As each one dropped, the airship rose a little higher in the air.

"An ingenious distraction, I'll admit," Mr. Tesla said. "Of course, if you'd brought this food earlier, I'd still have an airship."

Deryn gave him a hard look. He'd spoken so lightly of what he'd done, feeding not only his airbeast, she realized now, but also the horses and mammothines of his cargo train to the fighting bears. And all to stay a few more weeks in this blighted place.

"What were you doing here, anyway, Mr. Tesla?"

"I should think that would be obvious, boy. I am studying the phenomenon around us."

"Did you find out what caused it?"

"I have always known the cause. I was only curious about the results." The man raised a hand. "I must remain secretive at the moment, but soon the world will know."

He had a mad gleam in his eye, and as Deryn turned away toward the *Leviathan*, a twitchy feeling came over her.

This was, of course, the same Mr. Tesla who'd invented the Tesla cannon, a lightning weapon that had twice almost destroyed the *Leviathan*. He was a Clanker boffin, a maker of German secret weapons, and yet the czar had given him free run of Darwinist Russia.

None of it made sense.

She thought of the mysterious device hidden below-decks back on the *Leviathan*, and wondered why this man had wanted it smuggled here. It certainly wouldn't have been much use for fending off bears.

The airship's engines changed pitch. The bomb run was finished.

"They'll be coming about now," Deryn said. "We should head for the clearing."

Mr. Tesla waved his walking stick in the air, calling out in what Deryn reckoned was Russian. A group of the men ran into one of the buildings and came back with large packs on their shoulders.

"I'm sorry, sir, but you can't bring all that gear. We're too barking heavy as it is!"

"I am hardly going to abandon my photographs and samples, young man. This expedition took years to prepare!"

"But if the ship can't take off, it's all lost anyway. Along with us!"

"You shall have to make room, then. Or leave my men behind."

"Are you mad?" Deryn cried, then shook her head. "Listen, sir, if you want to stay here with your samples until the bears eat you, that's fine. But these men are coming with me, *without* any of that extra weight!"

Mr. Tesla laughed. "You'll have to explain that to them, I'm afraid. How good is your Russian, Mr. Sharp?"

"It's barking *fluent*," she lied, then turned to the men. "Do any of you speak English?"

They stared back at her, looking a bit confused. One offered up a choice curse in English, but then shrugged, apparently having exhausted his vocabulary.

Deryn clenched her teeth, wishing Alek were here. For all his useless knowledge, he could speak a fair number of languages. And this mad boffin might listen to another Clanker.

She looked at the men again. Some of them must have crewed the dead airship, so they would have to understand weight limits. . . .

But there wasn't time to put on a pantomime. The

howls of the bears were echoing through the still, stripped trees. They'd already found the first of the food, and had fallen to fighting over it.

"Just get your men moving, sir," she said. "We'll discuss this at the ship."

It took a few minutes to reach the edge of the standing trees, and another ten to find a level field large enough for the *Leviathan* to land upon. "Level" was hardly the word for it, though. Here near the center of the destruction, the fallen trees weren't laid out so neatly. They were jumbled together like in a game of Spellican sticks, with jagged splinters thrusting up from their stumps.

Deryn scrambled across the fallen trunks, hoping she could estimate distances properly in all this muddle. She pointed and waved at the Russians, like a cricket captain setting a field, and she soon had them arranged in a long oval a little larger than the *Leviathan*'s gondola.

"The ship's light after dropping all that beef," she explained to Tesla. "Normally the captain would vent hydrogen to land, but not if he wants to get back up quickly. We'll have to use ropes to drag it down."

The man lifted an eyebrow. "Are there enough of us?"

"Not a chance. If a gust of wind came along, we'd all be yanked into the air. So when the ropes fall, have your men tie them to the trees." She pointed at a fallen pine as big around as a rum barrel. "The bigger the better."

"But we won't be strong enough to pull the ship down."

"Aye, the ship pulls *itself* down, with winches inside the gondola. Once it's low enough, we'll go aboard and cut the ropes, and the ship pops back up like a cork in water."

Deryn paused, listening. Low growls rolled through the forest, setting her small hairs on end. The bears sounded a squick closer now, or maybe it was just her nerves.

"If you hear a Klaxon ringing in pairs, tell your men to throw anything they can out the windows—including your precious samples—or the bears will be having us all for dinner!"

The man nodded and began to instruct his men in Russian, waving his walking stick as he called to them. Deryn guessed he was leaving out the part about the ballast alert, but there was nothing she could do about that. She pulled out a short length of line and began to tie herself a friction hitch, in case she needed to climb.

Soon the airship was overhead, its engines rumbling as the crew pulled it to a halt. Heavy cables fell from the cargo deck portholes, a swaying forest of rope tumbling into place around them.

The Russians began to scramble about, gathering the cables and tying them onto the trees. Deryn could tell the airmen among them by their knots—at least a dozen of the men had been in the fallen airship's crew. Surely they would understand that if the bears were on their way and the ship wasn't rising, the boffin's precious baggage would have to go overboard. And no decent airman would hesitate to disobey Mr. Tesla, after what he'd done to that airbeast.

When the last man had stepped back from his knots, Deryn pulled out her semaphore flags and sent the ready signal. The ropes went taut, shuddering and creaking as the winches started to turn.

At first the airship didn't seem to move at all. But a few of the smaller trees began to stir, shifting along the ground. Deryn ran toward the nearest and jumped on to add her weight to it. The Russians understood, and soon all the nervously stirring trees had men standing on them. Mr. Tesla watched impassively, as if the operation were some sort of physics experiment and not a rescue mission.

It was almost noon, and the *Leviathan*'s shadow lay over them all, slowly widening as the airship descended.

Deryn listened again, and frowned. The sounds of bears in the distance had faded. Were they so far away she couldn't hear them anymore? Or had the last scrap of beef been found and eaten, and now the creatures were charging toward the scent of airbeast?

"Quite large, your hydrogen breather," Mr. Tesla said, then frowned. "Does that say '*Leviathan*'?"

"Aye, so you've heard of us."

"Indeed. You've been in the—" The wind gave a violent start, and the tree Deryn was standing on was pulled into the air, knocking Mr. Tesla to the ground. The *Leviathan* drifted twenty feet or so, dragging along a small host of Russians on their fallen logs.

They clung on gamely, though. Soon the wind died, the airship settling earthward again.

"Are you all right, sir?" Deryn called.

"I'm fine." Mr. Tesla stood, dusting off his traveling coat. "But if your ship can lift these trees, then why complain about a bit of extra luggage?"

"That was a gust of wind. Do you want to bet your life on getting another one!"

Deryn looked up. The *Leviathan* was close enough for her to see one of the officers leaning out of the front bridge window. There were semaphore flags fluttering in his hands. . . .

B-E-A-R-S—H-E-A-D-E-D—T-H-I-S—W-A-Y—F-I-V-E—M-I-N-U-T-E-S.

"Blisters," Deryn said.

The airship was still a dozen yards up when Deryn spotted the first fighting bear.

It was loping through the area of standing trees, huffing coils of condensation into the freezing air. The bear was a small one, its shoulders barely ten feet high. Perhaps the others had kept it away from the spoils of dried beef.

It certainly didn't *look* like a beastie that had already eaten lunch.

"Climb!" Deryn shouted, pointing up her own rope. "Tell them to climb!"

Mr. Tesla didn't say a word, but his men needed no translation. They began to pull their way up toward the portholes, hand over hand on the thick mooring ropes. None of them thought to drop his pack, or perhaps they were too scared of the Clanker boffin to leave anything behind.

But there was nothing Deryn could do for them now. She scampered up her own line, glad for the friction hitch she'd tied earlier.

As the men's weight was added to the ropes, the lines began to slacken, the airship settling closer to the ground. This was the situation Deryn had wanted to avoid—another gust of wind would pop the ropes taut again, flinging off the men holding them.

She looked over her shoulder. The small bear had

broken into the open, and larger shapes loomed behind it.

"Sharp!" Mr. Rigby's voice called from the porthole above her head. "Get those men to drop their packs!"

"I've tried, sir. They don't speak English!"

"But can't they *see* the bears coming! Are they mad?"

"No, just afraid of that fellow there." She jerked her chin toward Mr. Tesla, who still stood on the ground, impassively regarding the approaching bear. "*He's* the mad one!"

The *whoosh* of a compressed air gun split the air, and Deryn heard a howl. The anti-aeroplane bolts had hit the closest bear and sent it tumbling among the fallen trees.

A moment later it stood again and shook its head. A fresh mark gleamed on the beastie's scarred and patchy fur, but it let out a defiant roar.

"I think you've just made it *angry*, sir!"

"Not to worry, Mr. Sharp. We're putting that tranquilizer to good use."

Deryn glanced backward as she climbed, and saw that the bear looked unsteady on its feet now, ambling across the fallen trees like an airman full of too much drink.

When Deryn reached the porthole, Mr. Rigby stuck out a hand and pulled her in.

"The spare cargo's ready to drop," the bosun said, "so we've plenty of lift. But with bears closing in, the captain won't take us any closer to the ground. Can the rest of those men climb?"

"Aye, sir. About half of them are airmen, so they should—"

"Good heavens," Mr. Rigby interrupted, peering out the porthole. "What in blazes is that man doing?"

Deryn crowded in beside the bosun. Mr. Tesla was still on the ground, facing three more bears that had broken from the trees.

"Barking spiders!" Deryn breathed. "I didn't think he was *this* mad."

The largest of the creatures was hardly twenty yards from Tesla, leaping across the fallen trees in huge bounds. The man calmly raised his walking stick. . . .

A bolt of lightning leapt from its tip, with a sound like the air itself tearing. The beast reared onto its hind legs and howled, trapped for a split second in a jagged cage of light. The brilliance faded instantly, but the bear howled and turned to flee, the other beasties following in its wake.

Mr. Tesla inspected the end of his walking stick, which was black and smoking, then turned toward the airship.

"You may land your ship properly now," he called up. "Those beasts will be wary for an hour or so."

The bosun nodded dumbly, and before he could call

"REPULSION OF THE STARVING WAR BEASTS."

for a message lizard, the winches started up, inching the ship lower again. The officers were in agreement.

Mr. Rigby found his voice a moment later. "It's not just the bears that should be wary, Mr. Sharp."

She nodded slowly. "Aye, sir. We'll have to keep an eye on that fellow."

◦ EIGHT ◦

Alek awoke to a thunderclap, a buzzing sound, and then a monstrous roar.

He sat up and blinked his eyes, convinced for a moment that some awful dream had shaken him from sleep. But the sounds kept coming—shouting, the creak of ropes, and beastly growls. The air smelled of lightning.

Alek swung his boots to the floor and ran to his stateroom window. He'd only meant to doze for an hour, but the sun was high and the *Leviathan* had arrived at its destination. Dozens of mooring lines stretched to the earth below. The figures manning them were dressed in furs instead of airmen's uniforms, all of them shouting in . . . Russian?

The ground was littered with fallen trees—hundreds of them, maybe *thousands*. Chimney smoke rose from a distant cluster of buildings. Was this some sort of logging camp?

Then Alek heard another roar, and saw fighting bears among the fallen trees. They had no riders, not even harnesses, and their matted fur looked wild. He took an involuntary step back from the window. The ship was low enough for the giant beasts to reach it!

But they seemed to be running away.

Alek remembered the thunderclap that had woken him. The ship's crew must have scared the creatures off somehow.

He leaned out the window as the *Leviathan* settled to the ground. Gangways were dropped, and the Russians, at least two dozen of them, climbed aboard. Soon a wailing siren swept through the ship, warning of a fast ascent.

Alek pulled himself back inside just in time. The air crackled with the sound of ropes being cut, and the airship shot straight up, rising as fast as the steam elevators he'd ridden in Istanbul.

What *was* this place? The jumble of fallen trees stretched as far as the horizon, the area far more vast than any logging camp could be. Even as the *Leviathan* climbed into the sky, no end to the destruction came into sight.

Alek turned toward his cabin door, wondering where to go for answers. The Darwinists might involve him when they needed his Clanker expertise, but they wouldn't be calling for him now.

Where would Dylan be at a time like this? In the cargo bay?

At the thought of the boy, Alek remembered the newspaper lying by his bed. The questions he'd fallen asleep asking welled up again. But this was hardly the time to wonder about the mysterious Dylan Sharp.

The corridors of the ship were teaming with the Russians who'd come aboard. They were unshaven and haggard, half starved beneath their thick furs. The *Leviathan*'s crew was trying to relieve them of their heavy packs, but the men were resisting, English and Russian colliding with little effect.

Alek looked about, wondering how the ship could lift them all. The crew must have dumped every last bit of spare supplies.

A gloved hand landed on his shoulder. "It's you, Alek. Perfect!"

He turned to find Dylan before him. The boy was wearing a flight suit, his boots muddy.

"You were out there?" Alek asked. "With those bears?"

"Aye, but they're not so bad. Can you speak any Russian?"

"All the Russians I've met have spoken French." Alek

looked at the starving, unkempt men around him and shrugged. "And I think they were a different class of Russian."

"Well, ask them anyway, you ninny!"

"Of course." Alek began to push his way through the corridor, repeating, *"Parlez-vous français?"*

A moment later Dylan was imitating him, calling out the phrase with a distinctly Scottish lilt. One of the Russians looked up with a spark of recognition, and led them both to a small man wearing pince-nez glasses and a blue uniform beneath his furs.

Alek bowed. *"Je suis Aleksandar, Prince de Hohenberg."*

The man bowed in return and said in perfect French, "I am Viktor Yegorov, captain of the Czar's Airship *Empress Maria*. Are you in charge here?"

"No, sir. I'm only a guest on this ship. You're the captain of these men?"

"The captain of a dead airship, you mean!" The man glared over Alek's shoulder. "That fool is in charge."

Among the crowd was a tall man dressed in civilian clothes, being led away by two of the ship's officers.

Alek turned to Dylan. "This man is Yegorov, an airship captain." He pointed. "But he says that fellow is in charge."

Dylan snorted. "Aye, *him* I've met already. That's Mr. Tesla, the Clanker boffin, and he's barking mad!"

"Tesla the inventor?" Alek asked. "You must be mistaken."

Captain Yegorov heard the name and spat on the floor. "He cost me my ship, and almost got us all killed! An utter fool, with the czar's men behind him."

Alek said in careful French. "It isn't Nikola Tesla, is it? I thought he was working for the Clankers."

"Of course he was!" the captain said. "The Germans funded his experiments when no one else would, and he designed plenty of weapons for them. But now that war is here, he's seen what they've done to his motherland! He's a Serb."

"Ah," Alek said softly. "Of course."

This Great War might have stretched across the world, but it had all started with the invasion of Serbia, for which Alek's family was to blame. His father—heir to the Austro-Hungarian throne—and mother had been killed by a group of Serbian revolutionaries, or so everyone thought. In reality the murders had been plotted by Alek's own granduncle and the Germans. But tiny Serbia had been the first victim of Austria's revenge.

Captain Yegorov's eyes narrowed. "Wait. Is that . . . an Austrian uniform?"

Alek looked down at himself, and realized he was wearing his piloting jacket thrown over grease-stained mechanik's overalls.

"Yes. Hapsburg Guards, to be precise."

"And you're the prince of Hohenberg, you said?" Captain Yegorov shook his head. "The archduke's son, on a British airship? So the newspapers were telling the truth."

Alek wondered how Eddie Malone's ridiculous articles had made it to Siberia. "Some measure of it, anyway. I am Aleksandar."

The man let out a dry laugh. "Well, I suppose if a Clanker inventor can switch sides, why not an Austrian prince?"

Alek nodded, the words finally sinking in. Nikola Tesla—inventor of wireless transmission, the Tesla cannon, and countless other devices—had joined the Darwinists. Count Volger would be fascinated to hear this bit of news.

"What are you two blethering about?" Dylan asked. "Has he told you yet why that Clanker boffin is here?"

"Mr. Tesla appears to have joined the Darwinists," Alek said in English. He turned to the captain again. "But why are you all in Siberia? Mr. Tesla is an inventor, not an explorer."

"He was searching for something in that fallen forest." Captain Yegorov shook his head. "I have no idea what."

Alek remembered the strange device in the ship's belly. "Something metal?"

The man shrugged. "It could be. A few days ago his soldiers excavated a huge hole, and he was quite excited. After that we retreated inside the wire to wait for rescue."

Alek turned to Dylan, roughly translating. "Tesla was looking for something here, something secret. He may have found it a few days ago, whatever it was."

"Blisters. That means it's come aboard." Dylan looked down the crowded corridor, full of men with heavy packs but no Tesla. "They've taken him forward to speak with the officers."

"Do you suppose they'd want to meet Captain Yegorov?" Alek asked.

"Aye, they would." Dylan smiled. "And they might need a translator as well."

A marine guard stood at the entrance to the forward corridor, keeping back the Russians. But he saluted when Dylan approached, and listened as the boy explained who Captain Yegorov was, and how he spoke no English. A few minutes later Alek found himself and the captain being taken forward.

"Watch out for that bum-rag!" Dylan called, then turned away to face the throng.

In the navigation room were Captain Hobbes, Dr. Barlow, Dr. Busk, and the famous Mr. Tesla. The inventor was elegantly dressed, considering he'd just been rescued from the middle of Siberia, but he had a wild gleam in his eye. He clutched a walking stick that looked as though it had been thrust tip-first into a fire.

"I see no reason for this man to be here," Tesla said, giving Captain Yegorov a cold stare. The man said something short and sharp in Russian back at him.

Dr. Barlow spoke in a calming voice. "This is a difficult moment for us all, gentlemen. Our ship is full of men and empty of supplies. The expertise of another airship captain is welcome here."

Tesla gave a snort, which the lady boffin politely ignored.

"If you please," she added to Alek. "My French is a bit rusty."

As he translated her welcome for Yegorov, Alek heard a murmuring overhead, and glanced up to see both Bovril and Dr. Barlow's loris hanging from the message lizard tubes. They were repeating everything, relishing the sounds of a new language.

Captain Yegorov bowed. "You have my thanks for rescuing us, and I appreciate the dire situation you are in. But it's no fault of mine. That madman ordered his soldiers to kill my airship. Food for the bears!"

Alek translated the last part into English haltingly, not quite believing what he was saying. The *Leviathan*'s officers looked horrified as well.

After a moment's silence Dr. Busk cleared his throat. "It is not our place to pass judgment on what has happened here. We are on a rescue mission, nothing more. Perhaps we should all introduce ourselves." He turned to Captain Yegorov and said in slow, untidy French, "I am Dr. Busk, head science officer aboard His Majesty's Airship *Leviathan*."

As Dr. Barlow introduced herself and the captain, Alek noticed that her French was flawless. He wondered why she really wanted him here.

Mr. Tesla looked bored and irritable, tapping his cane and grimacing as pleasantries went around the table. But when Alek introduced himself, the inventor's eyes lit up.

"The famous prince!" he said in English. "I've been reading about you."

"Ah, you, too," Alek sighed. "I had no idea the *New York World* was so popular in Siberia."

Mr. Tesla laughed at this. "My laboratory is in New York City, and you were the talk of the town when I left. And by the time I passed through Saint Petersburg, the czar's court was also buzzing about you!"

An unpleasant feeling came over Alek, as always when he thought of thousands of strangers discussing the details of his life. "Don't believe everything you read in the newspapers, Mr. Tesla."

"Indeed. They claim you're pulling strings in the Ottoman Republic, and yet here you are aboard the *Leviathan*. Are you concealing the fact that you've become a Darwinist?"

"A Darwinist?" Alek dropped his eyes to the table, suddenly aware of the *Leviathan*'s officers in the room. "I don't know if you could say that. But if you've read about me, you know that the Clanker Powers plotted my parents' death. The Germans and my granduncle, the Austrian emperor, are to blame for this war. I only want to end it."

Mr. Tesla nodded slowly. "We are both servants of peace, then."

"A noble sentiment, gentlemen," Captain Hobbes said.

"But at the moment we are at war. We have twenty-eight extra mouths to feed, and we have dropped most of our supplies onto the tundra to make room for them."

"Airships certainly have their limitations," Mr. Tesla said.

Alek ignored the man, quickly translating Captain Hobbes's words into French.

"If we head straight toward the airfield at Vladivostok, we'll all survive," Captain Yegorov said. "It's two days away. We won't starve, and for water we can scoop up snow without landing, as Russian airships have done for years."

Alek translated, and Captain Hobbes gave a firm nod.

"We're grateful that you have joined our side in this conflict, Mr. Tesla, and the czar has asked us to offer any assistance we can. But I'm afraid Captain Yegorov is right. We can't take you back to Saint Petersburg just yet. We'll have to keep heading east."

The inventor waved his hand. "It doesn't matter. I haven't decided yet where I wish to go."

"Thank heaven for small favors," Dr. Barlow said quietly.

"After we resupply in Vladivostok, we may have to complete our mission in Japan," Captain Hobbes said. "But I won't be sure until the Admiralty's orders reach us from London."

"If you only had wireless," Tesla muttered. "Instead of those ridiculous birds."

Captain Hobbes ignored this. "In the meantime we shall have to ration our food carefully." He looked at Captain Yegorov, and Alek repeated his words in French.

"We are airmen. Of course we understand," Yegorov said. "We've all missed a few meals since arriving in Tunguska."

"Tunguska," said Bovril from the ceiling.

Dr. Barlow glanced up at the beast, then asked in French, "Is that the name of this place?"

Captain Yegorov shrugged. "The Tunguska River passes through this forest, but it hardly has a name."

"Not yet," Tesla muttered. "But soon everyone will know what happened here."

Dr. Barlow turned to him, switching to English. "If I may ask, Mr. Tesla, what *did* happen here?"

"To put it simply, the greatest explosion in our planet's history," the man said softly. "The sound broke windows hundreds of miles away. It flattened the forest in all directions, and threw such dust into the air that the skies went red for months around the world."

"Around the world?" Dr. Barlow asked. "When was this exactly?"

"The early morning of June 30, 1908. Back in the civilized world the atmospheric effects were barely noticed. But if it had happened anywhere except Siberia, the event would have filled all mankind with astonishment."

"Astonishment," Bovril whispered softly, and Tesla paused to give the beast an irritated stare. Alek glanced out the navigation room's slanted windows. Even at this height, he could see that the fallen trees stretched out endlessly.

"I came here to study what happened, and soon I shall report my results." As the inventor continued, he placed a heavy hand on Alek's shoulder and turned his gaze to him. "When I do, the world will shudder, and perhaps at last find peace."

"Peace? Because of an explosion?" Alek asked. "But what caused it, sir?"

Mr. Tesla smiled, and tapped his walking stick three times upon the floor.

"Goliath did."

◦ NINE ◦

"He is quite mad, of course," Alek said.

Count Volger drummed his fingers on his desk, his eyes still locked on Bovril. Dr. Barlow had handed the creature to Alek as the meeting had broken up, and Alek hadn't stopped to leave it in his own stateroom. The news was simply too extraordinary to wait. But now Volger and the beast were staring at each other, a contest that Bovril appeared to be enjoying.

Alek pulled the creature from his shoulder and placed it on the floor. He stepped closer to the stateroom window. "Mr. Tesla says he did all this from America, with some kind of machine. Six years ago."

"In 1908?" Volger asked, his eyes still fixed on the beast. "And he's waited until *now* to tell the world?"

"The Russians wouldn't allow a Clanker scientist into their country," Alek said. "Not until he switched sides. So he couldn't study the effects firsthand. But now that he's seen what his weapon can do, he says he's going to make the invention public."

Volger finally tore his eyes from Bovril. "Why would he test this weapon on a place he couldn't visit?"

"He says this was an accident, a misfire. He only wanted to 'create some fireworks' and didn't realize how powerful Goliath was." Alek frowned. "But surely you don't believe any of this."

Volger turned to stare out the window. The *Leviathan* was nearing the edge of the devastation, where only the youngest trees had fallen. But the massive extent of the explosion was still apparent.

"Do you have another explanation for what happened here?"

Alek sighed slowly, then pulled out a chair and sat down. "Of course I don't."

"Goliath," Bovril said softly.

Count Volger gave the beast an unfriendly look. "What do the Darwinists think?"

"They don't question Mr. Tesla's claims." Alek shrugged. "Not to his face, at any rate. They seem quite pleased that he's joined their side."

"Of course they are. Even if the man's lost his mind, he can still show them a trick or two. And if he's telling the truth, he could end the war with the flick of a switch."

Alek looked out the window again. The magnitude of the fallen forest, and the fact that Volger wasn't laughing outright at Tesla's absurd claim, made him feel queasy. "I suppose that's true enough. Imagine Berlin after such an explosion."

"Not Berlin," Volger said.

"What do you mean?"

"Tesla is a Serb," Volger explained slowly. "*Our* country attacked his homeland, not Germany."

Alek felt the weight of the war settling on his shoulders again. "My family is to blame, you mean."

"Tesla might well think so. If this weapon of his really works, and he uses it again, it will be Vienna that lies in splinters."

Alek felt something dreadful rising up inside him, like the hollow feeling he'd carried inside since his parents' murder, but greater. "Surely no one would ever use such a weapon against *a city*."

"There are no limits in war," Volger said, still staring out the window.

Then Alek recalled the dead airbeast, sacrificed to the fighting bears so that Tesla could complete his mission. The man was determined, it seemed.

Bovril shifted on the floor, saying, "Splinters."

Volger gave the beast another withering look, then turned to Alek. "This may be an opportunity for you to serve your people, Prince, in a way few sovereigns can."

"Of course." Alek sat up straighter. "We'll convince him that Austria is not his enemy. He's read about me in those newspapers. He understands that I want peace too."

"That would be the best solution," Volger said. "But we must be certain of his intentions before we let him leave this ship."

"*Let* him leave? I hardly think we can convince the captain to arrest him."

"I wasn't thinking of an arrest." Count Volger leaned closer, his hands splayed across the map of Siberia on the desk. "How close were you standing to him in that meeting? How close might any of us find ourselves to this man over the next days?"

Alek blinked. "Surely you're not suggesting violence, Count."

"I am suggesting, young prince, that this man is a danger to your people. What if he wants revenge for what Austria has done to his homeland?"

"Ah. Revenge again," Alek muttered.

"Two *million* of your subjects live in Vienna. Would you not lift a hand to save them?"

Alek sat there, uncertain of what to say. It was true—half an hour ago he'd been standing next to the famous inventor, close enough to put a knife into him. But the whole idea was barbaric.

"He thinks Goliath can end the war," Alek managed at last. "The man wants peace!"

"As do we all," Count Volger said. "But there are many ways to end a war. Some more peaceful than others."

There was a knock on the door.

"*Mr.* Sharp," Bovril said, then gave a giggle.

"Come in, Dylan," Alek called. The lorises had very keen hearing and could tell people apart by their footsteps or door knocks, even the particular rasp of how they drew a sword.

The door swung open, and Dylan took a step inside. He and Volger exchanged a cold glance.

"I thought I'd find you here, Alek. How was the meeting?"

"Quite illuminating." Alek glanced from Dylan to Volger. "I'll tell you all about it, but . . ."

"I need to get some sleep first," Dylan said. "Up all night, and out with the bears while you were napping."

Alek nodded. "I'll keep Bovril, then."

"Aye, but get a squick more sleep yourself," Dylan said. "The lady boffin wants us to do some skulking tonight, to find out what Mr. Tesla's been up to."

"Skulking," Bovril said, quite happy with the word.

"An excellent idea," Alek said. "There's no telling what he's brought aboard."

"Then, I'll see you after nightfall." Dylan made an

infinitesimal bow at Volger. "Your countship."

Volger nodded in return. Once the door was closed again, a tiny shiver went through Bovril.

"Have you two had some sort of a falling-out?" Alek asked.

"A falling-out?" Volger snorted. "We were hardly friends in the first place."

"In the first place? So you *are* on the outs with each other." Alek let out a dry laugh. "What happened? Did Dylan talk back during his fencing lessons?"

The wildcount didn't answer, but rose from his desk and began to pace about the room. Alek felt his smile fade, remembering what they'd been discussing.

But when the wildcount finally spoke, he said, "How important is that boy to you?"

"A moment ago, Count, you were suggesting cold-blooded murder. And now you're asking about Dylan?"

"Are you trying to avoid the question?"

"No." Alek shrugged. "I think Dylan's an excellent soldier and a good friend. A good *ally*, I might add. He helped me get into that meeting today. Without him we'd be sitting here without a clue as to what's happening on this ship."

"An ally." Volger sat back down, dropping his gaze to the map on his desk. "Fair enough. Does Tesla say he can fire this weapon at any spot on earth?"

"I'm having trouble following your leaps in conversation today, Volger. But yes, he says he can aim it now."

"But how can he be certain, if this first event was an accident?"

Alek sighed, trying to cast his mind back to the meeting. Tesla had gone on at length about the matter. Despite claiming to be keeping secrets, the inventor had a gift for disquisition.

"He's been working on that problem for six years, ever since the accidental firing. He knew from newspaper accounts that something had happened in Siberia, something extraordinary. And now that he's measured the explosion's exact center, he can adjust his weapon accordingly."

Volger nodded. "So that device you and Klopp put together, it was meant to find the center of the explosion?"

"Well . . . that doesn't make sense. Klopp says it's a metal detector."

"When a shell lands, aren't there traces of metal left?"

"But it isn't that *kind* of weapon." Alek cast his mind back, trying to remember how the great inventor had described it. "Goliath is a Tesla cannon of sorts, one that becomes part of the Earth's magnetic field. It casts the planet's energy up through the atmosphere and around the world. Like the northern lights, he said, but a million times more powerful. The way he described it, the air itself caught fire here!"

"I see." Volger let out a slow sigh. "Or rather, I don't see at all. This may all be a case of madness, of course."

"Surely," Alek said, feeling himself relax. The notion of murdering Tesla to stop some imaginary event was too absurd to contemplate. "I'll ask Klopp what he thinks. And Dr. Barlow will also venture an opinion, no doubt."

"No doubt," Bovril said thoughtfully.

Count Volger waved his hand at the beast. "Is that *all* this abomination does? Repeat words at random?"

"Random," Bovril said, then chuckled a bit.

Alek reached down to stroke the creature's fur. "That's what I thought, at first. But Dr. Barlow claims that the beast is quite"—he used the English word—"*perspicacious*. And it does make a good suggestion every now and then."

"Even a stopped clock is right twice a day," Volger muttered. "Clearly those creatures were nothing but an excuse to have a snoop around Istanbul. Bringing the behemoth down the strait was always the Darwinists' plan."

Alek lifted the beast back up to his shoulder. He'd thought the same thing himself, back in Istanbul. But just that morning in the cargo hold, the creature had borrowed Dr. Barlow's necklace to show how the mysterious device worked.

Surely *that* couldn't have been random.

But Alek didn't mention it. No point in making the wildcount even more uneasy around the beast.

"I may not understand Goliath," he said simply. "But I understand Darwinist fabrications even less."

"Keep it that way," Volger said. "You're the heir to the Austrian throne, not some zookeeper. I'll talk to Klopp about all this. In the meantime you should follow Dylan's advice and get some sleep before tonight."

Alek raised an eyebrow. "You don't mind me skulking with a commoner?"

"If what Tesla says is true, your empire faces grave danger. It's your duty to learn everything you can." Count Volger stared at him a moment, a look of resignation coming over his face. "Besides, Your Serene Highness, sometimes skulking in the dark can prove most enlightening."

Making his way back to his stateroom, Alek felt his missed night of sleep again. The perspicacious loris sat heavily on his shoulder, and too many thoughts buzzed in his mind—images of the ruined forest beneath the ship, the notion that a madman could destroy the Austro-Hungarian Empire, and the awful possibility that Alek himself might have to prevent it with the blade of a knife.

But when he slumped onto his bed, Alek found Volger's newspaper still there, opened to the story about Dylan.

Volger had been so strange today, his questions zigzagging between Tesla's weapon and Dylan. They *must* have had a fight, but about what?

Alek picked up the newspaper, staring at the photograph of Dylan swinging from the *Dauntless*'s trunk. The wildcount had seen the story too, of course. He read every newspaper Barlow gave him from cover to cover.

"You know something you shouldn't, don't you, Volger?" Alek said quietly. "That's why you and Dylan are fighting."

"Fighting," Bovril repeated thoughtfully. Then it crawled from Alek's shoulder onto the bed.

Alek stared at the beast, recalling what had happened in the cargo bay. The creature had sat on Klopp's shoulder all night, listening to everything, rolling words like "magnetism" and "electrikals" around in its mouth. And then it had plucked Dr. Barlow's necklace from her and demonstrated the purpose of the strange device.

That was how the beast's perspicaciousness worked. It listened, then somehow drew everything together into a neat bundle.

Alek flipped the newspaper back to the first page,

and began to read aloud. Bovril spoke up now and then, repeating new words happily, digesting it all.

> ... He surely has bravery running in his veins, being the nephew of an intrepid airman, one Artemis Sharp, who perished in a calamitous ballooning fire only a few years ago. The elder Sharp was posthumously awarded the Air Gallantry Cross for saving his daughter, Deryn, from the hungry flames of the conflagration.

Alek sat back up. He blinked away sleep, still staring at the words. *His daughter, Deryn?*

"Reporters." Alek took a deep breath. It was amazing how they could get the simplest facts wrong. He'd explained to Malone several times that Ferdinand was his father's middle name. And yet the man had referred to Alek as "Aleksandar Ferdinand" in several places, as if it were a family name!

"His daughter, Deryn," Bovril repeated.

But why would anyone change a boy into a girl? And where had the unlikely name Deryn come from? Perhaps Malone had been misled by someone in Dylan's family, to hide the fact that two brothers had entered the Air Service together.

But Dylan had said that was all a lie, hadn't he?

So this Deryn had to do with the real family secret, the one Dylan refused to talk about.

For a moment Alek felt dizzy, and wondered if he should put down the paper and forget all about this, out of respect for Dylan's wishes. He needed sleep.

But instead he read a little further. . . .

At the time of the tragic incident, the *Daily Telegraph* of London wrote, "And as the flames exploded overhead, the father cast his daughter from the tiny gondola, and in saving her life sealed his own fate." Surely our brothers across the Atlantic are lucky to count brave men such as the Sharps among their airmen during this terrible war.

"Sealed his own fate," Bovril said gravely.

Alek nodded slowly. So the mistake had been made two years ago, by a British paper, and had been merely copied by Malone. That had to be it. But why had the *Telegraph* made such an odd error?

A cold feeling went through Alek then. What if there really was a Deryn, and Dylan was lying about it all? What if the boy had only watched the accident, and had inserted himself into the story in his sister's place?

Alek shook his head at this absurd idea. No one would embellish the story of his own father's death. It had to be a simple mistake.

Then, why was Dylan lying to the Air Service about who his father was?

A strange feeling, almost a kind of panic, was coming over Alek. It had to be exhaustion, compounded by this reporter's odd mistake. How was he supposed to believe anything he read, when newspapers could get reality so completely wrong? Sometimes it felt as though the whole world were built on lies.

He lay down, forcing his eyes closed and willing his racing heart to slow down. The details of a years-old tragedy hardly mattered anymore. Dylan had seen his father die and his heart was still broken from it, of that Alek was sure. Perhaps the boy didn't know himself what had happened on that terrible day.

Alek lay there for long minutes, but sleep wouldn't come. Finally he opened his eyes and looked at Bovril. "Well, you've got all the facts now."

The creature just stared up at him.

Alek waited another moment, then sighed. "You're not going to help me with this mystery, are you? Of course you aren't."

He kicked off his boots and closed his eyes again, but his head was still spinning. He wanted more than anything to get some rest ahead of tonight's skulking. But Alek could feel sleeplessness nestling in beside him, like an unwelcome visitor in the bed.

Then Bovril crept up beside his head, seeking warmth against the chill that pushed through the ship's window-panes.

"*Mr.* Deryn Sharp," the creature whispered into his ear.

◦ TEN ◦

Tazza's ears perked up. The beastie strained at his leash, pulling Deryn forward in the darkness of the gut. Just ahead of them a strange two-headed silhouette was emerging from gloom.

"*Mr.* Sharp," came a familiar voice, and Deryn smiled. It was only Bovril, riding on Alek's shoulder.

Tazza leaned back onto his haunches and bounced with excitement as the two approached. Bovril chuckled a bit at the sight, but Alek didn't look happy. He was staring at Deryn, his eyes hollow.

"Did you not get any sleep?" she asked.

"Not much." He knelt to pet the thylacine. "I looked in your cabin. Newkirk said you'd be here."

"Aye, this is Tazza's favorite place for a walk," Deryn said. The great airbeast's gut was where all the organic matter of the ship came together to be processed and separated into energy-making sugars, hydrogen, and waste. "I think he likes the smells."

"Mr. Newkirk seemed quite at home there," Alek said.

Deryn sighed. "It's his cabin too now. We're short of bunks for the next few days. Still, it's better than back when there were three of us middies to a cabin."

Alek frowned, his gaze lingering on her again. Even in the faint wormlight of the great airbeast's gut, his face looked pale.

"Are you all right, Alek? You look as if you've seen a ghost."

"My head's been spinning, I suppose."

"It's not just you. Since meeting with that Clanker boffin, the officers have been as twitchy as a box of crickets. What in blazes did Tesla *say* in there?"

Alek paused a moment, still giving her the strange look. "He claims that he destroyed that forest himself. He has a weapon of some kind in America, called Goliath. It's much bigger than the one we tore down in Istanbul, and he wants to end the war with it."

"He said he . . . w-with a *what?*" Deryn sputtered.

"It's like a Tesla cannon, which he says can set the air on fire anywhere in the world. Now that he's seen firsthand what it can do, he wants to use it to force the Clankers to surrender."

Deryn blinked. The boy had said the words so simply,

as if repeating a duty roster, but they hardly made sense.

"Surrender," Bovril said. "Mr. Sharp."

"A barking *weapon* did all that?" She could recall with perfect clarity the night of the battle with the *Goeben*, when the Tesla cannon's lightning had spread across the *Leviathan*'s skin, threatening to set the whole ship aflame. An astonishing sight, but a fly's fart compared to the destruction here in Siberia.

Deryn felt dizzy. The news was staggering, and it didn't much help that supper hadn't been served that night. Tazza nuzzled her hand, whining hungrily.

"No wonder you couldn't sleep," Deryn said.

"That was part of it." The boy looked her in the eye again. "It could all be a lie, of course. You can never tell when people are lying."

"Aye, or mad. No wonder the lady boffin wanted us to do a little skulking tonight." Deryn stood, pulling on the thylacine's leash. "Come on, beastie. It's back to the cabin with you."

"We should take the loris with us," Alek said as he stood up. "It's been quite perspicacious lately."

"*Mr.* Sharp," Bovril added, and Deryn gave it a hard look.

"Well, all right," she said. "But I hope it knows when to shush."

"*Shushhh,*" the loris said.

◉   ◉   ◉

The belowdecks were full of snoring men.

The *Leviathan* might not have had enough bunks for its guests, but the ship's empty storerooms had plenty of space. Except for their captain the Russians were all down here, packed together like a box of cigars. But Deryn reckoned they were happy enough, getting their first night of sleep in weeks without the lullabies of hungry fighting bears.

It was drafty in the belowdecks, and the men were still wrapped in their furs. Deryn saw no glimmer of watching eyes as she slunk past. Sitting on Alek's shoulder, Bovril softly imitated the sounds of snoring, breathing, and the wind of the airship's passage.

Near the rear of the ship, she and Alek reached a locked door, its wooden frame bound with metal. She pulled out the ring of keys that Dr. Barlow had given her that afternoon.

The door swung open on silent hinges, and Deryn and Alek slipped inside. "Some light, your princeliness?" she whispered.

While Alek was fiddling for his command whistle, she relocked the door behind them. His shaky tune came through the dark; then Bovril joined in, and the green light of glowworms sprang up around them.

It was the airship's smallest storeroom, the only one

with a solid door. The officers' wine and spirits were kept here, along with any other cargo of special value. At the moment it was empty except for the captain's lockbox and the strange magnetic device.

"The crew saved this machine?" Alek asked. "Even when they threw all our food away?"

"Aye. The lady boffin had to yell a bit to make it happen. She's a clever-boots, thinking ahead like that."

"Clever-boots," said Bovril with a chuckle.

Alek's eyes opened wider. "Of course. This device was meant to find whatever Tesla was looking for."

"Aye. But he's already found it! Captain Yegorov said that Tesla's men dug something out of the earth a few days ago. So whatever they discovered must be aboard the *Leviathan* right now!" She looked down at the device. "And he's supplied us with a way to find out exactly where."

Alek's smile grew as his hands took the machine's controls.

Typical, Deryn thought, that it took a clever scheme and a Clanker device to lift Alek's spirits. But it was good to see the boy happy at last, instead of moping about as if the world had ended.

"These walls are solid," she said. "The Russians won't hear if you turn it on."

Alek tapped at one of the dials, then gave the power switch a flick.

The low whine of the machine built, filling the tiny room. The three glass spheres began to shimmer, a wee sliver of lightning sparkling to life in each one. The electricity flickered aimlessly for a moment, then steadied.

Deryn swore, leaning closer. "That's exactly the same as this morning—two pointed upward and one astern. It's detecting the engines again."

"One moment," Alek said.

Deryn watched as he fiddled with the elegant controls. The machine's parts looked handmade, more like the *Leviathan*'s equipment than a Clanker device. She remembered Klopp complaining about its fanciness as they'd put it together.

"It almost looks like it belongs here," she murmured.

Alek nodded. "Mr. Tesla has lived in America for some time. It must be difficult to escape the Darwinist influence there."

"Aye, poor man. I'm sure he *wished* he'd made it barking ugly."

"There!" Alek said. "It's got hold of something!"

The slivers of lightning had faded for a moment, but now they were flickering back to life. All three of them pointed in the same direction—up and toward the bow.

Deryn frowned. "That's the officers' staterooms, or maybe the bridge. Could it be detecting the metal in the ship's instruments?"

"Perhaps. We'll have to triangulate to be sure."

"What, you mean *move* it?"

Alek shrugged. "It's designed to be carried, after all."

"Aye, and we're supposed to be skulking, not waltzing about with this noisy contraption sparkling in the dark."

"Sparkling!" Bovril announced, then began to imitate the sounds of the machine.

"Well, I can turn the current down," Alek said, and fiddled with the controls a bit. The glass spheres dimmed. "How's that?"

"It's still barking noisy," Deryn muttered, but there was no way around it. With only a single direction to go on, they'd have to search a quarter of the ship. "You shush, beastie!"

"*Shush*," Bovril whispered, and a moment later the sound in the room began to change. The whining grew flatter and dimmer, as if the machine were being carried away down a long corridor. But it was still there, right in front of Deryn.

"Did you do that?" she asked Alek.

The boy shook his head, holding a hand up for silence. He turned to stare at the perspicacious loris on his shoulder.

Deryn squinted in the green-tinged darkness, and soon she saw it. Every time Bovril paused for breath, the whine of the device grew in volume for a moment, then faded again.

"Is *Bovril* doing that?" she asked.

Alek placed a hand over his ear on one side, closing his eyes. "The creature's whine is making the machine's quieter somehow, as if the two sounds were fighting each other."

"But *how?*"

Alek opened his eyes. "I have no idea."

"Well, I suppose that's a question for the lady boffin." Deryn reached for the machine's handles. "We've got skulking to do."

The device was easy enough for the two of them to carry, but once out in the cargo bay, Deryn realized how tricky this would be. Only a narrow sliver of floor was visible among the sleeping bodies, like a path of paving stones through a carpet of brambles.

Alek led the way, taking slow deliberate steps. Deryn followed, her palms growing sweaty on the machine's metal handles. She was certain of one thing—if the device slipped from her grasp, whoever it landed on was going to make a ruckus.

The whine of the machine seemed even quieter out here, stifled by the packed bodies and Bovril's mysterious vocal trick. What sound remained was lost in the rush of wind slipping past the airship's gondola.

"A CAREFUL EXTRACTION."

As she and Alek made their way toward the bow, the slivers of lightning in the glass spheres gradually shifted, until they pointed directly up. Deryn stared at the ceiling, recalling the deck plans she'd copied a hundred times from the *Manual of Aeronautics*.

One deck up was the officer's baths, and above that . . .

"Of course," she hissed. Over the baths was Dr. Busk's laboratory, which the head boffin was letting Mr. Tesla use as a stateroom.

The realization froze her midstride, just as Alek took a long step over a sleeping Russian. Too late Deryn felt cool metal slipping from the fingers of her right hand. . . .

She stuck out a boot just in time—the right rear corner of the device landed on it, sending a jolt of pain through her foot. She choked back a shriek, grabbing for the bars to steady the contraption before it toppled onto a sleeping Russian.

Alek turned back to give her a questioning look.

Deryn jerked her chin back at the storeroom, afraid that if she opened her mouth, the stifled cry of pain would leap out. Alek looked at the glass spheres, then up at the ceiling, and nodded. He steadied the machine, then reached out and turned it off.

The way back was even trickier. Deryn led this time, her foot throbbing, her steps slow and painful across the sleeping bodies. But finally the machine was inside the storeroom again. She and Alek slipped back out into the cargo bay, then locked the door behind them.

As they made their way toward the central stairs, Deryn scanned the sleeping men. None stirred, and a squick of relief competed with the drumbeat of pain in her foot.

But as she climbed the stairs, Bovril shifted on Alek's shoulder and made a soft sound, like whispers in the dark.

● ELEVEN ●

"Let me do this," Alek whispered again.

Deryn rolled her eyes. "Don't be daft. I know every squick of this ship. You've never even been in the laboratory."

"But you can't just sneak into a man's room while he's sleeping," Alek said, his voice breaking from a whisper.

"And you can? You're a barking prince. I hardly think that qualifies you for burglary."

Alek started to sputter something else, but Deryn ignored him, glancing up and down the hallway. After a day that had included a rope-and-winch landing and twenty-eight unexpected new passengers, the exhausted crew was mostly asleep, the airship's corridors empty and dark.

"Just stay out here and keep quiet."

"Mr. Tesla is quite unbalanced," Alek whispered. "Who knows what he'll do if he wakes up? Volger said his walking stick was quite dangerous."

"Aye, there is that," Deryn murmured. Tesla had promised the captain that he wouldn't fire the stick inside the airship. But what if she startled the inventor, and he forgot that he was hanging from a giant bag of hydrogen? "I'll have to make sure I don't wake him, I suppose."

"Why don't we simply tell Dr. Barlow that he's got something in his cabin?" Alek whispered. "The ship's marines can search for it in the morning."

Deryn shook her head. "You know what a sneaky-beak the lady boffin is. She wants it all done quietly, so Tesla won't *know* she's on to him."

"Of course. The simplest path is completely beyond that woman."

"Listen, if you want to help, wait out here and give the door a wee scratch if anyone's headed this way." She pointed at the beastie. "And keep your eye on Bovril. It'll hear any footsteps before you do."

"Don't worry. I'm not moving from this spot."

"Except to hide if you hear anything." Deryn recalled the whispering sound Bovril had made as they'd left the belowdecks. "If any of Tesla's Russians saw us down there, they might pop up to tell him."

Alek opened his mouth to protest again, but Deryn silenced him with a stern look, pulling Dr. Barlow's keys from her pocket. The largest was labeled LABORATORY, and fit perfectly into the lock.

"*Shush,*" Bovril said with a quiet, anxious rush of breath.

As the door opened, a wedge of the corridor's green light spilled into the room, and Deryn's breath caught. Of course, being discovered right away would be easiest. She was simply a dutiful middy checking on an important passenger.

But Mr. Tesla was asleep in his bunk, his breathing heavy and slow. The moon shone through the window, three quarters full, and the glass instruments that Dr. Busk had left behind glittered with the moon's pearly light.

Deryn stepped inside and leaned back against the door, her heartbeat taking up residence in her bruised foot. The door shut behind her with a soft *click*, but still Mr. Tesla didn't stir.

A shiny leather suitcase lay open on the floor, revealing a neatly folded white shirt that glowed in the moonlight. The electrical walking stick lay on a laboratory bench, its handle pulled off to reveal a pair of wires. As Deryn's eyes adjusted, she saw they were connected to the airship's power lines. So the bum-rag was recharging his stick, despite his promise to the captain.

Deryn took a few slow steps into the room, her foot still pounding from the contraption landing on it. She knelt by the suitcase and slipped a hand beneath the shirt on top, feeling layer by layer. Nothing but clothing.

She frowned, looking about the room. Dr. Busk had cleared most of his boffin gear away, so the lab wasn't in its usual cluttered state. There wasn't much space to hide anything, at least not anything big enough to create an explosion forty miles across. But the little slivers of lightning had pointed straight at this cabin, so whatever Tesla had found *had* to be here.

She swore under her breath. It was just like the lady boffin, sending Deryn to search for something without saying what it was.

As she knelt there pondering, a soft scratching sound came from the door. It was Alek, alerting her that someone was coming. . . .

There was nowhere else to hide, so Deryn dropped to her hands and knees and scuttled beneath the bed.

She waited there in the darkness, her heart pounding. There were no sounds from the corridor, nothing except the rush of wind and Mr. Tesla's steady breathing.

Maybe it had been only a crewman walking past. . . .

But then a soft knocking came from the door. Deryn squeezed herself farther under the bed as the sound grew louder. Finally the door opened, spilling wormlight into the room.

Deryn swore silently—she hadn't locked the door behind her.

A pair of fur-lined boots strode to the side of the bed, and she heard Tesla's name amid a stream of whispered Russian. Tesla's voice answered, sleepy and confused at first. Then a pair of bare feet descended before her eyes, and a quiet conversation began in Russian.

Lying there, Deryn realized that something was poking into her back. She reached a hand around and felt an object wrapped in a canvas sack. It was as hard as stone.

Deryn swallowed. This had to be what she was looking for, but it wasn't much bigger than a football. Would Tesla have come six thousand miles to find something so small?

She would make too much noise if she turned over to take a closer look, so she slowed her breath and waited, staring at the fur-lined boots and trying to ignore her own throbbing foot.

Finally the whispered conversation ended. The boots walked away and through the door, and the pair of bare

"A SKULK INTERRUPTED."

feet shifted as Tesla stood up. Deryn clenched her fists. Was he going to check on his precious cargo beneath the bed?

But the feet padded over to the door, and Deryn heard the knob jiggle. Tesla was probably wondering how his Russian friend had simply walked in. But after the long and frantic day, could he be certain he'd locked the door before going to bed?

The rasp of a key reached her ears, then the click of a dead bolt sliding closed. The bare feet came back to the bed, which creaked above her as the man climbed back in.

Deryn lay there, listening to his breathing, realizing that she would have to wait for ages to make sure he was asleep again. At least her throbbing foot would help her stay awake.

The mysterious object was still jabbing into her back, and its size still bothered her. How had that contraption detected something so small from the other end of the ship?

Magnetic fields, Klopp had said.

Deryn reached into a pocket and pulled out her compass. She inched it out from beneath the bed until its face caught a squick of moonlight. . . .

Her eyes widened. The needle was pointing straight

at the object, toward the bow of the ship. But they were headed south-by-southeast, not due north.

The mysterious object was magnetized. It *had* to be what Tesla had been looking for.

Deryn counted a thousand slow heartbeats before daring to turn over. She felt the canvas sack in the darkness, and when her fingers slipped inside, they touched a cool metal surface. Not smooth, like cast metal, but as knobbly as a piece of old cheese.

She tried to test the object's weight, but it wouldn't budge from the floor. Solid metal was barking heavy, of course. Even hollow aerial bombs took two men to lift.

What in blazes was this thing?

Dr. Barlow might know, if Deryn could get a sample somehow.

She remembered the chapter from the *Manual of Aeronautics* on compasses. Iron was the only magnetic element, and a great spinning blob of it at the earth's core was what made compasses work. She rubbed the metal and sniffed her fingers, and caught a tang almost like fresh blood. There was iron in blood, too. . . .

And iron was much softer than steel.

She pulled out her rigging knife and slipped it into the sack. Her fingers searched until she found a wee sliver jutting up from the object's rough surface. Tesla was snoring by now, so Deryn began to saw away at the sliver, the canvas sack muffling the rasp of her knife.

As she worked, her mind spun with questions. Had Tesla's weapon used a projectile of some kind and this was all that was left? Or had the electrical explosion somehow fused all the iron in the frozen Siberian ground?

One thing was certain—Mr. Tesla's claim of having caused all that destruction suddenly seemed more credible.

At last the sliver broke free, and Deryn slipped it into a pocket. She stretched her muscles carefully one by one. It wouldn't do for her legs to cramp as she was sneaking out of the room.

She crawled from beneath the bed and slowly stood, watching the rise and fall of Tesla's chest as she pulled her keys out. The door unlocked with a soft *click*, and a moment later Deryn was in the corridor.

Alek stood there looking pale, a drawn knife in his hand. Bovril still perched on his shoulder, wide-eyed and tense.

Deryn put her fingers to her lips, then turned and relocked the door. With a beckoning wave of her hand, she led Alek to the middies' mess. He followed, his expression still anxious, his eyes darting down every corridor.

"You can put that away," Deryn said when she'd closed the door to the mess.

Alek stared at his knife a moment, then slipped it back into his boot.

"It was maddening," he said, "standing out there. When that other man stayed so long, I almost burst in to make sure you were all right."

"Good thing you didn't," she said, wondering why Alek was so twitchy tonight. "You'd have started a ruckus for no reason. And look, while I was hiding under the bed from that Russian, I found something!"

She pulled the shard of metal from her pocket and placed it on the mess table. It didn't look like much here in the light, just a shiny black blob the size of Bovril's little finger.

"That can't be what Tesla came here for," Alek said. "It's too small."

"That's just a wee piece of it, *Dummkopf*. The rest is as big as your daft head."

Alek pulled out a chair and sat at the mess table, looking exhausted. "That still seems awfully small. How did that device detect it?"

"Watch this." She pulled out her compass and set it close to the sliver of metal, which set the needle shivering. "It's magnetized iron!"

Bovril crawled down from Alek's shoulder, getting close enough for a sniff.

"Magnetized," the beastie said.

"I don't understand," Alek said. "What has magnetism to do with an explosion?"

"I reckon that's one for the boffins to ponder."

"I'll ask Klopp as well. We have to know if Tesla's telling the truth before he gets off this ship."

Deryn frowned. "Why's that, exactly?"

Alek drummed his fingers on the table a moment, then shook his head. "I can't tell you."

Deryn's nerves twitched a bit. There was something odd about the way Alek was looking at her, not just exhaustion and nerves. He'd been tense all night, but now there was something stormy in his eyes.

"What do you mean you can't tell me?" she asked. "What's wrong, Alek?"

"I need to ask you a simple question," he said slowly. "Will you listen to every word? And answer me truthfully?"

She nodded. "Just ask."

"All right, then." He took a slow breath. "Can I trust you, Deryn? Really trust you?"

"Aye. Of course you can."

Alek breathed out a sigh as he stood up. He turned without another word and walked from the room.

Deryn frowned. What in blazes was he . . . ?

"Can I trust you, Deryn?" repeated Bovril, then it sprawled across the table, chuckling to itself.

Something coiled, tight and hard, in her chest. Alek had called her *Deryn*.

He knew.

◉ TWELVE ◉

She was a girl. Her name was Deryn Sharp, and she was a girl disguised as a boy.

Alek walked toward his stateroom with steady, determined steps, but the floor was shifting beneath his feet. The soft green wormlight of the corridors looked all wrong, as sickly as when he'd first come aboard the *Leviathan*.

He raised a hand to guide himself, his fingers sliding along the wall like a blind man's. The fabricated wood trembled against them, the whole ghastly airship pulsing with life. He was trapped inside an abomination.

His best friend had been lying to him since the moment they'd met.

"Alek!" came a frantic whisper from behind.

Part of him was pleased that Deryn had followed. Not

because he wanted to talk to her, but so he could walk away again.

He kept walking.

"Alek!" she repeated, breaking into a full-voiced cry, loud enough to wake the sleeping men around them. Alek had almost reached the officers' cabins. Let the girl keep yelling where *they* could hear.

She'd lied to all of them, hadn't she? Her captain, her officers and shipmates. She'd sworn a solemn oath of duty to King George, all lies.

Her hand grabbed his shoulder. "You daft prince! *Stop!*"

Alek spun about, and they glared at each other in silence. It stung him to finally see her sharp, fine features for what they really were. To see how completely he'd been fooled.

"You lied to me," he whispered at last.

"Well, that's pretty barking obvious. Anything else obvious to say?"

Alek's eyes widened. This . . . *girl* had the nerve to be impertinent?

"All your talk of duty, when you're not even a soldier."

"I *am* a barking soldier!" she growled.

"You're a girl dressed up like one." Alek saw that the

words cut deep, and he turned away again, shards of satisfaction mixing with his anger.

Until this moment he hadn't believed it. The newspaper article, her lies to the crew about her father, even
the whispered words of the perspicacious loris hadn't
convinced him. But then Deryn had answered to her real
name without blinking.

"Say that again," she spat from behind him.

Alek kept walking. He didn't want to have this absurd
discussion. He wanted only to go inside his stateroom and
lock the door.

But suddenly he was stumbling forward. His feet
tangled, and he landed on his hands and knees, staring
at the floor.

He turned to look up at her. "Did you just . . . *shove* me?"

"Aye." Her eyes were wild. "Say that again."

Alek got to his feet. "Say what again?"

"That I'm not a real soldier."

"Very well. You aren't a real—*oof!*"

Alek staggered backward, the breath driven from
his lungs. His back thumped against a cabin door—she'd
punched him in the stomach. Hard.

He clenched his fists, anger coursing through his
blood. In a flash he saw an opening, how her fists were
held too low, how she favored her injured foot . . .

But before he could swing, he realized that he couldn't

hit back. Not because she was a girl, but because she *wanted* so much to fight. Anything to make herself feel like a real boy.

Alek straightened himself. "Are you proposing that we settle the matter with a fistfight?"

"I'm proposing that you say I'm a real soldier."

He saw a glimmer in the darkness, and his lips curled into a thin smile. "Is that how real soldiers cry?"

Deryn swore extravagantly, her thumb squashing the single tear on her left cheek, her fists still clenched. "That's not crying; that's just—"

Her voice choked off as the door behind Alek opened. He stumbled a moment, then turned and took a hasty step back. A sleepy-looking Dr. Busk stood in the doorway, wearing his nightgown and an annoyed expression.

His eyes darted back and forth between them. "What's going on here, Sharp?"

Her fists dropped. "Nothing, sir. We thought we heard one of the Russians wandering about. But it might be that a sniffer's got loose."

The boffin glanced up and down the empty hallway. "A sniffer, eh? Well, whatever it is, keep it *quiet*, boy."

"Our apologies, sir," Alek said, giving the man a small bow.

Dr. Busk returned the bow. "Not at all, Your Highness. Good night."

The door closed, and Alek met Deryn's eyes for a moment. The naked fear in them sent a pang through him. She had expected him to tell the boffin everything. Was *that* what she thought of him?

Alek turned and walked toward his stateroom again.

Her quiet footsteps followed, as if she'd been invited along. He sighed, the rush of anger fading into the dull throb where she'd punched his stomach. There was nothing else to do but have this out with her.

When Alek reached his stateroom door, he pulled it open, extending his hand. "Ladies first."

"Get stuffed," she said, but went in ahead of him.

He followed, shut the door softly, and sat down at his desk. Out the window the snowy ground glowed in patches, moonlit islands in a black sea. Deryn stood in the center of the room, shifting her weight, as if still ready for a fight. Neither of them whistled for the glowworms to light up, and Alek realized that they'd left the loris behind in the middies' mess.

For a moment he brooded on the fact that a mere beast had figured Deryn out before him.

"That wasn't a bad punch," he finally said.

"For a girl, you mean?"

"For anyone." It *had* hurt rather a lot; it still did. He turned to face her. "I shouldn't have said that. You are a real soldier—quite a good one, in fact. But you aren't much of a friend."

"How can you say that?" Another tear gleamed on her cheek.

"I told you everything," Alek said in a slow, careful voice. "All my secrets."

"Aye, and I've kept them all too."

He ignored her, making a list on his fingers. "You were the first member of this crew to know who my father was. You're the only one who knows about my letter from the pope. You know everything about me." He turned away. "But you couldn't tell me about *this*? You're my best friend—in some ways my *only* friend—and you don't trust me."

"Alek, it's not that."

"So you lie simply to amuse yourself? 'Sorry, Dr. Busk, it might be that a sniffer's got loose.'" Alek shook his head. "It's as natural to you as breathing, isn't it?"

"You think I'm here for my amusement?" Deryn stepped closer to the window, her fists clenching again. "That's a bit odd. Because when you thought I was a boy, you said it was barking *brave* for me to serve on this ship."

Alek looked away, remembering the night Deryn had told him about her father's accident. She'd wondered if it was madness for her to serve on a ship full of hydrogen, as if she secretly wanted to die like him.

Perhaps it was both brave *and* mad. She was a girl, after all.

"All right. You're an airman because your father was." Alek sighed. "That is, if he really *was* your father."

She glared at him. "Of course he was, you ninny. My brother's crewmates knew Jaspert had a sister, so we made up another branch of the family. There's no more to it than that."

"I suppose all your lies have a certain logic to them." As he thought it through, Alek felt his anger building again. "So in my case you thought I'd be a stuffy, arrogant prince who'd turn you in!"

"Don't be daft."

"I saw your face when Dr. Busk caught us in the corridor. You thought you were done for. You don't trust me!"

"You're being a *Dummkopf*," she said. "I only thought he might have heard us arguing. We'd said enough for him to figure it out."

Alek wondered what Dr. Busk *had* heard, and found himself hoping it hadn't been too much.

Deryn pulled out the chair and sat down across from him. "I know you'll keep my secret, Alek."

"As you have kept mine," he said coldly.

"Always."

"Then, why didn't you *tell me?*"

She took a long, slow breath, then spread her hands on the desk, staring at them while she talked. "I almost told you when you first came aboard, when you thought I might get in trouble for hiding you. They'd never hang a girl, you see?"

Alek nodded, though he doubted that was true. Treason was treason.

That thought made him shake his head—this *girl* had committed treason for him. She'd fought by his side, taught him how to swear properly in English, and how to throw a knife. She'd saved his life, and all while lying to him about what she was.

"When we were in Istanbul," Deryn went on, "and I thought we'd never get back aboard the *Leviathan*, I tried a dozen times to tell you. And just a week ago in the rookery, after Newkirk mentioned my uncle, I almost told you then, too. But I didn't want to . . . to ruin everything between us."

"Ruin everything? What do you mean?"

She shook her head. "It's nothing."

"It's obviously *not nothing*."

She swallowed, pulling her hands back from the

surface of the desk, almost as if his sharp tone had frightened her. But nothing scared Dylan Sharp, nothing
but fire.

"Tell me, Deryn." The name tasted strange in his
mouth.

"I thought you couldn't stand to know."

"You mean you thought I was too *delicate*? You thought
my fragile pride would crumble, just because some girl
can tie better knots than me?"

"No! Volger may have thought that, but not me."

Alek squeezed his eyes shut, fresh anger rising
in him. Tossing and turning that afternoon, wondering if the loris's hints were true, he'd forgotten about
Deryn's falling-out with Volger. But it was all so obvious
now. . . .

"Why didn't he *tell me*?"

"He didn't want to upset you."

"That's another lie!" Alek stood up. "I see it all now.
This is why you helped us escape—why you've kept my
secrets. Not because you're my friend. But because Volger
was blackmailing you all along!"

"No, Alek. I did all that because I'm your friend and
ally!"

Alek shook his head. "But how can I *know* that? All
you've done is lie to me."

For a long moment Deryn didn't answer, staring at

him across the desk. Fresh tears rolled steadily down her cheeks, but she seemed frozen in place.

Alek began to pace about the stateroom. "That's why Volger never told me, so that he could hold it over you. Everything you've done was to protect yourself!"

"Alek, you're being daft," she said softly. "Volger might have tried to blackmail me, but I was your friend long before he knew."

"How can I believe you?"

"Volger wasn't with us in Istanbul, was he? Do you think I jumped ship and joined your barking revolution for *him*?"

Alek clenched his fists, still pacing the room. "I don't know."

"I didn't go to Istanbul because of Volger, or because of any mission. I was never meant to reach the city, just The Straits. You know that, right?"

Alek shook his head, trying to order his thoughts. "Your men were caught, and you were cut off from the *Leviathan*. So you had no choice but to join me."

"No, you daft prince! That's just what I told the officers. There were a hundred British ships at harbor in Istanbul. I could've taken one into the Mediterranean anytime I wanted. But Volger said you were in danger, that you'd stay in the city and fight instead of hiding. And I couldn't let you do that all alone. I had to save you!" Her voice broke on the last word, and she steadied herself with a ragged breath. "You're my best friend, Alek, and I couldn't lose you. I'd do anything not to lose you. . . ."

He stared at her, frozen midstride. Her voice sounded so different now, like another person's altogether. He wondered if she'd been putting on a voice before, or whether he somehow *heard* her words differently, now that he knew she was a girl.

"What do you mean, lose me? I'd already run away."

She swore, then stood and walked to the door. "That's all you need to know, you daft prince, that I'm your friend. I have to go collect the beastie, before it starts looking for us. It might wake somebody up."

She left without another word.

Alek watched the door close. Why was it so important that she'd joined him in Istanbul? She'd taken the fight to the enemy, helped the revolution, and saved the *Leviathan* in the process. That was simply the kind of soldier she was.

But then it came back to him, that first moment when he'd seen her in the hotel in Istanbul. The way Deryn had looked at Lilit with such suspicion. Even jealousy.

And then, without a perspicacious loris whispering the truth into his ear, he finally understood. She hadn't come to Istanbul as a soldier at all. And she never would have revealed her secret to Alek, for the simplest reason in the world.

Deryn Sharp was in love with him.

⊙ THIRTEEN ⊙

The crooked fingers of inlets stretched from the sea into the city of Vladivostok, slicing it into winding peninsulas toothed with piers. Hills rose up from the water's edge, crisscrossed by avenues where mammothines trudged, bearing cargo from the ships scattered across the harbor.

As the *Leviathan*'s shadow rippled along the rooftops, traffic slowed, with people looking up and pointing. Clearly they had never seen an airship so huge. The airfield looked paltry to Alek, barely half a kilometer across.

"We're in the middle of nowhere," he said. "Exiled."

"Vladivostok," Bovril answered from the windowsill, and Alek wondered where the beast had heard the city's name.

Bovril rubbed its paw against the window glass,

"A SHOWER TO CLEAR THE HEAD."

which was always fogging up here in the officers' baths. The plumbing was integrated into the airbeast's circulatory system, the air as warm and moist as a steam bath in Istanbul, an unpleasant reminder that the ship was a living thing. But at least the room was empty during the day. The officers were on duty, the crewmen not allowed to enter.

Since finding out Deryn's secret, Alek had steered clear of her and Newkirk. The rest of the crew had little time for him, so he'd taken to wandering the ship alone. It had been an education, seeing places where the middies' duties rarely took them—the ship's electrikal engines, the darkest reaches of the gut. But after two days of skimpy rations, Alek no longer had the energy to explore. Loneliness and hunger were natural allies, together carving an emptiness inside him.

"Middle of nowhere," said the perspicacious loris.

Alek frowned. The beast had sounded almost sad.

"Do you miss her?" he asked.

Bovril was silent for a moment, staring down at the airship's shadow slipping across the ground. Finally it said, "Exiled."

Alek couldn't argue. He was truly on the outside now, hiding from the crew, his own men, and especially Deryn. He had only Bovril for company.

But a fabricated beast was better than nothing, he

supposed. And its company was much simpler than trying to untangle Deryn's feelings for him. She of all people knew that he could never love a commoner.

The *Leviathan* was coming about, turning its nose into the wind, slowly descending. The tiny figures on the airfield resolved into view. Half a dozen cargo bears waited with supplies, and two mammothine-drawn omnibuses stood ready to carry the Russians away. A lone Siberian tigeresque stood sentinel, its fangs as long and curved as scimitars.

Alek dimly recalled that the fangs of a tigeresque came from the life threads of some extinct creature. But surely no dinosaur had been armed with such teeth. Were they from some ancient great cat? For the hundredth time while wandering the ship alone, Alek wished that Deryn were here to provide the answer.

The door opened behind him, and he turned, half expecting to find her there, ready to deliver a biology lesson. But it was Count Volger.

"I am sorry to disturb you, Your Highness, but I need you."

Alek turned back to the window. The man had betrayed him far worse than Deryn had. She, at least, had her reasons to lie.

"I have nothing to say to you."

"I doubt that very much, but we haven't time in

any case. We must deal with Mr. Tesla before we land."

"Deal with him?" Alek shook his head. "What do you mean?"

"He's dangerous. Have you forgotten our discussion?"

Alek's mind processed the words, and a chill cut through the warm air of the officers' baths. In the last two days he'd forgotten to worry about Tesla and his city-destroying weapon, or Volger's plan to stop him. The possibility of murdering the inventor had never seemed quite real, but the look on the wildcount's face was deadly serious.

Bovril shifted nervously on the windowsill.

"So you're on your way to kill a man, and thought you'd stop by and ask for help?"

"I didn't want to involve you in this, Alek. But we have to know if Tesla is leaving the ship today. He has refused to meet with me, but he'll talk to you." Volger's face showed a hint of a smile. "You *are* in all the newspapers."

Alek only glared, though the man was right. In the navigation room Tesla had been excited to meet him—the famous prince. And an invitation to dinner had been slipped under Alek's stateroom door yesterday morning. He had ignored it, of course.

"You want me to find out if he's staying on board."

"If you please, Prince."

"And what if he's about to leave? Will you and Klopp gut him on the gangplank?"

"Neither Klopp nor I will be anywhere near the spot. Nor shall you."

"Gut him on the gangplank," Bovril said gravely.

Alek swore. "Have you gone mad? If Bauer and Hoffman murder someone on this ship, the Darwinists will know who ordered it!"

"I may not have to order anything." The wildcount gestured toward the door. "But it's up to you to find out."

"And you waited until *now* to tell me?" Alek spat, but Volger's cold smile didn't shift. The man had picked this moment on purpose, when Alek wouldn't have time to argue. "What if I just stand here?"

"Then Hoffman and Bauer will follow their orders. They're already in place."

Alek lifted Bovril from the windowsill and put the beast on his shoulder. He took a step toward the door, ready to find his men and tell them to stand down. But where were they lying in wait? And worse, what if they ignored his commands? Now that they were all back aboard the *Leviathan*, Volger was in charge again.

Alek's two days of sulking had made certain of that.

"Damn you, Volger. You shouldn't concoct plans without me. And you shouldn't keep secrets from me either!"

"Ah." For a moment the man looked genuinely sorrowful. "That was regrettable. But I did warn you not to make friends with a commoner."

"Yes, but you left out something rather *important*. Did you really think I was too fragile to know what Deryn was?"

"Fragile?" Volger looked about. "I hadn't thought so, but now I find you brooding in a bathroom. This doesn't speak well of your sturdiness."

"I haven't been brooding! I've been exploring the ship."

"Exploring? And what have you discovered, Your Serene Highness?"

Alek turned back to the window, feeling a fresh wave of emptiness in his gut.

"That I can't trust anyone, and that no one has any faith in me. That my best friend was . . . a fiction."

"Brooding," Bovril said.

Count Volger was silent. Alek almost added that his suspicion was that Deryn Sharp was in love with him, but he didn't want to see the scorn on Volger's face.

"I've been a fool," he finally said.

Volger shook his head. "But hardly a singular fool. That girl has tricked her officers and crewmates for months, and has been decorated in the line of duty. She even fooled me for some time. In her way, she's quite impressive."

"You admire her, Count?"

"As one does a bear riding a bicycle. One sees it so rarely."

Alek shook his head. "And along with your admiration, you decided to blackmail her."

"I needed her help to get off this ship. I thought I could prevent you from joining in that pointless revolution and getting yourself killed." The annoyance in Volger's voice faded a bit. "Of course, who knows? We may have need of her help again."

"Are you saying I should stay friends with her?"

"Of course not. I'm saying that we can still blackmail her."

"Get stuffed," Alek said, and suddenly he had to get out of the steam and heat. He strode toward the door, halting with one hand tight around the knob. "I'm going to Tesla's cabin. If he intends to disembark today, I shall call the ship's marines to escort him off in safety."

"It's your right to betray us, of course." Volger bowed. "We are at your disposal."

"I won't betray you aloud, Volger, but the captain might draw unfortunate conclusions. Unless you promise me right now that—"

"I can't, Alek. Tesla's claims may be madness, but it isn't worth the risk. Two million of your people live in Vienna, and that's probably only the first city on his list. You saw what his machine can do."

Alek pulled the door open. He didn't have time for this argument, and he couldn't let a man be killed over some imaginary threat. He had to stop this now. But he found himself pausing to say one more thing.

"If you threaten Deryn Sharp again, Volger—in any way at all—I'm done with you."

The man only bowed again, and Alek left, slamming the door behind him.

Mr. Tesla was still in his stateroom, but a leather suitcase lay on the bed. One of the Russians was packing while Tesla worked at the laboratory bench. The electrikal walking stick lay before him, partly disassembled.

Alek knocked on the open door. "Excuse me, Mr. Tesla?"

The man looked up with irritation on his face, then brightened. "Prince Aleksandar. You appear at last!"

Alek returned the bow. "I apologize for not answering your note. I've been indisposed."

"No need, Prince," Tesla said, then his eyes narrowed at Bovril. "So you really have become a Darwinist."

"Oh, this beast? It's . . . a perspicacious loris. 'Perspicacious' meaning 'wise or canny.'"

"Get stuffed," Bovril said, then giggled.

"And it insults people," Tesla said. "How peculiar."

Alek gave the creature a sharp look. "Bovril is usually more polite, as am I. It was an oversight not to join you last night. We have much to discuss."

The man turned back to his walking stick, his long fingers twisting a coil of wire round and round. "Meals are a dismal affair on this ship, at any rate."

"The food isn't so bad when the galley has supplies." Alek wondered why he was defending the *Leviathan*, but he went on. "The vegetables are grown fresh in the gut, and sometimes the strafing hawks bring their prey back for us."

"Ah, that would explain the braised hare. The highlight of the evening."

Alek raised an eyebrow. This man had eaten fresh meat while Alek had been chewing on old biscuits? Of course, if the Darwinists believed that Goliath worked, they'd happily feed Tesla caviar three times a day.

"I'm sorry I wasn't here to share it with you. But now that the ship is resupplied, perhaps dinner tonight?"

Mr. Tesla's face darkened. "I must return to New York as quickly as possible. At last I have the data to complete my work."

"I see." Alek took a slow breath, then looked at the Russian, who was folding a pair of trousers. "Might we have a moment alone, Mr. Tesla?"

Tesla waved a hand. "I have no secrets from Lieutenant Gareev."

Alek frowned. Tesla had a Russian officer as his valet? No doubt one of the czar's confidants, sent to keep an eye on the inventor.

Then Alek realized that he recognized Lieutenant Gareev. He was the man who'd interrupted Deryn's burglary two nights before. And it was possible that he'd spotted the two of them carrying the metal detector in the cargo bay that night.

Alek switched from English to German. "Mr. Tesla, can this weapon of yours really stop the war?"

"Of course it can. I have always been able to see with absolute clarity how my inventions will operate, how every piece fits into another, even before I put the designs onto paper. Since this war began I have worked to extend this ability into the realm of politics. I am certain the Clanker Powers will yield to me, if only because they have no other choice."

Alek nodded silently, struck again by the peculiar effect of listening to Tesla. Half of Alek rebelled at the wild claims; the other half was swept along by the man's certainty. What if Count Volger had got it backward? If Goliath really worked, then Tesla could end the war in a few weeks. It would be *mad* to plot against him.

But then Alek recalled the forest of fallen trees and scattered bones, a nightmare landscape stretching in all directions. What if it took the destruction of a whole city to convince the Clanker Powers to surrender?

All Alek knew for certain was that he couldn't see the future, and he didn't want blood on his men's hands today.

"Stop the war," Bovril said quietly.

Tesla leaned in to inspect the loris. "What an odd beast."

"Sir, if there's any way you could stay aboard, I might be able to help you. I want peace too."

The man shook his head. "My steamship leaves for Tokyo this afternoon, and I'm catching a Japanese airbeast for San Francisco in two days, then straight to New York by train. Missing a connection could cost me a week, and every day this war goes on, thousands die."

"But you can't leave yet!" Alek clenched his fists. "You need my help, sir. This is politics, not science. And my granduncle is the emperor of Austria-Hungary."

"The same granduncle you just accused of murder in the newspapers? My dear prince, you and your family are hardly on the best of terms." Tesla smiled gently as he said this, but Alek could hardly argue.

There was no other way, then. He reached for his command whistle and blew the notes to call a lizard. One popped from a message tube in seconds, but as Alek started to speak, his stomach twisted. He couldn't betray his own men, and he could hardly ask for an armed escort without explanation.

Mr. Tesla glanced up at the lizard, raising an eyebrow.

"Straight to New York," Bovril said.

Alek finally found the right words. "Captain Hobbes,

Mr. Tesla and I need to see you at once. We have an important request. End message."

The creature scampered away.

"A request?" Tesla asked.

The plan formed in Alek's mind as he spoke. "Your mission is too important to waste time with steamships and trains. We should leave for New York immediately, and the *Leviathan* is the fastest way to get there."

FOURTEEN

"Are Japanese sea beasties as big as ours?" asked Newkirk.

"Aye, they've got a few krakens," Deryn said through a mouthful of ham. "But their wee beasties are deadlier. It was kappa monsters that captured the Russian fleet ten years ago."

"Aye, I remember that lesson." Newkirk was pushing his potatoes across his plate, feeling a bit twitchy here in enemy territory. "Funny how the Japanese and Russians are on the same side now."

"Anything to beat those Clanker bum-rags." Deryn reached over to spear one of Newkirk's potatoes, but the boy didn't complain.

Deryn couldn't see any point in not eating. She'd had four huge meals since the *Leviathan* had resupplied at

Vladivostok, and she still felt empty from those two awful days of no rations.

Of course, there was another void inside her, one that food couldn't fill. She and Alek hadn't spoken since he'd learned her secret. Whenever they bumped into each other, he only looked away, his face as pale as a mealyworm.

It was as if she'd transformed into something awful, a stain on the deck of the *Leviathan* that someone—not a prince, of course—ought to clean up. Alek had thrown their friendship straight out the window, just because she was a girl.

And, of course, he'd taken Bovril for himself. Bum-rag.

"Where's Alek, anyway?" Newkirk asked, as if reading her thoughts.

"Clanker business, I suppose." Deryn tried to keep the anger from her voice. "I saw him with Mr. Tesla this morning, in a meeting with the officers. All very hush-hush."

"But we haven't seen him in days! Did you two have a fight?"

"Get stuffed."

"I knew it," Newkirk said. "He's been hiding from us, and you're as grumpy as a bag of wet cats. What in blazes happened?"

"Nothing. It's just that, now that everyone knows

he's a prince, he's too important to hang about with us middies."

"That's not what Dr. Barlow thinks." Newkirk stared down at his food. "She asked me if you two'd been fighting."

Deryn let out a groan. If the lady boffin was ordering *Newkirk* to spy for her, she had to be barking curious. And for a sticky-beak like Dr. Barlow, there wasn't much distance between curiosity and suspicion.

"It's none of her business."

"Aye, nor mine. But you have to admit it's a bit odd. After you two got back from Istanbul, you seemed as close as . . ." Newkirk frowned.

"As a prince and a commoner," Deryn said. "And now that he has Mr. Tesla to scheme with, he's got no more use for me."

"That's Clankers for you," Newkirk said. "I suppose."

Deryn stood and went to the window, hoping the conversation was at an end. The Sea of Japan spread out beneath the ship, glimmering with the afternoon sun, and beyond it the coastline of China. Scouting birds dotted the blue horizon, on the lookout for enemy craft.

The *Leviathan* was headed toward Tsingtao, a port city on the Chinese mainland. The Germans had a naval base there, whose warships could raid shipping across the entire Pacific. The Japanese were already besieging the city, but it seemed they needed a hand.

Newkirk joined Deryn at the window. "It's funny how Mr. Tesla didn't get off in Vladivostok. When I was laundering his shirts, he wanted them folded for packing."

Deryn frowned, wondering what had caused the change in plans. She'd spied enough to know that Alek was spending a lot of time with his new friend. According to the cooks the two of them had eaten at the captain's table last night.

What in blazes were they all up to?

"Ah, Mr. Sharp and Mr. Newkirk. Here you are."

As the two middies turned from the window, Tazza bounded forward through the door. Dr. Barlow was behind him, her loris sitting primly on her shoulder. The dark stripes under its eyes somehow gave the beastie a snooty expression.

Deryn knelt to give Tazza's head a rub, glad for once to see the lady boffin, who might know something about Tesla and Alek's plans. Sticky-beaks could come in handy sometimes.

"Good afternoon, ma'am. I hope you're well."

"I am annoyed, at present." Dr. Barlow turned to Newkirk. "Would you be so kind as to give Tazza his morning walk?"

"But, ma'am, Dylan already—," the boy began, but a look from Dr. Barlow silenced him.

A moment later Newkirk was gone, having shut the door behind him without being told. The lady boffin sat down at the mess table and gestured at the remains of the middies' lunch. Deryn set to clearing them, her brain spinning.

Was Dr. Barlow here to ask about her fight with Alek?

"If you would, Mr. Sharp, please describe the object you discovered in Mr. Tesla's room."

Deryn turned away with a stack of empty dishes, hiding her relief. "Oh, that. As I said, ma'am, it was round. A bit bigger than a football, but much heavier—probably solid iron."

"Most certainly iron, Mr. Sharp, perhaps with some nickel. What of its shape?"

"Its shape? I didn't get *that* good a look at it." Deryn cleared away a pair of aluminum tea mugs. "I was under a bed in the dark, trying not to get caught!"

"Trying not to get caught," the boffin's loris said. "*Mr. Sharp.*"

Dr. Barlow waved a hand. "At which you succeeded admirably. But roughly what form did this iron football take? Was it a perfect sphere? Or a misshapen lump?"

Deryn sighed, trying to recall those long minutes of waiting while Tesla had drifted back to sleep. "It wasn't perfect at all. It was knobbly on the surface."

"Were these 'knobbles' smooth or jagged to the touch?"

"Mostly smooth, I suppose, like that bit I sawed off." Deryn reached out a hand. "If you've still got it, ma'am, I'll show you what I mean."

"The sample is on the way to London, Mr. Sharp."

"You sent it to the Admiralty?"

"No, to someone with intellect."

"Oh," Deryn said, a bit astonished that even Dr. Barlow needed help to solve this mystery.

The loris crawled down to sniff at the empty milk jug. The lady boffin's eyes followed the beastie, her fingers drumming on the table.

"I am a species fabricator, Mr. Sharp, not a metallurgist. But what I'm asking is simple enough." She leaned forward. "Would you say that Mr. Tesla's find was natural or man-made?"

"You mean, was it cast iron?" Deryn remembered her hands on the object in the darkness. "Well, it was close enough to a sphere. But it was awfully banged up. Like a cannonball, I suppose, *after* it's been shot through a cannon."

"I see. And a cannonball is man-made."

Dr. Barlow fell into silence, and the loris picked up the teacup in its tiny paws and studied it.

"Man-made," it repeated softly. "*Mr.* Sharp."

Deryn ignored the beastie. "Begging your pardon, ma'am, but that doesn't make sense. To cause all that wreckage, a cannonball would have to be as big as a barking cathedral!"

"Mr. Sharp, you are forgetting a basic formula of physics. When calculating energy, mass is only one variable. And the other?"

"Velocity," Deryn said, recalling the bosun's lectures on artillery. "But to knock down a whole forest, how fast would a cannonball have to fly?"

"Astronomically fast. My colleagues will know exactly." The lady boffin leaned back in her chair and sighed. "But London is a week away, even for our swiftest courier aquilines. And in the meantime Mr. Tesla spins his tales and takes us on a wild goose chase."

"But we're headed to fight the Germans, aren't we?"

Dr. Barlow waved a hand before her face, as if a fly were bothering her. "We may briefly show the flag, but Mr. Tesla and Prince Aleksandar have convinced the captain to proceed to Tokyo. From there we can contact the Admiralty by underwater fiber."

"What in blazes for?"

"Tesla will try to convince them to order us to New York." The lady boffin snapped for the loris, which scampered back up her arm and onto her shoulder. "Where Goliath waits to stop the war."

"What . . . go all the way to *America?*"

"Indeed, and all for a delusion."

Deryn's mind was spinning at the thought of crossing the Pacific, but she managed to ask, "You think Mr. Tesla's lying?"

The lady boffin stood, straightening herself. "Lying, or simply mad. But at the moment I have no proof. *Do* keep your eyes open, Mr. Sharp."

She turned and swept out the door, the loris on her shoulder staring back through slitted eyes.

"Mr. Sharp!" it said.

Deryn went back to the window, fretting over what the lady boffin had said. If Mr. Tesla were up to some deception, then he must have tricked Alek into helping him. And little wonder—Alek was angry and alone, feeling betrayed by everyone he'd trusted. Tesla had appeared at just the right moment to take advantage.

And it was all Deryn's fault. . . .

But there was no point telling him that Tesla was lying. Alek would never take her word for it, especially as Dr. Barlow had admitted that there wasn't any proof. Deryn stood there for a long minute, her fists clenched, trying to think of what to do.

It was almost a relief when the Klaxon began to sound, calling her to battle.

◎   ◎   ◎

The ratlines were full, the ropes groaning with the weight of men and beasts. The whole crew seemed to be scrambling topside, eager to fight after a week of flying across the Russian wasteland. The sun was bright, the wind blowing across the Sea of Japan crisp and cool, nothing like the freezing gales of Siberia.

Deryn paused to scan the horizon. A dark silhouette lay ahead—two tall funnels, and turrets bristling with guns—a German warship for certain. To her relief there was no sign of a spindly Tesla cannon on its decks. The ship was making for the Chinese coast, which stretched across the horizon, the haze of a Clanker city rising from a nest of steep-sided hills.

She continued climbing, following the sound of the bosun's voice.

"Reporting for duty, sir!" she called when she reached the spine.

"Where's Newkirk?" Mr. Rigby asked.

"Last I saw, he was seeing to the lady boffin's pet, sir."

The bosun swore, then pointed down at the water. "There's a Japanese submarine somewhere down there, in pursuit of that warship. It's tending a school of kappa, so we can't put any fléchette bats into the air. Let the men on the forward gun know, then report back here."

Deryn saluted and turned, running for the bow, where

two crewmen were erecting an air gun. She jumped in to help when she arrived, tightening the screws and cleats, feeding a belt of darts into the weapon.

"There are kappa in the water, so the captain doesn't want any spikes." Deryn spun the shoulder stock into place. "Mind you don't scare the bats when you fire!"

The men looked at each other dubiously. Then one said, "No bats, sir? But what if the Clankers have got aeroplanes?"

"Then you lads will have to shoot straight. And we've still got the strafing hawks."

She returned the men's salutes and headed aft, passing the word along. By the time she got back to Mr. Rigby, Newkirk had arrived with a pair of field glasses. Mr. Rigby was staring at the horizon through them.

"Pair of zeppelins over Tsingtao," he said. "Never seen them this far from Germany."

Deryn shielded her eyes. Twin squicks of blackness hovered above the city harbor, where the warship was coming to a halt. But the guns of Tsingtao would offer no protection from the kappa.

As she watched, the zeppelins seemed to lengthen against the horizon.

"Are they turning away, sir?" she asked. "Or toward us?"

"Away, I'd think. They're tiny compared to the *Levia-*

than. But that warship won't be happy to see them go. Without air cover the kappa will make short work of her."

Deryn stared down at the sea, her heart beginning to race. Except for the doomed sailors of one unlucky Russian fleet, no Europeans had ever seen kappa in action. The *Manual of Aeronautics* contained no photographs of the beasties, only a few paintings based on rumors and stories.

"The attack signal will come soon," Mr. Rigby said, handing Deryn the field glasses and scanning the city below with his naked eyes.

She raised the glasses and peered at the Clanker warship. The name *Kaiserin Elizabeth* was painted on its side, and it flew an Austrian flag.

"Not German after all," she murmured, wondering if Alek had spotted that, and if he'd go back to dithering over which side he was on. Of course, he had a new Clanker friend to share his worries with, so he didn't need Deryn's shoulder to cry on.

"Not German?" Newkirk asked. "What do you mean?"

"It's an Austrian ship," Mr. Rigby said. "The Germans have got their own ships out and left their allies here to face the siege. Not very kind of them."

Deryn squinted through the glasses. The sea around the *Kaiserin Elizabeth* was starting to look unsettled, like water coming to a boil. The kappa swam just beneath the surface, like dolphins riding the waves.

With a distant roar the smaller deck guns of the *Kaiserin* opened up, a torrent of bullets chopping the water into a white froth. Austrian sailors stood at the rails, peering down and fixing bayonets to their rifles.

Suddenly Deryn was very glad to be up in an airship, and not down there.

"Have you spotted the Japanese submarine?" Newkirk asked.

"We won't," Mr. Rigby said. "Her periscope must be up, but it's too small. All we'll see is . . ."

His voice faded as a sliver of a wave slid across the water, like a ripple in a cup of tea.

"That's the submarine now," Mr. Rigby said, nodding. "As the boffins suspected, they use an underwater explosion to send the kappa into a battle frenzy."

As Deryn watched, the first beastie scrambled out of the water and up the side of the ship. It climbed with both hands and feet, four sets of webbed fingers splaying wide on the metal. Somehow the kappa ascended the smooth expanse as easily as it would a ladder, and was upon the men at the railing almost before they'd seen it.

Its long fingers grasped the ankle of a sailor, and a dozen shots rang out, his fellows on either side blasting away at the monster. The poor beastie twisted for a moment in the volley of lead, but its claws stayed locked on its victim. Finally the kappa fell dead into the sea, dragging the unlucky Austrian along.

Deryn held the field glasses tighter, ignoring Newkirk's pleas for them. The kappa were swarming up by the dozens now, their wet green skin shining in the sunlight. A

"KAPPA SURFACING."

few larger ones shot from the water and arced through the air, descending on the Austrian sailors from clouds of spray.

From the blazing guns of the defenders, a veil of smoke arose, like some makeshift, flimsy barrier. More sailors were pulled into the sea, and a few kappa broke past them and bounded across the deck. Soon the broad windows of the bridge were shattered, and as the beasties leapt through them, Deryn saw the flash of drawn cutlasses within.

Her stomach twisted, and finally she handed the field glasses to Newkirk, wondering why she'd watched for so long. Battle was always like this, excitement and fascination turning to horror as the reality of bloodshed set in.

And this wasn't a proper battle at all, just the extermination of an overmatched foe.

"Are they coming about?" Mr. Rigby cried, pointing across the water to the zeppelins.

Newkirk lifted the glasses a bit. "Aye, they're turning back. And from the way their engine smoke is carrying, there's a wind at their tails."

"Of course," Deryn said, and swore. "They were waiting for the kappa!"

Now that the water was swarming with Japanese beasties, the *Leviathan* couldn't deploy its fléchette bats.

There was nothing to stop the smaller, faster zeppelins from closing in and using their rockets. . . .

"Blisters," Deryn said.

This was turning into a real battle, after all.

◎ FIFTEEN ◎

"Quick, lads, to the strafing hawks!" shouted Mr. Rigby.

He picked up a coil of rope and flung it into Deryn's arms, then set off for the aft end of the ship. The two middies followed, lugging the heavy line as fast as they could.

As the three headed for the airship's tail, the spine sloped away beneath them. They hurtled down the decline, Mr. Rigby roaring at the other crewmen to jump aside.

Directly above the rookery he slid to a halt and pulled the rope from the middies' arms. Kneeling to tie one end off, the bosun clutched his side in pain. He'd taken a bullet there two months before, just before the *Leviathan*'s crash landing in the Alps.

"Are you all right, sir?" Deryn asked.

"Aye, but I won't be sliding down with you." Mr. Rigby

thrust a handful of carabiners at her and Newkirk. "Half the hawks are fitted with aeroplane nets, which are barking useless against zeppelins. Get down there and help the rook men switch them into talons. And hurry!"

"Aye, sir," Deryn said. "Me first!"

Snapping her safety harness to the rope with three carabiners, she turned and ran straight for the edge. The great whale was narrow here, halfway to the tail, and within seconds she was flying off into thin air.

Rope hissed through the carabiners like an angry viper, and Deryn let herself fall fast. The first moments of descent were glorious, her worries about Tesla, his iron football, and barking Prince Aleksandar of Hohenberg all left behind. But soon Deryn twisted in midair, tightening the grip of the carabiners, and came to a long and skidding halt. Momentum swung her inward toward the airship's underbelly, where she reached out and grabbed the ratlines with one gloved hand.

As she climbed down toward the rookery, the cilia were in furious motion beneath her hands. The *Leviathan* was nervous about the zeppelins closing in. Deryn wondered how the great whale saw the Clanker airships. Did they look like a pair of fellow airbeasts? Or like inexplicable things, in a familiar shape but queerly devoid of life?

"Don't worry, beastie," she said. "We'll take care of them."

⊙   ⊙   ⊙

The rookery was in a state, the birds squawking like mad inside their cages. Somehow they always knew when battle or bad weather was afoot. As she hauled herself through the aft window, Deryn called out to rearm the hawks.

"Aye, the bridge sent orders!" answered Higgins, the head rook man. He was inside one of the cages already, pulling an aeroplane net harness from a large and fluttering bird. "We've launched all the hawks we had in talons, and we're switching the rest!"

"I'll give you a hand, then." Deryn slid down the access ladder, fighting a squick of nerves. She'd handled birds of prey before, but only one at a time. And she'd never set foot in a cage full of stirred-up strafing hawks.

With a deep breath Deryn opened a cage door and stepped into a blizzard of wings. It was hard to keep her eyes open, hard not to leap back out, but she managed to grab one of the hawks and smooth its wings. She worked quickly then, unclipping the tiny harness that held a folded net of spider silk. Its acidic strands would slice through the fragile wings of an aeroplane in an instant but had little effect on a huge and stately airship.

Once the harness was off, she moved on to the next bird, leaving it to the rook men to attach the talons. Every rook man she'd ever met carried nasty-looking scars from handling razor-sharp steel, and she wasn't keen to learn the art in the heat of battle. As Deryn moved on to her third hawk, she saw Newkirk at work in the cage beside hers.

Long minutes later the first aerie of hawks had been fitted, and Mr. Higgins opened a chute to discharge them into the air. The rook men gave a quick cheer before setting back to work. Deryn felt the ship climbing, and she wondered if the captain had turned tail and run, or stayed to guard the kappa from the Clanker zeppelins.

Suddenly a *boom* shook the floor beneath her feet, and the frenzy of the birds redoubled. Deryn was blinded by beating wings but managed to grope her way out of the cage. She climbed up to the rookery windows and peered sternward.

One of the zeppelins was a few miles behind and a thousand feet below, a horde of strafing hawks swirling around it, tearing at its skin with their talons. But as Deryn watched, a streak of red fire shot from its gondola straight at her. The distance was too great, though—the rocket began to arc away before it could reach the *Leviathan*. It burst well below the ship, throwing out burning tendrils in all directions.

"Another close one, but they missed!" Deryn cried down to the rook men, but as she turned back to the window, her eyes went wide.

One of the sputtering tendrils was reaching up from

the center of the explosion, climbing straight toward the rookery!

At the last moment the bright ember veered away, drawn toward the ventral engine pod by its whirling propeller. Fire struck metal, and a sheet of sparks shot out from the pod. The engine ground to a halt, spilling a cloud of smoke into the ship's wake.

The Clanker airship was losing altitude quickly now, its shredded gasbag fluttering in the breeze. The other zeppelin was much farther back, hovering over the *Kaiserin Elizabeth* and raining metal darts onto the frenzied kappa.

The *Leviathan* was safe from the two zeppelins, but the ventral engine was still spitting smoke and flame. Deryn spun about and called to Newkirk, "We're hit! I'm headed aft. But keep those birds coming!"

Not waiting for an answer, she hoisted open the window and looked down. A stabilizing boom connected the gondola to the engine pod, wide enough to walk on in a pinch. But it was a good ten yards below the rookery, and Deryn didn't fancy jumping. If she missed the boom, nothing would stop her fall but the open sea.

Luckily Mr. Rigby had made her draw the ship in profile a hundred times, and she remembered a steel cable connecting the rookery to the boom. It was anchored just overhead, almost close enough to reach. . . .

Almost, but not quite.

Deryn swore. With smoke still pouring from the ventral engine pod, this was no time for caution. Crawling out the window, she saw a set of handholds leading up to her goal—some poor blighter had done this trick before!

Deryn grabbed the nearest hold and swung off into the air. She pulled herself hand over hand up to the cable and threw out her legs to wrap them around it. Then she was sliding down fast, the steel cable as hot as a teakettle in her gloves. Half a mile below, the plummeting zeppelin fired again, but the rocket burst uselessly low, sending a dozen sizzling threads into the sea.

Her boots landed with a *clang* against the boom.

Ahead of Deryn the hatches and windows of the engine pod were all thrown open, and smoke was gushing out and spilling back into the *Leviathan*'s wake. She entered through the nearest hatch, her eyes stinging.

"It's Middy Sharp. Report!"

An engineer appeared from the smoke, wearing goggles and an ember-tattered flight suit. "It's bad, sir—we've called for a Herculean. Grab on to something!"

"You called for a . . . ," Deryn began, her voice fading. A rushing sound was building overhead. She stared up at the belly of the airbeast, and saw the ballast lines swelling.

She'd never seen a Herculean inundation before. They were called only when the ship was in serious danger of

"FIREFIGHT IN THE AIR."

burning, because they were barking dangerous themselves.

"It's coming!" Deryn cried, pushing into the pod to look for a handhold.

The engineer turned and stepped through the thick smoke to a rack of gears and parts, where another man with engineering patches stood. Deryn knelt behind the main turbine, taking hold as the first spume of water exploded into the engine pod. The inundation came straight from the gut, briny and fouled with the clart of a hundred species. The torrent grew, the burning engine spitting white steam to mingle with the smoke and brackish water.

The inundation lifted Deryn from her feet for a moment, trying to sweep her out the open hatch and into the void. The water filled her boots, churning up to force itself into her nose and eyes. But she held fast until the last sparks in the engine sputtered out and the flood finally began to slacken. The briny water slowly drained from the engine pod, dropping below her waist, then her knees.

One of the engineers let out a sigh of relief, letting go to take a step toward the blackened mass of gears.

"Keep hold, man!" Deryn said. "We've lost our rear ballast!"

He grabbed the rack again just as the ship began to

"A HERCULEAN INUNDATION."

tilt. With thousands of gallons of ballast gone from its stern, the *Leviathan* was out of balance, tipping the airship into a steep dive.

The remaining water coiled past Deryn's feet, pouring out the forward hatch. She heard the creak of the ratlines overhead as the airbeast strained, bending its nose upward against the dive. But out the nearest porthole she saw the glittering sea rushing toward them.

Then Deryn heard a growl like a pair of hungry fighting bears—the Clanker engines shifting into reverse. The whole ship shuddered, its descent slowing to a crawl. The *Leviathan* hovered aslant in the air for a moment, until the ballast lines began to swell again with water pumping toward the tail. Gradually the floor of the engine pod leveled off.

A lizard popped its head from a message tube and spoke with the captain's voice. "Ventral engine pod, help is on the way. Please report your status."

The two engineers looked at Deryn, perhaps a bit nervous that they'd just sent the whole ship plummeting toward the sea.

She cleared her throat. "Middy Sharp, sir, just arrived here from the rookery. The pod was set aflame, so the engineers called for a Herculean. The fire's out, but by the looks of things, we won't be giving you any power for a while. End message."

The lizard blinked, then scampered away. Deryn turned to the men. This was her station for the rest of the battle, it seemed.

"Don't look so sheepish," she said. "You may have saved the ship. But if you want to be proper heroes, let's get this engine running again!"

· SIXTEEN ·

"Hard to starboard," the captain said, and the pilot sent the master wheel spinning.

As the *Leviathan* turned, the deck shifted beneath Alek's feet, but it was nothing like the sickening dive of a moment before. The ocean had filled the front windows of the bridge, and he and Mr. Tesla had skidded forward on their dress shoes. Not for the first time Alek was envious of the crew's rubber-soled boots. Bovril was still clinging tight to his shoulder, scared into silence.

The zeppelin that had fired at the *Leviathan* swung into view below, still falling. A swarm of strafing hawks had spilled its hydrogen from a thousand cuts, and the German airship settled on the ocean like a feather on a pond. As the *Leviathan*'s shadow passed across it, a pair of canvas lifeboats emerged from beneath the billowing membrane.

An awful thought occurred to Alek. "Will the kappa attack those lifeboats as well?"

Dr. Barlow shook her head. "Not unless the submarine sends out another fighting pulse."

"And we're close enough to shore," Dr. Busk added. "Those chaps should be fine, as long as they don't mind a bit of rowing!"

"A bit of rowing," repeated Dr. Barlow's loris from the ceiling, and had a chuckle. Bovril looked up and joined in, relaxing its grip on Alek's shoulder a little.

"The others aren't so lucky," Mr. Tesla said, staring at the *Kaiserin Elizabeth* in the distance. She looked like a haunted ship. Her decks were awash with blood and were glittering with spikes, and kappa roamed freely across them, searching for prey. If any crew had survived, they must have hidden belowdecks behind metal hatches.

The second zeppelin hovered over the warship, sending a last shower of darts down onto the kappa. But the first strafing hawks were arriving, hacking at the zeppelin's fragile skin. Its engines soon fired up, and the German airship began to pull away.

"We won't pursue them, will we?" Alek asked.

"I doubt we shall bother." Dr. Busk nodded to Tesla. "Getting you to Japan is more important than this sideshow."

Alek let out a quiet sigh. As Count Volger had suspected, this long voyage had all been for show. The Admiralty wanted to prove that British air power was global, and that the Great War was a contest among European powers, not upstart empires in Asia.

But at least now that the Union Jack had been waved, the *Leviathan* could turn around and head for Tokyo—and then America, if the Admiralty allowed it.

"I don't suppose those creatures recognize the white flag," Tesla said.

"The submarine will call them off," Dr. Barlow replied. "Exactly how is known only to the Japanese, for obvious reasons."

"Wouldn't want the enemy figuring out how to turn your beasties peaceable, would you?" Dr. Busk scanned the ocean's surface through a telescope. "Some sort of sound would be my guess. One that humans can't hear, a bit like a dog whistle."

"Quite a vicious dog," Mr. Tesla said.

"Vicious," Bovril repeated gravely.

Alek found himself nodding. He'd seen plenty of Darwinist creatures in battle before, but nothing as horrifying as these kappa. The beasts had sprung from the water so quickly, like something from a nightmare.

But in a way it was a relief, seeing Mr. Tesla so unsettled. If he was appalled to see Austrian sailors slaughtered like this, surely he would think twice before unleashing his weapon on a defenseless city.

"And yet the ship is undamaged," Dr. Busk said. "She'll join the Japanese navy now, like the Russian fleet did ten years ago. A most efficient form of victory."

Alek frowned. "The Japanese can operate a Clanker warship?"

"They are adept with both technologies," Dr. Barlow said. "An American named Commodore Perry introduced Japan to mechaniks some sixty years ago. Almost made Clankers of them."

"Lucky we put a stop to that, eh?" Dr. Busk said. "Wouldn't want these fellows on the other side."

Mr. Tesla looked as though he were about to say something impolitic, but instead cleared his throat. "Your damaged engine, is it electrikal?"

"All the *Leviathan*'s engines are," Dr. Busk said, then bowed to Alek. "Except for the two that His Highness kindly lent us."

"So you aren't entirely against the machine," said the inventor. "Perhaps I could be of assistance."

"Allow me," Alek said. In his two days of sulking, he had explored all of the ship's engine pods. "It's a bit tricky, but I know the way."

"Thank you, Prince," said Dr. Busk, bowing. "You'll be pleased to see that we use your alternating current design, Mr. Tesla. A truly ingenious concept."

"You are too kind." Mr. Tesla bowed to the two boffins, and Alek led him from the bridge, heading for the aft end of the gondola.

As they walked, Bovril shifted nervously on Alek's shoulder.

"A bit tricky," it whispered into his ear.

Even in the heat of battle, the boom that ran from gondola to ventral engine pod was unmanned. It was cramped inside, designed more to stabilize the ship than as a passageway, and the leggy Mr. Tesla had to stoop as he walked.

"That was a ghastly business," Alek said once they were alone.

"War is always ghastly, whether conducted with machines or animals." Tesla paused in his stride, watching a message lizard scuttle past overhead. "Though at least machines feel no pain."

Alek nodded. "Even the great airbeast itself has feelings, which can be a good thing. It retreated from one of your Tesla cannons when the *Leviathan*'s officers would not."

"Useful, I suppose." Tesla shook his head. "But the slaughter of animals is destructive to human morals."

Alek remembered an argument Deryn had made in Istanbul. "But don't you eat meat, Mr. Tesla?"

"A personal weakness. One day I shall give up that bar-baric practice."

"But you sacrificed your airbeast back in Siberia!"

"Not without my reasons," Tesla said, tapping his walking stick against the floor. "I couldn't endure those bears starving to death, so I simply let nature take its course."

Bovril shifted on Alek's shoulder, murmuring. The loris was always quiet around Tesla, as if cowed by the man. Or perhaps it was listening carefully.

Alek didn't know what to make of the inventor's words. Perhaps it made sense, sacrificing one creature to save many. But what if Tesla applied that same logic to stopping the war?

As they neared the engine pod, the floor of the passageway grew wet and sticky, and Alek smelled a foul, briny odor. Through an open hatchway ahead came the clang of tools.

"Hello?" Alek called.

A figure in a grimy flight suit appeared, sodden and smelly. As she snapped a salute, Alek realized with a start who it was beneath the muck.

"*Mr.* Sharp!" exclaimed Bovril, leaning forward on Alek's shoulder, reaching out for her.

Of course. Deryn Sharp could always be counted on to be in the thick of any mayhem aboard the *Leviathan*.

Alek stiffly returned her salute. "Mr. Tesla, I believe you've met Middy Sharp?"

"He was kind enough to drop in on me in Siberia," the inventor said. "Are those feathers?"

Deryn looked down at herself. Trapped in the engine grime on her flight suit were, indeed, a few feathers.

Deryn flicked one off and snapped her heels, as if she were at a formal dance instead of in an engine room covered with bilge. "I was tending to the strafing hawks. Very kind of you to visit, Mr. Tesla."

Tesla waved his walking stick. "I'm not visiting; I'm here to help. This engine is based on my design, you know."

"What exactly happened here?" Alek asked.

"The propellers sucked in a bit of rocket," Deryn said, avoiding Alek's eyes. "Started a fire, so the engineers called for a Herculean inundation. Watch your step, please."

Inside, the engine pod smelled like the gut of the ship. The floor was covered in gunk, the machinery blackened by fire. The engineers stopped their work and stared at Mr. Tesla, their eyes wide.

"A Herculean inundation?" the inventor asked. "As in the seven labors?"

Deryn looked puzzled, so Alek jumped in. "They must have flushed the rear ballast through the pod. Hence that sudden dive that sent us all sliding across the bridge."

Tesla lifted one shoe to peer at its grimy sole. "Both

ingenious and unhygienic, like so much Darwinist technology."

Deryn stiffened a bit, but her voice stayed level. "You
say you invented this particular engine, sir?"

"I created the principles of alternating current." Tesla
poked at the machine with his walking stick. "Much safer
on an airship."

Alek nodded. Visiting the pods a few days ago, he'd
noticed how the electrikal engines didn't spit smoke or
sparks, and ran almost silently.

"Alternating current," Bovril repeated happily.

"But you don't have a boiler room aboard," Tesla said.
"Where does the power come from?"

"These fuel cells here." Deryn looked down at a pile of
small metal kegs. "Hydrogen made by wee beasties in the
whale's gut."

"A biological battery!" Mr. Tesla exclaimed. "But they
can't have much power."

"They don't have to, sir." Deryn gestured out the pod's
high windows. "Darwinist airships get most of their push
from cilia—those wee hairs along the flanks. The engines
just give it a nudge in the right direction, and the airbeast
does the rest."

"But the *Leviathan* is special. It has two Clanker
engines as well," Alek added. "It will get you to New York
faster than anything else in the sky."

"Excellent." Mr. Tesla pulled off his jacket. "Well, let's get to work, then. The more engines the better!"

As Mr. Tesla worked, he held forth on a variety of topics—from world peace to his fascination with the number three—but Alek found it all a bit hard to follow. Master Klopp had never taught him much about electrikal engines, which weren't powerful enough to use in walkers.

At first Alek tried to help by handing Tesla his tools, but the engineers soon crowded him out for the honor. Just like Bovril, they hung on the great man's words. Alek found himself reduced to a waste of hydrogen, as usual.

Then he noticed that Deryn had stepped out onto the stabilizing boom. Of course, Alek had been avoiding her the last few days. But it was childish, pretending not to know each other. Their sudden falling out might start Dr. Barlow asking questions, and the last thing Alek wanted was for Deryn to be found out thanks to him.

He took a deep breath and stepped out through the hatchway.

"Hello, Dylan."

"Afternoon, your princeliness." Deryn didn't look up. She was staring down at the passing ocean, the wind barely ruffling her muck-matted hair.

For a moment Alek wondered if she were upset about him seeing her like this, covered in grime. But that was nonsense. Ordinary girls worried about that sort of thing, not Deryn.

"Mr. Tesla should get your engine working soon," he said.

"Aye, he's a barking genius. You should hear the engineers go on about it." She looked aft. "And it seems he's got the captain's head spinning too."

"What do you mean?"

Deryn pointed at the glare of sunlight in the airship's wake. "We're headed due east. We'll be in Tokyo tomorrow."

"Of course," Alek said. "Now that we've lent the Japanese navy a hand, we can depart with Britain's honor intact."

"The lady boffin said the same thing, but I thought she was blethering!"

"Dr. Barlow doesn't blether. Your Admiralty couldn't let Tsingtao fall without British aid, because the Japanese aren't properly . . ." He spread his hands, looking for the right word. "European. It wouldn't do for them to beat the Germans without our help."

For the first time Deryn looked straight at him. "You mean we came halfway round the world just for show? That's the biggest load of yackum I've ever heard!"

"Yackum," Bovril said, and leapt down onto the handrail.

Alek shrugged. "More or less. But there was a higher purpose, it seems. Now we can help Mr. Tesla stop the war."

Deryn gave him the same exasperated look she did whenever he mentioned his destiny.

"DRAINING."

"Are you going to punch me again?" Alek asked. "Because I'd like to get a good grip. It's a long fall."

A smirk flashed across her face, but her eyes didn't soften.

"You are rather strong," Alek said.

"Aye, and I'm taller than you too."

Alek rolled his eyes. "Listen, Deryn—"

"It's not a good habit, you calling me that."

"Perhaps not. But I've been calling you the wrong name for so long, I feel I should make up for it."

"It's not your fault I've got two names."

Alek looked down at the water slipping past. "So whose fault is it? I mean, even Volger thinks you're a fine soldier, and yet you have to hide who you are."

"It's just the way things are." She shrugged. "It's no one's fault."

"Or everyone's," Alek said. "Deryn."

"Deryn Sharp," said Bovril quietly.

Both of them stared at the perspicacious loris in horror.

"Brilliant," Deryn said. "Just barking *brilliant*. Now you've got the beastie saying it!"

"I'm sorry." Alek shook his head. "I didn't realize—"

Suddenly her hand was across his mouth. He smelled engine grease and brine on her palm, then saw the message lizard making its way along the underbelly of the ship.

Deryn let her hand fall, gesturing for silence.

The lizard spoke with Dr. Barlow's voice. "Mr. Sharp, tomorrow afternoon you shall accompany me to Mr. Tesla's meeting with the ambassador. I seem to recall, however, that you have no formal uniform. We shall have to remedy that when we arrive in Tokyo."

Deryn swore, and Alek recalled that her only dress uniform had been destroyed in the battle of the *Dauntless*. Going to a tailor to replace it would be tricky enough, even without the lady boffin along.

"Um, but—but, ma'am," Deryn sputtered. "I'll have to—"

"Dr. Barlow," Alek broke in, "this is Prince Aleksandar. I know you want young Dylan to look his best, but gentlemen's tailoring is hardly your area of expertise. It would be my pleasure to go with him. End message."

The beastie waited a moment, then blinked and scuttled away.

Deryn gave him a long stare, then shook her head. "You're both daft. I can see to my own clothes, right?"

"Of course." Alek pulled at his own threadbare sleeve. "But I could use a bit of tailoring myself."

"True. You're looking a bit less than princely." Deryn straightened with a sigh. "Well, I have duties to attend to. See you when we get to Tokyo, I suppose."

"I suppose so." He smiled at her.

Deryn turned and strode back into the engine pod, shouting at the engineers to give Mr. Tesla some peace. Alek stayed out on the boom, staring down at the water a little longer and wondering at what he felt inside.

Whatever her name was, he had missed his good friend these last few days, rather a lot.

"A bit of tailoring," Bovril said thoughtfully. "End message."

◉ SEVENTEEN ◉

Alek pulled on another jacket, then scowled at the mirror. His Hapsburg Armor Corp uniform was just as threadbare as the others, shiny at the elbows and missing two buttons. Had he really spent the last weeks walking about in such a disreputable state?

"This seems unwise," Count Volger said.

Alek fingered the jacket's frayed epaulettes. "I have an ambassador to impress, and I doubt the tailors in Tokyo are expensive."

"I'm not talking about the cost, Alek. You're practically penniless, in any case." The wildcount glanced out the window—one of the spires of Tokyo was sliding by, alarmingly close to the gondola. "I'm talking about that girl."

Alek picked up the silk piloting jacket he'd worn the night of the Ottoman Revolution. "Her name is Deryn."

"Whatever she calls herself, you've managed to escape her influence at last. Why risk another entanglement?"

"Deryn isn't an entanglement." Alek pulled the jacket on and considered the effect. "She's a friend, and a useful ally."

"Useful? Only in that she's taken that beast away."

Alek didn't answer. Deryn had dropped by his stateroom the night before to "borrow" Bovril. Alek found that he missed the creature's weight on his shoulder and its murmurs in his ear. The perspicacious loris had offered comfort when everyone else had betrayed him.

"You can't trust her," Volger said.

"Nor can I trust you, Count. And Deryn, at least, can tell me what the *Leviathan*'s officers are thinking."

"Tesla does their thinking for them these days. Imagine, trying to requisition this whole ship to take him to America! It's madness to believe that the Admiralty will allow it."

Alek raised an eyebrow. "That was my idea, you know."

"Ah, of course." With a sigh Volger stood up from the desk and went to his traveling trunk. "This is a diplomatic affair, not a costume party."

Alek pulled off his Ottoman piloting jacket. "Perhaps it is a bit too colorful for a British ambassador."

"You're taking a risk, believing in Tesla."

"He wants peace, and has the power to make it happen."

"Let's hope so, Your Serene Highness. Because if you support him publicly and he turns out to be mad, the whole world will think you're a fool. Do you think the people of Austria-Hungary will want a young fool for an emperor?"

Alek's glare was wasted on Volger, who was rummaging in his trunk. He pulled out a deep blue tunic with a red collar.

"My Hapsburg House Cavalry uniform."

Alek said, "Do you think I'm being a fool?"

"I think you're trying to do something good. But doing good is rarely easy, and no weapon has ever stopped a war." Count Volger handed over the cavalry tunic. "But who knows. Perhaps the great inventor has changed all that."

"And you wanted to murder him." Alek pulled the tunic on. The sleeves were too long, of course, but a decent tailor could fix that. "Or was that whole business just an idle threat to shake me out of my sulk?"

The wildcount smiled. "Two birds, one stone."

The streets of Tokyo teemed with steam trams, pedestrians, and beasts of burden. The morning sun had crested the buildings, but the strings of paper lanterns hanging overhead still glowed. Each was filled with a little swarm of flickering insects, like a handful of stars.

Alek was always uncomfortable in crowds, and here in Tokyo he felt especially conspicuous. There were no other Europeans about except the pair of marine guards following him. Many of the Japanese men wore western clothing, but the women were dressed in long dresses dyed in indigo and scarlet patterns, with broad silk belts that gathered into bundles on their lower backs. Alek tried to picture Deryn in such a getup, but failed completely.

The two technologies mixed more elegantly than he'd expected. Streetcars huffed out clouds of steam, but the most crowded were yoked to oxenesques for extra power. A few rickshaws putted along behind diesel two-legged walkers; the rest were pulled by squat, scaly creatures that reminded Alek disturbingly of kappa. Telegraph lines crisscrossed the sky overhead, but messenger lizards scampered along them, and carrier eagles wheeled against the clouds.

"Are we lost yet?" Deryn asked.

"Lost," declared Bovril from her shoulder, then went back to burbling snatches of Japanese.

Alek sighed, unfolding Dr. Barlow's map for the fortieth time since they'd left the airfield. It was exasperating, not being able to read street signs. On top of which, addresses worked differently here in Japan. Instead of the numbers running along the avenues, they went clockwise around city blocks. Pure insanity.

According to a local scientist friend of Dr. Barlow's, a whole street of tailors catering to Europeans was hidden somewhere in this madness.

"I think we're close," Alek said. "You don't suppose those two could help?"

Deryn glanced at the marine guards shadowing them. "They're only here to keep you from running away."

"Hardly necessary. I'm quite happy to be on the *Leviathan* these days."

Deryn gave a snort. "Aye, thanks to your new boffin pal."

"He's a genius, and he wants to stop this war."

"He's a complete nutter, you mean. Dr. Barlow says his talk of Goliath is daft!"

"Nutter," Bovril said with a chuckle.

"Of course she would say so," Alek said. "Mr. Tesla is a Clanker scientist, and she's a Darwinist—and a *Darwin* to boot! They're natural enemies."

Deryn started to reply, but her head swiveled as a food stall drifted slowly past. The whole thing was drawn, customers and all, by a squat two-legged walker. One of the cooks was chopping thin layers of dough into fine noodles; the others were slicing mushrooms, fish, and eels. The smell of buckwheat and prawns carried on the steam rising from the boilers, along with the tang of vinegar and pickles.

"Might want some of that later," Deryn mumbled.

"Want," Bovril said.

Alek smiled. He'd learned in Istanbul that food could always distract Deryn from an argument. But she wasn't done yet.

"Have you forgotten what I found in Mr. Tesla's room?"

"You found a rock," Alek said flatly.

"If it was only a rock, why did he bring it aboard?"

"He's a scientist. They *like* rocks. Didn't Dr. Barlow know what it was?"

Deryn shook her head. "She isn't certain, but it's all very suspicious. Mr. Tesla's weapons all use electricity, and it was a sort of . . . cannonball."

"No cannonball could destroy half of Siberia, *Mr.* Sharp."

"*Mr.* Sharp!" Bovril repeated.

"Perhaps I'll simply ask him myself." Alek gave a snort. "Though he might wonder why you were hiding under his bed at night."

"Forget it. If he knows we were spying on him, he won't trust you."

Alek shook his head—as if Deryn could offer advice on trust and friendship. "Once we get to New York and reveal Goliath to the world, I'm sure these minor details will all make sense."

"You think the Admiralty will really let us head off to America?"

"Mr. Tesla can be quite convincing," Alek said. "Besides, this is my destiny."

"Aye," Deryn said, and snorted. "Your destiny."

She was about to say more, when Bovril interrupted. "A bit of tailoring!"

"The beastie's right." Deryn was looking over Alek's shoulder. "Your destiny is a better-fitting jacket, looks to me."

He turned. Beneath the awning of an open shop front whirred a spidery machine, bristling with spindles of thread. Squeezed onto a hanging banner full of Japanese characters were a few recognizable words: WELCOME TO SHIBASAKI TAILORS.

Alek folded up the map. "For the moment that will do."

"Irasshai," came a call as Alek stepped beneath the awning. Two men stood up from behind sewing machines, one robed in white cotton with a flowered print, the other in a European waistcoat and jacket.

"Welcome, gentlemen," the robed man said in practiced English.

Alek and Deryn returned his bow.

"We've just arrived here, sirs," Alek said slowly. "We have no money, but we can pay with gold."

The man looked embarrassed at this forwardness, but Alek could only bow again, holding out Volger's cavalry uniform.

"If you could make this fit me."

The other tailor took the jacket by the shoulders and shook it open. "Of course."

"And my friend needs a dress shirt in the British naval fashion, by this afternoon."

"We have many shirts for British gentlemen, if we

make alterations." The man turned to Deryn. "May we measure you, sir?"

She glanced at the marine guards waiting just outside— close enough to hear any exclamations of surprise.

"I'm afraid not," Alek said. "He has a . . . skin condition. Perhaps you could measure me, and adjust a little."

The tailor frowned. "But you are shorter, sir."

"Not *that* much shorter," Alek said, and heard Bovril chuckling.

The tailor bowed gracefully, then extended a length of string between his hands. Alek took off his jacket and turned around, holding out his arms wide.

Deryn leaned back to watch, wearing the first smile Alek had seen on her face in days.

After the measurements were done, the tailors told Alek and Deryn to return in two hours. Deryn unerringly tracked down the moving food stall they'd seen earlier, and soon they were seated on a long bench that faced the cooks, shoulder to shoulder with the other customers. The marine guards took up station just behind the stall, watching from a distance.

A dozen pots of noodles bubbled on the boilers, which Deryn said were burning an oil made from fabricated peanuts. The fuel let off a sweet scent that mingled with the briny smell of salmon slices edged with orange, a black vinegar sauce in small bowls, and tiny dried fish curled into silver half-moons.

As Deryn pantomimed for the cooks, Alek realized how hungry he was. He watched the other customers eating with chopsticks, wishing he'd brought a fork and knife from the *Leviathan*'s mess.

"Did you hear?" Deryn asked. "The meeting's been moved to the Imperial Hotel."

"Why a hotel?"

"It's got a barking theater! Seems the ambassador wants to show the whole world that the great Nikola Tesla has changed sides." Deryn inspected her chopsticks. "Maybe that will get the Clankers quaking in their boots."

"Hopefully," Alek said. Two bowls were set before them, full of tangled noodles half covered in a thick broth. Atop the noodles sat a spoonful of white mush and a cluster of tiny orange spheres, as translucent as rubies. A plate of fresh salmon was set before Bovril.

As the beast started in, Alek stared at his dish. "What have you ordered us?"

"No idea," Deryn said, picking up a wooden spoon. "It looked good, so I pointed at it."

Alek lifted his chopsticks and attempted to pick up

one of the pearly orange spheres. The first exploded, but he managed to get a second into his mouth. It popped like a tiny balloon between his teeth, tasting of salt and fish.

"It's like oversize caviar."

"Which is what?" Deryn asked.

"Fish eggs."

She frowned, but the revelation didn't slow her eating.

Alek tasted the white substance, which turned out to be pickled radishes chopped into mush. There were also slivers of a pearly fruit, as tangy as lemon rind. He swirled his chopsticks in the bowl, mixing the sharp flavors of radishes, citrus, and fish eggs with the thick buckwheat noodles.

As he ate, Alek finally took a proper look at the slowly passing city. The rooftops of Tokyo curved and swelled like ocean waves, terra-cotta tiles rippling their surfaces. Miniature potted trees crowded the windows, growing in twisted shapes that mirrored the strokes of calligraphy decorating every shop. Canopies of vines overhead spilled pink blossoms onto the ground, and the hanging paper lanterns seemed to be everywhere, bobbing in the breeze.

"Quite beautiful, considering," Alek said.

"Considering what?"

"That the same culture fabricated those horrid kappa."

"Less horrid than a phosphorous shell, if you ask me."

Alek shrugged, not in the mood to revisit the argument he'd had with Tesla. "You're right. Killing is ugly, whatever shape it takes. That's why we have to stop this war."

"It isn't up to you to fix the world, Alek. Maybe your parents' murder set it off, but the world was ready enough with war machines and beasties!" She stared into her bowl, twirling noodles onto her chopsticks. "A fight would have happened one way or another."

"None of that changes the fact that my family started it."

Deryn turned to face him. "You can't blame a match for a house made of straw, Alek."

"A nice turn of phrase." All that was left of Alek's meal was broth. The other customers seemed to think nothing of drinking from their bowls, so he lifted his with both hands. "But it doesn't change what I have to do."

Deryn watched him drink, then said simply, "What if you can't stop it?"

"You saw what we did in Istanbul. Our revolution kept them out of the war!"

"It was *their* revolution, Alek. We just helped a bit."

"Of course, but Mr. Tesla can do much more. Destiny

brought me to Siberia to meet him, so clearly his plan *has to work!*"

Deryn sighed. "What if destiny doesn't care?"

"Why can't you admit that providence has guided my course at every turn?" Alek counted the points on his fingers. "My father prepared a refuge for me in the Alps, in the very same valley where the *Leviathan* crashed! Then, after I escaped, I wound up back on your ship—just as it was headed for the siege of Tsingtao. And that brought me to the wastes of Siberia in time to meet Tesla. All those connections have to *mean* something!"

Deryn opened her mouth to argue, then hesitated, a half smile crossing her face. "So you must think that we're meant to be together."

Alek blinked. "What?"

"I told you how I wound up on the *Leviathan*. If a freak storm hadn't carried me halfway across Britain, I'd be serving on the *Minotaur* with Jaspert. Never would have met you, then."

"Well, I suppose not."

"And when we crashed, and you came to help us on those silly snowshoes, you walked straight up to where I was lying in the snow." Her smile grew broader. "You saved me, first thing."

"Only from a frostbitten bum." Alek stared into the empty bowl before him; a fish egg was stuck to one side.

He picked it up with his chopsticks and regarded it.

"And when you jumped ship in Istanbul, you thought you'd got away from me." Deryn gave a snort. "Not likely."

"You do have a habit of showing up."

"Must be rough for you. Having your destiny mixed up with a barking commoner's!" She shoveled in her last mouthful of noodles, chuckling to herself.

Alek frowned. In two days of brooding it somehow hadn't crossed his mind that without Deryn Sharp the Ottoman Revolution might have failed, and Alek certainly would never have come back aboard the *Leviathan*. Thus he wouldn't have met Tesla, and would be no closer to stopping the war.

Deryn had been there every step of the way.

"We are connected, aren't we?"

"Aye," she said, still chewing. "And for us to meet at all, I had to pretend to be a boy. Fancy that."

"Barking destiny," Bovril said, then burped.

Alek put his hands up in surrender. There were worse things than being connected to Deryn Sharp. In fact, the simple fact that she was smiling sent a wave of relief through him—she was his ally again, his friend. Providence seemed to be saying that she always would be.

All at once a fist around his heart loosened its grip.

"It was awful, being at war with you."

Deryn laughed. "I missed you, too, daft prince." She started to say more, but then cast a look over her shoulder at the two marine guards, and sighed. "We should go fetch our clothes. Tesla will be starting in a few hours."

Alek nodded. "It should be quite a show."

○ EIGHTEEN ○

The theater of the Imperial Hotel was filling up; there were at least a hundred in the audience already. Deryn wondered if the Clanker boffin had invited them all, or if the British embassy had, or whether the news was spreading on its own across Tokyo.

The British ambassador was easy to spot, a man in a posh civilian suit surrounded by admirals and commodores. Not far away a dozen Japanese naval officers wore black tunics and hats with red piping. Deryn recognized other uniforms—French, Russian, even a handful of Italians, though Darwinist Italy had yet to join the war. A gaggle of boffins, European and Japanese, stood about in bowlers, some with recording frogs perched on their shoulders.

Of everyone there, only Deryn was alone. Dr. Barlow had abandoned her for the other boffins, and Bovril was

sneaking beneath the chairs, listening for new snippets of language.

Most of the audience seemed to be reporters, some already snapping photos of the stage. All sorts of electrical apparatus waited there, metal spheres and glass tubes, coils of wire, a generator the size of a smokehouse, and a large glass bulb hanging from the ceiling. How Tesla had put all these contraptions together so quickly was beyond Deryn. The *Leviathan* had made good speed and had landed just before midnight, and the man had left in a whirlwind shortly after. He must have spent the whole night and morning hunting for electrical parts.

Deryn spotted Master Klopp off to one side, working on a tangle of wires. Hoffman stood beside him, tools at the ready. Alek had put his men at the disposal of the great inventor, of course. And at the moment, Alek himself was busy chatting to a group of officers in unfamiliar blue uniforms. Americans, perhaps.

Deryn was still surprised at her own words from that morning, about her and Alek being meant to be together. She still didn't really believe any of his claptrap about providence. Blethering about destiny was simply a way for Alek to accept her as a girl, by fitting her into his grand plan to save the world. He'd swallowed it, of course, because deep down Alek knew that he was stronger with her than without.

The lights flickered, and the audience began to settle into their seats. Bovril returned to Deryn's shoulder, and Dr. Barlow made her way back across the room, taking a seat beside her.

"Mr. Sharp, have I mentioned it's good to see you so well dressed?"

Deryn fingered her shirt, which was made out of a thicker, softer cotton than she was used to. It fit marvelously, despite the tailors never having touched her.

"They take their tailoring seriously here, ma'am."

"And a good thing too. You are in the presence of greatness."

Deryn frowned. "I thought you didn't like this bum-rag."

"Not Mr. Tesla, young man." She gestured with a white-gloved hand. "There is Sakichi Toyoda, the father of Japanese mechanics. And, beside him, Kokichi Mikimoto, the first fabricator of shaped pearls. Clankers and Darwinists, working together."

"To-yo-da," Bovril said softly, separating each syllable.

"Better than fighting each other, I suppose," Deryn said. "But what's the point of all this? The Admiralty's not even here to see it."

"In a way, they are." Dr. Barlow nodded her head toward the wings of the stage, where a Royal Navy officer sat at a telegraph key. "Tokyo is connected to London by underwater fiber. According to the ambassador, Lord Churchill himself has awoken early to follow the proceedings."

Deryn frowned. The underwater fiber system, which stretched from Britain to Australia to Japan, was one of the more uncanny creations of Darwinism. Made from mile-long strands of living nervous tissue, it bound the British Empire together like a single organism, carrying coded messages along the ocean floor.

"But they won't be able to *see* anything," Deryn said.

"Mr. Tesla claims otherwise." Dr. Barlow's voice

faded as the lights dimmed and a hush settled over the crowd.

A familiar tall figure strode to the center of the darkened stage, holding a long cylinder in one hand. He flourished it in the air, like a swordsman saluting, and then his voice boomed across the theater.

"Time is pressing, so I shall begin without prologue. I hold a glass tube full of incandescent gasses." Tesla pointed at the ceiling. "And here is a wire conveying alternating currents of high potential. When I touch both . . ."

He took the wire in one hand, and the glass tube suddenly illuminated in the other. There was a slight gasp from the audience, and then a scattering of laughter, as if some of them had known the trick was coming.

Shadows shifted across Tesla's features as he rested the glowing tube across his shoulder, like a phantasmal walking stick. "This is merely an electric light, of course, except for the novelty of using my body as a conductor. But it reminds us that electricity can travel through more than wires. Through the atmosphere, for example, or the Earth's crust, and even the ether of interplanetary space."

"Oh, dear," Dr. Barlow said softly. "Not *martians* again."

"Martians," Bovril said, chuckling, and Deryn raised an eyebrow.

Tesla placed the tube at the edge of the stage, the light extinguishing the moment his fingers left it. He let go of the wire and straightened his jacket.

"In some ways our planet itself is a capacitor, a giant battery." He reached up to touch the bulb hanging from the ceiling, and a light spread inside it. "In the center of this sphere is another, smaller, globe. Both are filled with luminous gases, and together they can show us the engine of our planet at work."

The man fell silent then, standing back and saying nothing. The globe stayed lit, but nothing else happened as minutes passed in silence. Deryn shifted in her seat. It was a bit uncanny to see so many important people sitting quietly for this long.

Her mind began to drift, wondering why Dr. Barlow had mentioned martians. Did Tesla believe in them? It was one thing to call the great inventor a nutter, but quite another if he was truly mad.

Alek wanted to stop the war so badly, he was willing to believe any promise of peace. And after all he'd lost— his family, his country, and his home—how would he carry on if this hope were dashed as well? But there was not much she could do, Deryn supposed, except show him that there were other things to life besides saving the world.

A murmur went through the crowd, and she looked

up. The light in the glass sphere had formed a shape, a tiny finger of lightning, just like those inside Tesla's metal detector. The flicker was moving, sweeping slowly around the globe like the second hand on a clock.

"The rotation is clockwise, as always," Tesla said. "Though in the Southern Hemisphere it would go in the other direction, I suppose. You see, this finger of light is set in motion by the spinning of our planet."

Another murmur traveled across the room, a bit unsettled. Deryn frowned. How was that so different from a pendulum or a compass needle?

"But we are not limited to the brute forces of nature." Tesla took a step closer to the hanging light, a small object in his hand. "With this magnet I can wrest control of this flicker from the earth itself."

He stepped still closer, and the light stopped spinning. Tesla began to walk around the bulb, and the flicker began to move again, always pointing away from him, no matter how he paused or hurried.

"Strange, isn't it? To think that one can aim lightning as easily as a pistol." He pulled out his pocket watch and checked it. "But now it is time for a larger demonstration. Much larger. A few days ago I sent a message from the *Leviathan* to Tokyo by courier eagle. The message was forwarded by underwater fiber to London, and finally by radio waves to my assistants in New York, more than halfway around the world. There, a few minutes from now, they will follow my instructions."

He signaled to Klopp, who began to make adjustments in one of the black boxes. A moment later all the devices onstage began to flicker and hum. Mr. Tesla stood among them, his hair standing on end like an angry cat's. Deryn felt her own hairs tingle, as if a summer storm were in the air.

"The results will be visible on these instruments here," Tesla said, then turned toward the Royal Navy officer at the telegraph key. "And also in the early morning sky of London, if you would kindly ask Mr. Churchill and the Sea Lords to step to a window?"

Another murmur went through the room, and Deryn whispered to the lady boffin, "What's he on about?"

"His machine in New York is going to send a signal into the air. Like a radio wave, but far more powerful." Dr. Barlow leaned closer. "It's daylight here, so we need instruments to see its effects. But in London the sun isn't up yet."

"You mean, he thinks Goliath can change the *sky*?"

The lady boffin nodded silently, and Deryn stared at the stage, where needles of light had begun to flicker from every object. Even Mr. Tesla's pocket watch was glowing, and a buzzing filled the air, like the bees in the gut of the *Leviathan* when they needed feeding.

"The transmission will begin in ten seconds," Tesla said, then snapped his watch closed. "It will not take long to reach us."

"Transmission," Bovril said, shifting unhappily. The loris began to keen softly, and suddenly the buzzing wasn't so bad in Deryn's ear. She reached up to scratch the beastie's head gratefully.

For a long moment nothing happened, and Deryn let herself hope that the experiment was failing. The great Tesla would be humiliated, and all this yackum about going to America would end.

But then the fingers of lightning in the hanging globe grew stronger, flickering across the inside surface of the glass. Then they spun aimlessly for a moment, then turned strong and steady, pointing to the left side of the stage.

All the other instruments had come to life, filling the theater with light. The glass tubes were filled with rainbows of color, the metal spheres covered with a thousand needles of electricity. The antennae on Klopp's black box had erupted, sending shoots of lightning climbing up them, only to sputter out in the air. The officer at the telegraph still tapped away, the buttons on his coat alight with tiny sparks.

Gradually the countless fingers of light began to align, all of them pointed to the left. Deryn could feel the hairs on her head pulling in that direction.

"North-northeast," Dr. Barlow muttered. "Directly toward New York, by great circle."

"As you can see," Tesla cried above the buzzing, "I am able to control the currents in this room, even from ten thousand kilometers away. Imagine a thunderstorm brought to heel at such a distance. Or even the electrical charges of the earth's atmosphere itself, focused and aimed like a searchlight!"

Bovril was burbling madly. The creature's fur stood on end, and its eyes were open wider than Deryn had ever seen.

"Don't worry, beastie," she said. "He's on our side."

"Let's hope so," Dr. Barlow said.

Tesla lifted his hands into the air, waving them to and fro. Tendrils of lightning clung to his fingertips, but then went shooting off in the same direction—north-northeast.

"This is the power of Goliath, that no one on earth, Clanker or Darwinist, can escape. So we all must learn to share the globe, or perish together!"

He waved a hand, and Klopp cut a master switch. All the lightning disappeared at once, leaving the room in darkness. The silence was quickly filled with gasps and mutterings. Then came a halting applause that slowly grew in strength.

A thousand flickers seemed to hover in the air, burned like sunbeams into Deryn's vision. Through them she saw Tesla reaching up to grab the hanging wire again. He picked up the simple glass tube, which sprang to life.

"Any word from the Admiralty?" he asked, silencing the applause.

The Royal Navy officer stood up from his telegraph, a piece of paper in his quivering hand. "Lord Churchill and the Sea Lords send their greetings, and wish to report that your experiment was a success. Subtle but strange colors appeared in the dawn sky over London."

The crowd went dead silent.

"They offer hearty congratulations." The officer cleared his throat. "Pardon me, ladies and gentlemen, but the rest of the message is for the captain of the *Leviathan*."

Dr. Barlow leaned back into her seat. "Well, that's not

much of a mystery, is it, Mr. Sharp? It looks as though we're headed for New York."

"New York," Bovril said thoughtfully, and began to smooth its frizzled fur.

· NINETEEN ·

The Pacific Ocean was nearly half the world, as Mr. Rigby liked to say. It certainly looked vast now, spread out beneath the ship like a rippling sheet of silver. The Japanese home islands were less than a day behind them, but already the very notion of land seemed distant and obscure.

The *Leviathan* was at full-ahead, making airspeed of sixty miles an hour. The wind blew down the spine at whole gale force, thrumming along the ship's surface like a surging river.

"Is it always like this?" Alek shouted over the wind.

"Aye," Deryn replied. "Brilliant, isn't it?"

Alek just scowled at her. His gloved hands clutched the ratlines in a death grip, and Hoffman's eyes were wide with fear behind his goggles. The two Clankers had been at full-ahead in their engine pods before, but never out here on the open spine.

"This is *real* flying!" Deryn leaned closer. "But if you're afraid, your princeliness, you can go back down."

Alek shook his head. "Hoffman needs a translator."

"My German's good enough," Deryn said. "I had a whole month of your Clanker jabbering in Istanbul!"

"*Weißt du, was ein Kondensator ist?*"

"That's easy. You asked me if I know what a *Kondensator* is!"

"Well, do you?"

Deryn frowned. "Well, it's some sort of . . . condenser. Obviously."

"No," Alek said. "A capacitor. You just blew up the ship, *Dummkopf.*"

She rolled her eyes. It seemed a bit unfair, expecting her to know German words for contraptions she'd never seen before. But she couldn't argue the point. Hoffman was the engineer best able to follow Tesla's orders, and only Alek could translate Clanker technical jargon into English.

This whole trip topside was at the bidding of the great inventor. He wanted a radio antenna stretching the length of the *Leviathan*, but he didn't want the ship slowing down. The captain had little choice but to obey—the

Admiralty's orders were to cooperate with Tesla, and to get him to America as quickly as practical.

Working on the spine at top speed wasn't impossible, after all, just a bit tricky. And also dead good fun.

"Take the wire to the bow, Sharp!" Mr. Rigby shouted above the wind. "And before you head back, make sure that end is secure."

"I'll go along," Alek said.

"No you *won't*, boy!" Mr. Rigby shouted. "It's too dangerous for princes up there."

Alek scowled, but didn't argue. Up here on the spine, the bosun was the only royalty.

Deryn waved for Hoffman, then began to make her way toward the great airbeast's head. Reattaching her safety clip every yard or so made progress slow, and the spool of wire was barking heavy. But the trickiest thing was crawling into a sixty-mile-an-hour headwind.

Hoffman followed, carrying his tools and a small device that Mr. Tesla had been tinkering with all day. He claimed that with a thousand-foot-long antenna at this altitude, he could detect radio signals from anywhere in the world—even beyond.

"So he can talk to bloody *martians*," Deryn cried. "That's what we're up here for!"

Hoffman didn't understand, or chose not to comment.

At full-ahead the bow was bare of life. The fléchette bats were all hidden away in their nooks and crannies, the birds safe in the rookery. Soon the last set of ratlines disappeared, and Deryn crawled still more slowly, lying flat, her palms spread across the rough, hard surface of the airbeast's bowhead.

She was glad for the weight of the spool now. At least with sixty pounds of wire strapped to her back, the wind was less likely to blow her into the ocean. She yelled at Hoffman to keep himself flat. At this speed, rushing air could find a grip in any space between a crewman's body and the airbeast's skin, like a knife prying up a barnacle, and fling him off into the sea.

At last Deryn reached the mooring yoke, the heavy harness at the extreme bow of the airship. She snapped her safety clip to it and sighed with relief. Hoffman joined her there, and together they began to secure one end of the wire.

As they worked in the relentless wind, Deryn found herself wondering if Hoffman knew what she really was. She doubted Volger would have told anyone; the man always kept secrets for his own uses. But what about Alek? He'd promised not to tell anyone that she was a girl, but did that include hiding the truth from his own men?

When the wire was tied fast and Tesla's device attached,

Hoffman clapped Deryn on the shoulder, muttering a few choice German curses into the wind. She smiled, suddenly certain that he didn't know.

Alek might be a *Dummkopf* sometimes, but he was always true to his word.

The two started back, unspooling wire as they went, securing it to the ratlines every few yards, to keep it from flapping about. Crawling was much quicker with the wind at their backs, and they soon reached Alek and Mr. Rigby again. Together the four of them headed aft.

The journey grew easier as they neared the tail. The roar of the Clanker engines lessened with distance, and past the airbeast's middle its body narrowed, the great hump sheltering them from the wind. When the first spool emptied, they halted. Mr. Rigby and Hoffman spliced it to another five-hundred-foot wire.

While they waited, Alek turned to Deryn. "Are you excited about seeing America?"

"A bit," she said. "But it sounds like an odd place."

The United States was another half-Darwinist, half-Clanker country. But unlike Japan, the technologies weren't happily combined there. The two halves of America had been fighting a vicious civil war when old Darwin had announced his discoveries. The South had adopted Darwinist agricultural techniques, while the industrial North had stayed loyal to the machine. Even fifty years later the nation remained split in two.

"Isn't that why people join the Air Service?" Alek asked. "To see the world?"

Deryn shrugged. "Me, I just wanted to fly."

"I'm beginning to see the appeal," Alek said, smiling. He stood up halfway, the airflow thrashing at his hair and flight suit, and he leaned forward at a precarious angle, letting the force of the wind keep him upright.

"Blazes, Alek. Sit yourself down!"

The boy just laughed, splaying his hands like a bird's wings. Deryn leaned forward to grab the safety harness of his flight suit.

The bosun looked up from his work. "Quit that skylarking!"

"Sorry, sir!" Deryn pulled at Alek's harness. "Come on, you dafty. Sit *down*!"

Alek stopped laughing, dropping to one knee. He pointed ahead. "Is that what I think it is?"

Deryn turned to face the wind. The *Leviathan*'s nose was tipping down a bit, and the great hill of the whale's hump seemed to descend before them, revealing the sky ahead.

"Mr. Rigby!" Deryn called, pointing at the bow. "You should see this, sir."

A moment later the bosun swore, and Hoffman let out a low whistle. Ahead of the airship was a towering mass of

"THE COMING STORM."

thunderclouds, framed by a dark wall that stretched across the horizon. It was a huge storm, right in the *Leviathan's* path.

Deryn caught the scent of rain and felt lightning in the air. "What should we do, Mr. Rigby?"

"We finish this job, lad, unless we get new orders."

"Begging your pardon, sir, but there's no way they'd send a message lizard up. Even a hydrogen sniffer would be blown off at this speed!"

"The captain can always send up a team of riggers, if he wants." The bosun pointed at the second spool of wire, still full. "In any case we can't stop now, or we'll hit that storm with loose wire flying about!"

Deryn swallowed. "Aye, of course, sir."

Hoffman finished off the splice, and the four of them headed toward the tail again. Crawling along the spine was even trickier now. The wind was shifting unpredictably, the currents of the storm mixing with the airflow of the ship's great speed.

Deryn felt the membrane moving beneath her, rolling to one side. She glanced over her shoulder at the bow.

"We're turning, sir," she said. "Angling to starboard."

Mr. Rigby swore, waving them on.

"That's good, isn't it?" Alek asked her. "They're aiming to avoid the center of the storm."

Deryn shook her head. "Hurricanes always spin anti-clockwise, so we're headed into a massive tailwind. We're not missing the storm—we're using it to move faster. A brilliant idea from Mr. Tesla, no doubt."

"Is that dangerous?"

"The ship should be fine. It's us I'm worried about." Deryn snapped her safety clip down with a vengeance. "If they'd just slow down a bit, we could get this barking job done!"

"Settle yourself, Mr. Sharp," came the bosun's grumble. "We have our orders, and the captain has his."

"Aye, sir," Deryn said, then set herself to crawling as fast as she could.

Having a boffin in charge was getting to be annoying.

They were still out in the open when the airship hit the storm. The rain didn't build gradually but arrived in a silvery wall hurtling down the *Leviathan*'s length at sixty miles an hour.

"Take hold!" Deryn cried as the chattering tumult surrounded them. The membrane rippled beneath her, stirred by the wave of cold air that came with the rain, no doubt pulled down from the northern Pacific by the great spinning engine of the storm. Suddenly the driving wind seemed full of ice and nails, the freezing drops hitting her goggles like tiny stones.

"Don't anyone move!" Mr. Rigby shouted. "The captain should slow down for us now!"

Deryn clung to the ratlines with both hands, gritting her teeth, and it was only moments later that the roar of the Clanker engines went silent.

"Aye, I didn't *think* the officers had gone mad," the bosun muttered. He rose slowly, holding his side where he'd been shot two months before. A wave of fresh annoyance swept through Deryn. It was all very well for Tesla to send men up topside at full-ahead, when he was safe and sipping brandy in his cabin!

With the engines off, the airship quickly matched the speed of the wind, and a strange calm settled around the four of them. They headed for the steering house at a jog, the membrane slick with rain beneath their feet. Deryn kept one eye on Mr. Rigby, ready to grab him if he slipped. But the old man was as sure-footed as always, and soon they were crowding into the dorsal steering house, the aftmost shelter on the ship.

"Get that wire secure," Mr. Rigby ordered.

Alek translated for Hoffman, who set to work. The bosun plunked down heavily on a box of spare engine parts, and Deryn pulled off her gloves and rubbed her hands together, then whistled for glowworm light.

The dorsal steering house wasn't luxurious. It was full of parts for tending the ship's rear engines, and had its own master wheel if the bridge somehow lost rudder control. Thankfully it was connected by passageways to the airbeast's gut, so a squick of warmth rose from an open hatchway in the floor.

Once the wire was tied fast, Hoffman said a few words to Alek, then descended into the airship, unspooling still more wire behind him.

"Where's he off to?" Deryn asked Alek.

"Mr. Tesla wants the antenna to run down through the ship, all the way to his laboratory."

"Aye, anything to keep *him* dry," Deryn muttered. She wondered exactly what the Clanker boffin was up to. Back in Tokyo he'd proven he could send radio waves around the world. What more could he do from up here in the sky?

The bosun still wore a pained expression, so the three waited a few minutes before moving on. Every gust of wind made the steering house shudder, the rain-spattered windows rattling in their frames. Deryn felt the floor shifting beneath her. The airbeast was flexing its body, turning its face away from the force of the storm. This close to the tail, it was easy to feel the giant body shift, like being at the end of a vast, slow whip.

The ratlines creaked around them, and an unfamiliar metal groan came through the sounds of wind and rain.

The wire leading out into the storm went taut beside Deryn, then shuddered and fell slack.

"Blast it," the bosun sighed. "That wire must have been too short."

"But Mr. Tesla's measurements were quite precise!" Alek said.

"Aye, of course they were." Deryn shook her head. "*Too* precise. He was thinking of the *Leviathan* as a zeppelin, a dead thing, rigid from bow to stern. But an airbeast bends, and more than usual in this barking storm."

Alek stood up, looking out. "Perhaps someone might have *mentioned* that to him!"

"Your Mr. Tesla never bothered to ask," the bosun said flatly. "But repairs will have to wait. They'll be starting the engines up again soon."

Alek looked as though he were going to argue, but Deryn put a hand on his shoulder.

"They're idle for now, Mr. Rigby." She stepped to the windows, shielding her eyes with her hands. "And the break might be close by."

The bosun snorted. "All right. Pop out and take a look."

Deryn opened the door a bit and squeezed out onto the blustery expanse of the topside. A moment later something caught her eye. At least five hundred feet away, near the base of the hump, a glimmer of silver danced in the rain.

"One end of the wire's got loose, sir," she called over her shoulder. "Maybe twenty yards of it. And it's flailing about in the wind!"

Mr. Rigby got to his feet and joined her at the door, then swore.

"When the engines come back, that'll get a bit lively! Could even cut into the membrane!" He crossed to the gut hatchway. "I'm afraid you've got to go back out, lad, and secure both loose ends. I'll find a message lizard and tell the bridge to hold the engines still for a bit longer."

"Aye, sir." Deryn pulled her gloves back on.

The bosun paused halfway down into the hatch. "Wait a few minutes to make sure they've got the message, then get it done fast. Whatever happens, I don't want you out there at full-ahead!"

The bosun dropped away, and Deryn began to search the parts drawers. All she needed was some pliers and a short length of wire.

"I'm going with you," Alek said.

She started to say no. The bosun hadn't given orders one way or the other, and she could handle the job herself. But if Mr. Rigby's message arrived too late and the ship went to top speed again, anyone alone out there could be swept away into the sea.

Besides, who knew what Alek would get up to if she left him here alone?

"I'm not afraid," he added.

"You should be," Deryn said. "But you're right, it's better if we stick together. Hand me that rope."

⊙ TWENTY ⊙

"Ready?" Deryn asked.

"I suppose so." Alek looked down at the rope tied to his flight suit's harness. He wondered what Count Volger would say about him being bound to a common girl. Probably something unpleasant.

But it was certainly better than letting a friend go out there on her own.

Deryn opened the hatchway, and a rush of cold air sent a fresh chill through Alek's sodden flight suit. As he followed her out into the rain, the five meters of rope between them grew heavy with water.

"If the engines start up, drop flat and hold on to the ratlines," Deryn said.

Alek didn't argue. The few moments of downpour at full-ahead had been convincing enough.

He followed Deryn toward the bow, keeping to the

middle of the spine, his hands out for balance. Down below, the ocean's surface was in furious motion, the wind tearing whitecaps off the waves like they were plumes of steam.

"'Pacific' means 'peaceful,'" he said. "So far, this ocean isn't living up to its name."

"Aye, and believe me, it's much worse down there than it looks. We've matched the speed of the wind, so all we're feeling is the odd gust."

Alek nodded. The sky was dark, the rain still falling, and he could smell a deadly hint of lightning. But the air was eerily calm. It was like being in the placid eye of a storm, with its energies boiling all around them, waiting to be unleashed.

"Then, why's that loose wire blowing about?

Deryn's hand described an arc in the air. "The hump always has an untidy bit of airflow behind it when the ship's free-ballooning, ever since the earliest airbeasts were fabricated. The boffins have never been able to fix it."

"You mean Darwinism has its flaws?"

"So has nature. Ever seen a red-footed booby try to land?"

Alek frowned. "I'm afraid I have no knowledge of red-footed boobies."

"Well, I've never actually *seen* one myself. But everybody says they're barking hilarious!"

They were drawing near the airbeast's hump, and Alek felt the air growing restive around them. The loose section of antenna looked like a glint of silver dancing on the ratlines.

"Step carefully here," Deryn called.

With every meter the troubled airflow grew worse, driving the rain into a blur against Alek's goggles. But he didn't dare take them off. The loose wire was flailing like the tentacle of some dying creature, and he didn't fancy leaving his eyes unprotected.

Deryn came to a halt. "Do you hear that?"

Alek listened. Above the chattering of rain he heard a distant thrum.

"The rear motivator engines?"

"Aye, on low speed." She shook her head. "Just a bit of steering, let's hope. Come on!"

She jogged toward the flailing wire, dragging Alek by his harness. The wind shifted every few seconds now, sending the falling rain into a dozen little whirlwinds. The wire skittered away as Deryn made a jump for it, but Alek managed to plant a boot down to bring its thrashing to a halt.

Deryn reached into her tool bag. "I'm going to splice another ten yards on to the antenna. That should be loose enough to keep it from snapping again. Go find the other end of the break."

"I can't *go* anywhere, Deryn. We're tied together, remember?"

She looked down at the rope. "Ah, right. Best to keep it that way, though."

Alek didn't argue. If Mr. Rigby hadn't got word to the officers, the engines could come back on at any time. Deryn worked swiftly with the pliers, her hands as sure as they were with knots and cable. Alek noticed how rough they were. Of course, any sailor's hands were calloused and scarred, but now that he knew she was a girl . . .

He shook the thought out of his head. At times like this it was best just to think of her as a boy. Anything else was too confusing.

"Done," she said. "Let's go find the other loose end."

As Alek rose to his feet, a chill went through his wet flight suit.

"Has the wind gotten stronger?"

Deryn cocked her head to listen. "Aye, the rear engines are running a bit faster."

"And we're losing altitude." Below, the towering waves were clearly visible now, their whitecaps glowing against the dark water.

"Blisters, we might be in trouble." Deryn knelt again, putting one finger into the water building on the airship's surface. "Almost half an inch already!"

"Of course. It's *raining*."

Her eyes closed. "Just let me remember my sums. Every inch of water spread across the membrane adds . . . eight tons to the ship's weight."

Alek opened his mouth, but it took a moment to speak. "Eight *tons?*"

"Aye. Barking heavy stuff, water." She started down the spine toward the tail, letting out the added length of wire behind her. "Come on. Let's find the other end and get this job done!"

Alek dumbly followed, his gaze traveling down the endless length of the ship. The *Leviathan*'s topside was huge, of course, so of course a thin layer of water would add up to thousands of liters. And though water was running down the sloped sides and off the ship, the rain was constantly adding more to replace it.

"They'll have dropped all the ballast by now," Deryn said. "But I reckon the weight's still building. That's why we're losing altitude."

Alek's eyes went wide. "You mean this ship can't fly in the rain *without crashing?*"

"Don't be daft. We can still use aerodynamic lift, but that's what I'm worried about. There it is!"

She knelt and picked up a loose end of wire tangled in the ratlines, the other end of the break. Her fingers worked quickly, splicing it together with the added length.

Alek stood close, sheltering her from the rain. "Aerodynamic lift? Like when we took off in the Alps and had to fly for a bit to get off the ground?"

"Right. The *Leviathan* is like a big wing. The faster we go, the more lift we generate. Done!" She stretched the wire between her hands once, snapping it hard—the new splice held.

"So when it rains, your ship has to keep moving to stay aloft." Alek looked down at the ocean. The waves were building in strength, the tallest of them almost reaching the bottom of the ship. "Aren't we getting a bit close to the water?"

"Aye," Deryn said. "The captain's been waiting as long as he can. But I doubt we have much . . ."

Her words faded as the Clanker engines roared to life. Deryn swore, then stood there for a moment listening.

"What do you reckon, Alek? Quarter speed?"

He knelt to press his palm against the membrane. "I'd say half."

"Blisters. We'll never make it back to the wheelhouse before the wind gets too strong to walk." She looked around. "Might as well stay here, where the ship's wider. It'll be harder to fall off."

Alek glanced down at the roiling black sea. "Very sensible."

"But we need to get out of the flooding channel."

"The *what*?"

"You'll see." Deryn started jogging toward the stern.

Alek hurried to catch up. The ship's speed was building fast, the wind at his back pushing him harder and harder. The rain felt like cold needles now, and the view through his goggles was a blur.

He slowed down to wipe them, forgetting the rope stretched between him and Deryn. It yanked tight, and Alek's boots skidded on the wet surface of the spine. He landed badly, the air driven from his lungs, his head cracking hard. With the blow echoing in his ears, Alek realized that he was still moving, sliding along in the flow of rainwater. He clawed at the ratlines, but his cold fingers wouldn't close. For an awful moment the slope of the airbeast's flank dropped away from beneath him.

Then the rope around his waist went taut again, snapping Alek to a halt. He lay there, uncertain of up and down, his heart pounding.

A voice was in his ear. "This is no use! Clip yourself!"

Alek nodded, feeling blindly for his safety clip. He snapped it onto the grid of ropes beneath him, then sat up, his head spinning. Every second the engines roared louder, and as their power built, so did the driving power of the rain. His goggles were blurred, and his head still reeled from the impact of his fall.

"Sorry I fell." Talking hurt his head.

"No worries. We're far enough aft. Just wanted to stay out of *that*."

Alek pulled his goggles off, following Dylan's gaze. Pushed along by the airship's passage, a channel of water was spilling down the backside of the hump, like a waterfall forming after a downpour.

"The flooding channel?"

Dylan laughed madly. "Aye, I've never seen it like that. And this is only three-quarter speed!"

Alek squeezed his eyes shut, suddenly uncertain how he'd gotten out here in this storm. It felt as if he'd just woken up to find himself magically transported from his bed out onto the topside.

"Blisters, Alek, you're bleeding!"

"I'm what?" He blinked. Dylan was staring at his forehead. Alek reached up to touch the painful spot, then looked at his fingers. They were stained by a thin, watery hint of blood.

"It's nothing."

"Are you dizzy?"

"Why would I be dizzy?" Alek reached up to pull his goggles off, but found them already in his hand. His vision stayed blurry, though, as if a layer of glass hovered between him and the world.

"Because you just cracked your head, you dafty!"

"I did what?" It was hard to think with the engines roaring like this.

"Barking spiders, Alek." Dylan grasped both his hands, staring straight into his eyes. "Are you all right?"

"I'm cold." All the heat in his body was trickling out into the storm, the strength in his limbs carried away by the cold water rushing past. Alek wanted to stand up, but the wind was too strong.

A vast *boom* rang out, the whole ship shuddering beneath them.

"Blisters!" Dylan swore. "A wave just smacked our underside! The officers left the engines too late."

Alek stared at Dylan, the shock wave echoing in his head. He wanted to ask a question about the engines and the storm, but all at once the blurry layer across his vision seemed to clear away.

"You're a *girl*, aren't you?"

"What in blazes?" Deryn's eyes grew wide. "Did your brain get cracked that bad? You've known that for a barking week!"

"Yes, but I can...*see* it now!" Even after he'd known the truth, the lie had remained stuck in his mind, like a mask over Deryn's face. But suddenly the mask had shaken free.

He touched his forehead. "Did you always look like this?"

Deryn's answer was drowned out by the engines. Alek knew the sound from his long hours in the pods, the distinctive roar of full speed ahead. The wind drove even harder, the rain suddenly like hailstones. He pulled his goggles on again.

"You fell and cracked your head!" Deryn shouted. "The ship's heavy with rain, remember? So they're throwing every engine to full speed." She turned into the gale, her arm thrown across her face, and stared up at the hump rising over them. "And that's not all!"

Alek squinted into the wind and saw it—a white sheet rippling toward them down the slope of the spine.

"What on earth is *that*?"

"The water from the bowhead—all being blown back at once!" She wrapped her arms around him. "Take hold of the ratlines before it hits, in case your safety line snaps!"

As Alek dug his fingers into the ropes beneath them, another *boom* shook the airship. A vast ripple passed through the membrane, bucking Deryn and Alek half a meter into the air, but her arms held tight around him. Her body was a shadow of warmth in the freezing wind.

"We're still too low!" she cried. "A tall enough wave could hit the—"

The surge of rainwater struck at that moment, hardly knee height but moving fast. It swept across them where they lay, filling Alek's nose and mouth. He clutched the ratlines with all his strength, and felt Deryn's arms around him tighten. His safety line pulled taut as the torrent tried to carry them both down the sloping flank of the airbeast.

After a few long seconds the flood passed by, the water spilling away in both directions from the spine. Deryn let him go, and Alek sat up sputtering and coughing.

"We're gaining altitude," she said, looking down the flank. "Our speed has pushed a bit of water off."

Alek huddled in his soaking flight suit, wondering if the world had gone mad. The wind was roaring with the fury

"SPINE SPOUT."

of a hundred engines, a rain like cold gravel was tumbling from the sky, freezing rivers were pouring down the *Leviathan*'s length . . .

And his friend Dylan was a girl.

"What's *wrong* with everything?" he said, curling up against the cold and shutting his eyes. The world had broken the night his parents had died, and it just seemed to keep breaking.

Deryn shook him. "You've got a head wound, Alek. Don't fall asleep!"

He opened one eye. "It's a bit cold for a nap."

"Aye, but don't pass out!" She leaned closer, their heads almost touching. "Keep talking to me."

Alek lay there shuddering, trying to think of what to say. The rumble of the engines seemed to be inside his head, tangling his thoughts.

"I forgot you were a girl, just for a moment."

"Aye. That fall scrambled your attic, didn't it?"

He nodded, her strange way with words setting off an old memory. " 'My attic's been scrambled.' You said that the first time we met. After you crashed in the Alps."

"Aye, I was a bit loopy that night. But you sounded mad yourself, pretending to be a Swiss smuggler."

"I didn't know what I was pretending to be. That was the problem."

She smiled. "You're a hopeless liar, your princeliness. I'll give you that."

"Lack of practice." Alek shivered, and they huddled closer, her face only centimeters from his. The hood of her flight suit was pulled up, her wet hair pasted to her forehead, baring the angles of her face.

She frowned. "Are you going daft again?"

Alek shook his head, but his eyelids were heavy. He felt his body stop shivering, giving up its struggle against the cold. His thoughts began to fade into the roar of the world around him.

"Stay awake!" Deryn cried. "Talk to me!"

He searched for words, but the rain seemed to strip away his thoughts before they could form. Staring at Deryn, Alek felt his mind switch back and forth, seeing her as a girl, then as a boy.

And he realized what he had to say.

"Promise you won't ever lie to me again."

She rolled her eyes.

"I mean it!" he shouted above the wind. "You have to swear it, or we can't be friends."

Deryn stared hard at him another moment, then nodded. "Aleksandar of Hohenberg, I promise never to lie to you again."

"And you won't keep any secrets from me either?"

"Are you *sure* you want that?"

"Yes!"

"All right. I won't hide anything from you again, for as long as I live."

Alek smiled, and let his eyes finally drift closed. That was all he'd wanted, really, for his allies to trust him with the truth. Was it so much to ask?

Then a warmth pressed against his mouth, lips touching his. Soft at first, then harder, trembling with an intensity that lofted above the storm. A quiver went through him, like the shudder of a dream-fall pulling him from the edge of sleep. He opened his eyes and was staring into Deryn's face.

She pulled away a little. "Wake up, you daft prince."

He blinked. "Did you just . . ."

"Aye. I did. No secrets, remember?"

"I see," Alek said, and another shiver went through him, not from the cold. His head was clear now, and the rain chattered in the silence between them. "You know I can't . . ."

"You're a prince, and I'm a commoner." She shrugged. "But this is what no secrets means."

He nodded slowly, wondering at the warmth of her secret still on his lips.

"Well, I'm certainly awake now."

"So it works on sleeping princes, too?" Deryn asked, then her smile faded. "I need a promise from you also, Alek."

He nodded. "Of course. I won't keep secrets from you, I swear."

"I know, but it's not that." Deryn turned away, staring off into the blackness, her arms still around him. "Promise that you'll lie for me."

"Lie for you?"

"Now that you know what I am, there's no way to escape it."

Alek hesitated, thinking how strange it was to make an oath to lie. But the oath was to Deryn, and the lies would be to . . . anyone else.

"All right. I swear to lie for you, Deryn Sharp, whatever it takes to protect your secret." Saying it aloud made Alek's breath quicken, and the feeling bubbled up into a laugh. "But I can't promise I'll be any good at it."

"You'll probably be rubbish. But that's the mess we're in."

He nodded, though he wasn't sure at the moment exactly what *kind* of mess it was. She had kissed him, after all. He found himself wondering if she was going to kiss him again.

But Deryn was staring off into the storm. Her expression grew serious.

Alek could see nothing but darkness and rain. "What is it?"

"Rescue, your princeliness. Namely, the four biggest

riggers in the crew, crawling straight into a sixty-mile-an-hour headwind on their hands and knees. Risking their barking lives to make sure you're all right." She turned back with a scowl. "Must be nice to be a prince."

"Sometimes, yes," he said, finally letting his eyes close. Another shudder passed through him, shaking every muscle.

Deryn held him tighter, lending him a sliver of her heat until the strong hands of the riggers picked him up and carried him somewhere warm and quiet.

· TWENTY-ONE ·

"That will, I trust, be the last of your heroics." Count
Volger said this too softly to make Alek's head hurt, but
the words were brittle and precise.

"There weren't any heroics. I was only there as a
translator."

"And yet here you are with bandages round your
head. Rather tricky translations, I should think."

"Rather tricky," said Bovril with a chuckle.

Alek took a drink of water from the glass beside
his bed. He was fuzzy on much of what had happened
last night. He remembered the airship free-ballooning
through the strange calm of the storm, and then the
engines roaring to life, lashing the rain into a tempest.
Things had gotten complicated after that. He'd fallen
and hit his head, then almost drowned in a surge of rainwater.

And Deryn Sharp had kissed him.

"There were important repairs to be done," he said. "A loose antenna."

"Ah, yes. What could be more vital than Tesla's giant flying radio?"

"Is it working?" Alek asked, wanting to change the subject. Thinking about last night made his head spin, though it pleased him to have a secret from Count Volger.

"Apparently. Tesla sits in his laboratory, tapping out messages." The wildcount drummed his fingers. "Instructions to his assistants in New York, to prepare Goliath for our arrival."

Bovril began to rap out Morse code on the frame of the bed.

Alek shushed the beast. "Maybe we've done some good, then, getting him home so quickly. If he stops the war . . ."

Hundreds were dying every day. Rescuing Tesla from the wilderness and getting him to America quickly might save thousands of lives. What if something so simple had been Alek's destiny all along?

"'If' is a word that can never be said too loudly." Volger stood up, looking out at the still cloudy sky. "For example, *if* you had died last night, the last decade of my life would've been altogether wasted."

"Have a little faith in me, Volger."

"I have great faith, tempered with vast annoyance."

Alek smiled weakly, falling back into his pillows. The ship's engines were still at full-ahead, the stateroom rumbling around him. The world was unsteady.

It wasn't *fair* of Deryn, kissing him. She knew the story of how his father had married a woman of lesser station, and all the disasters that had resulted. It had torn Alek's family apart, and in turn had upset the balance of Europe. His father's one selfish act of true love had cost more than anyone could count.

The pope's letter might make Alek the heir to his granduncle's throne, but it didn't alter the fact that he'd been rejected by his own family. The slightest mark against him would cast his legitimacy into doubt. Alek couldn't allow himself to think about a commoner that way. He had a war to stop.

He made a fist and wiped his lips with the back of his hand.

"Great faith," Bovril repeated. "Vast annoyance."

Giving the beast a withering look, Volger said, "The captain asked me to mention that he'll be coming to see you."

"He must be annoyed as well. He had to risk four men just to rescue me." Alek closed his eyes and began to rub his temples. "I hope he doesn't shout."

"I shouldn't worry." Volger began to pace, his footsteps echoing in Alek's head. "Unlike mine, his annoyance will be well hidden."

"What do you mean?"

"The Darwinists see you as a link to Tesla. You're both Clankers, and both of you have switched sides in this war."

"Tesla doesn't think much of my political connections."

"Not to the Austrian government, no. But he sees you as a way to broadcast the news of his weapon." The man mercifully stopped pacing. "You were famous already, thanks to those ridiculous articles. And soon you will arrive in America on the world's greatest airship."

Alek sat up again and stared at Volger, trying to figure out if the man was serious.

"He's always been a showman. Dr. Barlow told me about his spectacle in Tokyo." Volger gave a shrug. "It makes sense, I suppose. The best way to keep Goliath from being used is to tell everyone what it can do, and that means creating a sensation. So why not promote his weapon to end the war with you, the boy whose family tragedy started it?"

Alek rubbed his temples again. The pounding was getting worse with every word. First Deryn, now this. "It all sounds quite undignified."

"You wanted a destiny."

"Are you saying I should let him put me on display?"

"I'm suggesting, Your Serene Highness, that you get as much sleep as possible over the next few days." Volger smiled. "Your headaches have only begun."

The ship's officers came a few hours later, just when Alek had managed to fall back asleep.

A marine sergeant shook him awake, then snapped to attention with a painful *smack* of his boot heels against the floor. Dr. Busk took Alek's pulse, staring at his watch and nodding sagely.

"You appear to be recovering nicely, Prince."

"Someone should tell my head that." Alek nodded at the assembled visitors. "Captain, First Officer, Dr. Barlow."

"Good afternoon, Prince Aleksandar," the captain said, and the four of them bowed together.

Alek frowned. This all seemed oddly formal, given that he was lying here in his nightshirt. He wished they would go away and let him sleep.

Dr. Barlow's loris dropped from her shoulder to the floor and crawled under the bed, where Bovril joined it. The two beasts began to mutter snatches of conversation to each other.

"What can I do for you?" Alek asked.

"You've already done it, in a manner of speaking." The captain was beaming, his voice altogether too loud. "Middy Sharp told us how bravely you assisted him last night."

"Assisted him? Dylan made the repairs. I only fell and hit my head, from what I can recall."

The officers all laughed at this, loudly enough to make Alek wince, but Dr. Barlow's expression remained serious.

"Without you, Alek, Mr. Sharp would have been untethered on the spine." She looked out the window. "In gale conditions nothing is more dangerous than working topside alone."

"Yes, I make excellent deadweight."

"Most amusing, Your Majesty," said Captain Hobbes. "But this modesty is falling on deaf ears, I'm afraid."

"I only did what any member of the crew would have done."

"Exactly." The captain nodded vigorously. "But you are *not* a member of this crew, and yet you performed heroically. A copy of Mr. Sharp's report has already been dispatched to the Admiralty."

"The Admiralty?" Alek sat up straighter. "That seems a bit . . . excessive."

"Not at all. Reports of heroism are sent to London as a

matter of course." He clicked his heels together and made a small bow. "But whatever they decide, you have my personal thanks."

The officers made their good-byes then, but the lady boffin remained behind, snapping her fingers for her loris. The beast seemed reluctant to come out from beneath the bed, where Bovril was babbling the names of German radio parts.

"Excuse me, Dr. Barlow," Alek asked. "But what was that all about?"

"You really don't know? How charming." She gave up on her loris and sat down on the end of the bed. "I think the captain means to give you a medal."

Alek felt his jaw drop open. A week ago it would have overjoyed him to be made one of the crew, much less decorated as an airman. But Volger's warnings were still fresh in his aching head.

"To what purpose?" he asked. "And don't tell me it's in recognition of my heroism. What does the captain *want* from me?"

The lady boffin sighed. "So jaded for one so young."

"Jaded, heh," came a small voice from beneath the bed.

"Don't be tiresome, Dr. Barlow. The captain already knows I'll help Mr. Tesla's cause. Why must he bribe me with medals?"

She looked out the window at the boiling clouds. "Perhaps he fears you'll change your mind."

"Why would I do that?"

"Because someone might convince you that Mr. Tesla is a fraud."

"Ah." Alek remembered Deryn's words in Tokyo. "And might that someone be you?"

"We shall see." Dr. Barlow reached down and snapped her fingers again, and finally her beast emerged. She lifted it onto her shoulder. "I am a scientist, Alek. I do not deal in surmise. But when I have proof, I'll let you know."

"It was awful, being at war with you," said the loris on her shoulder.

Alek stared at it, recalling when he'd said the words to Deryn in Japan. Had Bovril recounted that entire conversation to the other loris? The thought of all their secrets being traded between the creatures was most unsettling.

Dr. Barlow shook her head. "Pay no attention. These two beasts were clearly damaged in their eggs. Years wasted, all thanks to one bumpy landing in the Alps." She reached out to straighten Alek's bandages. "And speaking of bumps, do get some sleep, or you shall wind up as simpleminded as they."

After she left, Bovril emerged from beneath the bed. It crawled up onto Alek's stomach, chuckling to itself.

"What's got you amused?" he asked.

The creature turned to Alek, suddenly wearing a serious look.

"Fell from the sky," it said.

TWENTY-TWO

It took five days for the sky to clear again.

The storm had pushed the *Leviathan* across the Pacific swiftly, carrying the airship well to the south. The coast of California stretched across the windows of the middies' mess. A few white cliffs caught the sun, and behind them were rolling hills, grassy and patched with brown.

"America," Bovril said softly from Alek's shoulder.

"Aye, that's right." Deryn reached up to stroke the beastie's fur, wondering if it was only repeating the word, or if it had a real sense that this was a new place with its own name.

Alek lowered his field glasses. "Looks rather wild, doesn't it?"

"Here, maybe. But we're halfway between San Francisco and Los Angeles. Put together, those two cities have got almost a million people!"

"Most impressive. Then, why is it so empty between them?"

Deryn gestured at the maps on the mess table. "Because America's barking huge. One country, as big as all of Europe!"

Bovril leaned forward on Alek's shoulder, pressing its nose against the glass. "Big."

"And growing stronger," Alek said. "If they enter the war, they'll tip the balance."

"Aye, but which way?"

Alek turned, revealing the fresh scar on his forehead. His color had returned since the accident, and he no longer complained of headaches. But sometimes he got that daft look in his eye again, as if he didn't quite believe the world around him was real.

At least he hadn't forgotten again that Deryn was a girl. Kissing him had made certain of that.

She still wasn't quite sure why she'd done it. Maybe the energies of the storm had brought on an unsoldierly madness in her. Or maybe that's what oaths were all about, keeping your word even when it made everything go pear-shaped. No more secrets between them, no matter what. . . . That had a scary ring to it.

Neither of them had spoken of that moment again, of course. There was no future in kissing Alek. He was a prince and she was a commoner, and she'd made her peace with that back in Istanbul. The pope didn't write letters turning Scottish girls dressed as boys into royalty. Not in a million years.

But at least she'd done it once.

"They'd never take up arms against Britain," Alek was saying. "Even if they are half Clanker."

Deryn shook her head. "But Americans aren't just a mix of Clanker and Darwinist; they're a mix of nations. Plenty of German immigrants fresh off the boat and still loyal to the kaiser. And plenty of spies among them, I'll bet."

"Mr. Tesla will end the war before any of that matters." Alek handed the field glasses to Deryn and pointed. "On those cliffs."

It took her a moment to spot the mooring tower, rising up from an odd cluster of buildings on the seaside hills. They were a mishmash of styles—medieval castles, ramshackle houses, modern Clanker towers, all half finished. Massive building machines moved among them, huffing steam into the clear sky, and cargo ships swarmed the long pier jutting into the sea below.

"Blisters, that's this fellow's *house?*"

"William Randolph Hearst is a very rich man," Alek said. "And a bit odd as well, according to Mr. Tesla."

"Which is saying something, coming from him."

"But he's the right man for the job. Hearst owns half a dozen newspapers, a newsreel company, and a few politicians as well." Alek said this firmly, then let out a sigh. "It was a lucky storm that blew us this far south, I suppose."

"News," Bovril said softly.

Deryn handed back the field glasses and put a hand on the boy's shoulder. Back in Istanbul, Alek had spilled his secrets to Eddie Malone to keep the reporter from sniffing out the revolution, about fleeing his home after his parents' murder and joining the *Leviathan*'s crew. Everything except the pope's letter that promised Alek the throne, his last secret. He had hated every minute of being in the limelight. And now Tesla wanted to exhibit Alek's story on a much larger stage.

"Doesn't seem fair, making you go through all that palaver again."

Alek shrugged. "It can't be any worse a second time, can it?"

They watched in silence as the sprawling mansion drew nearer. The *Leviathan* came about and turned its nose into the steady breeze coming off the sea, approaching the mooring tower from the landward side.

A lizard popped its head out of a message tube overhead.

"Mr. Sharp, report to the topside," it said in Mr. Rigby's voice.

"Right away, sir. End message." She looked at Alek. "I'll be down helping with the landing. Maybe I'll get to see your big entrance from the ground."

He gave her a smile. "I shall try to look dashing."

"Aye, I'm sure you will." Deryn turned to the window, pretending to make a quick survey of the landing field, the obstacles of machines and men, the wind's patterns in the ruffling grass. "They're just reporters, Alek. They can't hurt you."

"I'll try to remember that, Deryn," he said.

"Deryn Sharp," said Bovril with a chuckle as she headed toward the door. "Quite dashing."

She hit the airfield softly, her gliding wings stiff with ocean air. A dozen ground men waited to steady her, and a young man in civilian clothes presented himself.

"Philip Francis, at your service."

"Midshipman Sharp, of His Majesty's Airship *Leviathan*," Deryn said, giving him a salute. "How many ground men do you have?"

"Two hundred or so. Is that enough?"

She raised an eyebrow. "Aye, that's loads. But are any of them trained?"

"All trained, and they've got lots of practice. Mr.

Hearst has his own airship, you know. It's in Chicago at the moment, undergoing repairs."

"He has his own barking *airship*?"

"He dislikes train travel," the man said simply.

"Aye, of course," Deryn managed, turning to take stock of the airfield. The swarm of ground men was already in position, arranged in a perfect oval beneath the *Leviathan*'s gondola. They looked sharp enough in their red uniforms, and most wore sandbags on their belts for extra weight, no doubt to guard against the gusty ocean breeze.

She heard the growl of Clanker engines, and turned to find a trio of strange machines lumbering forward— six-legged walkers. Their pilots rode out in the open, and metal arms rose up from their backsides, carrying some sort of contraption.

"What in blazes are those?" she asked Mr. Francis.

"Moving-picture cameras, on the latest walking platforms. Mr. Hearst wants the *Leviathan*'s arrival captured for his newsreels."

Deryn frowned. She'd heard about the Clanker obsession with moving pictures but had never seen one herself. The cameras whirred and shuddered, a bit like the sewing machines back in Tokyo. Each one had three lenses like insect eyes, all staring up at the airship overhead.

"That's the door on the starboard side, correct?" Mr. Francis asked. "We'll want to shoot them coming out."

"You want to *shoot* them?"

"Photograph them." He smiled. "Figure of speech."

"Of course. Aye, the gangway drops from starboard," she said, feeling like a traitor to Alek for helping. This Mr. Francis wasn't an airman at all, calling the gangway hatch a *door*. He was some sort of moving-picture reporter!

Behind the walkers waited more men in civilian clothes, recording frogs on their shoulders, cameras in their hands. They surged forward as the airship dropped its lines to the waiting ground men.

"You might want to pull those reporters back," Deryn said. "In case there's a gust."

"Mr. Hearst's crew can handle it."

She scowled. The ground men looked sure enough in their duties, but how dare they call her down here just to help with barking camera angles!

The ground men took hold of the lines and began to spread out, pulling the *Leviathan* downward. When the gondola was a few yards above the airfield, the gangplank lowered itself to the ground, revealing Captain Hobbes, Mr. Tesla, and Prince Aleksandar. The captain saluted smartly, and the inventor waved his walking stick, but Alek looked unsteady. His eyes flicked between the cameras and the crowd for a moment, until he managed a halfhearted bow.

The walking platforms plodded closer, their cameras rising up, and suddenly they looked predatory, reminding Deryn of the scorpion walker that had captured her men at Gallipoli. The cameras even looked a bit like Clanker machine guns.

A plump man with a broad hat and pin-striped pants detached himself from the scrum of reporters, making his way up the gangplank. He reached out and pumped the captain's hand.

"Is that Mr. Hearst?" Deryn asked.

"The man himself," Mr. Francis said. "You're lucky to find him at home. With the war boiling over, he's been in New York since late summer, tending to his newspapers."

"Lucky us," Deryn said, watching Alek greet Mr. Hearst. In the cavalry tunic he'd borrowed from Volger, Alek did in fact look quite dashing. And with his host before him, his aristocratic reflexes seemed to take over. He bowed again, gracefully this time, and even smiled for the cameras looming overhead.

Deryn was glad to see him getting into the spirit of

"THE MOGUL."

things, but then she had a disturbing thought. What if he started to enjoy all this attention?

No, it would take more than a knock on the head to change Alek *that* much.

She tore her gaze from the spectacle and checked the landing field once more. To her relief a tangle was developing among the ropes.

"Looks as though your men might need some help after all," she said to Mr. Francis, and took off at a run.

The snarl of cables was near the bow of the ship, where the breeze was strongest. Overhead the topside crew had already cast a line across to the mooring tower, but they were waiting for the chaos below to settle before hitching the airship fast.

As Deryn approached, two groups of ground men were shouting at each other. Someone had pulled in the wrong direction, crossing the ropes, and now no one wanted to let go. She waded in, barking orders while making sure the men didn't all drop their lines at once. It was sorted out soon enough, and Deryn pulled out her semaphore flags to flash a quick R-E-A-D-Y to the topside crew.

"I'm afraid that was my fault," came a voice from behind her.

She turned to find a man in an ill-fitting uniform, a bit older than the other crewmen. Behind his mustache his face was somehow familiar.

"Are you . . . ," she began, but then a croak came from one of the sandbags on his belt.

"Shush, Rusty," he hissed. "Good to see you again,

Mr. Sharp. Do you suppose we might have a quick word in the privacy of your ship?"

She squinted at his face, and recognized him just as he stuck out his hand.

"Eddie Malone. Reporter for the *New York World*."

◦ TWENTY-THREE ◦

"What in blazes are *you* doing here?"

Malone considered the question. "Why am I in California? Or why am I in disguise, instead of snapping photos with the other reporters?"

"Aye, both!"

"Happy to explain everything," Malone said. "But first we need to get aboard your ship. Otherwise those fellows are about to give me a thrashing."

Deryn turned to follow Malone's gaze, and saw a trio of burly men in dark blue uniforms striding across the airfield.

"Who in blazes are *they*?"

"Pinkertons—security guards in the employ of Mr. Hearst. You see, my paper was owned by a fellow called Pulitzer, and he and Hearst weren't exactly pals. So let's not dawdle." The man started to drag her toward the *Leviathan*'s gondola.

"Surely they won't set upon you in broad daylight!"

"Whatever they do, it won't be pretty."

Deryn looked at the men again. They carried truncheons in their hands. Perhaps it was better to be safe than sorry.

The *Leviathan*'s gondola was still too high to jump aboard, and she and Malone would never make it past the Pinkertons to the gangplank on the other side. But where the navigator's bubble bulged downward beneath the bridge were two steel mooring rings, just out of reach.

"Get ready to grab one of those handholds," she ordered Malone, then turned to the ground men she'd just untangled, shouting, "Give me a good heave in one . . . two . . . *three!*"

The men pulled back in a mass, and the ship's nose dipped just enough. Eddie Malone and Deryn jumped to grab the mooring rings, then hauled themselves up as the ship bobbed back to level.

"This way," she said, scrambling toward the forward cargo bay windows. Malone followed, his shoes almost slipping from the metal rail around the bottom of the gondola.

The Pinkertons had arrived below them, and were peering up at Deryn and Malone with annoyed expressions.

"PINKERTONS' PURSUIT."

"Come down here!" one shouted, but Deryn ignored him. She rapped on a cargo bay porthole.

The ship shifted a squick beneath her—the ground crew was bringing it slowly down. In another minute she and Malone would be within reach of the Pinkertons' truncheons.

An airman's face appeared at the porthole, looking a bit perplexed.

"Open up. That's an order!" Deryn shouted, and the porthole popped open.

As she shoved Eddie Malone through, she wondered why she was helping him. Maybe he'd done them a favor back in Istanbul by not spilling the revolution's secrets, but only for a price.

In any case he was aboard now. It was the captain's decision whether to throw him back or not.

Deryn scrambled after him, not waiting to see if the Pinkertons would take out their frustration on her. She climbed down from the barrels of the ship's honey stacked by the window, then gave the confused airman who'd let them inside a salute. "Carry on, lad."

Malone was looking about the darkened cargo bay, his pencil already scribbling in his notepad.

"So this is what belowdecks looks like?"

"I'm afraid we haven't time for a tour, Mr. Malone. Why were those men after you?"

"As I said, I work for the *New York World*, and Hearst owns the *New York Journal*. Archrivals, you might say."

"And here in America rival newspapermen attack each other on sight?"

The man barked a laugh. "Not always. But Hearst didn't exactly send me an engraved invitation. I had to disguise myself just to snap a few pictures. Speaking of which . . ."

He pulled a camera from one of his sandbags, then reached into the other for his recording frog. As he placed the beastie on his shoulder, it made a burping noise, blinking at Deryn.

"I thought you were the Istanbul bureau chief," she said. "Again, what are you doing here? Istanbul is seven thousand miles away!"

The reporter waved his hand. "Prince Alek's the best scoop I ever had. I'm not about to let a couple of oceans get in my way. Once I found out the *Leviathan* was headed east, I sailed back to New York. Been there for two weeks now, waiting to see where you popped up again."

"But how did you get *here*?"

"After Mr. Tesla's shindig in Tokyo made the papers, I jumped on a train for Los Angeles. That's where the biggest airfield on the West Coast is. But last night I got a tip that you were coming here instead."

Deryn shook her head. Mr. Tesla had only convinced

the officers yesterday to resupply at Hearst's. "A tip? From whom?"

"From the great inventor himself. Radio waves aren't like carrier pigeons, Mr. Sharp. Anyone with an antenna can pick them up." The man shrugged. "You shouldn't be surprised that Tesla sent uncoded messages. Why let one newspaper have all the fun?"

Deryn swore, wondering who else was following the *Leviathan*'s movements. Clanker spies had radios too. She also wondered why she'd been so anxious to rescue Malone. Sticky-beaks like him would only cause trouble in the end.

"Well, however you got here, Mr. Malone, we'll have to ask the officers if you can stay aboard. Follow me."

She led the man to the central staircase, then up and forward toward the bridge. The ship's corridors were buzzing; the cargo bay was already open to take on fuel and supplies. It was only a matter of time before Malone's pursuers found their way aboard.

But the bridge was just as hectic as the rest of the ship, and Deryn found herself shunted from one officer to the next. The captain was busy being photographed for the newsreels, and no one else wanted to take responsibility for a wayward reporter. So when Deryn spotted the lady boffin and her loris taking tea in the officers' mess, she pulled Malone inside and shut the door behind them.

"Afternoon, ma'am. This is Mr. Malone. He's a reporter."

The lady boffin nodded. "How kind of Mr. Hearst, remembering that there are more than just Clanker scientists to interview aboard this ship!"

"Clankers!" said the loris with a snooty tone.

"Sorry, ma'am," Deryn said. "But it's not what you think. You see, Mr. Malone doesn't work for Mr. Hearst."

"I'm with the *New York World*," Malone said

"A trespasser, then?" Dr. Barlow's eyes traveled over his ground crew uniform. "And in disguise as well, I see. Do you realize, Mr. Sharp, that there are German spies here in America?"

"You're right about that, ma'am," Malone said with a smile. "Stacks of them!"

"Mr. Sharp, how exactly did this man get aboard?"

Deryn's voice felt small in her throat. "Um, I sort of let him in a porthole, ma'am."

Dr. Barlow raised an eyebrow at this, and her loris said, "Spies!"

"But he can't be a German agent!" Deryn cried. "I met him back in Istanbul. In fact, you did too! On the ambassador's elephant, remember?"

Malone stepped forward. "The boy's right, though we didn't chat much. And of course I wasn't wearing this."

He reached up and took one end of his mustache,

yanked it off in a single jerk, and threw it onto the table. The lady boffin's eyebrows shot up, and her loris crawled over to inspect the false mustache.

"Ah, you're *that* Malone," she said slowly. "The one who's been writing those dreadful articles about Prince Aleksandar."

"The very same. And as I was just explaining to young Sharp here, I don't intend to stop. If you Darwinists think you can do an exclusive deal with Hearst's operation, you've got another think coming!"

"There is no 'deal' between us and Hearst." Dr. Barlow waved a hand. "This detour was Mr. Tesla's idea."

"Hmph, Tesla," said the loris, affixing the mustache to its own face.

"I've been trying to talk to the captain, ma'am," Deryn said. "It might get a bit tricky for Mr. Malone. Hearst's men are after him."

"Well, of course they are." Dr. Barlow stroked her loris, which was now posing with the mustache. "This land is private property, which makes him a trespasser."

Deryn groaned, wondering why the lady boffin was being so bothersome. Had those articles about Alek upset her, too?

"Oh, so that's how you're going to play it?" Eddie Malone said; then he pulled out a chair and sat down across from her. "Let me tell you something, Doctor. You

don't want to get mixed up with this Hearst fellow. He has some mighty unsavory friends."

"I should think, sir, that having unsavory friends was the defining attribute of newspapermen."

"Hah! You got me there!" Malone slapped the table, making the loris jump. "But there's unsavory, and there's dangerous. A fellow called Philip Francis, for example."

"Mr. Francis?" Deryn said. "I just met him. He was in charge of the ground crew."

Malone shook his head. "What he's in charge of is the Hearst-Pathé newsreel company. At least, that's what most people think." He leaned closer, his voice dropping. "But what they don't know is that his real last name isn't Francis. It's Diefendorf!"

There was a moment of silence, and then the lady boffin's loris spoke up.

"Clankers!"

"He's a German agent?" Deryn asked.

Malone shrugged. "He was born in Germany, that's for sure, and he hides the fact!"

"Many immigrants to America change their names," Dr. Barlow said, her fingers drumming the table. "On the other hand, not all of them create propaganda films for a living."

"Exactly," Malone said. "You must know how Hearst uses his papers and moving pictures to rail against the British, and against Darwinism, too. And now, all of a sudden, he's being friendly with you?"

Deryn turned to Dr. Barlow. "We should tell the captain about this."

"I shall make the proper introductions." She waved a hand at her tea dishes. "You may clear these, Mr. Sharp, and you shall come with me, Mr. Malone. If the captain is done with his theatrics, perhaps he can spare us a moment. I might be able to explain the wisdom of not putting all our eggs in one basket."

"Madam, I think we understand each other," said the

reporter, rising to his feet. He clapped Deryn on the back. "By the way, Sharp, thanks for your help back there. Much appreciated."

"Happy to be of service," Deryn said. She began to stack the dishes, glad that they'd run into the lady boffin, after all. Everybody else aboard seemed overawed by the famous Tesla, and this Hearst fellow with his cameras and newspapers could only make things worse.

But then something quite unsettling happened.

As Malone pulled out Dr. Barlow's chair for her, the loris yanked off the mustache and dropped it into a teacup, fixing Deryn with its haughty stare. Without thinking, she stuck her tongue out at the beastie.

"Deryn Sharp," it said as it rode the lady boffin's shoulder out the door, quite pleased with itself indeed.

· TWENTY-FOUR ·

Mr. William Randolph Hearst certainly knew how to host a banquet.

His dining room looked like the great hall of a medieval castle, with tapestries on the walls and saints carved into the ceiling. The chandeliers were sixteenth-century Italian, but flickered with tiny electrikal flames, and the marble fireplace was large enough for Alek to walk into without stooping. It was all quite garish and a bit of a muddle, as if Hearst's decorators had gone plundering across Europe, heedless of cost and tradition.

The dinner itself, however, was impeccable. Lobster Vanderbildt, roasted partridges with *salade d'Alger*, *grouse chaud-froid*, and for dessert *succès de glace* in the style of the Grand Hotel. It was, in fact, the first proper meal Alek had eaten since stealing away from home. Bovril had sampled every course, and was now curled up asleep on the high back of Alek's chair, though the creature's ears still twitched now and then.

Though Alek had always hated formal dinners with his parents, this was altogether different. As a child he hadn't been allowed to utter a word once the conversation turned to politics, but now he was an indispensable part of the discussion. At a table that held thirty people, Alek had been seated at Mr. Hearst's right hand. Tesla sat to the host's left, with the captain beside him and the other officers of the *Leviathan* trailing off into the distance. Dr. Barlow sat unhappily at the far end of the table with the other ladies, one a newspaper reporter, the rest moving-picture actresses. Alek had been introduced to them before dinner with cameras looking on, the actresses smiling at the whirring machines like old friends. Deryn, of course, a common crewman, wasn't here at all.

As the meal wound down, Mr. Hearst was giving his views on the war. "Wilson, of course, will side with his British friends. He won't protest the Royal Navy blockading Germany. But he'll scream bloody murder if German submarines do the same to Britain!"

Alek nodded. President Wilson was from the South, he recalled, and a Darwinist by upbringing.

"But he claims to want peace," Count Volger said. He was seated across from the *Leviathan*'s first officer, close enough to join in. "Do you believe him?"

"Oh, certainly, Count. The only decent thing about the man is that he wants peace!" Hearst stabbed at his dessert with a spoon. "Imagine if that cowboy Roosevelt had been elected. Our boys would be over there already!"

Alek glanced at Captain Hobbes, who was smiling and nodding politely. The British would no doubt welcome the Americans fighting at their side, if they could arrange it somehow.

"This war will draw in the whole world sooner or later," Mr. Tesla said gravely. "That's why we must end it now."

"Exactly!" Hearst clapped him on the back, and the inventor grimaced, but his host didn't seem to notice. "My cameras and newspapers will be following you every step of the way. By the time you get to New York, both sides will have had fair warning that it's time to stop this madness!"

Alek noticed that Captain Hobbes's smile froze a little at this talk of "both sides." Of course, Mr. Tesla's weapon could be used against London just as easily as against Berlin or Vienna. Alek wondered if the British had plans for making sure that didn't happen.

"I have faith that the world will find my discovery hopeful," Mr. Tesla said simply. "And not a cause for fear."

"I am certain that we Darwinists will," Captain Hobbes said, and raised his glass. "To peace."

"To peace!" Volger said, and Alek quickly joined him.

The toast went round the table, and as the waiters stepped forward to pour the gentlemen more brandy, Bovril murmured the words in its sleep. But Alek wondered if any of the American guests were truly worried about a war thousands of miles away.

"So let's get down to brass tacks, Captain," Mr. Hearst said. "Where will you be stopping on the way to New York? I have papers in Denver and Wichita. Or will you just hit the big cities like Chicago?"

"Ah," the captain said, setting his glass carefully down on the table. "We won't be stopping at any of those places, I'm afraid. We aren't allowed."

"The *Leviathan* is a warship of a belligerent power," Alek explained. "It can stay in a neutral port for only twenty-four hours. We can't simply fly across your country, stopping wherever we take a fancy to."

"But what's the point of a publicity tour if you don't stop to make appearances!" Hearst cried.

"That is a question I'm not qualified to answer," Captain Hobbes said. "My orders are simply to get Mr. Tesla to New York."

Count Volger spoke up. "And how do you intend to do that without crossing America?"

"There are two possibilities," the captain said. "We had planned to go north—Canada is part of the British Empire, of course. But after the storm pushed us this way, we realized that Mexico might be easier."

Alek frowned. No one had mentioned this change of plan to him. "Isn't Mexico neutral as well?"

The captain turned his empty palms up. "Mexico is in the midst of a revolution. As such, they can hardly assert their neutrality."

"In other words, they can't stop you," Tesla said.

"Politics is the art of the possible," Count Volger said. "But it will be rather warmer, at least."

"A brilliant idea!" Mr. Hearst waved at a servant, who scurried over to light his cigar. "Flying across a war-torn country on a journey for peace is a cracking good story!"

Everyone stared at Mr. Hearst, and Alek hoped the man was joking. During the Ottoman revolt Alek and Deryn had lost their friend Zaven, one among thousands killed. And from what Alek understood, the Mexican Revolution was a rather bloodier affair.

When the uncomfortable silence stretched a bit, he cleared his throat. "You know, a granduncle of mine was once emperor of Mexico."

Hearst stared at him. "I thought your granduncle was the emperor of Austria."

"Yes, a different uncle," Alek said. "I'm speaking of Ferdinand Maximilian, Franz Joseph's younger brother. He lasted only three years in Mexico, I'm afraid. Then they shot him."

"Maybe you could fly over his grave," Hearst said, blowing on the tip of his cigar. "Toss some flowers down or something."

"Ah, yes, perhaps." Alek tried not to show his astonishment, wondering again if the man were joking.

"The emperor's body was returned to Austria," Count Volger said. "It was a more civilized time."

"There still might be a news angle somewhere." Hearst turned to the man sitting between Alek and Count Volger. "Make sure to get some shots of His Majesty on Mexican soil."

"I shall indeed, sir," said Mr. Francis, who had been introduced to Alek as the head of Hearst's newsreel company. Along with a young lady reporter and a few camera assistants, he would be coming along to New York on the *Leviathan*.

"We shall cooperate in any way possible," Captain Hobbes said, saluting Mr. Francis with his glass.

"Well, enough of politics," Mr. Hearst said. "It's time for this evening's entertainment!"

At this command the waiters swooped in and plucked the last dishes from the table. The electrikal flames in the chandeliers flickered out, and the tapestry on the wall behind Alek slid away, revealing an expanse of silvery white fabric.

"What's going on?" Alek whispered to Mr. Francis.

"We're about to see Mr. Hearst's latest obsession. Possibly one of the best moving pictures ever made."

"Well, it will certainly be the best I've ever seen," Alek murmured, turning his chair to face the screen. His father had forbidden all such entertainments in their home, and public theaters had of course been out of the question. Alek had to admit he was curious to see what all the fuss was about.

Two men in white coats wheeled a machine into place across the table, pointing it at the screen. It looked rather like the moving-picture cameras that had stalked Alek all day, but with only a single eye in front. As it whirred to life, a flickering beam of light burst from the eye, filling the screen with dark squiggles. Then words materialized. . . .

The Perils of Pauline, said the shuddering white letters, which lingered long enough that a child of five could have read them a dozen times. The logotype of Hearst-Pathé pictures followed, the projector carving its shape into the cigar smoke hanging over the dinner table, like a searchlight lancing through fog.

The actors appeared at last, hopping about madly. It

took Alek long minutes to recognize that the actress sitting beside Dr. Barlow was Pauline herself. In person she'd been quite pretty, but the glimmering screen somehow transformed her into a white-faced ghoul, her large eyes bruised with dark makeup.

The moving images reminded Alek of the shadow-puppet shows that he and Deryn had seen in Istanbul. But those crisp black shadows had been elegant and graceful, their outlines sharp. This moving picture was something of a blurry mess, full of muddy grays and uncertain boundaries, too much like the real world for Alek's taste.

The light show was intriguing the perspicacious lorises, though. Bovril was awake and watching, and the eyes of Dr. Barlow's beast glowed, unblinking in the darkness.

On-screen the characters kissed, played tennis in absurd striped jackets, and waved their hands at one another. The scenes were punctuated by words explaining the story, which was also something of a mess—blackmail, fatal diseases, and deceitful servants. All quite dreadful, but somehow Pauline herself caught Alek's fancy. She was a young heiress who would inherit a fortune once she married, but who wanted to see the world and have adventures before settling down.

She was a bit like Deryn, resourceful and fearless,

"DINNER WITH PAULINE."

though thanks to her wealth she didn't have to pretend to be a boy. By odd coincidence her first adventure was an ascent in a hydrogen balloon, and events unfolded just as Deryn had described her first day in the Air Service—a young woman set adrift all alone, with only her wits, some rope, and a few sacks of ballast to save herself.

Without a hint of panic, Pauline threw the balloon's anchor over the side and set to climbing down the rope, and Alek found himself picturing Deryn in her place. Suddenly the jittering imperfections of the film fell away, disappearing like the pages of a good book. The balloon sailed past a steep cliff, and the heroine leapt onto the rocky slant and began to scramble toward the top. By the time Pauline was hanging from the edge, her betrothed racing to save her in his walking machine, Alek's heart was pounding.

Then suddenly the moving picture ended, the screen going white, the film reels sputtering like windup toys set loose. The electrikal chandeliers sparked back to life overhead.

Alek turned to Mr. Hearst. "But surely that isn't the end! What happens next?"

"That's what we call a 'cliff-hanger,' for obvious reasons." Hearst laughed. "We leave Pauline in big trouble at the end of every installment—tied to some train tracks, say, or in a runaway walker. Makes the audience come back for more, and it means we never have to end the darn thing!"

"Cliff-hanger," Bovril said with a chortle.

"Most ingenious," Alek said, though in fact it seemed rather an underhanded scheme to him, making an audience wait for a conclusion that would never come.

"One of my better ideas!" Hearst said. "A whole new way to tell stories!"

"Only as old as *The Thousand and One Nights*," Volger muttered.

Alek smirked at this, but he had to admit that the moving picture had possessed a mesmerizing quality, like a tale written in firelight. Or perhaps it was only his mind still wavering—since he'd cracked his head, the boundaries between reality and fancy had been uncertain.

"Bet you two can't wait till you see yourselves up on the screen!" Hearst said, reaching out to take Alek and Mr. Tesla by their shoulders.

"Like a glimpse into the future," Tesla said with a smile. "One day we shall be able to transmit moving pictures wirelessly, just as we do sound."

"What an intriguing notion," Alek said, though the idea sounded dreadful.

"Don't worry, Your Majesty," Mr. Francis said quietly. "I'll make sure you look good. It's my job."

"Most reassuring." Alek remembered seeing his own photograph for the first time in the *New York World*. Unlike any decent painting, it had been unpleasantly true to life, even magnifying his too-large ears. He wondered how these moving pictures would rearrange his features, and if he would look as jittery and hurried on the screen as Pauline and her fellows.

The thought of the heroine made him turn to Mr. Francis again. "Do women in America really fly about in balloons?"

"Well, they must want to! *The Perils of Pauline* is so popular that our competitors are getting in on the act, making something called *The Hazards of Helen*. And we're already planning *The Exploits of Elaine*."

"How . . . alliterative," Alek said. "But outside of moving pictures, do women actually do these sorts of things?"

The man shrugged. "Sure, I suppose so. Ever heard of Bird Millman?"

"The high-wire walker? But she's a circus performer." Alek sighed. For that matter, Lilit had known how to use a body kite. But she was a revolutionary. "What I mean is, do *normal* women ever fly?"

Count Volger spoke up. "I think what Prince Aleksandar wants to ask is, do American women pretend to be men? It is currently a subject of intense study with him."

Alek gave the wildcount a hard look, but Mr. Francis only laughed.

"Well, I don't know about flying," he said, "but we've sure got a lot of women wearing trousers these days. And I just read that one in twenty walker pilots is female!" The man leaned closer. "You thinking of getting yourself an American bride, Your Majesty? One with some frontier spirit, maybe?"

"That was not in my plans, alas." Alek saw Volger's smug expression, and added, "Still, five percent is something, isn't it?"

"Do you want to meet Miss White again?" Francis asked with a wink. "She's quite a bit like her character. Does all her own stunts!"

Alek looked down the table at the actress who had played Pauline—she possessed the rather unlikely name of Pearl White, he recalled. She was deep in conversation with Dr. Barlow and her loris, and Alek wondered what the three were talking about.

"Could be newsworthy," Mr. Francis said. "A movie starlet and a prince!"

"Starlet," Bovril said, sliding down onto Alek's shoulder.

"Thank you, but no," Alek said. "Talking to her now might spoil the illusion."

"Very wise, Your Serene Highness," Volger said, nodding sagely. "It's best not to mix make-believe with reality. At the moment the world is too serious for that."

◎ TWENTY-FIVE ◎

The resupplied *Leviathan* took the air before noon the next day, hours ahead of the twenty-four-hour limit. Watching from his stateroom windows, Alek could see the strange truth behind Hearst's estate. The buildings weren't so much unfinished as flat and hollow, designed to be filmed from certain angles but never lived in.

They were false, in other words.

Alek kept to his cabin most of the day, avoiding the newsreel cameras roaming the ship's corridors. One of his grandaunts believed that photographs snatched pieces of the soul, and maybe she was right. At sixteen frames a second, a moving-picture camera would chip away like a machine gun. Perhaps it was only last night's brandy in his head, but Alek felt as empty as Mr. Hearst's false buildings.

The airship followed the coast of California southward

at three-quarter speed, angling against the cool ocean breezes that blew toward land. Los Angeles slipped past in the late afternoon, and a few hours later Alek felt the airship turn southeast. According to the map on his desk, the sprawling city below was Tijuana.

A sudden blaring of horns and drums cut through the engine noise, and Bovril scampered to the windowsill. Alek looked out—a huge stadium yawned below, packed with cheering spectators. Some sort of double-headed bull was kicking up dust in the arena's center, facing a matador almost too small to see in the fading light.

It occurred to Alek that however swift airship travel was, one missed a great deal of scenery from the lofty height of a thousand feet.

By the time he'd dressed for dinner, the desert below was wrapped in darkness. Bovril was still on the windowsill, gazing down. No doubt its large eyes could see by starlight.

"Meteoric," the beast said, and Alek frowned. It was the first word Bovril had said all day, and certainly not one that Alek had uttered.

But Alek was already late for dinner, so he placed the creature on his shoulder and headed out the door.

The lady boffin had commandeered the officers' mess for the evening, no doubt the first of many tiresome dinner parties. With so many civilians aboard, the *Leviathan*'s journey to New York was in danger of turning into a pleasure cruise. At least tonight's dinner was for only five, and not two dozen like Hearst's affair.

Deryn stood waiting at the mess door, dressed in her formal serving uniform. When Bovril reached out for her, she ruffled its fur and then opened the door with a deep bow. A smirk played on her face, and Alek felt briefly silly in his formal jacket, as if the two of them were children playing dress-up.

The other guests had already arrived—Count Volger, Mr. Tesla, and the lady reporter from Hearst's San Francisco paper. Dr. Barlow ushered the young woman forward. She was wearing a pale red dress with a frilled collar, and a pink ostrich plume curled up from her rose-colored felt hat.

"Your Serene Highness, may I present Miss Adela Rogers?"

Alek bowed. "I had the pleasure last night, but only briefly."

Miss Rogers extended her hand to be kissed, and Alek hesitated—she was hardly of his social standing. But Americans were famous for ignoring such notions, so Alek took her hand and kissed the air.

"You missed," she said with a baffled smile.

"Missed?" Alek asked.

"Her hand," said Dr. Barlow. "The custom in Europe, Miss Rogers, is that only married women are kissed directly on the flesh. You young things are thought to be too easily swayed by the touch of lips."

Alek heard Deryn snort, but managed to ignore her.

"Young? But I'm all of twenty," Miss Rogers said. "My hand has been kissed many times without injury!"

Dr. Barlow's loris laughed, and Alek coughed politely. "Of course."

"And I was *almost* married once," Miss Rogers said. "But an old suitor rushed in at the last moment and tore up the marriage license. I think he was still in love with me."

"Really?" Alek managed. "No doubt he was."

"Couldn't you have got another license?" the lady boffin asked.

"I suppose so. But the interruption gave me time to think. I have decided to put my writing first. One can *always* get a husband, after all."

Dr. Barlow laughed as she guided the young lady toward the table. Alek felt himself blushing and looked away, only to see a smirk on Deryn's face—and on Volger's as well. He wondered if all American women were this bold, as ready to embarrass men as they were to escape in balloons.

"Easily swayed," Bovril repeated; then it crawled beneath the table to join the lady boffin's loris. As Alek took his seat, he noticed a sixth table setting before an empty chair.

"We appear to be awaiting a mystery guest," Count Volger said, inspecting his wineglass for spots.

"Mr. Francis?" Alek asked Dr. Barlow.

"He was not invited. You shall soon see why." She nodded at Deryn, who opened the door. A man in a somewhat ill-fitting jacket entered. It took a moment, but then Alek gripped the table's edge, half rising from his chair.

"You!"

"Don't get up, Your Highness." Eddie Malone bowed. "Ladies and gentlemen, sorry I'm late."

Alek sank back into his chair.

"Mystery guest," the beast muttered.

"Mr. Malone, I believe you've met Count Volger and His Serene Highness." Dr. Barlow was all smiles. "Mr. Nikola Tesla and Miss Adela Rogers, this is Eddie Malone, reporter for the *New York World*."

"The *World*?" said Miss Rogers. "Oh, dear."

"Edward Malone," Tesla murmured. "Aren't you that reporter who interviewed Prince Aleksandar in Istanbul?"

"That was me, all right." Malone took his seat. "I've been tracking him ever since, you might say. And thanks to your flying radio, I've found him at last!"

The inventor smiled. "A most rewarding experiment."

The two men laughed, and Alek suddenly wished that he and Deryn had let the storm wreck the antenna. Its only purpose had been to generate more publicity.

Miss Rogers looked aghast. "Has anyone told the chief that one of Pulitzer's men is aboard?"

"Mr. Hearst didn't think to ask." The lady boffin gestured to Deryn, who stepped forward to pour the wine. "And you'll find that Mr. Malone has some interesting news."

Malone turned to Miss Rogers. "It has to do with your friend Philip Francis. We've been looking into him for some time now, and it turns out that's not his real name. He was born Philip Diefendorf, about as German a name as you could have!"

Alek frowned, recalling Mr. Francis from the night before. "He doesn't have a German accent."

"Maybe he also changed the way he talks."

Miss Rogers rolled her eyes. "Philip was born in New York."

"So he claims," Malone said.

"Hah! You boys at the *World* are always making out like the chief's a traitor. You just hate him because he sells more papers than you!"

"I didn't say Hearst knew anything about this," Malone said, raising his hands. "But the head of your newsreel operation is German, and he's taken pains to hide it."

"Don't most Americans come from somewhere else?" Count Volger asked.

Mr. Tesla nodded. "I am an immigrant myself."

"An excellent point," Dr. Barlow said. "But the captain is concerned. Last night we took aboard a large quantity of supplies in a great hurry, and not all of it has been searched yet."

"Searched for what?" Miss Rogers asked.

"Sabotage is the easiest way to destroy the *Leviathan*," Dr. Barlow said. "A small phosphorous bomb in the right place would bring us all to a fiery end."

The table went silent, and Alek felt his headache threatening to return.

"That's not likely, of course," Deryn spoke up. "We've

had the sniffers belowdecks all afternoon, and they'd have found any explosives. But something dangerous might've been smuggled aboard."

"Such as?" Count Volger asked.

Deryn shrugged. "A weapon of some kind?"

"Now, this is just preposterous," Miss Rogers said. "One man can't take on the whole crew, no matter what sort of weapon he has."

"With the right tool one man can do quite a bit," Mr. Tesla said, and let out a sigh. "I recently designed a device that would have been most useful in this situation. I had it built and shipped to me in Siberia, but, alas, it didn't arrive before your ship was kind enough to rescue me."

Alek glanced at Deryn, remembering the contraption still sitting in the officers' storeroom.

"That sounds like a fascinating machine," Dr. Barlow said with a smile. "Perhaps you could give us a demonstration, Mr. Tesla."

"A demonstration? But it never . . ." He narrowed his eyes at the lady boffin. "Ah, I see. I would be happy to."

"After dinner, of course. Mr. Sharp?"

Deryn bowed, then turned to open the door again. The ship's stewards were waiting outside.

As the dishes came clattering in, their metal covers steaming out the scents of steak and potatoes, Alek pondered what had just happened. The lady boffin never let anything slip without a good reason, but she'd revealed her suspicions about Philip Francis to Miss Rogers, a fellow Hearst reporter. And then she'd let Mr. Tesla know that his metal detecting machine had been aboard the *Leviathan* all along.

Had she decided that cooperation was better than secrecy?

"Dinner," Bovril said happily, crawling up into Alek's lap.

The door to the officers' storeroom creaked open, revealing Mr. Tesla's machine among crates of sake and Japanese silks. The party had moved belowdecks after dinner, and the six of them looked out of place in their finery. Miss Rogers was still sipping sherry, and Volger and Malone had brought down their brandy snifters.

"This was here?" Tesla asked. "And you kept it from me?"

"Sir, it was you who kept it from us," Dr. Barlow said. "Why on earth did you have it smuggled aboard?"

Tesla sputtered for a moment, then threw out his arms. "Smuggled? Why would I do that? It must have been a misunderstanding with the Russians."

"Perhaps you merely asked them to exercise discretion?" Dr. Barlow said helpfully.

"Well, of course. So many ideas have been stolen from me. And you know the Russians, very secretive people." The inventor stepped forward, inspecting the control panel. "But how did you manage to put it together without plans?"

"My men and I found your design quite intuitive," Alek said. "We're still Clankers, you know."

"Clankers!" Bovril said.

"Well remembered," Count Volger muttered, but Alek ignored him.

"Just as I visualized it." Tesla's hands caressed the woodwork. "Not a bad job, Your Highness."

Alek clicked his heels. "I shall pass on your compliments to Master Klopp."

"What exactly *is* this doohickey?" asked Miss Rogers.

Tesla turned to her. "A magnetometer of the highest sensitivity, using principles of atmospheric conduction."

"In other words, it detects metal," Deryn said.

Tesla waved a hand. "One of its more mundane uses."

"But at the moment, the most pertinent." Dr. Barlow stepped forward and twisted the main control knob; the machine started up with a hum. The two lorises began to imitate its sound.

"It appears to be fully charged," said Tesla, squinting at the dials.

The lady boffin smiled. "Almost fully."

"Almost," her loris repeated.

Alek glanced at Deryn, who was smirking again. Dr. Barlow, of course, was letting Tesla know that they'd used the machine already. And to what purpose, he could certainly guess.

Alek recalled his argument with Deryn in Tokyo, when he'd declared that the specimen in Tesla's cabin was nothing but an interesting rock. But if Tesla had created this machine for the sole purpose of finding metal, then the rock must have been the goal of the whole expedition. The mysterious hunk of iron might well be the key to Goliath.

And for some reason he'd wanted to keep it all a secret.

"Well," the inventor grumbled. "Let's see if it even works."

Tesla was a virtuoso with his machine's controls. He could set it to search for metal in amounts large or small, distant or near. Each of the three globes had slightly different properties, and each could be adjusted separately. As Alek watched, he realized that he'd employed the device in the most fumbling fashion, like a cat playing a piano.

Dr. Barlow summoned two crewmen to carry the machine, and soon the globes were dancing, guiding Tesla though the piles of supplies that had been loaded at Hearst's estate. The dinner party trailed behind, Mr. Malone's flashbulb occasionally sending the party's shadows flailing across the darkened cargo rooms.

The machine's flickers finally led them into the back

of a crowded storeroom, toward a stack of barrels buried beneath boxes of dates and apples.

Mr. Tesla squinted in the wormlight and tutted. "These barrels contain more than sugar, it seems."

"Oh, dear," Miss Rogers said.

Dr. Barlow gestured to Deryn, who ordered the crewmen to take the machine away. Alek helped her unstack the crates on top, and when the way was clear, she stepped forward with a crowbar in her hand. She split the wooden top of a barrel with one blow.

"Careful, Dylan," Alek said. "If this is sabotage, there might be a trap."

The others took a step backward, but Bovril sniffed and said, "Sugar."

Deryn knocked away the splintered wood, then slid the crowbar into the barrel—it stopped with a muffled *thunk.*

"Well, that's interesting." She pulled off her white gloves, rolled up a sleeve, and reached in. A moment later she tugged out something long and thin wrapped in oiled rags. Sugar streamed onto the floor as she pulled the object free.

Unwrapped, the metal cylinder gleamed in the wormlight. Alek looked at Count Volger, who nodded and said, "Yes, it looks a bit like the barrel of a Spandau. But it's a Colt-Browning, most likely the 1895."

"A machine gun?" Miss Rogers said. "Oh, dear."

Malone's camera flashed again, blinding Alek for a moment. By the time he'd blinked the spots away, Deryn had pulled out another prize. She unwrapped the rags to reveal a metal case the size of a dinner plate.

"An ammunition drum?" Alek asked.

Volger stepped forward. "Not one I'm familiar with."

"Wait. Don't open—," Miss Rogers began, but Deryn had already pulled the case into two halves. A black disk fell out and struck the floor with a *bang*, making them all jump. It rolled away into the darkness, unspooling a sliver of something shiny behind it.

Miss Rogers knelt to peer closer. "This is unexposed moving-picture film. Or it *was*, young man, before you opened it. Now it's ruined."

"Film?" Alek asked. "But why would anyone smuggle more of that aboard? There's already stacks of it in Mr. Francis's stateroom."

Count Volger nodded. "For that matter, why a machine gun? The Colt-Browning weighs fifteen kilograms. A bit large for a saboteur to use."

"And we won't find any bullets for it either," Deryn added. "Our beasties would've sniffed out the gunpowder."

"Rather a mystery," Dr. Barlow said, turning to Miss Rogers. "Though in a way I am relieved. Perhaps your Mr. Francis is merely an arms smuggler." She frowned. "And a supplier of . . . movie film."

Miss Rogers shrugged. "I have no idea what's going on, I promise. But I'll have a snoop around tomorrow, and see what I can find out."

"Just don't forget that this is my story," Malone said.

Miss Rogers frowned, but gave him a curt nod.

"We'll check the rest of these barrels, ma'am," Deryn said to the lady boffin. "Then I'll have the ship's carpenter seal them back up so no one's the wiser."

Alek nodded. If the ship wasn't in immediate danger, there was no need for a confrontation. The best way to uncover Mr. Francis's plans was to let him make the next move.

◦ TWENTY-SIX ◦

The next morning Deryn stayed close to Mr. Francis and his camera assistants.

She served them breakfast in the middies' mess, then took them on a tour of the ship—"scouting locations," they called it. The captain had given the newsmen free run of the upper decks, so as not to give away any suspicions, and the guards watching the barrels in the cargo room had been ordered to stay out of sight.

Deryn noticed that Adela Rogers, the young lady reporter, was also keeping an eye on Mr. Francis. She pretended to wander the ship on her own, but always stayed within earshot of Francis and his cameramen. And when Deryn left them in the middies' mess with lunch, she found Miss Rogers skulking outside.

Closing the mess door carefully behind her, Deryn

whispered, "Pardon me, miss, but we mustn't let Mr. Francis know we're on to him."

"Well, of course not." The woman adjusted her hat. Just as last night, she was immaculately tailored, this time in a matching pin-striped jacket and skirt, with a black fedora in fabricated beaver fur. "Do you think I was born yesterday?"

"No, but you're being a bit obvious, following him everywhere."

"*You're* the one trailing after him, not me."

Deryn pulled the reporter farther down the corridor. "It's my barking duty to escort him! But you're tagging along like some village lassie in love."

Miss Rogers laughed. "Really, young man, I doubt *you* would know the signs of that condition. In any case, it isn't Mr. Francis I've been following. It's you."

"Pardon me, miss?

"Because you're quite obviously the bell captain of this ship."

Deryn blinked. "What are you blethering about?"

The woman took a step back, looking Deryn up and down like a tailor sizing up a client. "I grew up in a hotel, you see. Daddy was hopeless at housekeeping, and my mother wanted nothing to do with us, so it was our only hope of a civilized life. I learned at a tender age that the most important person in a hotel isn't the owner, or the manager, or even the house detective. It's the *bell captain*. He's the one who knows where the bodies are buried. He got quite a nice tip for burying them, if you know what I mean."

"No, miss, I *don't* know what you mean," Deryn said. "I'm a midshipman, not a bellman."

"Oh, yes. I caught your act last night, all white gloves and merrily pouring the brandy. But underneath it you're in on everyone's *secrets*, aren't you? And everyone glances at you when they've got a pickle to deal with. Dr. Barlow, Prince Aleksandar, even that crusty old count—they all want to know what the bell captain thinks."

Deryn swallowed. This woman was either quite mad or dangerously canny. She'd proven quite deft at embarrassing Alek the night before, which had been amusing enough. But now she was being a bit too . . . perspicacious.

"I'm quite sure I don't know what you mean, Miss Rogers."

"The only thing my mother ever taught me is that the servants always have the keys."

"I'm *not* a servant. I'm a decorated officer!"

"So is the bell captain at any fine hotel! Note the employment of the word 'captain.' I wouldn't mistake you for a bell*boy*, not ever."

Deryn took a step back. What had she meant by that, exactly?

"Just because I'm a 'girl reporter,' don't think you can—" Miss Rogers's next words were cut off by the sound of an alert, single rings in quick succession.

Deryn frowned. "That's the 'enemy spotted' signal."

"What enemy? We're over neutral territory."

"Indeed, miss. You'll have to excuse me." Deryn turned away, grateful for any excuse to escape the reporter. As she headed toward the central stairs, the corridors filled with men rushing toward their battle stations.

"Mind if I come along?" asked Miss Rogers, who was, in fact, already coming along.

"No, miss! My post is on the spine, and passengers have to stay in the gondola. You should head back to your stateroom."

Not waiting for an answer, Deryn headed off through the bustling corridors. With the ship at high speed there would be no climbing the ratlines, so she made straight for the interior passages. For that matter, the wind topside would be too much for message lizards to be wandering about. Deryn snatched one up and shoved it into her jacket, in case she needed to get word to the bridge quickly. After all, there were German agents wandering about the ship, reporters everywhere, and now an enemy in the sky.

Neutral territory, indeed.

◉ ◉ ◉

The desert rolled past below, spotted with cacti and red-flanked gulches, and a few small farms cut into verdant rectangles. At three-quarter speed, the view swept past at almost fifty miles an hour, and only the master rigger, Mr. Roland, and a few of his men were topside. Deryn made her way toward them in a half crouch, ready to grab the ratlines if a gust sent her stumbling.

"Middy Sharp reporting, sir!"

Mr. Roland returned her salute, then pointed. "Spotted it twenty minutes ago. Some kind of manta airship. Local colors, Clanker engines."

A sleek, broad-winged form stood out against the western sky, the pontoon gasbags under its wings striped with red and green. Smoke trailed from it, though Mexico was a Darwinist power.

"Might that engine be German-made, sir?"

"Can't tell from this range," Mr. Roland said. "But they're matching our speed."

Deryn watched the Mexican airship's shadow rippling across the desert, and estimated a wingspan of no more than a hundred feet. "Too small to trouble us, though. Perhaps they're only curious, sir."

"Fair enough, as long as they don't get too close." Mr. Roland frowned, raising his field glasses. "Is that another one?"

A second winged shape had caught the sun, just behind

the first. Deryn shielded her eyes and swept the horizon, and soon spotted a third manta airship off to starboard.

She pointed at it. "More than just curiosity, sir."

"Perhaps," Mr. Roland said. "But even three to one, they don't stand a chance against us."

Deryn nodded. Stern chases were tricky in the air. Beasties or rockets launched from the trailing ships would be fighting a fifty-mile-an-hour headwind, while the *Leviathan* could drop an aerie of strafing hawks into their laps at any time.

A moment later the *Leviathan*'s engines roared up to full speed.

"It seems the captain has taken a dislike to them!" Mr. Roland shouted over the thunderous noise. Both of them knelt on the ratlines as the wind grew fiercer. The Mexican airships didn't seem to be losing much ground, though. Their smoke trails thickened, spreading across the horizon like storm clouds.

One of the riggers called from behind them, and Mr. Roland turned to face the headwind. "Who in blazes is that?"

Deryn turned and saw a figure making its way toward them along the spine. She held her hat on with one hand, and her skirts billowed around stockinged legs.

"Blisters! That lady reporter must have followed me! Sorry, sir. I'll tend to her."

"See that you do, Sharp."

Miss Rogers had the wind at her back, and looked sure-footed enough. But when Deryn made to stand up, the headwind sent her staggering backward. She swore and clipped her safety line to Mr. Tesla's antenna. It was easier than re-clipping herself every few feet.

She scuttled ahead in a crouch until she reached the reporter.

"What in blazes are you doing up here?"

"I'd like to interview you!" the woman yelled, then pulled out a notepad. The pages fluttered furiously, and her unsecured fedora lifted off and shot away. "Oh, dear."

"Now's not the barking time!" Deryn shouted. "As you can see, we've got a bit of trouble brewing!"

Miss Rogers peered into the distance. "Our 'enemy' ships would appear to be Mexican. Do you suppose they mean us harm?"

Deryn took the lady reporter by the arm, but pulling her back toward the hatchway proved impossible. The woman's skirts caught the headwind like a frigate at full sail. It was a wonder she was standing at all.

"You're not getting rid of me that easily, Mr. Sharp." Miss Rogers frowned. "Is there something moving in your jacket?"

"Aye, a message lizard."

"How odd. Now, please tell me about these airships."

Deryn glanced back at the *Leviathan*'s pursuers, then sighed. "If I answer a few questions for you, will you be sensible and go back down?"

"It's a deal. Let's say . . . three questions."

"All right, then! But *hurry!*"

"Who is following us?"

"Mexicans."

"Yes, but under which of the generals?" Miss Rogers asked. "You realize there's a revolution on, don't you?"

"I don't know which general, and yes, I do realize there's a revolution on. That was three questions. Now let's *go!*"

She tried to pull Miss Rogers toward the hatch, but the woman stood firm. "Don't be preposterous! That was only one question, which required two follow-ups due to your vagaries. My father was a lawyer, you know."

"Barking spiders, miss! Why can't you just—"

A metal shriek shattered the air, and a cloud of acrid smoke whipped across them both. Deryn turned into the wind, and saw the starboard Clanker engine spitting flame. With an awful groan its propeller seized, coughing out one last flurry of sparks.

"What in—," Deryn began, but with one engine halted, the ship went into a sudden starboard turn. The spine rolled beneath them, and Deryn grabbed Miss Rogers's arm and yanked them both to their knees. Tesla's antenna slithered beside them, stretching tighter as the airbeast bent hard along its length.

A moment later the port engine coasted to a halt, and the ship began to straighten again.

"What's going on?" Miss Rogers asked.

"No idea! But you'll have to wait here."

The airflow was already fading as the *Leviathan* slowed, and Deryn unclipped herself and ran forward toward the pods. Had the captain run the Clanker engines too hard this last week? Or was this sabotage?

But Mr. Francis had been followed from the first minute he'd come aboard, and the engines were manned at all times. It had to be a coincidence. . . .

Deryn reached the hump above the engines and pulled

the message lizard from her jacket. "Starboard engine pod, this is Middy Sharp. Report!"

She set the beastie down, and it scampered toward the pod, making good time. Even with the electrical engines still churning, the wind of the ship's passage was quickly dying. The airbeast's cilia never pushed while the Clanker engines were at full-ahead, so they'd been quiet for the better part of ten days. It might take an hour to wake them up again.

"Barking Clankers," she swore. Those contraptions had made the airbeast lazy.

To the west the Mexican airships were spreading out, taking time to surround their quarry. At this range Deryn could see their full wings and long whiplike tails, definitely based on the life threads of the manta ray. A brace of gasbags beneath the wings provided lift, with the Clanker engines slung in the middle. She recalled something like them from the *Manual of Aeronautics*, an experimental Italian craft, perhaps.

The manta ships weren't large; they didn't even carry a gondola. The crews rode in the ratlines on their backs, rifles in hand. The ships' only heavy armament was a pair of Gatling guns for each ship, mounted fore and aft.

A line of strafing hawks was streaming out from the *Leviathan*, but not in attack formation yet. The birds encircled their airship home with a glittering ring of talons.

The starboard engine had stopped belching smoke, and Deryn saw a familiar spiked helmet down in the pod—Master Klopp's. The Clanker machinery must have been acting up already, then. Since old Klopp's injury, the engineers never called him to the pods unless things were going pear-shaped.

The message lizard scuttled back up, speaking in the master mechanic's gruff German. "There's something wrong with the fuel, Dylan. It tastes funny."

Deryn frowned. Though she'd seen Klopp dip his finger into fuel and give it a sniff, she'd never seen him *taste* the stuff.

"The port engine will also be damaged if it keeps running," the lizard continued. "Tell them to shut down."

"What's wrong with that critter?" came a voice from behind her. "Sounds like it's talking German."

Deryn sighed as she picked up the lizard. "Yes, Miss Rogers. One of Alek's men is working down there. That's a Clanker engine, after all."

"And *you* understand German?"

"Well enough. I've worked with Master Klopp for more than two months now."

"What a fine coincidence! You've got a German fellow working on your engine *that just broke down!*"

"Master Klopp is Austrian!" Deryn said, pushing past the woman and heading across the hump.

Miss Rogers followed, notebook in hand. "Mr. Sharp, do you still suspect Mr. Francis of German sympathies? While ignoring the *actual* Clankers on your ship?"

Deryn waved at the riggers, hoping one would take the reporter away, but they were scrambling to set up an air gun. She swore, storming to the far side of the hump to set the lizard down again.

"Port engine pod," she told it. "This is Middy Sharp. Klopp says your fuel supply has something wrong with it. Don't go to speed unless absolutely necessary! End message."

As she shoved the lizard on its way, she realized the engineers would never obey her orders over the captain's. Maybe she should have sent the lizard to the bridge instead.

Miss Rogers was scribbling in her notebook. "Fuel supply, eh?"

"Exactly." Deryn stood up. "That's the fuel that Mr. Hearst gave us, and it's damaged our engines right in the middle of an ambush! Now does *that* sound like a coincidence to you?"

Miss Rogers scratched her nose with her pencil. "Hard to say."

Deryn looked back at the Mexican airships. One was drawing abreast of the *Leviathan*, no more than a mile away, a line of semaphore flags running out across its wings.

G-R-E-E-T-I-N-G-S—L-E-V-I-A-T-H-A-N, they said.

"So now you're being friendly," she muttered.

"Who is?"

Deryn pointed at the flags. "They've sent us greetings."

Another string followed, and she read them out to the reporter.

E-N-G-I-N-E—T-R-O-U-B-L-E—W-E—C-A-N—H-E-L-P.

"Well, that sounds friendly," Miss Rogers said.

Deryn frowned. "Maybe so, but this is all a bit convenient. They knew just where to find us, and this is a barking big desert."

"Young man, this is also a rather big airship."

Deryn started to retort, but another string of flags was running out. "It says these airships follow the orders of General Villa."

"Pancho Villa? Well, that's handy." The lady reporter scribbled. "The chief thinks quite highly of him."

Deryn snorted. "No doubt they're old pals. Now it says they've got an airfield nearby, with everything we need to make repairs. And they're happy to give us a tow." She squinted at the rest, then swore. "And all they want in return is one little thing."

"What's that?"

"A bit of sugar for their hungry beasts."

"Oh, dear," Miss Rogers said.

Deryn shook her head, remembering what Alek had

told her—Hearst had been delighted when he'd found out the *Leviathan* was headed across Mexico. And somehow he'd set all this in motion—the doctored fuel, the smuggled arms, the airships stalking them—in a single night.

She looked about. Men and sniffers were streaming up the ratlines now, and a few message lizards as well. She pulled out her command whistle and blew for a lizard. The bridge needed a full report.

"You say you know this General Villa?"

The lady reporter shrugged. "Only by reputation, but I know some of his business partners well enough."

"All right, then. Stay close to me, and keep your barking eyes open."

"Young man, you hardly need to tell me *that*."

· TWENTY-SEVEN ·

The cilia woke faster than Deryn had expected; maybe the mantas were giving the airbeast a fright. The motivator engines ran on organic batteries, of course, and hadn't suffered from Hearst's contaminated fuel. So the *Leviathan* was soon under its own power again, following the Mexican airships at a wary distance.

Deryn sent a message lizard down to the bridge, relating the news that Hearst and General Villa were on friendly terms. It came back and spoke in Captain Hobbes's own voice, telling her to take charge of docking. That was usually a rigger's job, but the captain wanted an officer on the bowhead. If the *Leviathan*'s hosts made any hostile moves, the ship would drop all ballast and shoot into the air. The mooring cables would have to be cut loose—and fast.

"I'll be ready, sir," Deryn said. "End message."

"That just proves my earlier point," Miss Rogers said as the creature scuttled away. "If you want something done right, always ask the bell captain."

"Stop barking *calling* me that."

"I assure you, young man, it's the highest compliment a hotel-raised girl can muster."

Deryn rolled her eyes. And she'd thought Eddie Malone was annoying.

Whoever had doctored the *Leviathan*'s fuel had done a precise job of it. The starboard engine had seized up only an hour away from Villa's airfield. The tip of a mooring tower rose up from a steep-sided canyon, deep enough for the *Leviathan* to hide itself in. The canyon had only one narrow entrance, but a hundred rocky nooks and crannies along its sides.

"A natural fortress," Deryn said. "I take it this General Villa is one of the revolutionaries."

"He's a rebel at heart." Miss Rogers shrugged. "Though it's complicated these days, more of a civil war than a revolution."

"But he's using Clanker engines. Do the Germans have a hand in all this?"

"All the powers are supplying one faction or another. The Great War has only raised the stakes."

Deryn sighed. Alek was right about one thing: One way or another, the war had sunk its claws into every nation on Earth. Even this distant conflict had been shaped by the war machines and fighting beasts of Europe.

Another reason for Alek to feel bad, to think all the world's troubles were his fault. Sometimes Deryn wished that she could burn the guilt out of his heart, or protect him from how awful the war was. Or at least make him forget somehow.

As the *Leviathan* slowed to a halt, the bottom of the canyon came into view. A few Clanker engines aside, these rebels were definitely Darwinists. Patches of fabricated corn covered the ground in bright colors, and a high stone wall penned a herd of fabricated bulls the size of streetcars. Six-legged donkeys carried packs down the steep trails leading into the canyon, and a pair of squidesque airbeasts grazed on the nearby cliff tops, their languid tentacles clearing scrub grass and cacti.

But on a high outcrop of rock a mile away was another bit of Clanker technology—a wireless tower.

"So that's how Hearst arranged all this."

Miss Rogers tutted. "Didn't someone tell me that your Mr. Tesla was a radio wiz?"

"Aye, but he's hardly arms-smuggling material. He can't stop blethering about peace."

"But his Goliath is a weapon, is it not?"

Deryn didn't bother to deny that.

The *Leviathan* angled itself into the wind, the cilia rippling to push it down. The manta ships drifted at a polite distance, but Deryn wondered if they had any hidden firepower. If the Mexicans were importing Clanker engines, maybe they'd got a few rockets in the bargain. The *Leviathan*'s strafing hawks were still in the air, of course, ready to strike in all directions.

Soon the sides of the canyon were rising up around Deryn, making her feel trapped. It was strange to be up on the spine and yet have stone walls to either side. If there was any treachery, the only way out would be straight up.

The airbeast's nose eased toward the tower, a team of riggers standing ready at the mooring crossbow. A grappling hook was set in the crossbow.

"Ready . . . ," Deryn called as the tower drew near. "Fire!"

The crossbow snapped, sending the grappling hook soaring. With a rattle of metal and chain, its prongs tangled in the struts of the tower.

"Draw her in!" Deryn cried, and the riggers wound

the cable fast, tightening the hook's grip. "Now tie her off!"

Soon the ship was secure, and from the canyon walls echoed the slither of cables dropping from the gondola below. The captain would be winching the ship down rather than venting hydrogen. That would keep the *Leviathan* buoyant, sitting in the canyon like a cork at the bottom of a bathtub, ready to pop up and out in case of danger.

Deryn's eyes swept the rocky ground below. The men gathering up the *Leviathan*'s ropes had rifles slung across their backs, but there was no sign of heavy arms, except for a half dozen cannon guarding the mouth of the canyon. They were pointed away from the airship, and looked like leftovers from a bygone war.

"Little wonder your boss wants to lend General Villa a hand," Deryn said, lowering her field glasses. "The general has got plenty of beasties, but no proper guns."

"I've heard the chief say exactly that." Miss Rogers sighed. "I just wish he'd told me what he was up to."

"Aye, he might have told us, too!"

The ground men below were pulling the ropes out in all directions. Deryn spotted Newkirk drifting down on gliding wings to help them. The boy was soon waving his arms as he tried to organize Villa's men.

"Do you know any Spanish, Miss Rogers?"

"As much as any girl from southern California. Which means more than a little but less than I'd like."

Deryn nodded. "You might be the only one on the ship who does. Stand ready."

"Much as I'd love to review my reflexive verbs, Mr. Sharp, it won't be necessary. I'm certain all of General Villa's motion picture contracts are in English."

"His *what*?"

"Didn't I tell you? That's how Mr. Hearst knows him. They're both in the movie business!" Miss Rogers swept her hand across the encampment. "That's how Villa finances all this. He takes moving pictures of his battles and sends them to Los Angeles. He's practically a motion picture star!"

"So Hearst has a *movie* deal with him?"

The reporter shook her head. "Villa's contract is with Mutual Films. But I suppose the chief wants to horn in. Crafty, isn't he?"

"A bit too crafty for my liking," Deryn muttered. If Hearst was such a peace lover, why was he sending weapons into Mexico? Or did he only care about making newsreels?

"There's something above us, sir," one of the riggers called. "Up on the cliffs!"

Deryn looked up. A column of smoke was rising from

the edge of the canyon. She closed her eyes to listen over the shouts of the men below, and heard it—the rumble of a Clanker engine.

Did the rebels have a walking machine up there? She'd seen nothing from the air, though any number of walkers might have hidden in the rocky terrain.

"And that way, sir!" called another man. Deryn turned and saw a second cloud of engine smoke rising from the far side of the canyon. There was dust rising as well, a sure sign of legs in motion. The tiny manta airships might have only Gatling guns, but walkers could carry heavy cannon.

Deryn pulled out her command whistle and blew for a message lizard. "We're being surrounded, and the officers down on the bridge can't see it!"

"But why would General Villa betray us?" Miss Rogers asked. "He wants those guns we're bringing him."

"He might also want the *Leviathan!*" Deryn cried. "It's one of the biggest airships in all of Europe. Think how powerful it would make him here in Mexico!"

Miss Rogers waved a hand. "But Mr. Hearst just wants a dramatic story. If the rebels destroy us, he'll get no story at all!"

"Aye, but has anyone explained that to the barking rebels?"

"These are *civilized* rebels, young man. They have *movie deals!*"

"That's no guarantee of sanity!" Deryn felt the tug of a message lizard pulling on her trouser leg. She knelt and said, "Bridge, this is Middy Sharp. Walkers on the cliffs above us, at least two. Could be an ambush! End message."

The beastie scampered away, but it would take at least a minute to reach the bridge. By then the vast topside of the *Leviathan* would be in the sights of the walkers' guns, as easy to hit as a cricket field.

She spun around, checking on the manta ships. They didn't seem to be closing in. Not yet, anyway.

"If only I could send up a scout," Deryn muttered. But all the Huxleys were stowed in the ship's gut to protect them from the winds of high speed.

"Sir," said the rigger beside her. "Mr. Rigby sent up a pair of gliding wings, in case the captain wanted you on the ground. You could use those."

"Aye, but I need to go *up* to—," Deryn began, but then she saw the dust rising from the ground crew's feet. It was climbing the sides of the canyon, carried by an updraft. . . .

"Get me those wings!" she shouted. "Now!"

As the man ran off, she watched the airflow in the canyon. The wind was rushing into the entrance, straight into the *Leviathan*'s nose. If Deryn took off dead ahead, she might gain enough altitude to rise above the cliff walls.

"I still say you're being entirely too suspicious," Miss Rogers said.

Deryn ignored her, turning to the crossbow crew. "If we blow even a squick of ballast, cut this cable. Don't wait for orders!"

"Aye, sir."

Two men arrived, gliding wings in hand, and Deryn struggled into the rig. She borrowed a pair of semaphore flags, then paced off ten yards from the bow, ready to take a running start. There was only one problem.

The mooring tower was in the way.

"Oh, sod it." She spread her arms and ran toward the edge. "Watch out!"

The riggers and Miss Rogers ducked beneath the wings, and Deryn sped past them and leapt from the edge of the bow, straight into the wind. The tower reared up before her, but she wrenched herself to starboard, barely clearing the metal struts.

Veering right had pulled her out of the headwind, and she went circling downward. But with another hard jerk the air filled the gliding wings again. She rose a little, climbing just above the canyon walls.

One of the walkers was in sight now—a two-legged machine the size of Alek's old Cyklop Stormwalker. It had the boxy look of a German contraption, and was rumbling straight toward the cliff edge.

Deryn pulled her wings hard toward it, but she slipped beneath the cliff tops again. She was flying straight into a wall of stone. . . .

At the last moment she swung her weight back, and the wings climbed hard, almost stalling in midair. Her momentum carried her the last few yards, and Deryn alighted on the edge of the rocky cliff. Her boots slipped on loose stone, but somehow she kept her feet.

The walking machine towered over her, its head bending down as if to take a closer look. The huge maw of a gun pointed straight at her.

"Barking spiders!" she said.

It wasn't a gun at all—it was a moving-picture camera. She heard the whir and snap of it capturing her image a dozen times a second.

The wind shifted, pulling her back toward the cliff's edge. Deryn spun about and took a look across the canyon. The other walker was just the same, a two-legged camera platform.

The rebels wanted to film the *Leviathan*, not destroy it.

Her message lizard would be at the bridge any moment now, and if the captain grew alarmed and dropped ballast, the landing ropes would rip through the hands of a hundred untrained men below. Worse, a few would hang

"THE WALKER SHOOTS DERYN."

on to be carried up into the sky, then fall back upon their fellows from a thousand feet. If General Villa didn't want to destroy the *Leviathan* now, he certainly would after that.

Deryn spun the gliding wings about and threw herself back off the cliff.

TWENTY-EIGHT

"Those men on the ropes look quite sharp," Captain
Hobbes said. "And this canyon keeps the wind steady
enough."

None of the officers answered. They were spread out
across the bridge, each at a different window, watching
for signs of treachery. Bovril shifted nervously on Alek's
shoulder, scenting disquiet in the air.

Outside, the rebels were hard at work, staking
ropes into the hard ground and tying them onto metal
posts driven straight into the rock. The lines trembled
as the *Leviathan* winched itself down, its huge shadow
spreading meter by meter across the canyon floor. The
captain hadn't vented any hydrogen, in case a quick
takeoff were necessary. To Alek it felt as though the airbeast were fighting the ropes, like Gulliver among the
Lilliputians.

"Do you really think these rebels will help us?" he asked Dr. Barlow.

"I should hope so, after putting us through all this bother." She sniffed. "I'm sure Mr. Hearst only wanted a bit of drama for his newsreel."

"Newsreel," her loris said softly, then *hmph*ed.

"And to think I trusted that man," Mr. Tesla said. He'd been in a dark mood since the breakdown, especially after the engine pod had reported that Hearst's fuel was to blame.

"He may want peace," Dr. Barlow said. "But conflict sells newspapers."

"I've heard of this Pancho Villa fellow, haven't I?" Alek asked.

"He's in all the papers at the moment." Mr. Tesla stared out the window at the ground men. "His name is Francisco Villa, but he goes by the nickname Pancho because he's a friend of the poor. He seizes wealthy plantations and gives them to the peasants."

"Quite a common habit among rebels," Dr. Barlow said, and her loris made a sniffing noise. "One hopes that he is above seizing airships."

Alek shook his head. However chaotic the world might be, he knew that providence was guiding him toward peace. His quest couldn't end here in this dusty canyon.

"Bridge, this is Middy Sharp!" came Deryn's voice from nowhere.

All eyes turned to the message lizard clinging to the ceiling.

"Walkers on the cliffs above us, at least two," it said. "Could be an ambush!"

A stir went through the bridge, and Bovril shivered on Alek's shoulder. The officers gathered around the captain.

"Walkers?" Alek said. "But they're Darwinists."

"Those airships had Clanker engines," Tesla said.

Dr. Barlow glanced out the window. "This is unsettling. The *Leviathan* is quite vulnerable to attack from above."

Alek tried to peer up at the surrounding cliffs, but the gasbag blocked out the sky. He felt trapped beneath the vast expanse of the airship.

Blast Hearst and his news-making games.

"Prepare to blow all ballast," the captain announced.

"Cut the landing lines, sir?" an officer asked.

"Don't bother. At this buoyancy they'll break."

"That's a bit unfriendly," Dr. Barlow muttered. "Those lines can decapitate a man when they snap."

Outside, the ground men were still working patiently to secure the ropes, not suspecting the chaos about to be unleashed. A flight-suited figure was among them, a pair of gliding wings folded across his back.

Alek turned to Dr. Barlow. "But Newkirk's out there. We can't leave him behind!"

"I fear we must." The lady boffin shook her head. "If this is an ambush, we can't afford to give them warning."

"You mean we'll just—," Alek began, but a dark shape was flickering across the ground—a small, winged shadow just beyond the starboard edge of the airship.

"On my command." Captain Hobbes raised his hand.

Alek squinted, watching the shadow wheel in ever-tightening circles. Its shape reminded him of the gliding wings on Newkirk's back.

"Deryn Sharp," whispered Bovril.

"Wait!" Alek cried, spinning about to face the captain. He took two steps closer, but a marine guard blocked his way. "It's Dylan!"

The captain turned, his hand still raised.

"Middy Sharp's gliding down!" Alek shouted. "There must be a reason!"

The officers stood ready, their eyes on the captain. The man hesitated a moment, then glanced at the first officer. "Take a look."

Alek crossed back to the windows, pointing at the flitting, wheeling shadow. The men on the landing lines had seen it now—they were looking up and calling to one another.

"How do you know it's Sharp?" the first officer asked.

"Because it's—it's . . . ," Alek sputtered.

"Mr. Sharp!" Bovril declared.

Deryn's winged form streaked into sight beneath the edge of the gasbag, careening downward at an absurd angle, two semaphore flags rippling in her hands. She shot past the bridge windows in an instant, arms flailing, and then she was gone.

"Did anyone catch that signal?" the captain asked.

"*A-M*, sir," one of the navigators said. "That's all I got."

"'Ambush,'" the captain said. "Stand ready, lads."

"Pardon me, sir," the first officer said. "But there was a *C* at first."

Captain Hobbes hesitated, shaking his head.

Alek ran to the far side of the bridge—Deryn's shadow wheeled about, and a moment later she swung back into view. She came in low across the front windows, sending the ground men scattering before her.

Her semaphore flags were still waving, but then her boots skidded on hard ground. Deryn reached up to regain control, the flags falling from her hands.

The wings pulled her up into the air one last time, then crumpled and twisted, dropping her into a stumbling halt. Ground men came running from all directions, and Deryn disappeared among them in a cloud of dust.

"Did anyone get that signal?" the captain shouted.

"*E-R-A?*" the first officer said.

"*C-A-M,*" Bovril muttered, and suddenly it all fell into place.

"The walkers on the cliffs," Alek said. "They're camera platforms!"

"Walker cameras?" The captain shook his head. "Why would rebels have that sort of equipment?"

"With Sharp flying about, they must know we're on to them," the first officer said. "Sir, we should blow—"

"The film!" Dr. Barlow cried. "Those barrels had unexposed rolls of film in them. So the rebels *must* have motion picture cameras. This isn't an attack!"

The bridge was silent for a moment, all eyes on the captain. He stood there with his arms crossed tight, fingers drumming.

"They haven't fired at us yet," he finally said. "But stand ready to blow all ballast if you hear so much as a gunshot."

Alek breathed out a slow sigh, and Bovril's claws eased

their grip on his shoulder. But then Dr. Busk spoke up: "Sharp looks hurt."

Alek ran to the front of the bridge, shoving his way past the marine guards. From the front windows he saw her lying curled on the ground a hundred yards away.

"I'm going out there."

The captain cleared his throat. "I can't allow that, Your Highness."

"Does anyone else on this ship speak Spanish?" Alek asked, trusting that between Italian and Latin he could manage.

The captain looked at his officers, then shook his head. "Perhaps not, but if the situation deteriorates, we'll have to blow our ballast."

"Exactly. Any misunderstanding could be a disaster, so give me a chance to sort this out!"

The captain thought another moment, then sighed and turned to Dr. Busk. "You go with him, and take five marines."

Newkirk was already at Deryn's side. A crowd of Villa's men surrounded them, one waving and calling "*Médico*," which certainly meant "doctor"—at least in Italian. A few landing lines swung freely, and an officer was trying to get the men back to their ropes.

"Dylan!" Alek shouted, pushing through the crowd.

The rebels pulled away, giving Bovril wide-eyed stares.

Newkirk looked up, his face streaked with dust. "He's conscious, but he's done his leg."

"Of course I'm barking conscious!" Deryn shouted. "It hurts like blazes!"

Alek knelt beside her. The left arm of her uniform was torn and bloody, and she clasped one knee to her chest. Her eyes were squeezed shut against the pain.

Bovril made a soft unhappy noise, and Alek took Deryn's hand.

"I've brought Dr. Busk," he said.

Her eyes sprang open, and she whispered, "You *Dummkopf!*"

Alek froze. Injured or not, Deryn couldn't afford to have a surgeon prying at her.

"Newkirk, get these men back on their lines!" Alek ordered. Then he whispered to Deryn, "Take my arm. If you can stand up, he might not look too closely."

"Stand on my right," she said, grasping his shoulder. Alek counted down from three under his breath, then stood, pulling her up onto one leg. Together they faced Dr. Busk, who was making his way through the crowd with the marine guards.

Deryn shifted on her good leg beside Alek, threatening to pull him over. She *was* rather taller than him, he realized, and heavier than she looked—muscles from climbing, he supposed. Bovril helpfully jumped down onto the ground.

Alek gritted his teeth and nodded at Dr. Busk. "Mr. Sharp seems well enough."

The surgeon looked Deryn up and down. "Should you be standing, Mr. Sharp? That was quite a spill."

"It's all right, sir. Just a banged-up knee." She skidded forward a bit, and Alek helped her take a step. "I'll walk it off."

"Blast it, Sharp. Sit down." Dr. Busk reached into his black leather bag and pulled out a pair of long scissors. "Let me take a look at that leg."

Deryn glanced at Alek, nodding just a bit, and the two struggled together to a nearby flat rock. Deryn sat down heavily, and Bovril crawled up into her lap. She grimaced at the beast's weight, but swallowed any cry of pain.

A metal stake had been pounded into the shaley stone beside her, and the landing rope that was lashed to it quivered with energy. Alek imagined it snapping with enough force to cut his head off, and glanced up at the bridge windows. He could just make out the captain peering down, his officers crowded around him.

"We got your message just in time," Alek said.

"C-A-M-E-R-A," Bovril said proudly.

"I wish I hadn't sent the first one." Deryn shook her head, stroking Bovril's fur. "According to Miss Rogers, General Villa's in the barking movie business! That's why Hearst is smuggling him arms and film. He wants battle scenes for his newsreels."

"Newsreels, fah!" Bovril said.

"Steady there, lad." Dr. Busk was cutting away Deryn's trouser leg above the knee. Her flesh looked pale around a purpling bruise.

She stared up at Alek, worry in her eyes. If the leg were broken, carrying off her deception would be impossible.

"Sir!" one of the marines called. "Someone's coming."

Dr. Busk didn't look up. "Some diplomacy, Your Highness, if you please."

"Of course." Alek gave Deryn what he hoped was a reassuring nod, then stood and turned. Two large creatures were approaching, sending a ripple through the ground men.

The crowd parted to reveal a pair of gigantic fabricated bulls. They stood at least three meters tall, their horns tipped with metal, their shoulders as broad as train engines. The bulls had riders on their backs, holding steel chains that ran down through silver rings in the beasts' noses. Behind each rider was mounted a platform with

"PANCHO VILLA."

another soldier; one bull carried a Gatling gun, the other a motion picture camera.

Almost lost between the two huge beasts was a man on horseback. He wore riding boots and pale trousers, a small-brimmed hat, and a short brown jacket crossed with two bandoliers of bullets. His clothes looked rumpled, as if he had just arisen from bed, and from above an unkempt, bristly mustache peered two lively brown eyes.

Alek knew only a few words of Spanish, but he bowed and gave it a try.

"*Sono Aleksandar, principe de Hohenberg.*"

The man laughed and said in a careful but clear English, "I think you mean '*soy.*' General Francisco Villa, revolutionary governor of Chihuahua, at your service."

"It is an honor, General," Alek said, bowing again.

So this was the famous rebel leader, the Robin Hood of Mexican peasants. Alek wondered what the man must think of the wealthy young prince before him, and if he had picked a side in the Great War in Europe.

The pistol on his belt was a Mauser—German made.

"Is your man hurt?" Villa asked.

Alek turned. Deryn was wincing in pain as Dr. Busk applied some sort of compress to her knee. "We hope not, sir."

"My personal doctor is coming. But please, why did he jump off your ship? He makes us very nervous for a moment."

"It was the camera walkers." Alek looked up. "There was some confusion about their purpose."

The man clicked his tongue. "Ah, I should have known. Last winter one of these walkers captures a whole platoon of *Federales*. They thought it would shoot them!"

Alek compared the Gatling gun and camera on the two monstrous bulls. "An understandable mistake. It seems an odd machine for an army to travel with."

The man pointed at the *Leviathan*'s gondola. "But okay for your airship?"

Alek looked up and saw Mr. Francis and his men filming the encounter through the open windows of the middies' mess. Here he was in front of the cameras, performing again.

"There seems to be no escaping them," Alek said. "Can you help us repair our engines?"

The man bowed low in his saddle. "Of course. All part of my deal with Señor Hearst. He sends his apologies for the inconvenience."

Alek was about to say something unpleasant, but a cry came from Deryn, and he spun about. Dr. Busk was pulling off her jacket now, revealing a red stain running down her left arm. In another moment he would have her shirt off.

Alek turned to General Villa. "Please, sir. If your doctor could be quick. I'm afraid our ship's surgeon is . . . a bit incompetent."

"You are lucky, then. Dr. Azuela is quite experienced with wounds of battle." Villa pointed at a man coming through the crowd. "Take him to your friend."

Alek gave a quick bow and raced back to where Deryn sat. He placed a firm hand on Dr. Busk's shoulder. "General Villa would prefer that his own doctor see to Mr. Sharp."

"Why, for heaven's sake?"

"He insists, as our host," Alek hissed softly. "We should not insult him."

"Most irregular," Dr. Busk said, but he stood and took a step back. Dr. Azuela was coming through the crowd. A man of less than forty, he was dressed in a tweed suit and string tie, his eyes behind small round glasses.

Alek went to him, wondering how to get Deryn hidden. He looked up at the bright sun, ransacking his brain for a few words of Spanish.

"*El sol. Malo.*"

The Mexican doctor glanced at Deryn, then at the

Leviathan's shadow only a dozen meters away.

"Can he walk?" he said in excellent English.

"We can't move him," Alek said. "Is there some way to get cover?"

"Of course," the man said, and began to shout orders. Soon the ground men were flinging canvas tarps across the landing lines, putting Deryn in the shadow of a makeshift tent and out of view of the *Leviathan*'s gondola.

As they worked, Alek pulled Dr. Busk aside. "General Villa wants a message taken to the captain. He says he'll do whatever he can to repair the ship."

"Well, that's good to hear, I suppose. I'll send one of the marines."

Alek shook his head. "He wants an officer to deliver it."

Dr. Busk frowned, looking at the tarps. "I see. Look after Sharp, will you?"

"Of course, Doctor," Alek said, turning away with a sigh of relief. The only remaining trick was to keep the rebel doctor from discovering Deryn's secret, or at least from making a fuss about it.

Halfway back to the makeshift tent, Alek realized that he had lied to three men in as many minutes. And worse, he'd done so rather skillfully.

He shook his head, ignoring the queasy feeling in his stomach. Deryn had warned him about this, after all, and he'd given his word. This was the battle that she fought every day, and he was part of her deception now.

◦ TWENTY-NINE ◦

When Alek slipped between the swaying tarps, he found only Deryn and Dr. Azuela inside. The ground men had swiftly thrown up a cot for Deryn and a case for the doctor's instruments. But now they had gone back to their ropes, and the growl of the winches drawing the ship down had started up again. Bovril was wrapped around Deryn's neck, purring softly.

"Are you all right?"

"I've had worse," Deryn said, but her eyes stayed fixed on the doctor's fingers as they probed her arm.

"It isn't broken," the man said. "But this cut is bad. I need to sew it up. Take off your shirt."

"I can't," Deryn said softly. "My arm won't move."

The doctor frowned, feeling carefully along her forearm again. "But a moment ago you made a fist."

"Just cut the sleeve off," Alek said, kneeling beside them. "I'll help you."

Dr. Azuela's wary gaze traveled from Deryn to Alek as he reached into his bag. He pulled out a pair of scissors and snipped through the cuff of the middy's uniform, then up her arm. Her pale skin was slick with blood.

Deryn drew in a sharp breath—the doctor's free hand had brushed her chest. Azuela frowned, hesitating a moment. Then, with a flash, the scissors had reversed in his hand. The points quivered at her throat.

"What's under your shirt?" he demanded.

"Nothing!" Deryn said.

"There's something strapped there. You're wearing a bomb! ¡Asesino!"

"You're wrong," Bovril said quite clearly.

Azuela stared at the beast, dumbfounded and frozen.

"It's all right, Doctor." Alek raised his hands in surrender. "Deryn, just take off your shirt."

She stared dumbly at him, shaking her head.

Dr. Azuela tore his eyes from the loris. "You're here to kill Pancho! You meant to fly down onto him with a bomb!"

"She isn't an assassin," Alek said.

The doctor stared up at him.

"She," Bovril said.

"Deryn is a girl. That's why she's bound like that." Alek ignored the look of despair on her face. "See for yourself."

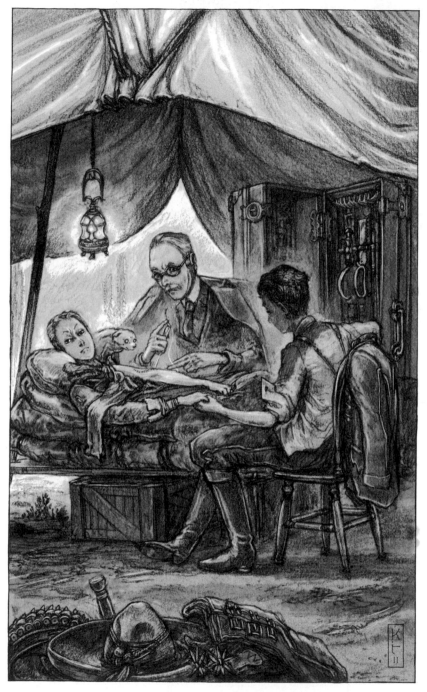

"THE DOCTOR'S SUSPICIONS."

With the scissors still at her throat, Dr. Azuela felt her again. Deryn flinched, and his eyes widened as he yanked his hand away.

"¡Lo siento, señorita!"

Deryn opened her mouth, but no sound came out. Her fists clenched, and she began to shake. Alek knelt beside her, gently opening one of her hands to hold it.

"Please don't tell anyone, sir," he said.

The doctor shook his head. "But why?"

"She wants to serve—to fly." Alek reached into his inner pocket, the one the pope's letter always occupied. Beside the scroll case his fingers found a small cloth bag and pulled it free.

"Here." Alek handed it to the man. "For your silence."

Dr. Azuela opened the bag, and found the sliver of gold—all that remained of the quarter ton that Alek's father had left him. He stared at it a moment, then shook his head. "I have to tell Pancho."

"Please," Deryn said softly.

"He is our commander." He turned to Deryn. "But only him, I promise."

Dr. Azuela called in one of the rebels from outside and gave an order in rapid-fire Spanish. Then he set to work, cleaning the wound with a rag and liquid from a small silver flask, sterilizing a needle and thread, then handing the flask to Deryn. As she drank, he drew the needle through the skin of her arm, pulling the wound closed stitch by stitch.

Alek watched, keeping his hand in Deryn's. She squeezed hard, her nails cutting half moons into his flesh.

"It'll be all right," he said. "Don't worry."

After all, why should a great rebel leader care if a girl had hidden herself in the British Air Service?

Before Azuela had finished, a gust of air from outside sent the canvas around them swaying. It was one of the great bulls snorting, like an exhalation of steam from a freight train.

The tarps parted, and General Villa stepped inside. *"¿Está muriendo?"*

"No, he will mend." The doctor's eyes didn't leave his work. "But he has an interesting secret to tell you. You may wish to sit down."

Villa sighed, settling cross-legged next to Alek. On horseback he had seemed quite graceful, but now he looked a bit thick about the middle. He moved deliberately, perhaps with a touch of rheumatism.

"Tell him," Dr. Azuela said.

Deryn looked exhausted, but her voice was firm. "I'm Deryn Sharp, decorated officer in His Majesty's Air Service. But I'm not a man."

"Ah." Villa's eyebrows rose a little as he looked her up and down. "Forgive me, Señorita Sharp. I didn't know the

British use women for their glider troops. Because you are small, yes?"

"That's not it, sir," Deryn said. "This is a secret."

"Deryn's father was an airman," Alek explained. "Her brother is too. She dresses as a boy because it's the only way she can fly."

General Villa stared at Deryn for a moment, then a snort of laughter rippled through his body. *"¡Qué engaño!"*

"Please don't tell anyone," Alek said. "At least not for a few hours, until we've gone. It's nothing to you, whether you turn her in. But to her it's everything."

The man shook his head in wonder, then raised an eyebrow at Alek. "And what is your part in this joke, little prince?"

"He's my friend," Deryn said. Her face was still pale, but her voice sounded stronger now. She offered Villa the flask.

He waved it away. "Only a friend?"

Deryn didn't answer, staring down at the fresh stitches in her arm. Alek opened his mouth, but Bovril spoke first: "Ally."

General Villa gave the loris a curious look. "What is this beast?"

"A perspicacious loris." Deryn reached up and stroked its head. "It repeats things, a bit like a message lizard."

"It does not only repeat," Dr. Azuela said. "It told me I was wrong."

Alek frowned—he'd noticed that as well. As the weeks had passed, the lorises' memories had grown longer. They sometimes parroted things from days before, or that they'd heard only from each other. It wasn't always clear now where a word or phrase had come from.

"That's because it's perspicacious," Deryn said. "In other words, it's clever."

"Dead clever," Bovril said, and Villa stared at it again, his brown eyes marveling.

"*Tienen oro,*" Dr. Azuela said into the silence.

Alek's Italian was sufficient for him to understand the word for "gold." He pulled out the small bag again. "It's not much, but we can pay for your silence."

General Villa took the bag and opened it, then laughed. "The richest man in California sends me guns! And you tempt me with this gold toothpick?"

"Then, what do you want?"

The man's eyes narrowed on Alek. "Señor Hearst says you are a nephew of the old emperor, Maximilian."

"A grandnephew, but yes."

"Emperors are vain and useless things. We did not need one, so we shot him."

"Yes, I know the story." Alek swallowed. "Perhaps it was a bit presumptuous, putting an Austrian on the throne of Mexico."

"It was an insult to the people. But your uncle was brave

at the end. In front of the firing squad, he wished that his blood should be the last to flow for freedom." General Villa looked at the red-stained rag in Dr. Azuela's hand. "Sadly, it was not."

"Indeed," Alek said. "That was fifty years ago, wasn't it?"

"*Sí.* Too much blood since then." Villa tossed the bag back to Alek and turned to Deryn. "Keep your secret, little sister. But be more careful the next time you jump off your ship."

"Aye, I'll try."

"And be careful of young princes. The first man I ever shot was as rich as a prince, and it was for my sister's honor." General Villa laughed again. "But you are a soldier, Señorita Sharp—you can shoot men for yourself, can't you?"

Deryn gave a one-shouldered shrug. "It's crossed my mind, once or twice. But pardon me, sir. If you don't like emperors, where did you get those German walkers?"

"The kaiser sells us arms." General Villa patted the Mauser pistol on his belt. "Sometimes he *gives* us arms, so we are his friends when the Yankees join the war, I think. But we will never bow to him."

"Aye, emperors are a bit pointless, aren't they?" Deryn sat up straighter and held out her right hand. "Thank you for not telling."

"Your secret is safe, *hermanita.*" General Villa shook

her hand, then rose to his feet, but suddenly his eyes narrowed and his hand went to his gun. A shadow loomed against the tarp.

Villa reached up and flung the canvas aside, pointing his pistol into the beaming unshaven face of Eddie Malone.

"Dylan Sharp, *Deryn* Sharp . . . of course! Well, I can't say I had a clue, but it sure explains a *lot*." The man rubbed his hands together and then thrust one at Pancho Villa. "Eddie Malone, reporter for the *New York World*."

• THIRTY •

The cut on Deryn's arm wasn't much in the end, just eleven neat stitches that hardly itched at all. But she was going to feel her injured knee for a long time.

Most often the ache was simple and honest, as if she'd bashed it on the corner of an iron bed frame. Other times the whole leg throbbed, like her growing pains back when she'd been only twelve and already taller than half the boys in Glasgow. But the worst agony came at night, when her kneecap buzzed and thrummed like a bottle full of bees.

The buzzing was probably thanks to Dr. Busk's compress. It wasn't mustard seed and oats like her aunties favored, but a wee fabricated beastie of some kind. It had attached itself to her skin like a barnacle, its tendrils creeping inside to heal the ligaments torn in the crash. The surgeon hadn't said what life threads the compress was fabricated from, but it lived on sugar water and a bit of sunlight every day—half plant and half animal, most likely.

Whatever the beastie was, it got annoyed when Deryn moved. Even a squick of weight on the leg was punished with an hour of angry bees. Walking was a nightmare and dressing was tricky, and of course she could hardly ask for help with that.

If it hadn't been for Alek, the whole crew would've learned her secret that first day. It was Alek who'd persuaded General Villa to stay silent, and had convinced the officers that Deryn could stay in her own cabin, not the sick bay, even though it meant Alek had to fetch meals from the galley himself. It was Alek who half carried her to the heads in the dark gastric channel several times a day, standing guard at a gentlemanly distance while she went. And it was Alek who kept her company so she didn't go stark raving mad.

He'd done so much, just to make sure that her last few days aboard the *Leviathan* were spent as a proper airman and not as some mad girl shunned by the officers and crew.

That bum-rag Eddie Malone hadn't told anyone, not yet. After Mr. Hearst's treachery, the reporters weren't allowed near Tesla's radio or the messenger birds, and Malone was too worried that Adela Rogers would steal his story. But New York was only two days away. Two more days in uniform, and then her secret would be revealed to the world. There was no escaping the fact that this was Deryn Sharp's last journey aboard the *Leviathan*.

It was like awaiting execution, every second slow and sharp-edged, but sometimes at night she was grateful to the bees for keeping her awake. At least she could spend a few more hours feeling the vibrations of the ship and listening to the whispers of airflow around the gondola.

Most of the time, though, Deryn wondered what she would do next. She'd have to make up some new lies, of course, to keep her brother Jaspert out of trouble for sneaking her into the Service. But her notoriety would eventually fade, and she'd have to find proper work.

Deryn still knew her aeronautics, even if the Service took away her uniform. And whether or not her knee healed completely, she'd grown strong enough to work alongside most men. Alek said she should stay in America, where, according to him, women who could handle hydrogen balloons were all the rage.

He'd explained about Pauline and her perils. The girl was nothing but a moving-picture character, a flicker of shadows on a screen, but she'd crawled inside Alek's daft attic somehow.

"She stands to inherit a lot of money," he was explaining the second day out of General Villa's airfield. "Millions of American dollars, I suppose. But here's the twist: She doesn't get a penny till she marries."

Deryn leaned back into her pillows and stared up. The Gulf of Mexico lay sparkling beneath the *Leviathan*, casting shimmers on the ceiling. Alek sat at the foot of Deryn's bed while Bovril perched on the head, waving its wee arms as if practicing semaphore signals.

"Poor girl," Deryn said. "Except for the millions of dollars part."

Alek laughed. "It's a melodrama, not a tragedy."

"Melodrama," Bovril said in the slow, clear way the lorises did when they learned new words.

"But instead of getting married," Alek went on, "she goes off to have adventures. And no one stops her, even though she's a girl!"

Deryn frowned. It didn't sound likely, though if you had a few millions in the bank, perhaps people treated you a bit more like a man. "Besides that palaver with the hydrogen balloon, what sort of adventures?"

"Well, I saw only the first episode. It didn't have a proper ending, just what they call a cliff-hanger." Alek thought a moment. "Though I think Mr. Hearst mentioned something about runaway walkers and being tied to train tracks."

"Tied to train tracks? Sounds like a brilliant career for me."

"Listen, Deryn. It doesn't matter if *The Perils of Pauline* is rubbish. The point is that it's terribly popular. So even if American women aren't piloting balloons yet, at least they *want* to. You could show them how it's done."

"Sometimes wanting isn't enough, Alek. You know that."

"I suppose I do." He leaned back against the cabin wall. "For example, you don't *want* to be cheered up, do you?"

Deryn shrugged. At the moment she knew exactly what she wanted: for Eddie Malone not to have eavesdropped on their conversation with General Villa. Or for her not to have crashed the gliding wings. Or better yet, for barking Hearst not to have gummed up the *Leviathan*'s engines in the first place!

If any of it had gone differently, no one would ever have found out she was a girl. Except Alek and that bumrag Volger, of course.

"Will you be staying in America?" she asked. "When the *Leviathan* heads on?"

Alek frowned at her. "Would the captain let me?"

"You're doing what the Admiralty wants, helping

Mr. Tesla talk up his weapon. Why should they drag you back to England?"

"I suppose you're right." He stood and went to the window, his green eyes bright as he stared at the sky.

It was obvious that he hadn't thought much about life after the *Leviathan*. Deep inside, Alek probably still hoped he could stay aboard. But even if he didn't disembark in New York, he and his men would be passengers only as far as London.

"You might be in love with the *Leviathan*, Alek. But the ship doesn't love you back."

A sad smile played on his lips. "It was a doomed relationship from the start. For you and me both, I suppose."

Deryn stared at the ceiling. A Clanker prince and a girl dressed as a boy—neither could last forever on this ship. Only dumb luck had kept them together this long.

"Did I ever tell you how I knew your real name?" Alek asked.

"You had plenty of clues," she said, then frowned. "But you tricked me by saying 'Deryn,' didn't you? Where did you hear that?"

"It was all Eddie Malone's fault," Alek said.

"That bum-rag!" Bovril exclaimed.

"He'd run out of my secrets," Alek went on, "so he wrote an article about you saving the *Dauntless*. I always meant to show you the photograph. You looked quite dashing in it."

"Wait, are you saying Malone knew my name *back then?*"

"Of course not. But he'd done some research on your family, your father's accident. He wrote about how you—that is, a daughter named Deryn—had survived."

"Oh, aye." She sighed. "That's why I never told that story to anyone but you. And that was enough for you to guess that Deryn was me?"

Alek glanced sidelong at the perspicacious loris. "Well, I had a bit of help."

"Barking traitor," Deryn said, and gave the head of the bed a thump.

Bovril teetered for a moment, its tiny hands out like a tightrope walker. Then it fell into her lap.

"Ooph," they both said together.

Alek took the beast from her. "You never told me, how did Volger figure you out?"

"Fencing lessons. All that touching and moving me about." Deryn scowled. "And I shouted at him too much."

"You shouted at him?"

"When you escaped in Istanbul and Volger was left behind, he was being a bit smug. As if he were *glad* to be rid of you!"

"I can imagine," Alek said. "But what's that got to do with you being a girl?"

"I was . . ." She stared at the wall. This was just embarrassing. "Maybe I got a bit screechy about you."

"Screechy," Bovril said with a chuckle.

Deryn forced herself to look at Alek. He was smiling.

"You didn't want me getting hurt?"

"Of course not, you daft prince." She found herself smiling back at him. For all her sadness about leaving the *Leviathan*, it was a relief being able to talk to him like this. What would it be like, once her secret was revealed to the whole world?

"We could both stay in New York, I suppose," she offered softly.

"That sounds perfect."

The simple words made Deryn's pulse quicken just a bit, enough to make the bees behind her kneecap stir.

"Really? You want to be immigrants together?"

Alek laughed, placing Bovril on the windowsill. "Not quite immigrants. Americans aren't allowed to become emperors, I seem to recall."

"But with Mr. Tesla's weapon, you don't need to be emperor to stop the war!"

He frowned. "Someone has to lead my people after all this."

"Aye, of course," Deryn said, feeling foolish.

Alek might pretend to be an airman now and then, but the pope's letter was always in his pocket, and he'd wanted his whole life to be his father's heir. Anything more than friendship with her would destroy his chances of taking the throne.

But every time one of them had fallen—in the snows of the Alps, in Istanbul, on the stormy topside, in that dusty canyon—the other had been there to pick them up. She couldn't imagine Alek leaving her for some daft crown and scepter.

"You're right, Deryn. We're both stuck in New York for the rest of the war." He turned from the window, his smile growing. "You should join me and Volger!"

"Aye, his countship would *love* that."

"Volger doesn't decide who my allies are." Alek stroked the loris's head. "If it were up to him, we would have strangled Bovril the night it was born."

"That bum-rag!" the beastie said.

Deryn frowned. Had Alek just likened her to *Bovril*?

"We don't even know where we'll live," he continued. "I've got hardly any gold left, and Mr. Tesla spent every penny he had building Goliath. But it'll be easy to raise more, now that he's proven what it can do."

"No doubt. But do you want to depend on that mad boffin's charity?"

"Charity? Nonsense. It'll be like Istanbul, all of us working together to put things right!"

Deryn nodded, though it was clear Alek barely knew

what charity was. His whole life had been spent in a bubble of wealth. He no more understood money than a fish understood water.

But a much worse notion had entered her mind.

"They might not kick me off the ship, Alek. They might take me back to London for trial."

"Have you broken any laws?"

She rolled her eyes at him. "About a dozen, you daft prince. The Admiralty might not want to make a fuss of it, but there's a chance they'll toss me into the brig. And if they do, we'll never see each other again."

Alek was silent for a moment, his eyes locked with hers. It was like one of his daft spells coming on, except his expression stayed dead serious.

She had to look away. "You should take Bovril with you. You were there when it hatched, and they won't let me keep a beastie in prison."

"You can escape," Alek said. "If I could manage to get off this ship, you certainly can!"

"Alek." She pointed at her knee. "It'll be days before I can walk properly, and weeks before I can climb."

"Oh." He sat down on the bed again carefully, staring at her injured leg. "I'm an idiot for forgetting."

"No." She smiled. "Well, aye. But not in a bad way. You're just . . ."

"A useless prince."

Deryn shook her head. Alek was a lot of things, but never useless.

"I've got it," he said. "I'll tell the captain that Mr. Tesla needs your help. He'll *have* to let you join me!"

"He'll ask for orders from London. It's not as though the *Manual of Aeronautics* has any chapters on girls dressed in trousers."

"But what if I . . . ," he began, then sighed.

She let out a dry laugh. "Barking *prince* Alek, always thinking you can fix everything."

"What's wrong with trying to fix things?"

"You always . . ." She shook her head. There was no point in dredging all this up. It would only make the boy angry—or worse, sad. "Nothing."

"Mr. Sharp," Alek said with a raised eyebrow. "Are you keeping secrets from me?"

"No secrets," Bovril said with a giggle.

"Barking stupid promises," Deryn groaned. Lying here in her cabin the last two days, countless mad notions had gone through her head. Was she meant to tell Alek *all* of them?

"*Mr.* Sharp?" Bovril prompted her.

Deryn gave the beastie a silencing glare, then turned to Alek.

"It's like this, Your Highness. The world fell apart after your parents died, and it's still falling apart. It must be awful for you, thinking about that every day. But I think you've got the two things muddled."

"What two things?"

"Your world, and everyone else's." Deryn reached out and took his hand. "You lost everything that night—your home, your family. You're not even a proper Clanker anymore. But stopping the war won't fix all that, Alek. Even if you and that boffin save the whole barking planet, you'll still need . . . something more."

"I have you," he said.

She swallowed, hoping he really meant that. "Even if they stuff me back into skirts?"

"Of course." He looked her up and down. "Though somehow I can't imagine that."

"Don't try, then."

They both glanced at Bovril, expecting it to weigh in. But the beastie only stared back at them, its large eyes glistening.

After a moment Alek said, "I have to stop this war, Deryn. It's all that's kept me going. Do you understand?"

She nodded. "Of course."

"But I'll do anything in my power to keep them from taking you away."

She took a shuddering breath, then let her eyes fall closed. "Promise?"

"Anything. As you said in Tokyo, we're meant to be together."

Deryn wanted to agree, but she'd promised him she wouldn't lie, and she wasn't certain whether that was true. If they were meant to *really* be together, why had they been born a prince and a commoner? And if they weren't, why did she feel this way inside?

But finally she nodded. Perhaps the daft prince's luck would hold and she wouldn't be hauled off to jail in London. And maybe it would be enough to stay by his side, an ally and a friend.

THIRTY-ONE

The East Coast of the United States had been in view all day, white beaches and salt-sheared trees, marshes and low green hills, a few small islands off the Carolinas. No delays for the last thousand miles, and the *Leviathan* was drawing near its goal. Deryn could hear the crew beginning to hustle about in the corridors. The sound made her heart sink.

Late tonight Eddie Malone would be at the offices of the *New York World*, handing in his story about Deryn Sharp, the brave airgirl who had fooled the British Air Service. By tomorrow her secret would be in the *World*, and by the next day it would be in every newspaper in America.

Deryn was exercising her knee, ignoring the buzzing bees, and readying herself to walk with the cane that lovely old Klopp had made for her. It was lathed from fabricated wood, but topped with a heavy Clankerish brass handle. She had no idea whether the captain would kick her off like a stowaway or throw her into the brig, but whatever happened, she didn't want to be helpless.

A knock came at the door.

It opened before Deryn could answer, and in strolled the lady boffin, her loris on her shoulder and Tazza in tow. The thylacine bounded over and buried its nuzzle in Deryn's palm.

"Good afternoon, Mr. Sharp."

"Afternoon, ma'am." Deryn lifted her cane into the air. "You'll have to forgive me for not standing."

"Not to worry. It looks as though Tazza misses you."

"Don't you miss me too, ma'am?"

Dr. Barlow sniffed. "What I miss is Tazza being walked at regular intervals. Mr. Newkirk has proven quite unreliable."

"Sorry to hear that, ma'am. But he's got my duties as well as his own," Deryn said, then frowned. There wasn't much point in bowing and scraping, now that her career was over. "Have you never thought of walking Tazza yourself?"

Dr. Barlow's eyes widened a bit. "What an odd suggestion."

"Mighty unsavory," her loris said.

"Poor beastie." Deryn stroked the thylacine's head.

"Well, send Mr. Newkirk round, and I'll tell him he's a bum-rag."

"Bum-rag," Bovril chuckled.

"Such *language*, Mr. Sharp!" Dr. Barlow exclaimed. "Are you sure you're feeling quite all right?"

Deryn stared down at her leg. Her uniform fit over the compress, but a lump was still visible. "The cut on my arm's fine, but Dr. Busk isn't sure about my knee."

"So he's told me." The lady boffin sat at Deryn's desk, snapping for Tazza to return to her. "If you've torn the ligaments behind the kneecap, your days of climbing the ratlines may well be over."

Deryn looked away, a sudden burning behind her eyes. Not that she would be let near any ratlines, once the officers knew she was a girl. But it still hurt to think that her ma and aunties could be right, after all. What if she *couldn't* be an airman anymore?

"Dr. Busk isn't sure about that yet, ma'am."

"No, he is not. But with misfortune may come opportunity."

"Pardon, ma'am?"

Dr. Barlow stood up again and began to inspect the cabin, sliding a white-gloved fingertip along the woodwork. "Over these past two months you have proven yourself useful, Mr. Sharp. You're quite handy in unpleasant situations, and most adept at improvisation. You even possess, when not brooding in your sickbed, a certain knack for diplomacy."

"Aye, I suppose."

"Let me ask, have you ever thought of serving the British Empire in a more illustrious capacity than scampering about on an airbeast tying knots?"

Deryn rolled her eyes. "It's a bit more than just tying knots, ma'am."

"Having seen your talents firsthand, I cannot disagree." The lady boffin turned to Deryn and smiled. "But if you accept my offer, you shall learn that *un*tying knots—figurative ones, of course—can be even more rewarding."

"Your offer, ma'am?"

"Am I so unclear?" the lady boffin asked. "I am offering you a position, Mr. Sharp. One outside the confines of the Air Service. Though I assure you, a certain amount of airship travel will be involved."

"A position, *Mr.* Sharp," her loris said, and Bovril made a low whistling noise.

Deryn leaned back into her pillows. Quite suddenly the buzz behind her kneecap had redoubled. "But what sort of position? You're the . . . head keeper of the London Zoo, aren't you?"

"Zookeeper, fah!" Dr. Barlow's beastie said.

"That is my title, Mr. Sharp. But were you under the

impression that our mission to Istanbul was zoological in nature?"

"Er, I suppose not, ma'am." It occurred to Deryn that she had no idea what Dr. Barlow's real position was, except that it involved ordering people about and acting superior. She was the great fabricator's granddaughter, of course, and had been able to requisition the *Leviathan* right in the middle of a barking war.

"Do you work for anyone in particular, ma'am? Like the Admiralty?"

"Those half-wits? I should think not. The Zoological Society of London is not a government agency, Mr. Sharp. It is, properly speaking, a scientific charity." Dr. Barlow sat down again, and began to stroke Tazza's head. "But zoology is the backbone of our empire, and so the Society has many members of high station. Collectively, we are a force to be reckoned with."

"Aye, I've noticed that." The lady boffin had practically run the ship, until Mr. Tesla had come aboard talking of superweapons. "But what sort of position would your Society have for *me*? I'm no boffin."

"Indeed not, but you seem a quick study. And there are times when my scientific work takes me into situations that are, as Mr. Rigby likes to say, quite *lively*." Dr. Barlow smiled. "At those times a resourceful personal assistant such as yourself might be useful."

"Oh?" Deryn narrowed her eyes. "How personal an assistant, ma'am?"

"You would hardly be my valet, Mr. Sharp." She swept her gaze about the cabin. "Though I see you are in need of one yourself."

Deryn rolled her eyes. It was barking hard keeping things tidy when you weren't allowed to stand up. But this position looked like a chance to escape prison— or worse, being sent back to Glasgow and stuffed into skirts.

"That sounds agreeable, ma'am. But . . ."

Dr. Barlow raised an eyebrow. "You have misgivings?"

"No, ma'am. But you may, after . . . You see, there's something you don't know about me."

"Do tell, Mr. Sharp."

"*Do* tell," her loris said. "*Mr.* Sharp."

Deryn closed her eyes, deciding to blazes with it all.

"I'm a girl."

When Deryn opened her eyes, the lady boffin was staring at her with no change of expression.

"Indeed," she said.

Deryn's mouth fell open. "You mean you . . . Did you barking *know*?"

"I had no idea at all. But I make it a policy never to appear surprised." Dr. Barlow sighed, staring out the window. "Though on this occasion it is proving rather more demanding than usual. A girl, you say? And you're quite certain?"

"Aye." Deryn shrugged. "Head to toe."

"Well, I must say this is extraordinary. And somewhat unexpected."

"*Mr.* Sharp," the loris on her shoulder said again, sounding quite smug.

Deryn found herself smirking a bit at the lady boffin's discomfort. It was rather pleasing, revealing a secret to such a know-it-all. It might not be so awful, seeing the surprise on all the faces of the crew. And what could the officers do to her, now that she had the lady boffin's protection?

"And why exactly have you perpetrated this hoax?"

"To fly, ma'am. And for the knots."

The lady boffin *hmph*ed. "Well, this *is* a new wrinkle, Mr. Sharp—or *Miss* Sharp, I suppose—but perhaps a useful one. The Society's efforts sometimes employ the art of disguise. Really, it's quite amazing that no one ever saw through your deception."

"Well, I'm afraid that's not the case." Deryn cleared her throat. "Count Volger did first, and then a lassie in Istanbul named Lilit. And more recently Alek. Oh, and Pancho Villa and his doctor, and finally that bum-rag reporter Eddie Malone."

The lady boffin's eyes were quite wide now. "Are you quite certain there aren't any more, young lady? Or am I the last person on this entire ship to know?"

"Well, that's just the problem, ma'am. Pretty soon the *World*—that is, Mr. Malone's newspaper—is going to know as well. He plans to tell them when we get to New York tonight."

"Well, that puts things into rather a tailspin." Dr. Barlow shook her head slowly. "I'm afraid I shall have to withdraw my offer."

Deryn sat up straighter. "What do you mean?"

"I mean, Miss Sharp, that you have attained some notoriety in certain circles. You helped foment a revolution in the Ottoman Empire. An ambitious effort, even by the standards of the London Zoological Society!" The lady boffin sighed. "But when the news of what you really are is made public, your celebrity will only heighten the scandal."

"Well, aye," Deryn said. "For a week or so."

"For some time, I'm afraid. Young lady, you have made a laughingstock of this ship and its officers. And you have picked a moment when all the eyes of the world are upon us. Think of what people will say of Captain Hobbes, not knowing that one of his own crewmen was a girl!"

"Oh." Deryn blinked. "There is that."

"And the shame won't end there, Miss Sharp. The Air Service is quite a new branch of the military forces, and the Admiralty . . . Well, *they* just gave you a medal!"

"But you said they were half-wits!"

"Very powerful half-wits, Miss Sharp, whom the Society cannot afford to antagonize." She shook her head. "But I'm sure that *someone* will be made happy by this revelation."

"You mean the suffragettes, ma'am?"

"No, I mean the Germans. What a boon to their propaganda efforts!" She stood. "I'm sorry, Miss Sharp, but I'm afraid this won't do at all."

Deryn swallowed, trying to come up with some sort of argument, but the crushing truth was that Dr. Barlow was right. Lying in bed these last two days, Deryn had thought only about what Malone's revelation would mean for herself, not for her captain and shipmates, much less the Air Service and the British Empire.

And worse, Alek hadn't thought about it either. Would he still want her in his life, once she was famous for humiliating her Service and her ship?

"Don't get me wrong, Miss Sharp, what you have done is quite brave. You are a credit to our gender, and you have my fullest admiration."

"Really?"

"Indeed." The lady boffin snapped for Tazza and opened the door. "And if you hadn't been caught, it would have been a pleasure working with you. Perhaps after this war is over, we can speak of this position again."

"Perhaps," said the loris on her shoulder. "*Miss* Sharp."

• THIRTY-TWO •

"There is still time to distance yourself from Tesla's madness."

Alek stared into the darkness outside his stateroom window. "Don't you think it's a bit late for that, Volger?"

"It is never too late to admit one's errors, even in front of a crowd."

Alek pulled on his dinner jacket and straightened it.

Sprinkled across the black waters below were at least a hundred small boats set out to greet the *Leviathan*, their navigation lights like shifting stars. Among them loomed a glittering cruise liner, her fog horn bellowing in the night. The low groan grew into a chorus as the other great ships in the harbor joined in.

Perched on Volger's desk, Bovril attempted to imitate the horns, but wound up sounding like a badly blown tuba.

Alek smiled. "But they're already singing our praises!"

"They are Americans," Volger said. "They toot their horns for anything."

Bovril went silent, pressing its nose against the window glass.

"Is that what I think it is?" Alek said, squinting into the darkness.

In the distance a towering human form was coming into view. She was as tall as the *Leviathan*, and her upheld torch glowed with both soft bioluminescence and a shimmering electrikal coil.

"The Statue of Liberty." Volger turned from the sight. "A few newsreels of you shaking hands with Tesla is one thing. But to stand beside him while he goes into raptures about this weapon seems unwise."

"You still don't think Goliath will work?"

"I spoke with Dr. Barlow this evening, and she says no." Volger's voice dropped. "But what if it *does* work, Alek? What if he uses it on a city?"

"I told you. He's promised not to attack Austria."

"So you'll happily preside over the destruction of Berlin? Or Munich?"

Alek shook his head. "I'm not presiding over anything. I'm helping to publicize Tesla's weapon so that he won't *have* to use it. The Germans will sue for peace when they realize what he can do. They aren't mad, you know."

"The kaiser's rule is absolute. He can be as mad as he likes. Your tie is crooked."

Alek sighed, adjusting his necktie in the reflection of the window glass. "You have a bad habit of listing everything that can possibly go wrong, Volger."

"I have always considered that a good habit."

Alek ignored this, staring at himself. It was refreshing to have proper clothes again. Mr. Hearst might have sabotaged the *Leviathan*, but at least he'd thrown a few decent dinner jackets into the bargain.

The floor shifted a bit beneath Alek's feet—the airship was turning north again. He leaned closer to the window and saw Manhattan ahead. A cluster of buildings erupted from the island's southern tip, some of them almost two hundred meters tall, as high as the steel towers of Berlin.

Alek imagined the dark sky above them bursting into flame, the buildings' glowing windows shattering, their metal frames twisting.

"Tesla will use his machine if he needs to, whether I stand with him or not."

"Exactly," Volger said. "So why not step aside? Is mass murder what you want to be remembered for, Your Serene Highness?"

"Of course not. But a chance of peace is more important to me than my reputation."

Volger let out a low hissing sigh. "Perhaps that's a good thing."

"What do you mean?"

"Dr. Barlow also mentioned Dylan to me—or rather, Deryn. It seems the doctor knows the girl's secret now."

"Deryn must have told her. The truth is coming out tomorrow at any rate, so it hardly matters now."

"Dr. Barlow seems to think it does. She says that the captain and this ship will be humiliated, the Admiralty outraged. And more important, your friend will become a point of German propaganda. The proud British Empire sending fifteen-year-old girls to fight their battles? Quite embarrassing."

"Deryn is hardly an embarrassment."

"They will make her into one. You would do well to keep your name out of the scandal. Tesla will thank you for it."

Alek set his jaw and didn't answer, watching the city draw nearer. From a thousand feet up he could see a grid of streets traced out in the glowing dots of electrikal gas lamps. The piers were thronging with people gathered to watch the great airship's approach.

Would everyone really turn on Deryn, once they knew? Perhaps the officers of the *Leviathan*, and of course the Admiralty. But surely lots of women would understand why she'd done it.

Of course, women couldn't vote.

The Klaxon rang in a long-short pattern, the signal for high-altitude docking. Volger pulled on his cavalry jacket, then held out an overcoat for Alek, gleaming dark sable from among Mr. Hearst's many gifts.

Alek didn't move, staring into Bovril's large eyes.

"Are you worried about Deryn?" Volger asked.

"Of course. And also . . ." He couldn't finish.

"This won't be pleasant for her. But if you insist on helping Tesla, it's best to keep your reputation intact for a bit longer."

Alek nodded, not saying the rest of what he'd realized. He and Volger were headed off into a whirlwind of diplomacy and publicity, while the *Leviathan* would be refueled at a proper airfield in New Jersey, leaving the country in only twenty-four hours. When would he see Deryn again?

They'd never said a proper good-bye. . . .

He closed his eyes, feeling the rumble of the engines, the faint tug of deceleration as the ship approached Manhattan.

"Let's go," he murmured; then he picked up Bovril and headed for the door.

"Might I have a few words, Your Highness?"

Alek turned. Miss Adela Rogers was dressed in a dark red winter coat; the fox around her shoulders was a fabricated pink. Its fur ruffled in the wind of the open cargo bay.

"A few more, you mean?" Alek asked. He had spent two hours with the woman the day before, recounting the *Leviathan*'s rescue of Tesla in Siberia. He'd borrowed from Deryn's version, of course, given that Alek had slept through the whole thing.

"Our interview was delightful." Miss Rogers stepped closer, her voice lowering. "But I forgot to ask you one thing. How do you feel about the danger you're in?"

Alek frowned. "Danger?"

Miss Rogers's gaze drifted over Alek's shoulder. Among the others waiting in the cargo bay were four of the ship's marines. They were armed with rifles and cutlasses, and one had a hydrogen sniffer on a leash.

"As you can see, the captain is concerned," she said. "There are German agents in New York, after all."

"There were more in Istanbul," Alek said. "Not to mention Austria. I've managed so far."

She scribbled in her notepad. "Mmm, quite brave."

"Quite," Bovril said. "He can be as mad as he likes."

"Are those critters' sentences getting longer?" Miss Rogers asked.

Alek shrugged, though it was true.

The gears of the cargo door growled into motion, and as it opened, the wind began to swirl, bringing in the salt smell of the harbor. Alek pulled his coat tighter, and Bovril shivered on his shoulder.

Through the widening door Alek saw the air jitney approaching. Four small hot-air balloons glowed beneath the passenger platform, and three vertical propellers thrust out from its sides. The jitney was big enough for no more than a dozen passengers. Alek and Miss Rogers were headed ashore tonight with Mr. Tesla, Count Volger, Eddie Malone, Dr. Busk, Captain Hobbes, and four marines. Dr. Barlow had announced that she did not wish to be photographed with Tesla, and was waiting until the *Leviathan* landed in New Jersey before she disembarked.

The jitney slowed to a halt ten meters away, and its gangplank began to unfold. The lifting propellers swayed a bit, their angles in lazy orbits, like juggler's plates spinning on sticks.

"I shall be glad to have my feet on solid ground," Miss Rogers said.

"I've been happy in the air," Alek replied, then saw her scribbling down his words, and resolved to remain silent.

The gangplank connected with the cargo bay with a *clunk*, and the riggers set to work binding it fast. Then, without ceremony or good-byes, the shore party hustled across to the jitney.

A moment later Alek was watching the *Leviathan* slip away.

The others crowded onto the far side of the platform, gawking at the Woolworth Building, the world's tallest, and the rest of Manhattan. But Alek stared back at the airship.

"Happy in the air," Bovril said.

Alek stroked its chin. "Sometimes you should be called the *obvious* loris."

As the beast had a chuckle at this, Alek felt the jitney lifting a bit beneath his feet, unbalanced by the scrum of passengers on the far side. The crew politely asked everyone to disperse their weight across the platform, and a moment later Alek found Eddie Malone at his side.

"Evening, Your Majesty. Nice and warm, thanks to these hot-air balloons, isn't it?"

Alek looked down. The burner of the balloon beneath him sent a ripple of heat up into the dark sky. Bovril was holding its hands out, like a soldier beside a campfire.

"Warm enough, Mr. Malone. But 'Your Majesty' is incorrect. 'Your Serene Highness' is proper. And if you're going to write about me, please remember that my last name isn't Ferdinand."

"It isn't?" The notebook was produced, its pages fluttering in the cold wind. "What is your last name, then?"

"Nobles don't have last names. Our titles define us."

"Well, that's one way to put it." A moment of scribbling later, the man spoke up again. "Perhaps you want to comment on Deryn Sharp?"

Alek hesitated. This was his chance to explain who

"ARRIVING IN MANHATTAN."

Deryn really was. He could tell Malone, and the world, about her bravery and skill, about *why* she'd taken to the air. But he saw Volger eyeing him from across the platform.

Deryn's scandal could only distract from Tesla's mission here in New York. And if he spoke on the matter, the headlines about her would only loom larger.

"I have no comment," Alek said.

"That seems a bit odd, considering how closely you two worked together in Istanbul."

Alek turned away from the reporter. He hated this, not helping tell her story, but no one's reputation was more important than peace. Or was that just a convenient excuse? A way to escape being caught up in an embarrassing revelation? At first he'd been so ashamed for not knowing who and what she really was. But there was no shame at all in being a friend of Deryn Sharp. Maybe he should forget Volger's warnings, and explain to Malone how he really felt about Deryn.

Alek swallowed. And how *did* he feel about her, exactly?

Up in the sky the *Leviathan* was moving away, now only a silhouette against the starry blackness. When would he see his best friend again?

Alek heard the growl of an engine, and dropped his gaze to the harbor. The jitney was descending quickly, heading toward the aero-piers at Manhattan's southern tip. Some sort of motorboat was skimming across the dark water, darting among the other bobbing lights.

"And from what I heard back in Pancho Villa's canyon," Malone went on, "you *sounded* like you already knew what she was. How long ago did you guess?"

Alek frowned. The motorboat below had turned hard, and was skimming directly toward the jitney now. A sudden flash sparked on its deck, and a cloud of smoke billowed out, hiding the boat for a moment.

"I think that's some sort of . . . ," Alek began, his voice fading as something climbed from the smoke, spilling flame behind it.

"Rocket," Bovril said, and crawled inside Alek's coat.

THIRTY-THREE

Alek spun about, but no one else was looking. Even Malone was staring into his notebook.

"There's a rocket," he said, not nearly loud enough. Then he found his voice and shouted, "We're under attack!"

Heads turned toward him, as slow as tortoises', but finally a crewman spotted the rocket climbing toward them. Shouts carried across the platform, and one of the lifting engines roared to life. The craft slewed to one side, Alek's boots skidding beneath him.

The rocket was almost upon them, hissing like a steam train. Alek threw himself down onto the platform deck, sheltering Bovril beneath his body, as the missile roared past.

An explosion cracked the air above him and flung tendrils of flame down upon the jitney. An ember the size of a pumpkin bounced across the deck, hissing and spilling smoke. It knocked down a crewman, then rolled off the platform and hit one of the hot-air balloons. The thin envelope full of superheated air burst into flame.

Alek's eyes were forced shut by the heat rolling up from below. He covered his face and peered out between gloved fingers. As the crew and passengers fled from the fire, the jitney rolled with their weight, dropping to one side. But a moment later the envelope was consumed, the fire having burnt itself into a ghost in seconds.

With only three balloons left, the jitney began to tip again, but now in the opposite direction—toward the corner with no lift. The passengers staggered back that way, then one fell and slid, and Alek saw in a flash how this would end. As their weight gathered on the damaged corner of the jitney, the tilt would increase until the craft flipped over.

Tesla had realized it too. "Grab on to something!" the man cried, taking hold of the platform rail. "Stay in this side!"

Lying beside Alek, Eddie Malone began to slide away, but Alek seized the man's hand. Around them other passengers were slipping; some managed to take hold of the rail, some spread their weight flat across the deck. Bovril mewled inside Alek's coat, and Malone's hand squeezed his hard. Captain Hobbes was shouting orders at the jitney's crew.

The craft began to gyrate, like a leaf falling through the air. Buildings spun past, alternating with empty sky. Would they fall into the freezing water? Or crash into Manhattan's steel and marble towers?

The fall seemed to take forever—the three remaining balloons were still full and functioning, and the jitney was not much heavier than the air around it. Alek saw Captain Hobbes at one of the lifting engines, trying to control the ship's descent.

Soon they were over solid ground. Buildings spun past on all sides, their lit windows streaking across Alek's view.

Then the jitney struck something solid, and the wooden deck beneath him split, hurling splinters into the air. The craft's underside shrieked, skidding sideways. Then came a crash like thunder, and a brick chimney shattered as the craft barreled through it. The captain had brought them down onto a large rooftop.

Brick fragments of the chimney scattered across the deck, but the jitney was still sliding. Ahead Alek saw a wireless aerial rushing at him. He covered his head, but the aerial bent away under the mass of the jitney. The groan of the skid continued for another few seconds, then ended with another crash. The ruined craft had finally run into something heavy enough to stop it.

Alek looked up. A short wooden tower loomed over

the jitney's deck. The bottom of the tower's struts were splintered, and it leaned precariously over him, but it didn't fall.

"Fire!" someone yelled.

Another of the balloons had burst into flame. The fuel in its burner was spilling from the jitney's deck, carrying the fire onto the rooftop. The marines and Captain Hobbes were beating the flames, but the blaze simply leapt onto their jackets, borne by the fuel.

"That's a water tower!" Malone pointed at the structure the jitney had half knocked over in its crash.

Alek looked about. The jitney carried no tools that he could see, but one of the lifting propellers had broken into pieces. He hefted one of the blades. It was a meter long and wasn't sharp, but it was heavy. Wielding it like an axe, Alek began to hack at the side of the water tower. The heat of the flames grew worse behind him.

The tower began to split beneath his blows. The wood was old and rotten, the nails rusted, and soon the planks were cracking open.

But no water rushed from the gap.

Malone stayed Alek's hand, then climbed up and looked in.

"It's empty, dammit!"

Alek groaned, turning back to the fire. It had reached the wooden deck of the jitney, and the *Leviathan*'s crewmen were retreating from the blaze.

"Your Highness!" the captain called. "This way! There's a fire escape!"

Alek blinked. They couldn't leave the building to burn, could they?

"Come on, Your Majesty!" Malone said, grabbing his arm.

Then Alek felt a drop of water hit his face, and he

reached up and touched a finger to it. More drops fell, and for a moment he thought that it was a perfect and improbable rain spilling from a clear sky.

But then Alek's nose caught the familiar scent. . . .

"Clart," said Bovril from inside his coat.

"Indeed." Alek breathed in the effluence of a hundred interlocked species, all of it mixed in the gut of a living airship. He shielded his eyes and looked up to see the underside of the *Leviathan* a hundred meters above, its ballast tubes swelling. The downpour built around him, its roar joined by the plaintive hissing of the blaze.

Someone aboard must have been looking back, watching the jitney disappear into a tiny flicker against the city lights. Someone had seen the attack and had told the bridge crew to come about.

"*Mr.* Sharp," said Bovril, then had a chuckle.

The heat of the fire was gone now, and Alek found himself soaking wet in a cold autumn wind. He cast aside the ruined sable coat, and Bovril scampered up onto his shoulder. The downpour was fading quickly now, and the *Leviathan* was growing smaller overhead. With its ballast spilled, it was climbing rapidly into the air, safe from any more rocket attacks.

"Two birds with one stone," Alek murmured, then looked about the roof. Dr. Busk was tending to Mr. Tesla and one of the jitney crewmen, but no one seemed seriously hurt. He heard the siren of a fire brigade from the streets below.

"Look over here, Your Majesty!" Eddie Malone was backing up, his free hand shielding his camera from the last of the falling ballast. He was taking a photograph of the crashed jitney, with Alek as the star.

It was pointless scowling, Alek supposed. He dutifully set his jaw. The camera flashed, and he was blinking away spots. When he could see again, he noticed how close Malone was to the edge of the roof.

An odd realization struck Alek. As the jitney had been crashing, he'd saved Malone from falling. If Alek hadn't seen him, or their fingers had slipped, the man might have slid to his doom. Then Deryn's secret would be safe again.

But Alek *had* saved Malone, just as he'd failed to say a word in her defense. It was as though he couldn't stop betraying her.

Then, quite suddenly, a simple and perfect idea entered his mind. Not letting himself think twice, Alek crossed the slick, broken deck of the jitney, until he was close enough to the reporter to speak softly. The camera flashed again.

"I saved your life during the crash," Alek said. "Didn't I, Mr. Malone?"

The man thought for a second, then nodded. "I suppose you did. Thanks for that!"

"You're welcome. Would you consider that payment for, say, *not* publishing what you know about Deryn?"

Malone laughed. "Not likely, Your Majesty."

"I didn't think so." Alek smiled, putting his hand on the man's shoulder. "Luckily, I have a backup plan."

THIRTY-FOUR

The nightmare had come again.

It was the same as always—the heat, the smell of propane, the awful crackle of ropes snapping. Then falling to the ground, pushed from the gondola by her da, and watching him soar away, burning in midair.

Deryn had known the dream was coming from the moment she'd closed her eyes. After all, she'd been watching as the rocket had climbed up from the dark water and struck the jitney, setting one of its flimsy balloons alight. The dreadful image hadn't left her mind even when the messenger eagle had arrived half an hour later, carrying the news that all hands had survived.

So she'd lain there all night, drifting in and out of conflagrations.

As the sun rose at last, Deryn flung the covers from

herself. It was no use pretending to sleep. Today was going to be its own nightmare.

"All hands" meant Eddie Malone was still alive. He'd no doubt made it to the offices of the *World* with his airgirl story in hand. The *Leviathan* was docked only forty miles from New York City. Once the British consulate spotted the story, the news would make its way here by the fastest messenger eagle they could find.

At least the captain was off the ship. Deryn doubted that the first officer would have the nerve to toss her into the brig without orders.

Still, the looks on her shipmates' faces would be bad enough.

Twisted knee or not, Deryn decided to wear a decent uniform for when the officers came calling. She had just dressed when a knock came at her door.

She stood there, staring out the window. Was this it, then? The end of everything she'd worked for?

"Come in," she said softly. But it was only the lady boffin, her loris, and Tazza.

"Good morning, Mr. Sharp."

Deryn didn't answer, just stuck out her hand for Tazza to nuzzle.

Dr. Barlow frowned. "Are you unwell, Mr. Sharp? You look a bit peaked."

"It's just . . . I had a bad night's sleep."

"Poor dear. Our welcome to New York was unsettling, wasn't it? But at least we had a bit of luck."

"Aye, ma'am," Deryn sighed. "Of course, if that bum-rag Eddie Malone had been a bit less lucky, I might be happier."

"Ah, I see." Dr. Barlow pulled out the chair from Deryn's desk and sat. "You find this morning's news dismaying."

Deryn swallowed. "News?"

"Of course. The whole ship is abuzz with the story." Smiling, the lady boffin produced a neatly folded newspaper from her handbag.

"So it's—it's already . . . ," Deryn sputtered. "And the officers sent *you?*"

"No one sent anyone, young man." Dr. Barlow handed the paper over.

Deryn spread it out, her heart thudding in her chest, the bees inside her kneecap awake and angry. In the middle of the front page was a photograph of Alek looking sodden before the wrecked sky jitney, and below that a huge headline said:

SECRET HEIR TO AUSTRIA'S THRONE SURVIVES ROCKET ATTACK

Little wonder that the attempt on Alek's life was the main story. And as her eyes traveled across the page, Deryn

The World.

"*Circulation Books Open to All.*" "*Circulation Books Open to All.*"

TTACK IN THE CITY

NEW YORK, SATURDAY, November 2, 1914.

ERVENTION D AT IN THE AMERICA PLEA HE MEXICANS

n Out at Washington
Note Was Prompted
Friendly and Unselfish
to Save a Sister Re-
from Present Distress
timate Destruction—
Wanted in Ten Days.

N AND CANNON
D TO BROWNSVILLE.

ants to "Strengthen
rison," and the War

NAL PARADE.

o Make Trip Aboard
ship Olympia.

nd Secretary Daniels
es upon the arrival of
xposition city. It is
l Dewey and Admiral
eak. The entire bri-
en will be taken to
the occasion. This
the place of their an-

the Olympia will be
 lly constructed wharf
Ibition throughout the
Behind them will be
ypical modern naval
ht of the New York
, a battleship of the
nnesota type, an ar-
he Tennessee or Mon-
the three scout cruis-

Chancellor, Amba
Agent and Ban
in Vast Scheme
ments Obtained
Fatherland Finan
Expenses Paid,
Press Associatio
Control News of

COST PUT AT $2,000,
BERNSTORF

Big Arms Plant and P
Outwardly Dicker
Owned by Germany
liver Munitions Sept
Carbolic Acid Taken
Plan to Buy Wrigl
Poisoned Gas Supp
Strikes in Munitions

OBREGON LEADS REB

Gen. Obregon,
German financiers
$500,000 to the bord
leads the revolt. If
overthrown Obrego
sume the presidency

WIFE AND GIRL FIN HIM SLAIN IN

John Hildenbrandt Blac
Then Shot, in His Apar
in Fifth Avenue.

John Hildenbrandt, a w
tired business man and
estate owner, was blackjack
before 11 o'clock last nigh
known man as he lay on t
No. 1446 Fifth Avenue, and
shot to death.

The murdered man's son,
of the Fifth Avenue Busine
Association, walked into
One Hundred and Tw
Street Station just after
and was complaining (acqu
out, peddlers in the nei
when the Lieutenant's
name. "The officer listened
sort of the murder

SECRET HEIR TO AUSTRIA'S THRONE SURVIVES ROCKET ATTACK

Diplomatic Revelation Immediately Compromised by Clandestine Agents — Act of War

New York November 2.— With the United States
formally neutral in this great war across the sea, foreign

"FRONT PAGE."

found articles asking whether German agents had been involved, asking whether they'd also meant to kill Nikola Tesla, and about an election for the city's mayor.

There was, however, not a single word on the subject of Deryn Sharp.

She flipped through the next few pages, finding photographs of the *Leviathan* over Tokyo, the airship's encounter with Pancho Villa, and the German ambassador denouncing the great inventor's threats against the Clanker Powers. There was even a somewhat mad allegorical illustration of Tesla taming the Darwinist and Clanker Powers with electricity.

But still no mad airgirl.

Deryn groaned. "Malone's just *waiting*, isn't he?"

"I think you're missing the point, young man. The first headline says it all."

Deryn turned back to the front page, and stared.

"'The Secret Heir to Austria's Throne,'" she murmured, the words finally sinking in. "But how did Eddie Malone find out about the pope's letter?"

Dr. Barlow tutted. "The pope's letter? Hah! I suspected you knew about all this!"

"Aye, ma'am. Alek told me back in Istanbul."

"Indeed. One might ask if *everyone* on this ship has a secret identity?"

"I hope not, ma'am. It's quite a bother, you know."

Deryn shook her head. "But why would he tell that . . ."

"That bum-rag," supplied the lady boffin's loris politely.

Then, all in a flash, Deryn understood. Alek had made another trade. Just like in Istanbul, when Malone had been about to reveal the revolution's plans, and Alek had agreed to tell his life story in exchange for the man's keeping silent.

But this time he'd given up his secrets for *her*.

"Oh," Deryn said softly.

"'Oh,' indeed," the lady boffin said. "That *was* rather slow, Mr. Sharp. Are you sure you didn't bump your head along with your knee?"

Deryn looked up from the newspaper. "Why are you calling me Mr. Sharp?"

"Because you would appear to be the midshipman of that name. And given *this*"—Dr. Barlow tapped the newspaper—"no one is likely to believe otherwise. Now please get ready. We shall be traveling within the hour."

"Traveling, ma'am?"

"To New York City. The Serbian consulate is giving a party for Mr. Tesla and Prince Aleksandar this afternoon. A formal uniform is required, of course. I see you've managed to dress yourself."

"Aye. But why are you dragging *me* along?"

"Mr. Sharp, you apparently have the ear—perhaps even the *affections*, though I shudder to think it—of the legal heir to the throne of Austria-Hungary." Dr. Barlow snapped for Tazza. "As long as your little skeleton remains in the closet, the Zoological Society of London shall have *many* uses for you. Now get ready, Mr. Sharp."

"*Mr.* Sharp," her loris said.

The ride across the Hudson River was splendid—the Statue of Liberty standing tall to the south, the towering skyscrapers of Manhattan ahead. Even the ferry's engine smoke pouring out across the blue sky looked rather grand. Deryn had grown used to Clanker engines over the last three months, she supposed, just as Alek had become a bit of a Darwinist. The rumble of the motors through her body felt almost natural now, and seemed to soothe her injured knee.

She and Dr. Barlow—and their marine escort—were met by an armored walker at the ferry docks. It was smaller than a proper war machine, nimble enough for the crowded streets of New York, but definitely bulletproof. After the attack last night, no one from the *Leviathan* would be venturing out unprotected. Deryn's rigging knife waited in a sheath inside her jacket, and the walking cane that Klopp had made for her was topped with a brass ball the size of an empress plum.

She might be dodgy in one leg, but Deryn reckoned she still had a bit of fight left.

The walker made its way through teeming crowds and beneath elevated trains. As they traveled north, the buildings grew shorter and were more like the row houses of London than skyscrapers. The air was clearer here than in Istanbul, the city driven more by electricity than steam, thanks to the influence of Tesla and the other great American inventor, Mr. Thomas Edison.

At last the walker reached the Serbian consulate, a large and solemn stone building with a line of policemen stretched along the footpath outside.

"Blisters. They look ready for trouble." Deryn turned from the small windows. "But the Germans wouldn't be daft enough to start a fight in the middle of Manhattan, would they?"

"The Germans will test President Wilson's patience, I'm sure," the lady boffin answered. "But the country is divided. There may have been hard words for Germany in the *New York World* this morning, but Mr. Hearst's papers called the attack the work of anarchists, not Clankers."

"Hmph," Deryn said. "Maybe that bum-rag really *is* a German agent."

"Mr. Hearst certainly dislikes the British." The walker lumbered to a halt, and Dr. Barlow began to straighten herself. "And the Germans know that one stray rocket won't drag America into war."

Deryn frowned. "Ma'am, do you reckon the Germans

were after Alek? Or are they more worried about Mr. Tesla?"

"Last night I'd guess they wanted Tesla." Dr. Barlow sighed. "But after reading this morning's papers, their priorities may shift."

Within the consulate walls it was easy to forget the armed policemen outside. White-gloved butlers in velvet tails took the lady boffin's hat and traveling coat, and the strains of dance music echoed from the marble walls. At a short staircase past the entryway, Dr. Barlow kindly took Deryn's arm, lifting a bit of weight off her bad knee.

The beastie on Deryn's wound had done its work quickly, and she could walk without limping now, but she was still glad for her cane. The sounds of voices and music grew as a butler guided them through the consulate to a large and crowded ballroom.

The party was in full swing. Half the gentlemen were in military uniforms, the other half in morning dress— striped trousers and tailcoats. The ladies wore soft pastels, a few hemlines rising to the daring height of midcalf. Deryn's aunties would have been scandalized, but perhaps it was only another sign that American women were changing fast.

Of course, that all mattered less to Deryn now that her secret was safe again. She wouldn't be staying here in

America, but heading off with Dr. Barlow to work for her mysterious Society. Deryn had been so relieved this morning that it had taken all day for that simple fact to sink in—when the *Leviathan* departed for London tonight, she would be leaving Alek behind.

Just as the thought struck her, there he was across the ballroom, with Bovril on his shoulder, standing beside Tesla in a group of fawning civilians.

"Pardon me, ma'am."

Dr. Barlow followed Deryn's gaze. "Ah, yes, of course. But do be . . . diplomatic, Mr. Sharp."

"Begging your pardon, ma'am," Deryn said. "But I've been *diplomatic* enough to fool you these last three months."

"Gloating is unchivalrous, young man."

Deryn only snorted at that, and made her way across the room. She was soon within earshot of Tesla, who was expounding about the commercial potential of Goliath— how he could use it not just to destroy cities, but to broadcast moving pictures and free power to the whole world.

She hovered at the edge of the circle of rapt listeners until she caught Bovril's eye. The beastie murmured something into Alek's ear, and soon the boy was easing himself away from Mr. Tesla, who hardly noticed.

A moment later they were alone together in a corner.

"Deryn Sharp," Bovril said softly.

"Aye, beastie." She looked into Alek's eyes as she stroked the loris's head. "Thank you."

Alek wore the same soft smile he always did when he was rather proud of something. "I promised to protect your secret, didn't I?"

"Aye, by *lying*. Not by telling the barking truth!'

"Well, I couldn't let you be disgraced. You're the best soldier I know."

Deryn turned away. There was so much she wanted to tell Alek, but it was all too complicated and unsoldierly to say here.

She began with, "Volger must be a bit angry with you."

"He's been oddly calm about it." Alek's gaze drifted over Deryn's shoulder, but she didn't turn to look. "In fact, he's at work charming the French ambassador as we speak. We'll need their recognition if I'm ever to take the throne."

"Hang the barking throne. I'm just glad you're not dead!"

Alek's eyes came back to her. "As am I."

"Sorry to be snappy," she mumbled. "I couldn't sleep last night."

"It was almost like your father's accident, wasn't it?" He displayed his hands. "But I emerged without a scratch. Maybe the curse is broken. Providence."

"Aye, there's no denying you've got a ruinous case of

good luck." She looked away. "But now that I'm Midshipman Dylan Sharp again, I'll have to leave with the *Leviathan*. Our twenty-four hours is up tonight."

"Ah, I'd forgotten that this is still a neutral port." Alek's stare faltered, as if he'd only just realized that by protecting her secret he'd sent her away. "Not much chance of them kicking you off now, is there?"

"No." She looked around at all the people in their fancy clothes. No one was watching her and Alek, but it still seemed wrong to say good-bye in a crowd.

"You could still . . ." He cleared his throat. "What if you stayed anyway?"

"What? You mean jump ship?"

"Why not? Sooner or later they're going to find out what you are, Deryn. And now that your secret's safe, you can join us without a scandal."

"Desertion is worse than a scandal, Alek. I can't abandon my shipmates."

"But if they knew what you were, they'd abandon *you*."

She stared at him for a long moment, then shrugged. He was right enough, but that wasn't what mattered. "My country's at war, and I'm no deserter."

"You can help your country by *ending* the war. Stay with me, Deryn."

She shook her head, unable to speak. She wanted to stay, of course, but not for any noble reasons. However awful this war might be, she wasn't guided by anything so grand as making peace. Being steered by providence was for barking *princes*, not common soldiers.

And what Deryn wanted was out of reach, whether she stayed here or went ten thousand miles away.

Alek couldn't read her thoughts, of course. He straightened and said in a small voice, "Sorry. That was foolish of me. We both have our duty. In fact, Mr. Tesla is talking to some very rich men over there. We'll need their money to make improvements to Goliath."

"You should go back and impress them with your Latin, then."

"The faster this war is over, the quicker we can . . ." His voice faded.

"See each other again, aye."

Alek clicked his heels. "Good-bye, Deryn Sharp."

"Good-bye, Aleksandar of Hohenberg." She felt a hard spot growing in her throat. This was really happening. They'd be apart for years now, and all she could think to say was, "You're not going to get soppy and kiss my hand, are you?"

"I wouldn't dream of it." Alek's bow turned into a slow step backward, as if he were trying to leave but couldn't. Then his gaze went past her, and he smiled with relief. "In any case, there's someone else who wants a moment with you."

Deryn closed her eyes. "Please don't tell me it's that bum-rag Malone."

"Not at all," Alek said. "It's the ambassador of the Ottoman Republic and his beautiful young assistant."

"The who and his what?" Deryn said as she turned around.

Standing before her were Lilit and the Kizlar Agha.

"OLD ALLIES."

THIRTY-FIVE

Lilit was the daughter of Zaven, the revolutionary who had befriended Alek and Deryn in Istanbul. The Kizlar Agha, on the other hand, had been the sultan's personal counselor. Zaven had been killed fighting for the revolution, and the sultan's government overthrown.

So, what were these two enemies doing here in New York . . . *together*?

"Mr. Sharp!" Lilit threw her arms around Deryn, hugging her tight.

For a moment Deryn feared the girl would kiss her, as she had the last time they'd laid eyes on each other. But when Lilit pulled away, she only flashed a knowing smile.

"Ah, the airsick airman," the Kizlar Agha said, stepping forward to shake Deryn's hand. He was dressed in formal evening clothes, a far cry from his Ottoman uniform. But the mechanical recording owl still sat on his shoulder, its clockwork spinning. "Pleasure to see you again."

"Aye, and you, too! Both of you." Deryn shook her head. "A bit unexpected, though."

"Unexpected for all of us, I think," Lilit said, watching Alek making his way back to Tesla's group. Deryn forced herself not to do the same.

Maybe the war really would end soon, and they could see each other again. But for the moment, thinking about Alek would only make her life more complicated, painful, and likely to fall apart.

"I thought you'd be busy ruling the Ottoman Republic," Deryn said to Lilit.

"So did I." The girl swore in unladylike fashion. "But the Committee says I'm more suited to rebelling than to governing. So they've sent me as far away as possible."

"Hardly a punishment, though," the Kizlar Agha said with a smile. "At least I hope not, as I am here too."

"Did Alek say you were the ambassador, sir?" Deryn asked.

The man straightened. "Ambassador of the Ottoman Republic to the United States of America. A rather long title to reward a tiny favor."

"Not so tiny, sir," Deryn said, bowing. On the night of the Ottoman Revolution, the Kizlar Agha had spirited away the sultan in his airyacht—kidnapping his own sovereign.

Thanks to that, the rebellion had ended in a single night. "I reckon you saved a few thousand lives."

"I simply did my job and protected the sultan. He lives happily in Persia now."

Lilit snorted. "He plots happily against the republic, you mean. His spies are everywhere!"

"He's not the only one," Deryn said. "As we found out last night."

"Indeed." The Kizlar Agha reached up to switch off the mechanical recording owl; the tiny wheels whirring within halted. His voice became a murmur. "As you may remember, Mr. Sharp, the kaiser was a close friend of my former sultan. I still have many contacts among the Germans."

Lilit stepped closer. "Recently we learned certain secrets from them. Secrets that the government of the republic can't pass on to the British. Not officially."

"But unofficially?" Deryn asked.

"As long as no one ever finds out where they came from . . ." The Kizlar Agha looked about the room. "Perhaps you two should take a walk and catch up on old times. Relive the splendor of the revolution!"

"An excellent idea." Lilit took Deryn by the shoulder.

"I shouldn't leave without telling Dr. Barlow."

"It's not a good idea to make a fuss," Lilit said softly. "We'll be back within the hour. And I promise, what I have to tell you is worth a bit of bad manners."

☉   ☉   ☉

Escaping unnoticed wasn't difficult. Dr. Barlow had found a group of bowler-hatted boffins to chat with, and Lilit seemed to know her way around the consulate. She led Deryn through the kitchens and out a back door, where a pair of policemen looked a bit surprised to see them, but apparently weren't under orders to keep anyone from leaving.

As they walked along the asphalt streets of Manhattan, Deryn began to feel her knee. It hadn't hurt all day, but the autumn chill and Lilit's quick pace had started it buzzing again. When Deryn shifted more weight onto her cane, Lilit raised an eyebrow.

"That isn't just for show?"

"I had a dodgy landing on glider wings. We probably shouldn't walk so fast."

"Of course." Lilit slowed a squick. "But can you still fight?"

Deryn snorted. "You haven't changed much, have you?"

"The world hasn't changed." Lilit shifted her daringly cut dress to reveal a tiny Mauser pistol gartered to her leg. "I wish you weren't in that Air Service uniform. It's a bit conspicuous."

Deryn looked about. The streets were full of bustling people, steam trams, and pushcarts. She'd heard snatches of several languages as they'd walked, and had even seen a few shop signs in German.

She shrugged. "I'm an airman. This is my uniform."

"I preferred you in Turkish clothes," Lilit said. "Perhaps we should get off the street and into someplace dark. Fancy a moving-picture show?"

"Aye, I would," Deryn said. She'd been curious about the whole business after Alek had become so enthralled. "Is there a cinema about?"

Lilit smiled. "In New York City? Yes, a few."

They took the next right turn, and a block away Deryn found herself looking up at a huge sign. It was covered in small electric lights that flicked on and off in sequence, as if wee beasties were skittering across it. In the center, giant letters spelled out EMBASSY CINEMA—NEWSREELS ALL DAY.

As they approached the ticket booth, Deryn's hands went to her pockets, but of course she hadn't a single coin.

"Sorry, Lilit, but I've got no American money."

"Well, you did risk your life fighting for the revolution," the girl said, producing a folded bill from a hidden pocket. "I suppose the Ottoman Republic can buy you a movie ticket."

The cinema was in most ways like an ordinary theater, with a few hundred seats spread out before a wide proscenium arch. But instead of a stage, a silvery white rectangle faced the audience. It was still late afternoon, and only a handful of people were present. As Deryn and Lilit made their way to seats near the back, the gaslights began to dim.

"Why exactly are we sneaking about?" Deryn asked once they were settled. "Are you afraid of making the Germans angry?"

"The Ottoman people have enjoyed the kaiser's generosity for a long time. We still need his engineers to make our machines work."

"Aye, of course." Every bit of Istanbul that Deryn had seen was wrapped in steam pipes and other mechanical contraptions.

"The Germans are desperate for more allies." Lilit leaned closer. "Austria-Hungary is falling to pieces. A few weeks ago they repulsed a Russian attack, but the fighting bears only scattered into the woods. And the creatures still have to eat."

Deryn swallowed, remembering the starving bears in Siberia. In a populated countryside the beasties would be much worse. It would be like living in some horrid old fairy tale, with every forest full of monsters.

Lilit gave a shrug. "So we pretend to consider joining the Clankers. A profitable ruse, so far."

A sudden clattering came from behind them, and

Deryn glanced back. Behind the audience a large machine with a single eye was sputtering and spinning. Light erupted from it to spill across the screen.

At first it was shadowy and blurred, just as Alek had said. But in a few moments Deryn's eyes adjusted, and a smoky auditorium appeared before her, two ghostly pale boxers in the ring cheered on by a silent crowd.

Lilit was settled back into her seat, her eyes wide and glittering. "It's not just Austria's weakness that has the Germans worried. They're convinced that Goliath will work."

"Aye. You should have seen what it did in Siberia. Not a tree left standing for *miles*."

"I've seen it. Everyone has." Lilit gestured at the screen. "Mr. Tesla was filming in Siberia, you know. The first of his newsreels appeared two weeks ago. We may see one today."

"Aye, he almost crashed our ship!" Deryn cried. "Bringing aboard all his cameras and scientific equipment."

But perhaps it made sense now. As Alek kept saying, the whole point of a weapon like Goliath was to scare everyone so much that you never had to use it.

Lilit was watching the boxing now, her shoulders twitching a bit, as if she were throwing the punches herself. But she went on talking.

"Last week the ambassador asked his German friends, 'How can we side with you now? We don't want Istanbul going up in a ball of flame.' They told him not to worry. They have plans for Mr. Tesla."

"Aye, that rocket attack."

"That was just a warning." Lilit swept her gaze across the audience. Two school-age girls sat a few rows away, but there was no one else within earshot. "And if Tesla doesn't heed it, they intend to destroy Goliath once and for all. With an invasion if necessary."

"An invasion! Right here? Won't that drag the Americans into the war?"

"An enemy across the ocean is better than their cities being leveled." Lilit's voice sank to a whisper. "A *Wasserwanderer* is on its way. That's all we know."

"A water-walker?" Deryn said.

"The ambassador thinks it's some sort of U-boat, but amphibious."

Deryn frowned. She'd never heard the word "amphibious" applied to a machine before, but it had a certain logic. Goliath was on an island near New York City—within a short stroll of the sea, Mr. Tesla always said.

Tesla might think to guard himself against saboteurs, but an armored walker popping out of the water?

"It will attack without warning one night," Lilit said.

"Then slip away into the ocean again, leaving only wreck-age and a mystery. The Americans might never realize what happened."

"Have you warned Tesla?"

Lilit shook her head. "He'd only blab to the press about it. He can't afford a private army, after all. And telling the Americans is pointless. They won't send a battleship to protect one man's property against a rumor. Especially when that man wants to wage war like some sort of demi-god!"

Deryn nodded. Some of the newspapers were already questioning whether Tesla should be allowed to wield such power. After all, if Goliath worked the way he claimed, he could become ruler of the world with the flick of a switch.

"So you want us to help?"

"You'll be helping yourself." Lilit turned from the screen. The boxing show had sputtered to a halt, and while the projector was being reloaded, the two nearby girls began to chatter about boys. "The *Leviathan* is powerful enough to stop a walker, and stealthy enough to lay in wait while Tesla completes his tests. And may I remind you, Mr. Sharp, that his success is entirely in British interests."

"Aye, true."

"Can you deliver this message without revealing who gave it to you?"

Deryn nodded. Only the lady boffin had to know. Now that Tesla was off the ship, she would have free rein to order people about again.

"I knew I could count on you." Lilit smiled. "You're still in love with Alek, aren't you?"

Deryn opened her mouth, but behind her the projector began sputtering again, filling the cinema with flickering light. She cleared her throat, her mouth too dry to speak.

"He seems to have grown up a bit," Lilit said. "Now that he's got a purpose in life."

Deryn found her voice. "Aye. He's convinced himself that he's destined to end the war. It's all part of a plan."

"Ah. So he's forgotten the most important rule of warfare."

"Which is . . ."

"That nothing *ever* goes to plan. But he finally knows your secret, right?"

Deryn took a sharp breath. She'd forgotten how annoyingly perspicacious Lilit could be. "Aye. It's made things a bit tricky between us."

"It shouldn't. Now you can tell him what you want."

"Aye, but to do that *I'd* have to know what I want," Deryn said.

Part of her wished more than anything to remain here in America with Alek, but that meant throwing away her career. She could take up the lady boffin's offer of working for the London Zoological Society, or even stay in the Air Service, but there would always be the danger of being found out and losing everything.

It was all a great barking mess.

She turned from Lilit's gaze and stared up as the next newsreel began. . . .

And there it was before her, the *Leviathan* soaring over a hilly expanse of desert, the image muddy and colorless on the screen, but vibrant in her memory. The point of view banked into a turn, and Deryn realized that there'd been cameras aboard General Villa's manta ships.

Then she was seeing the *Leviathan* from above, the camera peeking over a steep cliff as the airship descended into Pancho Villa's canyon. Crewmen and beasties scurried across the topside like bugs, the steel talons of the ship's ring of strafing hawks glittering in the sun.

Suddenly a winged figure rose into view, an airman staring wide-eyed into the camera. Deryn blinked, not quite believing—it was her own face up there on the screen.

The image was replaced by a sign . . . THE BRAVE AIRMAN TESTS HIS WINGS!

"*Tests* his wings?" she said aloud. As if she'd been lark-
ing about instead of preventing disaster! Giggles came
from the pair of girls nearby as the sign disappeared. They
were pointing up at her on the screen.

"They seem to think you make a dashing boy," Lilit
said. "Quite right too. When do you leave?"

"Our twenty-four hours will be up tonight."

"Too bad. And Alek's staying, isn't he?"

"Aye. He works for Tesla now."

"Oh, poor Dylan." The flickering screen showed Alek
now, standing face-to-face with Pancho Villa's massive
fighting bulls. "But Dylan isn't your real name, is it?"

Deryn shook her head but supplied nothing more.
Lilit seemed to have guessed everything else about her;
she might as well figure out the rest on her own.

"Do you want to stay a man forever?"

"It doesn't seem possible. Too many people know
already." Deryn looked at the schoolgirls, who were unes-
corted and didn't seem ashamed about it. "Though maybe
I don't have to. Women can ride in balloons here, and they
can pilot walkers. Dr. Barlow says that British women will
get the vote, once the war is over."

"Fah. The Committee promised the same thing,
back when we were rebels." Lilit shook her head. "But
now that we're in power, there seems to be no rush.

And when I complained, I was sent five thousand miles away."

"Aye, but I'm glad you're here," Deryn said softly.

She'd never talked about Alek aloud before, not to anyone. That was the problem with leading a secret life. The whole unsoldierly business of wanting him had all taken place between her own ears, except for that one brief moment on the topside.

"I kissed him once," she whispered.

"Well done. What did he do?"

"Um . . ." Deryn sighed. "He woke up."

"Woke up? Had you snuck into his cabin, Mr. Sharp?"

"No! He'd fallen and knocked his daft head. It was a medical emergency!"

Lilit snorted out a laugh, and Deryn turned from her to stare glumly at the screen. Maybe she should just confess to the world what she was. Then she could stop having secrets forever.

But the reason why she couldn't was right in front of her, written in flickering light. The air was the air, and every minute aboard the *Leviathan* was worth a lifetime of lies.

"Do you love him?"

Deryn swallowed, then pointed at the screen. "He makes me feel like that. Like flying."

"Then, you have to tell him."

"I told you, I kissed him!"

"It's hardly the same. I kissed *you*, after all. That wasn't love, Mr. Sharp."

"Aye, and what exactly was it?"

"Curiosity." Lilit smiled. "And as I said, you're quite a dashing boy."

"But I'm pretty sure Alek doesn't *want* a dashing boy!"

"You can't be sure until you ask."

Deryn shook her head. "You were raised to throw bombs. I wasn't."

"Were you raised to wear trousers and be a soldier?"

"Maybe not. But those are both dead easy compared to this!" One of the schoolgirls glared back at them, and Deryn lowered her voice. "At any rate it doesn't matter what he wants. He's the heir to the Austrian throne, and I'm a commoner."

"That throne may not exist once this war is over."

"Well, that's cheery."

"That's war." Lilit pulled out a pocket watch and read it in the jittering light from the screen. "We should get back."

Deryn nodded, but as she followed Lilit up the aisle, she took one last glance over her shoulder. The *Leviathan* was soaring again across the desert, its engines repaired.

She promised herself then to make everything clear,

the very next time she was alone with Alek. After all, she'd made a solemn vow never to keep secrets from him.

Of course that moment might not come until the war was over, years from now, when the world would be a very different place.

THIRTY-SIX

Alek's next two weeks were a whirl of cocktail parties, press conferences, and scientific demonstrations. Money had to be raised, reporters entertained, and diplomats introduced to the young prince with a shaky claim to the throne of Austria-Hungary. It was all so different from the rhythms of the *Leviathan*, the patterns of watches and bells and mealtimes. Alek missed the steady thrum of engines and the gentle sway of the deck beneath his feet.

He missed Deryn as well, even more than he had in those awful days after learning her secret. At least then the two of them had been walking the same corridors, but now the *Leviathan* was missing as well, all connections with his best friend and ally severed.

Instead of Deryn he had Nikola Tesla, a draining man

to spend long days with. Tesla wrestled with the secrets of the universe, but he also spent hours selecting the right wines for dinner. He lamented the war's daily toll of lives, but wasted time flattering reporters, wringing every drop of fame from these moments in the spotlight.

He lived in the grip of odd passions, none stranger than his love of pigeons. A dozen of the gray, warbling creatures inhabited Tesla's rooms at the Waldorf-Astoria hotel. He was overjoyed to see them again after his months in Siberia, during which the hotel staff had looked after them dutifully, and at great cost.

And yet Tesla knew how to turn his eccentricities into charm, especially when investors were present. He put on electrikal shows in his Manhattan laboratory and presided over lavish dinners at the Waldorf-Astoria, swiftly raising enough money to make the necessary improvements to his weapon.

But it felt like ages before Tesla and Alek completed their journey to Long Island. In a Pinkerton armored walker paid for by Hearst-Pathé Newsreels, the inventor finally brought Alek and his men to a huge tower looming over the small seaside town of Shoreham.

Goliath stood as tall as a skyscraper, a giant cousin to the sultan's Tesla cannon in Istanbul. Four smaller towers

"VISITING THE SECOND TOWER."

surrounded the central structure, which was crowned with a copper-sheathed hemisphere that shone brilliantly in the sun. Workmen scrambled over it, making the final adjustments before tonight's test. Beneath the towers was the brick powerhouse of the complex, its chimneys huffing.

The Pinkerton walker entered the compound through a tall barbed wire fence. The fence was enough to keep away tourists and trespassers, but Alek saw nothing that would stop a military walker.

Two days after the *Leviathan*'s departure, a messenger eagle had arrived bearing a letter from Deryn. She had passed on Lilit's warning, along with a promise that the *Leviathan* would be lurking off the coast, secretly watching for any sign of U-boats—or "water-walkers," whatever they were.

Deryn had asked Alek not to tell anyone about the German threat. But as Alek watched the pair of guards closing the gate again, with their antique rifles leaning against the guardhouse, secrecy didn't seem like such a good idea. If he and his men were going to sit here in harm's way, a bit more information might be useful.

Alek jostled the great snoozing form beside him.

"Master Klopp? We're here."

Klopp's sleepy eyes peered up at Goliath. "Looks like a child went mad with a mechanikal set."

"A child with very wealthy admirers," Volger muttered. He was fussing with the abundance of luggage he'd brought, dividing its weight between Hoffman and Bauer.

Alek glanced at Tesla, who was riding in front with the pilot, and lowered his voice. "Have you ever heard, Master Klopp, of something called a water-walker? A U-boat that can come onto land?"

"Water-walker," Bovril said.

The old man frowned, wiping sleep from his eyes. "I've seen a working model, quarter scale. But it's the other way round, young master."

"How do you mean?"

"A water-walker isn't a U-boat with legs. It's a land machine that's waterproof. It walks across the bottom of a river or a lake, like a metal crab."

Alek frowned. "A machine like that could never cross an entire ocean, right?"

Klopp looked at Hoffman, who said, "Impossible, sir. It would be crushed at a few hundred meters."

"Crushed!" Bovril said.

"So it's an empty threat," Alek said to himself, breathing a sigh of relief.

But then Hoffman spoke up again. "Of course, sir, you could take it across by ship. Then drop it onto the continental shelf."

Klopp thought a moment, then nodded. "And let it walk in from, say, fifty kilometers out?"

"I see." Alek doubted the Germans could sneak that large a ship past the British blockade, but the water-walker could be carried on some sort of U-boat.

"You see what, exactly?" Count Volger said. "Where did you hear of this machine?"

"In the newspapers." Alek found that lying had come easier lately. It was distressing but quite useful. "They were discussing the kaiser's threats against Tesla."

"And this penny paper knew of secret German weapons?" Volger asked.

Alek shrugged. "Only rumors."

Volger narrowed his eyes as the machine came to a halt. The gangway door opened, and Alek jumped out to help Klopp down. The reporters were piling out of the motorcar that had followed the walker, pointing their cameras up at Goliath.

The smell of salt was heavy in the air. The open sea was on the far side of the island, twenty kilometers distant, but Long Island Sound was a short walk away. According to the nautical maps Alek had checked, the sound was shallow, child's play for a water-walker to navigate.

Alek stared into the sky, though he knew the *Leviathan* was too far away, lurking near the narrow passage between the ocean and the sound. But perhaps from the top of

Goliath's central tower, with a pair of good field glasses, he could catch a glimpse . . .

Volger was staring at him, so Alek dropped his eyes and hurried ahead. Tesla was already bounding toward the tower, ready to put the weapon through its final paces. If the improvements to Goliath worked as expected, tonight's test would change the color of the sunrise in Berlin—fair warning for what was to come.

The Germans would have to take notice.

The control room of Goliath looked like a Clanker version of the *Leviathan*'s bridge. It jutted out from the roof of the power station, with tall windows offering a sweeping view of the towers and the darkening sky. In the room's center stood a huge bank of levers and dials; around it were clustered black boxes on wheels, covered with glowing tubes and glass spheres.

Tesla called out orders to his men, making use of a

dozen telephones connected to the other parts of the complex. Within a few minutes the smoke from the powerhouse
chimneys had redoubled. An electrikal buzz filled the control room, and Bovril's fur began to stand on end.

"Rather intoxicating, isn't it, Your Highness?"

Alek turned, and was surprised to find Adela Rogers
speaking to him. The Hearst reporter had spent the last
two weeks angry at him for leaking the pope's letter to
Eddie Malone, one of Pulitzer's men, instead of to her. But
she looked caught up in the excitement of the moment,
her eyes sparkling as the spheres and tubes began to glow
around them.

"It's a relief more than anything," Alek said. "We may
be coming to the end of this war at last."

"There's no maybe about it," Tesla boomed from his
controls. "Your faith in me will be rewarded tonight, Your
Highness."

Miss Rogers raised her writing pad. "Mr. Tesla, what
can we expect the test to look like from here?"

"Goliath is an earth resonance cannon, using the
planet itself as a capacitor. What you will see is a path of
pure energy stretching from the ground below us all the
way to the troposphere!"

Alek frowned. "Won't that be a danger to aircraft?"

"Not this test." Tesla's hands paused a moment on the
controls. "But if I ever fire Goliath in earnest, we'll warn

them to stay away. Ten kilometers in all directions, I should think."

"Let's hope that doesn't happen, sir," Miss Rogers said.

"Indeed," Alek said, and made a note to warn Deryn in his next letter.

Bovril was shifting nervously on his shoulder, trying to smooth its fur. Alek reached up and felt the crackle of static as he stroked the beastie. The air smelled of electricity, like when he and Deryn had been topside over the Pacific, facing the approaching storm. The night she'd kissed him.

"The kaiser can be quite cantankerous, you know," Miss Rogers said. "How long will you give him to submit?"

"That depends on tonight's experiment." Tesla gazed up at his machine, a smile on his face. "If Goliath works as it should, a single demonstration should prove convincing enough."

Even a test firing required vast amounts of energy, and it would be hours before the weapon's capacitors were full. So while the chimneys smoked and the dials nudged slowly upward, Mr. Tesla served his guests supper in an ornate dining hall just beneath the control room.

The inventor sat at the head of the table, as always ordering up several courses and wines, though it was quite late already. Alek had suffered through laboratory demonstrations in Manhattan that had lasted until the wee hours.

He turned to Volger beside him. "This will take all night, won't it?"

Across the table, Bauer cleared his throat. "Actually, sir, sunrise in Berlin is at seven. That's midnight here."

"Of course," Alek said. "An excellent point, Hans."

"Did you think he'd end the war with a flick of a switch?" Volger asked.

Alek didn't answer, leaning back as the first course of the evening was served, a consommé of turtle soup. Hoffman and Bauer looked down at their bowls dubiously. They'd been spared Tesla's feasts in Manhattan, but out here in the wilderness of Long Island, there were fewer reporters and investors about, so they had been promoted to dinner guests. Tesla's head engineers were also present, as immaculate in their formal jackets as they'd been in white coats.

As always at the inventor's table, fabricated beasts were banned. Alek found himself missing Bovril's weight on his shoulder and its nonsense mutterings, especially the snatches of Deryn's Scottish lilt.

"You seem less than serene, Your Highness," Volger said. "Perhaps a seaside stroll after dinner?"

"It's a bit cold for that."

"I suppose. And so many unpleasant things in the water."

Alek sighed. He'd said too much about the water-walker in front of Volger. The man wouldn't stop digging now until he knew.

"I was thinking about visitors," Alek said in a low voice. "Germans."

"I wasn't aware any had been invited."

"They have invited themselves."

Volger glanced at the other end of the table, where Tesla was amusing the handful of reporters by ordering that the cutlery be rearranged. He always insisted that the forks, spoons, and knives be laid out in multiples of three. The staff at the Waldorf-Astoria had grown used to his eccentricities, but the servants here in Shoreham were still learning.

"Who told you about these water-walkers?" Volger asked quietly.

"Deryn. And I can't say from whom. In any case there's not much we can do except wait."

"Have I taught you nothing?" Volger said. "There are always ways to prepare."

"The *Leviathan* is stationed nearby, ready to protect us. And preparations are overrated. The fact that we're here in America instead of the Alps is proof of that."

"The fact that you're alive at all is proof of quite the opposite," Volger said. Then he leaned away to murmur to Bauer, Hoffman, and Klopp.

Alek let himself relax and enjoy his food, relieved that he'd confessed the secret to Volger. The man might be a schemer at heart, a tight-lipped plotter who could never quite be trusted, but there was one oath he would never break—the one he'd made to Alek's father. Every infuriating thing Volger had ever done, from his grueling fencing lessons to his blackmail of Deryn, had been to protect Alek and see him one day on the throne.

When the wildcount turned back to Alek, leaving the other men still muttering, he said, "We'll be ready, Your Highness."

"I should have known you'd have something up your sleeve."

"I have no other choice," Volger said. "No matter how far from the war we run, it always catches up with us."

THIRTY-SEVEN

Deryn stood at attention against the wall of her cabin, taking deep, unhurried breaths. Finally she bent her knees, sliding her back down the wall until she was sitting on her heels. Her muscles quivered and her injury burned. But now came the hard part—pushing herself back up.

It was slow and agonizing, but Deryn managed it without crying out or toppling over. She stood there panting, her eyes shut against the pain.

"Exercising, Mr. Sharp?"

She opened her eyes to find Dr. Barlow framed in the doorway, Tazza at her side. The boffin's loris sat on its usual perch, looking imperiously about the middy's tiny cabin.

But Deryn was in no mood for the three of them. "It's traditional to knock, ma'am, even when the door's open."

"I stand corrected." Dr. Barlow rapped twice on the wooden frame. "Though you are hardly a slave to tradition yourself, *Mr.* Sharp."

The loris chuckled, but didn't repeat the words. It had grown quieter these last two weeks, almost thoughtful. Maybe it was missing Bovril.

"It's good to see you getting that knee into shape, Mr. Sharp."

"I've got to climb the ratlines again," Deryn said. "I'm going mad, stuck down here in the gondola."

"I see," Dr. Barlow said, then frowned. "You'll be wanting to muck about on the topside of every airship we travel on, won't you?"

"Aye, ma'am." Deryn took a breath and bent her knees again. "I do love tying those knots."

"In love," the loris said softly.

Deryn froze halfway down and stared at it.

Dr. Barlow smiled. "Aha. You *are* in love, aren't you, Mr. Sharp?"

"Ma'am?"

"With flying. You're in love with the air."

Deryn slid down the rest of the way, then pushed herself back up without a pause, letting pain hide her expression. Nosy boffins and their clever lorises.

Of course, it hardly mattered what Dr. Barlow was really thinking. Alek was gone, swept up in a distant world of power, influence, and peacemaking, maybe forever. How could someone who was in the newspapers every day have anything more to do with Deryn Sharp?

"Don't worry, young man. My duties with the Zoological Society involve a great deal of travel. You'll see plenty of airships."

"I'm sure, ma'am." Deryn sullenly reminded herself how lucky she was for the lady boffin's offer of employment.

Her close call with Malone had taught her one thing— if she were found out, it would humiliate her officers and shipmates. Deryn couldn't risk that, and it was clear that the lady boffin's shadowy Society was an easier place to keep secrets than the Air Service. In the Society, she reckoned, having more than one identity wouldn't be a problem at all. Dr. Barlow had even joked that Deryn might need to disguise herself as a girl, every now and then.

But it meant that Deryn hadn't just lost Alek; she'd lost her home as well.

She slid down the wall once more, ignoring the growing pain in her knee. She was desperate for one last climb in the ratlines before they headed back to London, Dr. Busk and his timid advice be damned. Nothing else in the sky measured up to the *Leviathan*.

"Disconsolate," the loris said softly.

Dr. Barlow shushed it. "You should join us on the bridge, Mr. Sharp. The view may be interesting tonight."

"That's right. They're testing Goliath, aren't they?" Alek's latest letter had been full of excitement. "But I thought you said it wouldn't work, ma'am."

The lady boffin shrugged. "I merely said that Goliath cannot call down fire from the sky. I would never suggest that Mr. Tesla is incapable of putting on a show."

When they were halfway to the bridge, the Klaxon began to ring.

"Is that battle stations?" Dr. Barlow asked. "How interesting."

"Aye, ma'am, it is." Deryn winced as she walked faster, wishing now that she hadn't worked her knee so hard. "But it's probably a drill. Sitting still for two weeks hasn't done much for morale."

"You could be right, Mr. Sharp." They both stepped aside as a squad of riggers thundered past. "But mightn't the Germans think this a fine evening to strike?"

"How do you mean, ma'am?"

They started walking again, and the lady boffin said, "Mr. Tesla has warned the world to expect alarms and eruptions in the sky. Any mishap might be written off as his machine going wrong, especially if there are no survivors to tell the tale."

"No survivors," the lady boffin's loris said, and Deryn redoubled her pace.

The Klaxon choked off in midring just as she and Dr. Barlow reached the bridge. The officers had gathered at the starboard windows, field glasses raised. A dozen message lizards were scampering across the ceiling.

This was no drill.

Dr. Busk turned from the windows and gave Deryn a nod. "I must admit, Mr. Sharp, I was beginning to doubt your story. But this is quite extraordinary."

Deryn stepped up beside him, following the stares of the officers. Below the *Leviathan* three trails of bubbles stretched across the water.

She shook her head, trying to imagine giant machines beneath the surface, their legs thrashing in the cold and dark.

"I'm a bit surprised myself, sir."

"The two escorts are no bigger than land corvettes, Captain," the first officer was saying. "But the one in the middle must be the size of a frigate."

Deryn leaned out over the handrail, wondering how the man could tell so much from mere bubbles. The water was as black as pitch, and the trails looked like scattered diamonds in the light of the rising half-moon, too delicate to be exhaust from huge Clanker engines.

The ruckus of battle stations filled the air, shouts and squawks and the roar of engines, and Deryn clenched the rail. She shifted her weight from foot to foot, her whole body outraged to be here on the bridge instead of top-side.

"Our faith in you has been rewarded, Mr. Sharp," the lady boffin said from just behind her. "But *do* stop jittering."

"Like a barking monkey," her loris said.

"Sorry, ma'am." Deryn settled herself. If they sent her back to her cabin, she might well explode.

"Less than a hundred feet deep here," the navigator spoke up. Charts were spread out before him on the decod-ing table. "This is the shallowest water for miles, sir."

The captain nodded. "Then, let us begin our attack. Slow to one quarter, Pilot. Let the wind carry us over."

The thrum of the engines softened, and the airship began to drift to starboard. The trails of bubbles were just reaching a narrow channel among the islands at the entrance to Long Island Sound.

"Those bubbles must be drifting as they rise," the cap-tain said. "How fast is that current?"

The pilot lowered his field glasses. "About five knots, sir."

"And how long does it take for bubbles to rise a hundred feet?"

No answer came, and everyone looked at the lady boffin.

"That depends on their size," she explained. "Champagne-size bubbles, as we've all seen, can take several seconds to travel an inch."

A moment of bemused silence stretched out, until Deryn

spoke up. "These aren't champagne bubbles, ma'am. They're exhaust from barking great diesel engines. The size of cricket balls at least!"

"Ah, of course." Dr. Barlow stared down at the black water. "Perhaps ten feet a second, then."

"Thank you, Doctor," the captain said. "Bombs away on my mark. Three . . . two . . ."

The deck shuddered a bit as the weight of the aerial bomb fell away, sending a twinge through Deryn's knee. She leaned out over the tilted windows, trying to see directly beneath the ship.

For a moment there was nothing but the dark, flat ocean, but then a column of water shot into the air as the bomb went in. The detonation followed seconds later, a silvery flower opening in the moonlight. Finally the gasses released by the explosion reached the surface, rising up in a frothing white dome. Ripples tumbled out across the water, full-blown waves cresting and storming as they rolled across the shallows.

"Bring us about," the captain ordered.

The *Leviathan* spun slowly in place until the bridge windows faced the channel again. The surface had stilled, and Deryn peered down, searching for exhaust trails.

One of the machines was in trouble—its stream of bubbles was swelling, filled with pops and splashes. And then another giant dome of water rose up, white and boiling.

"Secondary explosion," the first officer announced. "That's one of the escorts crushed by the shock wave."

"Fish in a barrel," said the captain.

Deryn tried to imagine the men inside the water-walker, fighting their hopeless battle to keep the ocean from gushing in. Now the other escort was failing, its exhaust stream sputtering in fits and starts. This one died with a whimper, though, its scattering of bubbles fading out to nothing.

"That's both the little ones, sir," the first officer said.

Deryn shuddered. It would be dark down there as lights and engines failed, and the water would be icy cold.

She'd never seen combat from the serene vantage of the *Leviathan*'s bridge before. Running about topside, the horror of battle was lost in a swirl of excitement and danger. This felt inhuman, watching men die when she felt no fear herself.

Not that her squeamishness made any difference to the sailors below.

"The frigate's made of sterner stuff, Captain." The first officer turned from the windows. "Shall we make another run?"

Captain Hobbes shook his head. "Stand by, but stay at battle stations."

Deryn turned to Dr. Barlow and asked softly, "Why aren't we finishing them off, ma'am?"

"BOMBS AWAY."

"Because they're underwater, Mr. Sharp. A German warship that can't be seen is of no use to us."

"No *use*, ma'am?"

"This is a Clanker attack upon sovereign territory of the United States. We can hardly let it go unnoticed."

Deryn looked down at Long Island Sound, her eyes widening. The exhaust trail of the surviving walker was still moving, following the coastline toward Tesla's machine.

"But we can't just . . ." Deryn's cry faded as she saw the eyes of the officers upon her. She dropped her eyes and said softly, "Alek's down there."

"Indeed." Dr. Barlow cleared her throat. "Captain, perhaps we should send a warning to His Highness."

Captain Hobbes thought a moment, then nodded. "If you would, Mr. Sharp."

Deryn snatched up a piece of paper from the decoding table and began to scribble. "It'll take an hour for an eagle to get there!"

"Steady, Mr. Sharp," the lady boffin said. "That walker's barely making fifteen miles an hour. Half the speed of an eagle at night."

"But Alek thinks we're protecting him, ma'am. He doesn't know we'll wait till that contraption's on his doorstep!"

The woman sighed. "It is unfortunate, but these are orders from Lord Churchill himself."

Deryn froze, making a fist around the writing pen. So this had been the plan all along, to destroy the last walker only after it emerged onto land. The Admiralty, of course, wanted a German war machine sitting on American soil for all the world to see, not some wreck lying beneath a hundred feet of water.

This was all about dragging the United States into the war.

But Goliath stood only half a mile from shore. The *Leviathan* would barely have time for one bomb run. If they missed, the water-walker would destroy Tesla's weapon and everyone within.

Alek was down there among the scattered lights of Long Island, without Deryn Sharp to protect him.

THIRTY-EIGHT

Dinner was unspeakably tedious. The turtle soup had led to saddle of lamb in *sauce béarnaise,* and that in turn to breast of hazel grouse. Now that the cheeses were done, dessert was "black cow"—ice cream floating in something called root beer, a concoction that had sparked a childish glee in Mr. Tesla and Master Klopp.

"A fencing lesson tomorrow, I should think," said Count Volger, leaning back from the table and loosening the lower buttons of his jacket.

"An excellent idea." Alek stared at his unfinished dessert, his ice cream melting into slurry. He'd been too impatient to eat much, but his reflexes were growing rusty from parties and dinners. He needed the feel of a sword in his hand.

Adela Rogers seemed to be in her element, though. She

was holding forth at Tesla's right hand, telling the host's end of the table how Hearst had managed to wrangle his new movie deal with the famous Pancho Villa. She didn't seem bothered that she was the only woman in the room. Indeed, she seemed to thrive on it. She was describing Hearst's flattery and bribes of Villa as if it were a romantic adventure, giving her female viewpoint incontestable authority.

Alek tried to imagine Deryn using the same strategy, if she were ever stuffed back into skirts. Could her swagger ever translate into the sort of flair and charm that Miss Rogers deployed?

Perhaps, Alek thought. But Deryn would also be ready with a good solid punch if one were needed. He could testify to that himself.

"Your Serene Highness?" It was a servant at his shoulder, presenting a letter on a small silver tray. "Just arrived by messenger eagle, sir."

The envelope was the apple green of the *Leviathan*'s stationery, and Alek's name was written in Deryn's hand. But she'd sent him a letter just yesterday. . . .

Miss Rogers had paused, and Tesla was staring at him. Alek nodded an apology to them, then ripped open the letter.

The writing was rushed, even worse than Deryn's usual scrawl.

Water-walker headed your way. You have an
hour at most.

    The Admiralty are bum-rags, so we won't
engage till it reaches the shore. But we'll be there.

Take care,
Dylan

"Ah," said Alek, his pulse quickening.

"News from our friends on the *Leviathan?*" Tesla said. "They must be in London by now."

"No, sir." Alek hesitated a moment, glancing at Miss Rogers—but every reporter in the world would know soon enough. "They're stationed only fifty kilometers away, at the mouth of Long Island Sound."

A stir went round the table.

"But why?" asked Tesla.

"They've been watching over us. There were rumors of a German surprise attack."

"A surprise attack?" Tesla said. Then his face broke into a smile. "Your Highness, please tell Dr. Barlow that she is invited to observe my experiments at any time, no excuses needed."

"I'm afraid that's not it, sir." Alek held up the letter. "Their fears have proven correct. A German underwater walker will be here within the hour."

The table went silent, and all the guests turned to Mr. Tesla. The inventor stared at Alek for a long moment, then dropped his gaze to the table and began to rearrange his forks. "An underwater walker? What an absurd notion."

"They exist, sir. My man Klopp has seen working models."

Tesla looked at Klopp, who appeared to be only half following the English, then brought his dark eyes back to Alek.

"How large is this machine?"

"Large enough to destroy Goliath. Otherwise, why would the Germans bother?"

Tesla spat out an angry noise and pushed away his dessert. "Pardon me, gentlemen and Miss Rogers, but unless this is some sort of joke, I must prepare my defenses."

Taking up his walking stick, he rose to his feet. The engineers jumped up from the table in unison.

"Defenses?" Miss Rogers asked.

"I am not naive, dear lady. I knew that the Germans would make plans against me." Tesla waved in the direction of the compound. "That's why Mr. Hearst provided us with that Pinkerton."

"But, sir," Alek said. "That Pinkerton machine is designed to frighten workers on picket lines. It can't stand up against a proper military walker."

The reporters had broken into a nervous hubbub,

some of them heading for the doors out to the observation deck. Others were asking the waiters to take them to a telephone.

Alek rose to his feet, waving Deryn's letter. "All of you, listen. I am assured that the *Leviathan* is on its way. It's more than capable of taking on a single walker."

Adela Rogers laughed. "So we should sit here and sip brandy?"

"Not at all, miss," Count Volger said. "We should retreat to a sensible distance and let the *Leviathan* handle this."

"That won't be necessary." Tesla turned toward the stairs up to the control room. "I shall stop them myself!"

"Sir . . . ," Volger said, but the inventor ignored him.

"It's no use," Alek sighed. "This is a man who took on three fighting bears with nothing but a walking stick."

"That hardly fills me with confidence," Miss Rogers said.

"Nor me. I'll talk to him." Alek made for the stairs. "If only to make sure he doesn't do anything rash."

"Your Highness," Volger said. "We can still put some distance between us and this place, even if we have to walk."

Alek shook his head. "That won't be necessary, Volger. The *Leviathan* will protect us."

◉　　◉　　◉

The control room was abuzz with shouted orders and sparking electrikals. The engineers were rushing about, wheeling equipment into a new configuration. Tesla was at the center of it all, a telephone receiver in each hand and several more tucked under his arms.

"Deploy the boats!" he shouted into one. "We'll destroy them as they come out of the water!"

He slammed a receiver down and glared at Alek.

"How long have you known about this?"

"As I said, it was only rumors," Alek said calmly. "Mr. Sharp heard something two weeks ago."

"The very day we arrived in New York." Tesla turned to the control room windows. The ocean was just visible in the distance, a silvery plane of reflected moonlight. "Every time I'm on the brink of a genuine discovery, someone tries to snatch it away."

"Sir, you needn't worry. Mr. Sharp has assured me that the *Leviathan* will deal with this walker."

"Then, more will come." The anger had left Tesla's voice all at once, and he only sounded tired now. "They'll keep coming for me, one way or another."

"That's a bit dramatic, sir. These water-walkers are experimental weapons. I can't imagine the Germans have too many of them."

"You don't know what smaller men are capable of, Alek. Edison, Marconi, and now the kaiser!" Tesla began

to place the telephone receivers back into their cradles, till only one was left in his hand. He lifted it to his mouth. "Boiler room? Please go to full."

"Mr. Tesla, we should abandon the test for tonight. Please!"

"I am abandoning the test."

Alek frowned. "But you told the boiler room—"

"Don't you understand? These men, these *little* men, want to destroy my life's work, to rob the world of everything Goliath will one day provide. Free power anywhere in the world, all of man's knowledge coursing across the airwaves! I can't allow that all to be snuffed out by this idiotic war."

The inventor turned to face the windows, his dark eyes gleaming, and Alek felt a cold drop trickle down his spine as Tesla placed the last telephone firmly back onto its cradle.

"I'm afraid this is no longer a test."

THIRTY-NINE

The walker was still half a mile from shore, but already its topside was cresting the surface. Water sluiced across its decks, swirling black with brine and seaweed. But beneath the ocean's detritus, wet metal gleamed. With a roar of its engines, the machine's kraken-fighting claws reared above the waves.

Deryn raised the field glasses to scan the deck for gun mounts.

"Doesn't look damaged at all," Dr. Busk was saying to the captain. "It must be designed for tremendous pressures."

The first officer snorted. "A direct hit should make it a bit less waterproof."

"Best to blow its legs off." Captain Hobbes lowered his field glasses. "Let's leave the Americans something menacing for tomorrow's papers, eh?"

A bit of laughter went about the bridge, but Deryn's mouth was dry. Tesla's tower was already visible in the distance, lights shining in every window. The great barking fool of an inventor hadn't evacuated, after all.

"Alek's still there, isn't he?"

"Our young prince would hardly leave an ally behind." Dr. Barlow stared out at Goliath and sighed. "I'd hoped that Mr. Tesla would not stoop to bravery."

"It'll be all right, ma'am," Deryn said, trying to keep her voice firm. "At least that walker hasn't any big guns."

The entire topside of the machine had cleared the surface now, and Deryn could see only a three-and-a-half-inch cannon, like the deck armament of a U-boat. The first crewmen were coming out of the hatches now, working to unplug the seals that kept the barrel waterproof.

"That's as we expected," the lady boffin said. "The Germans mean to tear down the tower with their kraken-fighting arms. Rather brutish of them."

"Aye, but it worked for us in Istanbul," Deryn said.

The captain had spotted the deck gun too. "A bit more altitude, Pilot. Ready in the bomb bay."

The *Leviathan* was almost on top of the enemy now; Deryn could feel the walker's great Clanker engines rumbling through her boots. The smokestacks had popped their water seals, and the machine was roaring at full power.

But there was something shiny in the surf, halfway

"REMOTELY FACING AN EMERGING THREAT."

between the shore and the walker. She raised her field glasses again.

It looked like a fleet of wee metal boats, each only a few feet long. Antennae whipped back and forth on their decks as the ripples from the emerging walker reached them. The boats were heading straight toward the German craft.

"Do you see those, ma'am?"

Dr. Barlow squinted into the darkness, then nodded. "Ah, yes. Mr. Tesla's remote controlled boats. He's been trying to sell them to the Royal Navy for years. How pleased he must be to finally make use of them."

As the first of the boats disappeared beneath the walker, light flared out across the water, and a jet of flame curled up around the metal. A few crewmen on the top deck cowered, but the machine hardly paused in its march toward the shore.

"A bit disappointing," the lady boffin said.

"A few sticks of dynamite and some kerosene, I reckon." Deryn frowned. "Did Mr. Tesla think he'd be fighting wooden ships?"

Dr. Barlow gave a shrug. "He never was one for chemistry."

"Not to worry," the captain said. "We'll show him how it's done. Starboard engine to half. Bomb bay, release when ready!"

Deryn stepped closer to the window, leaning out to see beneath the ship.

The water-walker's left foreleg was just stepping onto the beach when the shiver went through the deck. Deryn's knee twinged, and she held her breath until the bomb struck home.

It fell between the walker's two right legs, landing in a few yards of water. A dark column of sand shot into the air, fringed with silvery moonlit spray. Tesla's boats were tossed aside, bursting into flames that spilled across the surface of the sound. The Clanker machine was thrown sideways by the blast, almost tipping over. But finally it crashed back down, its right legs twisting and splitting.

The shock wave reached the *Leviathan* then, a great shudder traveling through the ship, the windows of the bridge rattling like teacups. Deryn kept her eyes trained on the walker. It was still trying to move, but its two working legs could only drag it a few yards with every step.

"Please give the bomb bay my compliments," Captain Hobbes said. "They've left her quite in one piece."

"What about her deck gun, sir?" the first officer asked.

"Keep an eye on it. If any more crewmen stick their heads out, we'll introduce them to our fléchette bats."

More orders were called, and a searchlight lanced out across the darkness. The burned and battered hulk of the walker suddenly shone brightly.

Deryn's eye caught a sparkle in the distance beyond. The central tower of Goliath was still dark, but the four smaller structures around it were starting to glow.

"Dr. Barlow?" she said. "I think Tesla's contraption is charging up."

"He means to complete his test?" The lady boffin tutted. "Captain, perhaps we should give Mr. Tesla some room. Even a test firing could prove unpleasant up here."

"Indeed, Doctor. Engines at one-half reverse."

The *Leviathan* hesitated for a moment in the air, then Deryn felt the gentle tug of the ship sliding backward. The black water of Long Island Sound pulled into view, and the tableau of the damaged walker and the sparkling towers spread out before them.

"Sir!" the pilot called. "There's another exhaust trail!"

The officers crowded the windows, and Deryn took a step forward. Something metal was breaking the surface near the shore.

It was a smaller walker, its four legs thrashing in the dark water of the sound, heading toward the beach.

"One of the escorts?" The captain shook his head. "But where's it been hiding?"

"It must have shut down after our attack," Dr. Barlow said. "Just long enough for us to follow the big one away. Or it may have ridden on the larger walker's back, mingling their exhaust streams."

"Who cares!" Deryn cried. "We need to stop that barking thing!"

"Well put, Mr. Sharp," the captain said. "Go to full-ahead."

A moment later the roar of engines rumbled through the bridge, and the *Leviathan* was moving forward again.

But the small walker had already made its way onto land. It was scrambling quickly through the trees, headed straight for the towers half a mile away. The machine hardly seemed large enough to tear Goliath apart, but it could certainly make a mess of things.

Suddenly a burst of sparks and flame ignited on the walker's back, arcing across the darkness. An explosion thudded in the distance.

"It's got a deck gun!" the first officer announced. "Captain?"

"Fléchette bats," came the answer. "We'll sweep them off the topside!"

Deryn's fingers curled into two fists. The airship was gaining on the walker, and the searchlights swung out to find it in the darkness. She heard the *pop* of an air gun overhead, and saw the first cloud of fléchette bats streaking away.

But as her eyes drifted past the German walker, Deryn's breath caught.

The outer towers of Mr. Tesla's weapon were glowing

brighter now, covered with nervous snakes made of fire and lightning. The tall central tower, Goliath itself, had begun to softly glow in the darkness, like the envelope of a hot-air balloon with its burner turned to full.

Deryn tasted acid in the back of her throat, and felt the awful, paralyzing fear of her nightmares. She remembered how the *Goeben*'s Tesla cannon had almost burned them all to a cinder. But Goliath was much more powerful, mighty enough to set the sky aflame thousands of miles away.

And the *Leviathan* was headed straight for it.

◦ FORTY ◦

The first shell landed at the edge of the compound, sending a length of barbed wire fence flailing and coiling in the air. A cloud of dust rolled outward from the explosion, and Alek heard pieces of torn metal hitting the rooftops around him.

He cupped his hands against the glass as the dust cleared, and saw the attacker striding through the trees—a smaller walker, a four-legged corvette. Two searchlights bore down from the *Leviathan*, revealing the deck gun on the machine's back, its barrel spilling smoke.

"Mr. Tesla," Alek called. "Perhaps we should evacuate."

"Your British friends may have deserted us, but I shall not abandon my life's work."

Alek turned. Tesla's hands were on the levers on the central bank of controls, his hair sticking out in all directions. Sparks flew about the room, and Alek felt the air humming with power.

"You haven't been abandoned, sir!" He pointed at the window. "The *Leviathan*'s still here."

"Can't you see they're too late? I have no choice but to fire."

Alek opened his mouth to argue, but another *boom* sounded in the distance, and the shriek of the incoming shell sent him into a crouch. This one landed inside the compound, throwing dirt and debris against the control room windows.

Suddenly the night turned red outside, the *Leviathan*'s searchlights changing color, and then glimmers of metal were streaking from the sky. The men on the deck of the walker twisted and fell as the fléchettes struck home. A moment later the gun was unmanned, rolling from side to side with the machine's gait.

The metal rain swept closer and closer, slicing through trees and sending up clods of dirt. As the torrent dwindled, one last fléchette hit the window with a *smack*. A crack slithered across the glass, and Alek scrambled a few steps backward, but the attack had ended.

He cleared his throat, willing his voice to stay firm. "The *Leviathan* has silenced that German gun, sir. We can stand down."

"But the walker is still coming, isn't it?"

Alek took a wary step closer to the window. The spikes had done nothing to the corvette's metal armor, of course. But in the sky above, the *Leviathan* was still closing in, its bomb bay doors already open.

Then he remembered what Tesla had said about firing Goliath in earnest—any aircraft within ten kilometers would be in danger. The *Leviathan* was no more than a kilometer distant, and Deryn was still aboard, thanks to Alek and his deal with Eddie Malone.

This madness had to stop.

Alek turned and strode to the main bank of controls, taking Tesla by the arm. "Sir, I can't let you do this. It's too horrific."

Tesla looked up. "Don't you think I know that? To destroy a whole city . . . It's the most horrible thing any human could conceive."

"Then, why are you doing it?"

Tesla closed his eyes. "It will take a year to rebuild this tower, Alek. And in that year, how many more will die in battle? Hundreds of thousands? A million?"

"Perhaps. But you're talking about Berlin . . . two million people."

Tesla stared down at his controls. "I can dampen the effect, I think."

"You *think*?"

"I won't destroy the whole city, just enough to prove my theories. Otherwise Goliath will be lost forever! No one will invest money in a smoking crater." He looked out the window at the walker scrambling across the dunes. "And the Germans will only grow bolder. If they aren't stopped now, do you think their assassins will let either of us live out the year?"

Alek took a step closer. "I know what it is to be hunted, sir. I have been hounded since the night my parents died. But proving your invention isn't worth this!"

A clamor of gunfire came from behind Alek, and he spun about. In the red glare of the *Leviathan*'s searchlights, the Pinkerton walker was venturing out to meet the German machine. A Gatling gun had popped up on its back and was chattering away.

But bullets were useless against steel armor, and the Pinkerton was far too small to stop the water-walker with brute force. It could only buy them time.

The *Leviathan*'s vast shape had slowed to a halt and was starting to reverse course. The corvette was inside the compound walls now—too close to Goliath for *Leviathan* to drop an aerial bomb. The airship's officers had to know that Tesla's weapon would be deadly to anything in the sky.

But there wasn't time to fly ten kilometers away. The air in the control room had begun to crackle, and Alek felt his hair standing on end. The buttons of his jacket softly glowed as the electrikal lights faded around them.

The weapon would be ready to fire soon.

Alek turned to Tesla. "The people of Berlin haven't had fair warning! You said we'd give them a chance to evacuate!"

The man pulled on a pair of thick black rubber gloves. "That chance has been stolen, but by their own kaiser, not by me. Please go back down to the dining room, Your Highness."

"Mr. Tesla, I insist that you stop this!"

Without looking up from his controls, Tesla waved a gloved hand at his men. "Show His Highness back to the dining room, please."

Alek reached for his sword, but he hadn't worn it tonight. The two men approaching were much larger than him, and there were another dozen that Tesla could call upon in the control room.

"Mr. Tesla, please . . ."

The inventor shook his head. "I've dreaded this moment for years, but fate has taken control."

The men took Alek firmly by the arms and led him to the stairs.

Most of the guests had fled the dining room, but Klopp was still there, a cigar in one hand, his cane in the other.

Miss Rogers sat with him, scribbling madly.

"Sounds like quite a battle up there," she said.

Alek sat heavily, staring at the empty chairs around the table, all askew. Even down here the floor was humming.

"He's going to fire at Berlin. Not a test, the real thing. What have I done?"

Klopp said in German, "The others should be back in a moment, young master."

"Back? Where in blazes have they gone?"

"To check on the luggage," Klopp said simply.

"*What?*"

"Your Highness?" Miss Rogers asked. "Would you say that Mr. Tesla has become unhinged?"

Alek spun to face her. "He means to destroy a city, without warning or negotiation. What would *you* say?"

"That this is what you signed up for. You and the chief, and all those investors in their motorcars, headed for Manhattan as we speak. This is something you all knew might happen."

"This is *not* what we planned!" Alek shouted. "This is murder!"

"The whole city of Berlin . . . ," Miss Rogers said, shaking her head and scribbling.

But Alek wasn't imagining a city leveled by fire. He

could think only of the *Leviathan* in the sky above, and of
Deryn's nightmares of her father's death.

The wine trembled in the abandoned glasses around
him. The whole table was vibrating.

"We can't let him do this."

"Don't worry, young master. Here they are."

Alek turned. Volger, Hoffman, and Bauer came storming in, carrying the long cases they'd brought from New
York.

The wildcount tossed one down onto the dining table.
Dishes smashed and clattered, and wineglasses fell over,
spilling red across the white table cloth.

"I take it we haven't much time?"

"Only a few minutes," Alek said.

"And you want to stop him?"

"Of course!"

"Glad to hear it." Volger popped the case open. Inside
was a pair of dueling swords.

Alek shook his head. "He has at least a dozen men up
there."

"Have you forgotten your father's watchword?" Volger
asked.

"Surprise is more valuable than strength." Klopp said,
and reached into the case that Hoffman had brought up,
drawing out a black cylinder with a long fuse. "I made

"THE AFTER-DINNER RAID."

this little surprise myself, in Tesla's own laboratory."

Klopp hobbled over to the staircase leading up to the control room, then touched the tip of his cigar to the fuse and grinned as it sputtered to life.

"Good heavens!" Miss Rogers looked up from her writing pad. "Is that a bomb?"

"Not to worry, young lady," Count Volger said, tying a dinner napkin across his nose and mouth. "It's only smoke. But lots of it!"

"Oh, dear," Miss Rogers said.

Hoffman threw a napkin to Alek as Bauer opened the other sword case.

A deeper rumble came up through the floor and set the walls quivering. The air itself seemed blurry now.

"Ready yourself, Your Highness." Volger hefted one of the swords.

Alek lifted the other sword from Volger's case. Its hilt was trimmed in gold, and its blade was carved with gears and clockwork. "Another of my father's heirlooms?"

"Hardly a century old. But sharp enough."

Alek thrust the sword through his belt and hurriedly tied the napkin across his mouth. The smoke bomb had begun to sputter and spark in Klopp's hand, and had only a few centimeters of fuse left. But the old man waited, calmly staring at it. Finally he heaved it up the stairs.

A *whoosh* came from above, and then a chorus of shouts

and cries. Klopp stepped back as a few engineers came stumbling down the stairs, coughing and spitting.

"Wish I could join you, sirs," the old man said, reaching for his cane.

Alek shook his head. "You've all done more for me than I can repay."

"We remain at your service, sir," Volger said, and bowed to Alek. Then he went charging up the stairs, with Hoffman and Bauer behind.

As Alek followed, the smoke rolled down to sting his eyes and lungs. The hum in the air grew with his every step.

The control room was smoke and bedlam. Electrikal sparks were flying, and someone was yelling "Malfunction," which only added to the chaos. Tesla's men seemed to think that the weapon itself had overloaded and set the room ablaze. The floor was shuddering, as if the whole building had turned into a vast engine.

Alek led Volger and his men through the smoke toward the central panel of controls. Tesla stood there calmly, ignoring the pandemonium around him.

"Sir, shut your machine down!" Alek ordered.

"You, of course." Tesla didn't look up. "I should have known not to trust an Austrian."

"Trust, Mr. Tesla? You've gone against all our plans!" Alek raised his sword, and his men followed suit. "Turn off your machine!"

Tesla glanced up at their sword tips, and laughed. "Too late for second thoughts, Prince."

With a rubber-gloved hand he spun a dial, then ducked behind the panel. The crackling in the air suddenly built to a *snap*, and a spiderweb of lightning leapt out of the smoke from all directions, striking the tips of the drawn swords.

The hilt of Alek's weapon turned searing hot, but he couldn't drop it—every muscle in his hand was suddenly clenched tight. A wild and unstoppable force seized him, twisting his heart in his chest. A lance of agony shot from his right hand down through his body, down to the soles of his feet.

Alek stumbled backward until he slipped, the dancing cord of electricity breaking as he fell to the ground. His lungs were seared by the smoke, and the palm of his sword hand was charred and stinging. The smell of burned hair and flesh filled his nose.

Alek lay there on his back a moment, but there wasn't time to be stunned. The floor was still shaking beneath him, stronger every second. He staggered to his feet, looking about for his sword, but the control room was a mass of smoke and flickering lights.

He stumbled over a prone form—Bauer, clutching his burned sword hand to his chest.

"Are you all right, Hans?"

"There, sir!"

Bauer pointed his blackened fingers at a silhouette in the smoke. It was Tesla, his long arms working the levers, and propped beside him on the controls was his electrikal walking stick. Alek lurched toward him and grasped the stick, then rose to his full height.

He nestled his finger around the trigger and pointed it straight at Tesla.

"Stop, sir."

The man stared at the metal tip a moment, then gave an arrogant snort and calmly reached for the largest lever among the controls. . . .

"No," Alek said, and pulled the trigger.

Lightning slashed out across the room. It took Tesla's body and shook him like a puppet. Fingers of white flame spilled out of the cane to dance across the controls. Sparks spat in all directions, and the smell of burned metal and plastic filled the room.

In seconds the walking stick sputtered out. Tesla lay slumped across the controls, not moving. Tiny bolts of lightning skittered across his body, and his hair twitched and quivered.

The rumble in the floor beneath Alek began to shudder, surging and falling, rattling the whole building in shock wave after shock wave, as if a giant were staggering past. Alek's vision blurred with every pulse, and he heard the windows shattering all around him.

He called out Volger's name, but the trembling air itself seemed to shred the sound apart. The smoke thinned as the smell of salt water rolled in through the broken windows, and Alek staggered toward the nearest one, his lungs crying out for fresh air. His boots skidded, shards of glass cutting him through his burned boot soles. But at least he could breathe.

He stared up at Goliath looming over the compound. The pulsing beat beneath his feet was echoed in the crackles of electricity coursing the tower's length. The whole machine was bursting with power, and Alek realized what he'd done. . . .

Goliath was like a steam boiler under pressure. It was ready to fire, but he had stopped Tesla from loosing the massive energies building up inside it. The chimneys were still spitting smoke, the generators sending more power to the already brimming capacitors. As Alek watched, he saw more windows shattering across the compound.

In the middle of it all, the German corvette stood over the wreckage of the Pinkerton walker. It had torn two of the smaller machine's legs off, and seemed to be performing a bizarre victory dance. Its legs were shivering, its body lurching back and forth.

Then Alek saw the webs of lightning on its metal skin—the walker's control systems had been addled by the wild energy that was setting the air aquiver. He looked into the sky.

The *Leviathan* itself was glowing, like a cloud catching the setting sun. The airship's cilia were rippling, slowly pulling it away, but the engines were silent, their electrikals also overwhelmed.

Would the hydrogen catch fire? Alek grasped the edge of the window, hardly feeling the broken glass against his palms.

"Deryn," he sobbed. Anything but this.

Then another shape loomed in the distance, something huge lurching over the horizon. It was the first walker, four times the size of the corvette, a tattered German naval jack fluttering from its spar deck. The machine was advancing slowly, its two right legs swinging uselessly. But the kraken-fighting arms were flailing at the ground, dragging the

walker across the dunes as though it were a dying beast.

Alek wondered for a moment how its electrikals hadn't shorted yet, but then the walker stumbled onto the tangled metal of the perimeter fence, and a circuit was completed. A single jittering finger leapt from the nearest small tower, striking an upraised kraken-fighting arm of the German machine.

The lightning from the other towers followed, their built-up charges hungry for a way out, and within an eyeblink five streams of electricity were pouring into the huge water-walker. The machine shuddered for a moment, its limbs rattling mindlessly as sparks swept across its metal skin. The air itself tore open in one long peal of thunder. The scrub trees around the walker burst into flame, the white fire consuming even the soil and sand beneath it.

The ammunition magazines must have caught then. The walker began to shake harder, and jets of fire burst from its hatches. Flames spat from the smokestacks as the fuel tanks caught all at once, and black smoke roiled out of the engine vents.

When the thudding of explosions had finally faded, Alek could hardly hear, but he could feel that the trembling beneath his feet was gone. The control room behind him was dark and silent, save for dazed human voices. Goliath had expended itself on the German walker.

Alek looked up again. The *Leviathan*'s glow was fading, the airship whole and alive with all its crew.

He shook with another sob, sinking to one knee and realizing that the survival of that one ship—one girl, really—had been for a moment more important than the war itself, or a city's millions. Then the wind shifted, and Alek breathed in the burnt-meat smells that filled the room behind him.

Important enough for him to kill a man, it seemed.

● FORTY-ONE ●

In their infinite wisdom, the Admiralty approved Alek's
medal for bravery in the air on the very same day the
United States entered the war.

The timing seemed suspicious to Deryn, and of course
the medal wasn't for anything useful, like shutting down
Tesla's weapon to save the *Leviathan*. Instead Alek was
to be decorated for blundering about on the ship's topside during a storm, and for his great skill in falling over
and knocking himself silly. That was the Admiralty for
you.

But at least it meant that the *Leviathan* was headed
back to New York, and she would see Alek one last time.

After fighting the German water-walkers on Long
Island, the airship had been invited to Washington, DC.
There the captain and his officers had testified before
the Congress, whose members were debating how to

respond to this outrageous attack on American soil.

It took a bit of droning and dealing, but finally the case was made that the Germans had gone too far, and Darwinist and Clanker politicians voted together to join the war. Already young men were swarming the enlistment offices, clamoring to go and fight the kaiser. As the *Leviathan* headed north, the streets below were choked with flags and parades and newsboys shouting war.

Deryn was on the bridge when a second message from London arrived, this one marked *Top Secret*.

She'd healed enough to put her cane aside, but Deryn hadn't dared the ratlines yet. She spent her time assisting the officers and Dr. Barlow. Being stuck in the gondola was still dead annoying, but bridge duty had taught Deryn more than a bit about how the *Leviathan* was run.

It would all be quite useful, if she ever got to command an airship herself.

The messenger eagle arrived just as the skyscrapers of New York City came into sight, on the day Alek was to receive his medal. The beastie shot past the bridge windows, then angled to the bird port on the starboard side.

The watch officer called out a moment later, "For Dr. Barlow's eyes only, sir."

The captain turned to Deryn and nodded.

She saluted him, then made her way to the lady boffin's stateroom with the message tube in hand. It rattled a bit.

Her knock was answered by Tazza whining from inside, which Deryn took as permission to go in.

"Afternoon, ma'am. Message from London for you." She squinted at the writing on the tube. "From a P. C. Mitchell."

The lady boffin looked up from a book. "Ah, at last. Please open it."

"Begging your pardon, ma'am, but it says 'Top Secret.'"

"I'm sure it does. But you have proven yourself adept at keeping secrets, *Mr.* Sharp. Proceed."

Her loris chuckled, then said, "Secrets!"

"Aye, ma'am." Deryn pulled open the message tube. It contained a single piece of translucent avian-mail paper scrolled around a small felt bag with something tiny and hard inside.

She unrolled the paper and read, "'Dear Nora, it is as you suspected: iron and nickel, with traces of cobalt, phosphorous, and sulfur. All quite natural in formation.' And it's signed, 'Regards, Peter.'"

"Just as I thought," the lady boffin sighed. "But too late to save him."

"Save who?" Deryn asked, but then realized the obvious—Nikola Tesla was the only person who'd needed saving lately. No one knew exactly what had happened the night he'd died. But it was fairly certain that the great inventor had been electrocuted by Goliath itself, the machine malfunctioning thanks to German shells and the general chaos of battle.

Deryn upended the felt bag onto her palm, and there it was—the tiny piece she'd cut from the object under Tesla's bed.

"So this is about that mad boffin's rock?" She looked at the letter again. "Nickel and cobalt and sulfur? What does it all mean?"

"Meteoric," the loris said.

Deryn stared at the creature. She'd read the word somewhere in the *Manual of Aeronautics*'s natural philosophy chapters, but couldn't quite place it.

"It means, Mr. Sharp, that Tesla was a fraud." Dr. Barlow shrugged. "Or perhaps a madman—he seemed to *think* he could destroy Berlin."

"You mean Goliath wouldn't have worked?" Deryn shook her head. "But what about Siberia?"

Dr. Barlow pointed at Deryn's hand. "In Siberia a stone fell from the sky."

"A wee stone did all that?"

"A meteor, to be precise. And not a small one but a giant piece of iron traveling at many thousands of miles per hour. What Mr. Tesla found was only a fraction of the whole." Dr. Barlow placed her book aside. "I suppose he was testing his machine when the meteor struck, and

he took it into his head that he himself wielded cosmic power. Quite typical of him, really."

Deryn looked at the tiny piece of iron in her hand. "But he had that metal detector sent to him, so he was looking for iron. He must have known it was a meteor!"

"The greater part of madness is hiding the truth from oneself. Or perhaps Tesla imagined that his machine could call down iron from the sky." She picked up the stone for a closer look. "In any case, what happened in Tunguska was merely an accident. A cosmic joke, so to speak."

Deryn shook her head, remembering the fallen trees stretching mile after mile in all directions. It was too much to believe that a mere accident could have created such ruination.

"It is fitting, though," the lady boffin said with a sad smile, "that Goliath should have been felled by a stone."

"But Tesla's machine made the sky change color. Lord Churchill himself saw it happen!"

The lady boffin laughed outright at this. "Yes, Tesla made the sky change color . . . at sunrise. Not such a difficult trick, if one has a gullible audience. Or perhaps Goliath really could change atmospheric conditions. But that's a far cry from destroying a city, Mr. Sharp."

"Gullible," her loris said with a snicker.

"You mean it was all rubbish? Everything we did, everything that Alek . . ."

Deryn closed her eyes. Alek had been duped, just as she'd always feared.

"An interesting point, Mr. Sharp. If a meteor falls in the forest and no one realizes it, does it end the war?" The lady boffin handed back the stone. "The Germans believed in Goliath, and in their belief they have propelled the United States to join our cause. That falling stone may have brought us peace, one way or another."

The black piece of iron suddenly felt uncanny in Deryn's hand. It was something from another world, wasn't it? She put it back into the bag, rolled the letter up, and slipped them both into the message tube. With a step forward she placed the tube on the lady boffin's desk.

"This will stay top secret, won't it, ma'am?"

"Of course," Dr. Barlow said. "With Goliath being rebuilt, the Zoological Society will have to keep the truth under wraps. Even His Majesty's Government mustn't know."

Deryn frowned. "But what about Alek? He's still raising money for the Tesla Foundation."

"Repairing Goliath will make the Germans anxious to sue for peace." Dr. Barlow fixed Deryn with her stare. "Telling Alek would be a mistake."

"But he's not your puppet, Dr. Barlow! Can you imagine what he's feeling? He thought the war would be over by now."

"Indeed," the lady boffin said. "So why make matters worse by revealing that Tesla made a fool of him?"

Deryn started to protest, but the lady boffin had a point. It would crush Alek to discover that his destiny was a lie, nothing but a cosmic accident.

"But Alek thinks it's *his* fault the war's still going, because he shut down the machine after Tesla was killed!"

"None of this is his fault, Deryn," the lady boffin said. "And the war will end one day. Wars always do."

◉   ◉   ◉

They pinned the medal on Alek in the cargo bay, with half the crew in formal dress and standing at attention. Captain Hobbes read the honors while a score of reporters snapped photographs, including a certain bum-rag from the *New York World*. Klopp, Hoffman, and Bauer were there in fresh civilian clothes, while Count Volger still wore his cavalry uniform. Even a few diplomats from the Austro-Hungarian consulate appeared, hedging their bets in case Alek's claim to the throne prevailed.

Deryn managed not to roll her eyes during the ceremony, even when the captain spoke of the grave injuries Alek had sustained.

"He fell and knocked his head," she muttered.

"Pardon me?" came a whisper from behind her, and Deryn turned. It was Adela Rogers, the Hearst reporter.

"Nothing."

"Surely it's *some*thing." The woman stepped closer. "The bell captain never speaks without reason."

Deryn bit her lip, wanting to explain that she was *not* a bell captain but a midshipman, a decorated officer. And soon a secret agent in the employ of the barking Zoological Society of London!

But she turned away, saying quietly, "He's done better things, that's all."

"You may be right about that. I was there the night Tesla died."

Deryn looked at Miss Rogers again, wondering what this was about.

"The last I saw of him," the woman said, "His Highness seemed *very* determined to stop Mr. Tesla."

"Alek saved this ship that night."

"And Berlin, too, I hear." The woman's notepad came out. "In fact, some people are saying the war might have been over already if Goliath had been fired, but Prince Aleksandar didn't want that. He is a Clanker, after all."

"No one even knows if that contraption—," Deryn began, but halted herself. That was too close to Dr. Barlow's new secret to say aloud.

Why couldn't everyone see that Alek had done more to end the war than anyone else? He'd given his gold to the Ottoman Revolution and his engines to the *Leviathan*, which had rescued Tesla from being eaten in the wilderness. That had all made a difference, hadn't it?

"You know something secret, don't you, bell captain?" the woman said. "You always have."

Deryn shrugged. "All I know is that His Serene Highness Aleksandar wants peace, just like he says. You can quote me on that."

· FORTY-TWO ·

After the ceremony, once all the photographs had been taken and the diplomats and notables had offered their congratulations, Alek went in search of Deryn. But before he could take two steps into the crowd, he found himself trapped between Captain Hobbes and the lady boffin.

"Your Serene Highness, congratulations again!" the captain said, and he offered a salute instead of bowing. As Alek returned the gesture, he imagined himself for a fleeting moment as a member of the crew. But that dream was over.

"Thank you, sir. For this and . . ." He shrugged. "For never throwing us into the brig."

Captain Hobbes smiled. "It was tricky for you in those first days, wasn't it? And a bit strange for us, having Clankers on the ship."

"But I always knew we'd make a proper Darwinist of you in the end," Dr. Barlow said, staring pointedly at Alek's medal.

He had been awarded the Air Gallantry Cross, the highest honor the British armed services could give a civilian, and right there on its face was a portrait of old Charles Darwin himself.

"A proper Darwinist," the lady boffin's loris said, and Bovril chuckled.

"I'm not sure what I am, these days," Alek admitted. "But I shall try to live up to this honor."

"A fine watchword in these strange times, Your Highness," the captain said. "If you'll excuse me, I must attend to our American guests. Their Clanker airships will be joining us on our way back to Europe. Most extraordinary."

"It certainly is." Alek bowed as the man strode away toward a clump of officers in dark American blue.

"How quickly things have turned," Dr. Barlow said. "The Ottomans remain neutral, Austria-Hungary is looking for a way out, and now the United States has joined the fray. Tesla may not have ended the war, but his death seems to have shortened it considerably."

"Let us hope so," Alek managed to say, and he looked about for a way to change the subject.

"Klopp!" said Bovril.

"Ah, yes." Alek waved his men over. "Master Klopp, Bauer, and Hoffman have left my service. They'll be staying here in America."

"The land of opportunity," the lady boffin said in excellent German.

Klopp nodded. "And the only place in the Clanker world that won't call us traitors and plotters, madam."

"That's only for the moment, Master Klopp," Alek said. "We'll all get home someday, I'm sure." The three men still looked odd to him in their civilian suits and ties, but they would be back in coveralls soon enough. "They're starting work Monday for a manufacturer of passenger walkers."

"Mightn't that be a bit boring?" the lady boffin asked. "After months of gallivanting about with your young prince?"

"Not at all boring, madam," Bauer said. "Mr. Ford pays five dollars a day!"

Dr. Barlow's eyes widened. "How extraordinary."

Alek smiled. He'd tried to give Klopp the rest of his father's gold, but the man hadn't taken it. In any case, the toothpick weighed less than twenty grams, no more than fifteen dollars' worth. Working for Ford Walkers, the three of them together would make that every day.

"Land of opportunity," the lady boffin's loris said with a sniff. The creature's German accent was also excellent.

"Where is your Count Volger?" Dr. Barlow said. "I've saved a number of periodicals for him."

"He's here somewhere." Alek looked about, and saw Volger skulking in a dark corner of the cargo bay. His eyebrows had been burnt off when Tesla's bolt of lightning had struck their swords, making his expression resemble a madman's in a motion picture show.

Or perhaps he was simply in one of his moods. When Alek had told his men to make new lives here in America, only Volger had resisted. The man had vowed to work for Alek's elevation to the throne of Austria-Hungary, whether Alek wanted him to or not.

But when Dr. Barlow went to the wildcount, his expression softened, and soon they were talking intently together in the privacy of the corner.

"Perhaps I'm speaking out of turn, sir," Hoffman said, looking at them. "But they are an odd pair, aren't they?"

Klopp snorted a laugh. "Quite suited to each other."

"You know what I've always thought, sir?" Bauer said. "That this war's been as good as over since they wound up on the same side!"

"Plotters," Bovril whispered into Alek's ear.

It took another hour for Alek to extract himself from all the well-wishers and interview-seekers, and to maneuver out of the cargo bay and into a smaller storeroom he'd seen Deryn make a quiet exit toward. She was still there waiting, sitting on a barrel of honey from the *Leviathan*'s fabricated bees.

It was the first time Alek and Bovril had seen her since they'd said good-bye at the Serbian consulate, and the beastie practically threw itself into her arms. Alek wished he could as well, but the crowded cargo bay was on the other side of an unlocked hatch. Instead he only nodded, wondering how to start.

He had expected it to be years before they met again, but even three weeks had seemed so long. He couldn't say any of that, though, not yet.

She was staring at his medal as she stroked Bovril's head. It was, of course, the same decoration that Deryn wore on her own dress uniform, and that her father had earned for saving her life.

"A bit daft," she finally said. "Getting a medal for falling down."

He swallowed. "I don't really deserve it, do I?"

"You deserve a *stack* of medals, Alek! For saving the ship back in the Alps, and in Istanbul, and again when you shut down Tesla's machine!" She paused a moment. "Not that the Admiralty would ever give you that last one, seeing as how you saved Berlin."

"You were there for all of those, Deryn, and I don't see medals filling up your . . ." He cleared his throat and glanced away.

"Chest!" Bovril said.

Deryn laughed aloud at that, but Alek didn't join her.

"I'm happy with just the one, thanks," she said. "And I wasn't beside you when you stopped Goliath."

"In a way you were," he said softly, staring at the floor. Only the fact that he'd been saving her had made pulling that trigger possible.

Deryn smiled and shook her head. "You never did recover from that knock to your head, did you?"

"A bit daft!" said Bovril.

"Maybe not. A lot of things have been a bit fuzzy since then." Alek looked up at her. "Of course, other things have gotten clearer."

Bovril chuckled at this, but Deryn looked away. A silence stretched out, and Alek wondered if it would always be like this between them now, halting and uncertain.

"There's something I should tell you," he said. "A secret about Tesla."

Deryn's eyes widened. "Blisters."

"Somewhere more private," Alek said, then wondered if he were only stalling. But suddenly he knew where he wanted to go. "I know I'm not serving on this ship, Mr. Sharp, but do you suppose they'd let me go topside one last time?"

"If you're escorted by a decorated officer, maybe." A grin spread across Deryn's face. "And I suppose it's time for me to try the ratlines."

"Your knee's still hurt? But your cane . . ." The first time he'd spotted her in the crowd, Alek had noticed she wasn't carrying it.

"It's much better, thank you. I'm still resting it, is all, and I'm forgetting all my knots!" She shrugged. "But if you don't mind climbing in your fancy clothes, I'm game to give it a try."

FORTY-THREE

The *Leviathan* was keeping station over the East River, making a show of patrolling for any German water-walkers that might attack Manhattan, unlikely as that seemed. The ocean breeze blew from the south, keeping the view of the city spires steady. Deryn wondered what the airbeast thought of the huge, uncanny skyscrapers—almost its own size, but planted in the ground sideways and pointing straight into the air.

Her knee hurt as they climbed the ratlines together, of course, but the burning was an old friend now. The feel of rope in her hands and the tremble of the airbeast beneath her weight overwhelmed everything else. And by the time they reached the spine, the muscles in her arms hurt worse than her injury.

"Barking spiders, I've gotten soft!"

"Hardly," Alek said, loosening the buttons on his formal jacket.

The U-boat spotters worked from the gondola, and half the crew had been to Alek's ceremony, so there was hardly anyone topside now. Deryn led Alek forward, away from the few riggers at work amidships. As they passed through the colony of fléchette bats, Bovril twitched on her shoulder, imitating the beasties' soft clicking sounds.

The bowhead was empty, but Deryn hesitated a moment before speaking. It was enough, just standing here with Alek in the salt breeze. And she suspected that his secret about Tesla concerned a certain bit of meteor, and talking about that would only make things sour.

But they couldn't stand here forever, however much she wished for it.

"All right, your princeliness. What's this secret?"

Alek turned away to face the darkening sky, in the direction of Tesla's ruined machine fifty miles away.

"The Germans didn't kill him," he said simply. "I did."

It took a moment for Deryn's mind to grasp the words.

"That's not what I . . . ," she began. "Oh."

"There was no other way to stop him." Alek looked down at his hands. "I killed him with his own walking stick."

Deryn stepped closer and took Alek's arm. He looked as sad as when he'd first come aboard the *Leviathan*, back when his parents' deaths still haunted him.

"I'm sorry, Alek."

"When I was helping Tesla, I never faced the truth of what Goliath was." He stared into her eyes. "But with the Germans storming up the beach, it all became real too fast. Suddenly he was standing there, ready to destroy a city, and I couldn't let him."

"You did the right thing, Alek."

"I killed an unarmed man!" he cried; then he shook his head. "But Volger keeps pointing out that Tesla wasn't exactly unarmed. Goliath was a weapon, after all."

"Quite," Bovril said.

Deryn swallowed, realizing that Dr. Barlow had been right. They couldn't tell Alek about the meteor now. He could never learn he'd killed a man to stop a weapon that didn't work.

But she'd promised not to keep secrets from him anymore. . . .

"It was Volger's idea to lie," Alek went on. "We told the truth about shutting down Goliath, because saving Berlin will make me a hero in the Clanker nations. But we can never say exactly *how* I did it."

"Aye, and he's right!" Deryn took both his hands,

remembering the suspicions that Adela Rogers had voiced. "Don't tell anyone you killed him, Alek. They'll think you were in league with the Germans, and they'll blame the rest of the war on you!"

He nodded. "But I had to tell you, Deryn. Because we promised not to keep secrets anymore."

She closed her eyes. "Oh, you daft prince."

There was no way out of it now.

"You're right enough about that." Alek was staring down at his formal boots, which were a little scuffed from climbing. "I thought it was my destiny to stop this war, and in the end all I had to do was step aside and it would've all been over. But instead I kept it going. So it really is my fault from now on."

"No, it isn't!" Deryn cried. "It never was. And you couldn't have stopped it anyway, because Tesla's machine *didn't work*!"

Alek blinked. He took a step back, but Deryn stopped him, squeezing his hands hard.

Bovril chuckled a bit and said, "Meteoric."

"Remember my bit of Tesla's rock?" Deryn said. "Dr. Barlow sent it to some boffin in London, and it was from a meteor. You know what that is, right?"

"A shooting star?" Alek shrugged. "Then, it's as I thought; it was only a scientific specimen."

"This wasn't just some shooting star!" Deryn tried to remember everything Dr. Barlow had said. "What Tesla found was just a wee bit of it, but the whole thing was huge, maybe miles across. And it was going so barking fast that it exploded when it hit the atmosphere. That's what knocked down those trees, not some Clanker contraption! Tunguska was just an accident, and Tesla was a rooster taking credit for the dawn!"

Alek stared at her, his eyes glittering. "Then, why did he try to fire Goliath?"

"Because he was *mad*, Alek, out of his mind with wanting to stop the war!"

"Just like you," she didn't say.

"And Dr. Barlow is certain of this."

"Completely. So it's *not* your fault the war's still going! It would have gone on, year after bloody year, no matter what you did." She flung her arms around him and squeezed hard. "But you didn't know that!"

Alek stood there motionless in her embrace, his muscles tight. At last he pushed her gently away, his voice barely a whisper.

"I'd have done it anyway."

She swallowed. "What do you mean?"

"I would have killed him to save the *Leviathan*. To save you." He put his hands on her shoulders. "It was the only thing in my mind, when it came time to choose—

that I couldn't lose you. That's when I knew."

"Knew what?"

He leaned forward to kiss her. His lips were soft against hers, but they kindled something sharp and hard inside her, something that had waited impatiently all the months since this boy had come aboard.

"Oh," she said after it was over. "That."

"Barking spiders," Bovril added softly.

"When we were topside in the storm, is this what you . . . ," Alek began. "I mean, have I gone mad?"

"Not yet." She pulled him closer, and they kissed again.

Finally she took a step back and looked about, worried for a moment that they might have been seen. But the nearest riggers on the spine were five hundred feet away, huddled around a hydrogen sniffer that had found a tear in the membrane.

"It's a bit tricky, isn't it?" Alek said, following her gaze.

She nodded silently, afraid that one wrong word could ruin everything.

He pulled something from his pocket, and as Deryn stared at it, her heart sank. It was the leather scroll case, the one with the pope's letter inside. She'd forgotten for a single, absurd moment that Alek was an emperor-in-waiting and she was as common as dirt.

"Tricky," Bovril said.

"Of course." Deryn dropped her gaze, stepping back from his embrace. "No one's going to write *me* a letter to turn me royal, are they? And I'd hardly make a proper princess, even if the pope himself sewed me a dress. This is all ridiculous."

Alek stared at the scroll case. "No, the answer's quite simple."

Deryn clenched her fists against too much hope. "You mean we could keep it all a secret? We'd have to hide ourselves for a bit anyway, given that I'm dressed in trousers. And you're a bit better at lying these days . . ."

"That's not what I mean."

She stared at him—the daft look was in his eyes again. "What, then?"

"We'll keep some secrets, for a while. And you may need your disguise until the world catches up with you." Alek took a slow breath. "But I have no use for this."

And with those words Prince Aleksandar of Hohenberg flung the scroll case hard to starboard, and it went spinning out across the Manhattan skyline, the shiny leather glittering in the sunlight. The ocean breeze caught it and carried it astern, but the whirling case still cleared the broadest part of the airbeast's body by some distance, and from the bowhead Deryn could plainly see where it struck the water with a tiny, perfect splash.

"Meteoric!" Bovril said a bit madly.

"Aye, beastie." The world had suddenly gone sharp and crackly, as if lightning were kindling the sky over Manhattan. But Deryn couldn't lift her gaze from the dark river. "That letter was your whole future, you daft prince."

"It was my past. I lost that world the night my parents died." He drew close again. "But I found you, Deryn. Maybe I wasn't meant to end the war, but I was meant to find you. I know that. You've saved me from not having any reason to keep going."

"We save each other," Deryn whispered. "That's how it works."

With a quick glance at the distant group of riggers, she kissed Alek again. This one was longer, better, their hands entwining at their sides, and the steady headwind made it feel as if the ship were underway, going somewhere new and wonderful with only the three of them aboard.

That thought made Deryn pull away. "But what in blazes are you going to *do*, Alek?"

"I expect I'll have to get a proper job." He sighed, staring down at the river. "My gold's run out, and it's not likely they'll let me join the crew."

"Emperors are vain and useless things," Bovril said.

Alek gave the beast a hard stare, but Deryn felt another smile on her face.

"Not to worry," she said. "I was thinking of leaving myself."

"What . . . you, leave the *Leviathan*? But that's absurd."

"Not quite. It turns out the lady boffin has just the job for me. For both of us, I'd think."

"AN END AND A KISS."

◦ FORTY-FOUR ◦

In a surprise announcement today, His Serene Highness Aleksandar of Hohenberg, putative heir to the empire of Austria-Hungary, renounced his claim to all the lands and titles of his father's line, including the imperial throne itself. This extraordinary news has shaken his war-ravaged country, many of whose embattled citizens have quietly embraced the fugitive prince as a symbol of peace.

It is unclear whether Prince Aleksandar would have taken the throne in any case. His claim is based on a papal bull that has not been verified by the Vatican, and which is contested by the current emperor, Franz Joseph. Indeed, as Russian victories mount on the eastern front, it is unclear whether the Austro-Hungarian Empire will exist at all once the Great War is over.

In a declaration of lesser importance, Aleksandar also renounced his ties to the Tesla Foundation, which is raising money to repair the late inventor's facility in Shoreham, New York. The prince's relationship with the organization had been under strain since the announcement that it was he who shut down the weapon after Nikola Tesla's death, fearing for the safety of nearby aircraft and the city of Berlin. According to his spokesman, Wildcount Ernst Volger, Aleksandar has taken a position with the Zoological Society of London, a scientific organization of royal patronage, best known for its upkeep of the London Zoo.

Rumors are flying as to why an heir to one of the great houses of Europe would trade his throne, lands, and titles for the post of zookeeper. But reached by this reporter while on his way to England via His Majesty's Airship *Leviathan*, Aleksandar had only this for comment: *"Bella gerant alii, tu felix Austria, nube."*

The phrase is the Latin motto of the Hapsburgs and refers to the house's tradition of gaining influence by alliance rather than conflict. It translates, "Let others wage war. You, lucky Austria, shall marry." What it might mean in this context is unclear, though it suggests to this reporter that the young prince has found the comfort of new and powerful allies.

Eddie Malone
New York World
December 20, 1914

AFTERWORD

Goliath is a novel of alternate history, so most of its characters, creatures, and machines are my own inventions. But the historical locations and events are modeled closely on the realities of the First World War, and some of the characters are real people. Here's a quick review of what's true and what's fictional in the novel.

At roughly 7:14 a.m. on June 30, 1908, a huge fireball exploded in the wilds of Siberia. Hundreds of kilometers away, people were knocked from their feet and windows were shattered by the blast. Due to its remote location, the Tunguska event wasn't studied by scientists for many years, and only recently has it been determined that a meteorite impact caused the destruction. (Or maybe it was a comet fragment. We're not *that* certain.) Many hypotheses about the cause were proposed in the intervening decades—from aliens to black holes to antimatter, and even experiments performed by the great inventor Nikola Tesla.

Tesla was world famous in 1914. A Serb immigrant

living in New York City, he was working on countless inventions, including a "death ray" that he hoped might make war impossible. His major project since 1901 had been Wardenclyffe Tower, a huge electrical device on Long Island, with which he hoped to broadcast free electrical power to the entire world (and much more). By 1914, however, Tesla's finances were unraveling, and he began to make wilder and wilder claims about what he could accomplish. The tower was never completed, and in 1915 the land it stood on was deeded to the Waldorf-Astoria hotel in lieu of money owed. (That's right, a mad scientist's lair was handed over to pay a *hotel bill*.) The tower was destroyed in 1917 by the U.S. government, who feared that Germans might use it as a transmitter or navigation landmark.

William Randolph Hearst and Joseph Pulitzer were rival newspaper moguls for many decades. Both were known for their so-called yellow journalism, stories that valued sensationalism over fact. As in *Goliath*, Hearst was steadfastly against U.S. entry into the First World War. He also loved motion pictures, and created the *Perils of Pauline* serial, the first of which is described herein, and which featured the original "cliff-hanger." (Let's just say I owe the guy.)

Adela Rogers St. Johns was a "girl reporter" for Hearst

newspapers and other papers from age nineteen well into her sixties. She is twenty years old in *Goliath*, and though she was married by then, I have somewhat capriciously changed history to keep her single. The story of her marriage license being torn in half is true, however. Her autobiography *The Honeycomb* (1969) is still widely available and is rather awesome.

Francisco "Pancho" Villa was a major figure in the Mexican Revolution of 1910–20. Villa really did have a Hollywood contract to film his battles, and German agents really did supply various revolutionary factions in hopes of gaining influence in Mexico. When the United States finally entered World War I in 1917, it was partly due to the discovery of the Zimmerman Telegram, an offer from the German Empire to assist Mexico if it attacked the United States. So I thought it would make sense to make the Mexican Revolution part of my story. Dr. Mariano Azuela was not really Villa's personal physician, but he was a fine writer, and his novels and stories are among the best about the Mexican Revolution.

The two Japanese boffins mentioned by name, Sakichi Toyoda and Kokichi Mikimoto, are both real; the former founded the company we now call Toyota. Hearst's lieutenant Philip Francis is also a historical figure, and it was discovered after his death that he had been born Philip Diefendorf. It is unlikely that he was a German agent—he isn't a German agent in *Goliath*, either—but many Americans with German names were persecuted during World War I, including one of my great-great-uncles.

The most important departures from history in this series, of course, lie not in these details, nor even in my fantastical technologies. The greatest changes are in the course of the war itself. In the real world, with no airship *Leviathan* to visit Istanbul, the Ottoman Empire joined the Central ("Clanker") Powers and cut off Russian food supplies. The long and bloody battle of Gallipoli failed to force The Straits, and the vigor of the Russian army was blunted. And of course there was no German attack on Shoreham, New York, so the United States remained neutral for three more years. In the meantime the war ground down into a horrific stalemate, and by its end Europe lay in ruins, setting the stage for the horrors of a second world war to follow.

At the end of *Goliath*, however, my fictional Great War would seem to be drawing to a close. The Germans have fewer allies and stronger enemies, mostly thanks to the brave officers and crew of the *Leviathan*. Europe may well emerge from this war less devastated than in our world, and therefore less vulnerable to worse tragedies to come. It's only too bad that Alek and Deryn have no way of seeing into our history and knowing how great a difference they made.

But then again, at the moment they have better things to do.

About the Author

Scott Westerfeld's first book in the Leviathan trilogy was the winner of the 2010 Locus Award for Best Young Adult Fiction. His other novels include the *New York Times* bestselling Uglies series, *The Last Days*, *Peeps*, *So Yesterday*, and the Midnighters trilogy. Westerfeld's newest book, *Uglies: Shay's Story*, is a graphic novel told from Tally's friend Shay's perspective. Westerfeld alternates summers between New York City and Sydney, Australia.

About the Illustrator

Keith Thompson's work has appeared in books, magazines, TV, video games, and films. See his work at KeithThompsonArt.com.

uglies

Read an excerpt from
the first book in SCOTT WESTERFELD's
groundbreaking dystopian series.

The early summer sky was the color of cat vomit.

Of course, Tally thought, you'd have to feed your cat only salmon-flavored cat food for a while, to get the pinks right. The scudding clouds did look a bit fishy, rippled into scales by a high-altitude wind. As the light faded, deep blue gaps of night peered through like an upside-down ocean, bottomless and cold.

Any other summer, a sunset like this would have been beautiful. But nothing had been beautiful since Peris turned pretty. Losing your best friend sucks, even if it's only for three months and two days.

Tally Youngblood was waiting for darkness.

She could see New Pretty Town through her open window. The

party towers were already lit up, and snakes of burning torches marked flickering pathways through the pleasure gardens. A few hot-air balloons pulled at their tethers against the darkening pink sky, their passengers shooting safety fireworks at other balloons and passing parasailers. Laughter and music skipped across the water like rocks thrown with just the right spin, their edges just as sharp against Tally's nerves.

Around the outskirts of the city, cut off from town by the black oval of the river, everything was in darkness. Everyone ugly was in bed by now.

Tally took off her interface ring and said, "Good night."

"Sweet dreams, Tally," said the room.

She chewed up a toothbrush pill, punched her pillows, and shoved an old portable heater—one that produced about as much warmth as a sleeping, Tally-size human being—under the covers.

Then she crawled out the window.

Outside, with the night finally turning coal black above her head, Tally instantly felt better. Maybe this was a stupid plan, but anything was better than another night awake in bed feeling sorry for herself. On the familiar leafy path down to the water's edge, it was easy to imagine Peris stealing silently behind her, stifling laughter, ready for a night of spying on the new pretties. Together. She and Peris had figured out how to trick the house minder back when they were twelve, when the three-month difference in their ages seemed like it would never matter.

"Best friends for life," Tally muttered, fingering the tiny scar on her right palm.

The water glistened through the trees, and she could hear the wavelets of a passing river skimmer's wake slapping at the shore. She ducked, hiding in the reeds. Summer was always the best time for spying expeditions. The grass was high, it was never cold, and you didn't have to stay awake through school the next day.

Of course, Peris could sleep as late as he wanted now. Just one of the advantages of being pretty.

The old bridge stretched massively across the water, its huge iron frame as black as the sky. It had been built so long ago that it held up its own weight, without any support from hoverstruts. A million years from now, when the rest of the city had crumbled, the bridge would probably remain like a fossilized bone.

Unlike the other bridges into New Pretty Town, the old bridge couldn't talk—or report trespassers, more importantly. But even silent, the bridge had always seemed very wise to Tally, as quietly knowing as some ancient tree.

Her eyes were fully adjusted to the darkness now, and it took only seconds to find the fishing line tied to its usual rock. She yanked it, and heard the splash of the rope tumbling from where it had been hidden among the bridge supports. She kept pulling until the invisible fishing line turned into wet, knotted cord. The other end was still tied to the iron framework of the bridge. Tally pulled the rope taut and lashed it to the usual tree.

She had to duck into the grass once more as another river skimmer passed. The people dancing on its deck didn't spot the rope stretched from bridge to shore. They never did. New pretties were always having too much fun to notice little things out of place.

When the skimmer's lights had faded, Tally tested the rope with her whole weight. One time it had pulled loose from the tree, and both she and Peris had swung downward, then up and out over the middle of the river before falling off, tumbling into the cold water. She smiled at the memory, realizing she would rather be on that expedition—soaking wet in the cold with Peris—than dry and warm tonight, but alone.

Hanging upside down, hands and knees clutching the knots along the rope, Tally pulled herself up into the dark framework of the bridge, then stole through its iron skeleton and across to New Pretty Town.

She knew where Peris lived from the one message he had bothered to send since turning pretty. Peris hadn't given an address, but Tally knew the trick for decoding the random-looking numbers at the bottom of a ping. They led to someplace called Garbo Mansion in the hilly part of town.

Getting there was going to be tricky. In their expeditions, Tally and Peris had always stuck to the waterfront, where vegetation and the dark backdrop of Uglyville made it easy to hide. But now Tally was headed into the center of the island, where floats and revelers populated the bright streets all night. Brand-new pretties like Peris always lived where the fun was most frantic.

Tally had memorized the map, but if she made one wrong turn, she was toast. Without her interface ring, she was invisible to vehicles. They'd just run her down like she was nothing.

Of course, Tally *was* nothing here.

Worse, she was ugly. But she hoped Peris wouldn't see it that way. Wouldn't see *her* that way.

Tally had no idea what would happen if she got caught. This

wasn't like being busted for "forgetting" her ring, skipping classes, or tricking the house into playing her music louder than allowed. Everyone did that kind of stuff, and everyone got busted for it. But she and Peris had always been very careful about not getting caught on these expeditions. Crossing the river was serious business.

It was too late to worry now, though. What could they do to her, anyway? In three months she'd be a pretty herself.

Tally crept along the river until she reached a pleasure garden, and slipped into the darkness beneath a row of weeping willows. Under their cover she made her way alongside a path lit by little guttering flames.

A pretty couple wandered down the path. Tally froze, but they were clueless, too busy staring into each other's eyes to see her crouching in the darkness. Tally silently watched them pass, getting that warm feeling she always got from looking at a pretty face. Even when she and Peris used to spy on them from the shadows, giggling at all the stupid things the pretties said and did, they couldn't resist staring. There was something magic in their large and perfect eyes, something that made you want to pay attention to whatever they said, to protect them from any danger, to make them happy. They were so . . . pretty.

The two disappeared around the next bend, and Tally shook her head to clear the mushy thoughts away. She wasn't here to gawk. She was an infiltrator, a sneak, an ugly. And she had a mission.

The garden stretched up into town, winding like a black river through the bright party towers and houses. After a few more minutes of creeping, she startled a couple hidden among the trees (it was a *pleasure* garden, after all), but in the darkness they couldn't see her face, and only teased her as she mumbled an apology and slipped away. She hadn't seen too much of them, either, just a tangle of perfect legs and arms.

Finally, the garden ended, a few blocks from where Peris lived.

Tally peered out from behind a curtain of hanging vines. This was farther than she and Peris had ever been together, and as far as her planning had taken her. There was no way to hide herself in the busy, well-lit streets. She put her fingers up to her face, felt the wide nose and thin lips, the too-high forehead and tangled mass of frizzy hair. One step out of the underbrush and she'd be spotted. Her face seemed to burn as the light touched it. What was she doing here? She should be back in the darkness of Uglyville, awaiting her turn.

But she had to see Peris, had to talk to him. She wasn't quite sure why, exactly, except that she was sick of imagining a thousand conversations with him every night before she fell asleep. They'd spent every day together since they were littlies, and now . . . nothing. Maybe if they could just talk for a few minutes, her brain would stop talking to imaginary Peris. Three minutes might be enough to hold her for three months.

Tally looked up and down the street, checking for side yards to slink through, dark doorways to hide in. She felt like a rock climber facing a sheer cliff, searching for cracks and handholds.

The traffic began to clear a little, and she waited, rubbing the scar on her right palm. Finally, Tally sighed and whispered, "Best friends forever," and took a step forward into the light.

An explosion of sound came from her right, and she leaped back into the darkness, stumbling among the vines, coming down hard on her knees in the soft earth, certain for a few seconds that she'd been caught.

But the cacophony organized itself into a throbbing rhythm. It was a drum machine making its lumbering way down the street. Wide as a house, it shimmered with the movement of its dozens of mechanical arms, bashing away at every size of drum. Behind it trailed a growing bunch of revelers, dancing along with the beat, drinking and throwing their empty bottles to shatter against the huge, impervious machine.

Tally smiled. The revelers were wearing masks.

The machine was lobbing the masks out the back, trying to coax more followers into the impromptu parade: devil faces and horrible clowns, green monsters and gray aliens with big oval eyes, cats and dogs and cows, faces with crooked smiles or huge noses.

The procession passed slowly, and Tally pulled herself back into the vegetation. A few of the revelers passed close enough that the sickly sweetness from their bottles filled her nose. A minute later, when the machine had trundled half a block farther, Tally jumped out and snatched up a discarded mask from the street. The plastic was soft in her hand, still warm from having been stamped into shape inside the machine a few seconds before.

Before she pressed it against her face, Tally realized that it was the same color as the cat-vomit pink of the sunset, with a long snout and two pink little ears. Smart adhesive flexed against her skin as the mask settled onto her face.

Tally pushed her way through the drunken dancers, out the other side of the procession, and ran down a side street toward Garbo Mansion, wearing the face of a pig.

Vi knows the Rules.
But Rules are made to be broken.

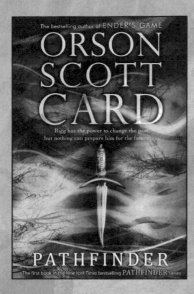
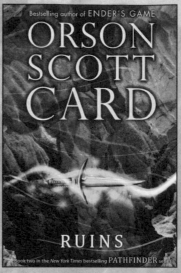

SIMONTEEN

Simon & Schuster's **Simon Teen**
e-newsletter delivers current updates on
the hottest titles, exciting sweepstakes, and
exclusive content from your favorite authors.

Visit **TEEN.SimonandSchuster.com** to
sign up, post your thoughts, and find out what
every avid reader is talking about!

Did you love this book?

Want to get access to
the hottest books for free?

Log on to simonandschuster.com/pulseit
to find out how to join,

get access to cool sweepstakes,

and hear about your favorite authors!

Become part of Pulse IT and tell us what you think!